BOOK ONE

— THE —
ABDUCTORS

A John Burton Novel

RICHARD LIPPARD

PAGE PUBLISHING, INC.
Conneaut Lake, PA

First originally published by Page Publishing 2019

ISBN 978-1-64584-033-6 (pbk)
ISBN 978-1-64584-034-3 (digital)

Printed in the United States of America

To Sharon, wife and companion. Thank you for your patience and perseverance.

THE ABDUCTORS

John Burton, ex-Special Forces and successful novelist, is on a mission. During the Vietnam conflict, he lost friends and buddies, some died, some were horribly maimed. John has devised a plan of revenge against those that made a profit in the war. With his handpicked team, his mission is to kidnap their young children for ransom. He has been successful twice. Phase three of this mission goes as planned until he makes his first mistake.

The FBI is called in and the chase is on. From Denver to Mobile, from Richmond to DC, the Feds chase him, always one step behind. Jack Donovan, head of the FBI's Kidnap Division, and Sally Martin, his assistant, lose him in DC.

Good investigative work by Sally leads her to Ellis Bay, Maine, but she is two days too late. John Burton is gone, said to be sailing on the Caribbean, along with his new wife, Jackie. Is she a part of John Burton's crimes?

Three months later, debris from the *Dram Bouie* is found, along with a skull. So what's happened to John Burton, his wife, and his friends? Sally is determined to find out.

CAST OF CHARACTERS

Major John Burton — Author and leader of the abductors
né John Parks
né James Pickett
né Jeffrey Matthews

Bobby — Bellhop at the Sheraton Hotel, Washington, DC

Tom Owens — Electrician, member of the abductors
né Allen Hodges

Amy Owens — Wife of Tom Owens

Cecil Montgomery — Weapons specialist, member of abductors
né Floyd King

Jacqueline "Jackie" Chandler — Makeup Artist, member of the abductors
né Julie Johnson

Kendra McArthur — Kidnapped child

Alexander McArthur — Kendra's father

Lisa McArthur — Kendra's mother

Richard Huard — Cherry Hills police officer

Don and Bob — Denver police detectives

Jack Donovan	DC FBI inspector
Sally Martin	DC FBI agent
Peter Jordan	Denver FBI SAC (special agent in charge)
Tom Richards	Denver FBI agent
Tony DeMarco	Denver police detective
Kevin McNally	Denver police officer
Richard Meade	Lakewood police agent
Bob Vincenza	Denver used-car dealer
Frank Cyr	New Orleans banker
Bertha	Housekeeper for Frank Cyr
Molly Stuart	Owner of Beauregard's Bed and Breakfast
Mike Morris	John Burton's Literary Agent
Marcie Blake	Assistant to Mike Morris
Dick Garcia	Head of East Virginia FBI Office
Bruce Sellier	Boston FBI SAC (special agent in charge)
Ian Bartholomew	President of Barclay's Bank, Cayman Isles
Ed Bodden	John Burton's driver on the Cayman Islands
Jorge Escovar	Pirate captain

PART I

CHAPTER 1

Washington, DC, Tuesday, May 22, 1990, 4:15 p.m.

Flight 1181 came in low on its final approach to Washington National Airport and taxied to a stop in front of the American Airlines terminal.

A man seated in the coach section on the aisle of the fifth row waited for the other passengers to deplane. Above him in the storage compartment was a brown briefcase, his only piece of carry-on luggage. His overcoat had been placed over it when he first boarded.

When the final passenger filed past him, he rose and retrieved these two items from the overhead compartment. He nodded to the flight attendant as he stepped onto the causeway connecting plane to terminal.

At the baggage claim, the man glanced at his watch. Four thirty-five. *Right on time.*

Twelve minutes later, his bags arrived. He grabbed them and walked out in search of a taxi.

"Where to?" the taxi driver asked as he placed the man's bags in the trunk.

"Airport Sheraton."

Fifteen minutes later, the driver pulled in front of the Sheraton. The man handed the driver a ten and said, "Keep the change."

The driver got out and retrieved the man's bags as he stepped out of the taxi.

A bellhop took the man's suitcases and led him to the reception desk.

"May I help you?" the receptionist asked.

"I need a room for a couple of nights but didn't have time to make a reservation."

"It happens all the time, the receptionist said. "Let's see…" She punched some keys before her, and a screen lit up.

"You're in luck," she said. "I've got a single room…or…a suite if you prefer something a little larger."

"The one room will do fine. I'm only going to be here until Thursday morning."

"And how will you be paying?" she asked, punching more keys.

"Cash."

"Very well." She punched more keys. "That will be, with tax… two hundred eighty-two dollars and fifty-six cents.

She returned with the change, glancing at the registration form.

"Have a nice stay, Mr. Parks.

The man nodded, then followed the bellhop to his room.

The bellhop put Park's luggage down in front of the open closet area and turned to the man. "My name's Bobby, Mr. Parks. If there's anything at all that you need, please don't hesitate to ask for me. I'm here to take care of you." With that, he bowed and left.

After he was gone, Parks unpacked, then sat on the bed and opened his briefcase. He removed a yellow legal pad and three sealed official-looking envelopes, each addressed to a different person in a different city in a different state. The only return address was a single line that read Washington, DC.

Inside each envelope were two pages full of jumbled letters, single-space, and both pages were filled from top to bottom.

He put the letters and envelopes on the nightstand and then stripped and went into the bathroom to shower.

The man was forty-two years old. He was not exceptionally handsome by any means but then again not bad-looking either. He had a rugged but indistinct face that blended into crowds. His most distinguishing features were his eyes—deep blue and penetrating. He had a square jaw with just the slightest dimple in the middle of the chin. He stood just under six feet tall in his bare feet. His torso was lean and fit. His hair was close-cropped, military style, and a light shade of brown, as were the beginnings of the stubble that covered his face. He rubbed his whiskers and decided to shave again.

His face now clean of stubble, he applied some Old Spice, put on deodorant, and dressed in a clean pair of slacks and a blue Oxford button-down shirt.

He retrieved the letters, putting his briefcase between the bed and the nightstand, and headed for the elevators. He pushed the button and waited while the elevator descended from an upper floor. When the door opened, there was Bobby, the bellhop, and off to his right and behind him was a blonde woman, probably in her mid to late twenties, Parks thought. She looked like she was dressed for a night out on the town, and when Parks looked at her and then back at Bobby, the bellhop grinned and winked at him.

Parks looked back at the woman, appreciating what he was seeing. His eyes met hers, and she smiled at him. He stepped into the elevator and stood next to her.

"Good evening, Mr. Parks," Bobby said. "Have you found everything to your liking?"

"The rooms are fine, Bobby." Bobby cleared his throat, and no other words were spoken as the elevator swiftly made its descent to the lobby.

Bobby and the man let the woman step out first. Parks stepped out next and slowed long enough to watch her head off in the direction of the bar.

Bobby stepped up beside him and mumbled softly, "Nice, huh?"

"Very," Parks said and turned in the opposite direction.

He found a blue mailbox outside and dropped the letters inside. One would go to Atlanta, one to Chicago, and one to Los Angeles. He took a deep breath, reentered the hotel, and went to the restaurant for dinner.

He ordered sea bass with steamed vegetables on the side, and a bottle of white wine.

It was just after eight when he paid his bill. In the lobby he observed the people milling about while he waited for an elevator, a habit he had picked up from his days with Special Forces. Even now, on what appeared to be a simple trip, he was careful—not paranoid—he told himself, just careful. He'd driven from Ellis Bay, Maine, to Boston, and then had flown to Washington, DC, just to mail three letters so that they couldn't be traced back to him.

Across the room, he saw the blonde woman coming his way, holding on to the arm of a much older man, their heads together, the man whispering something to her. She tossed her head back in quiet laughter. When they reached the elevators, she gave Parks a quick glance as the three of them entered the elevator. The older man mumbled something into the woman's ear that Parks did not quite hear, and then the two of them got off on the ninth floor. Parks continued to the eleventh floor.

The next morning, Parks arose, washed, dressed, and went downstairs for breakfast.

He ate leisurely, remembering a time long ago in a distant land when he'd been forced to eat roots and bugs, when he'd been both hot and sweaty and cold and wet. And he remembered how dirty he had been. He had sworn that when he got back to the States and finished with his tour, he would never be so uncomfortable again, nor would he be hungry. But especially, he had sworn that he would never be dirty again. And he promised himself, he would be rich.

In the jungles of Vietnam, he had first devised his plan. While he was in the jungles, fighting for his country over a questionable cause. There were "fat cats" back in the States who were making money off this accursed war. He decided to separate some of them from their money. He knew that he would need some help to achieve his objectives, and so he waited and watched until he found the three people he would need to fulfill his plans.

He approached each of them individually over an extended period and tested them carefully. When he was sure of their loyalty, he began laying the foundations for their future together. None of the three knew each other; they were enlisted into his confidence separately over a period of three years.

The play would begin when they were all discharged from the service. That had finally happened seven years ago, back in 1983. In

July 1986, their first endeavor had taken place in Houston, Texas. The four-year-old son from a very rich oil family had been abducted and held for ransom. Three days later, two million dollars in large unmarked bills was left at a drop site where it was quickly picked up by one of the team members. The son was found safe and unharmed. The whole plan had gone on without a hitch.

Each of the team members received $400,000, and he kept $800,000 for himself. That figure had been agreed upon beforehand. They all went their separate ways to wait for the next job. Parks had supplied them all with false identifications and places of origin. After two weeks of being together, they still did not know the real identities of each other. This also had been agreed upon beforehand.

In July 1988, the three-year-old daughter of a wealthy and influential banker disappeared in Detroit. She was found four days later, safe and unharmed, but not until the banker's wealth had been reduced by $2,000,000.

Each of the team members received $400,000, and the man had kept $800,000 for himself.

The man, who now called himself Mr. Parks, had taken his cut and retired to the small port town of Ellis Bay in southern Maine. There he lived among the locals and wrote of his experiences in Southeast Asia.

The waitress brought him more coffee and his bill. He sipped the last of the brew, checked his tab, put some bills on the table, and rose and left. Out in front, he waved for a cab.

"National Gallery of Art," he instructed the driver.

"You got it," the cabbie replied.

As the cab pulled into traffic, Parks glanced behind him, looking for *anyone* following him.

But of course not, he thought, *why should I be followed?* He chuckled. *Too cautious. Comes with the territory, I guess.*

Parks spent the day at the museum. At a quarter to five, he made his way back to the front entrance, performed a quick scan of the people and vehicles, and walked down the steps. Satisfied that all was right, he hailed a cab and rode back to the Sheraton.

Bobby was at the door when the cab pulled up.

"Evening, Mr. Parks. Did you have a good day?"

Parks was impressed with the bellhop's memory. "Yes, Bobby, thank you."

He walked through the doors with Bobby right behind him.

"Anything I can get for you, you just ask."

"I'll keep that in mind."

Parks walked to the elevators, checking the lobby as he went.

Bobby watched Parks enter the elevator from his spot next to the front desk.

The room was as he had left it. Parks called room service and ordered dinner, then he showered. Thirty minutes later, his dinner arrived. Parks tipped the man and closed the door behind him. He turned on the evening news and sat down and began to eat his meal. Bush's son, Neil, was speaking, defending his role as director in the failed Silverado Bank in Denver. Parks chuckled.

He finished dinner and pushed the cart outside. At his desk, he opened his briefcase, pulled out his legal pad, and began making notes—things he needed to do when he arrived in Denver.

At nine thirty, he put his notes back in his briefcase, stripped to his underwear, and went to bed.

In the morning, he checked out and took a cab to the United Airlines terminal.

He paid cash for a round-trip ticket. When asked to produce his driver's license, he produced a Massachusetts license with the name James Pickett and a fictitious Boston address, one of four he would be using on this trip. These he kept concealed in a secret compartment in his briefcase, along with an extra twenty thousand dollars.

"Thank you, Mr. Pickett. You'll be boarding from gate B-24. Have a nice flight."

He nodded to the attendant as she handed him his ticket, picked up his briefcase and coat, and headed off in the direction of the B concourse.

At the gate, Pickett's purchased a paper from a vending machine and found a seat, carefully placing his briefcase next to him.

Across from him, a young mother sat down with her two little children, a boy of about five and a girl of about three. Soon she was joined by her husband. He was carrying a baby. He handed her the child and sat down next to her. The two youngsters skipped their way over to the window, wide-eyed with excitement, after receiving a verbal warning from their mom not to stray too far. Outside, a United 707 was being directed to the gate to the left of theirs. The children watched as the man on the ground signaled for the aircraft to stop, and then squealed with delight as the telescope walkway was extended to the door at the side of the plane.

Pickett watched the two children with mild amusement. They were not unlike the children who would make him rich.

CHAPTER 2

Denver, Thursday, May 24, 1:10 p.m.

"Ladies and gentlemen," the captain announced over the intercom, "we will be arriving in Denver on time at one twenty local time. Skies are clear. Temperature is a pleasant seventy-four degrees. Please stow any loose luggage under your seats and return them to their upright positions. And once again, thank you for flying United."

The announcement interrupted his nap. Now, fully awake, he glanced out the window at the landscape below. He checked his watch, then kicked the briefcase stowed under his seat. The stewardess passed him and nodded, satisfied that his seatbelt was secure.

In five minutes, the aircraft touched down, lifted slightly, and resettled onto the runway, the roar of the big engines drowning out the chatter in the cabin as the plane began to slow. Again, as he had done in DC, Pickett waited until the others had gathered their things and were lined up to leave. When he was able to, he rose, gathered his things, and followed the last of the passengers out of the plane and into the airport.

He made a quick sweep of the waiting area. It was crowded, with people smiling and laughing as they greeted the arriving passengers. Sure enough, Grandma and Grandpa were there to greet the young couple with the three little children.

There didn't appear to be anyone there who shouldn't have been there. Still, ever cautious, Pickett walked over to one of the seats and sat down. He pulled out his newspaper and began reading. Soon the passengers and their greeters were gone, the noise and excitement of their greetings moving on down the concourse with them.

Only a few people were left, and none of them looked threatening. Pickett rose, threw his newspaper in the trash receptacle at the end of his row, picked up his coat and briefcase, and followed the signs to the baggage claim area. He stopped twice on the way and casually looked behind him. No one was following him.

Before retrieving his one piece of luggage from the carousel, he studied the different car rental counters. There, behind the National Car Rental agency were two men, one of whom was obviously new at his job. He grabbed his suitcase and approached the younger man and told him he would need a car for three days and would be paying for it with cash. He was asked to produce a driver's license and a major credit card, and this he did. The clerk looked at his license and ran the card through the imprinter, transferring the information onto the contract, then handed the contract to him and explained the terms.

Pickett nodded, signed the contract, and gave it back to the clerk, collected his license and credit card, and listened as the clerk explained that a bus would take him to his car.

He thanked the clerk, exited the terminal, climbed aboard the waiting bus, and sat with seven other passengers. The bus pulled up in front of a small building where the passengers got off. A young man took Pickett over to a burgundy four-door Pontiac sedan. After a brief walk-around, Pickett signed the inspection form, was given his keys, threw his things into the back seat, and climbed behind the wheel. He drove out of the airport area, crossed Quebec Street, and pulled into the Doubletree Hotel, where a valet greeted him and helped him unload his things.

Pickett checked his watch again. It was two twenty-five. The two entered and made their way to the counter. Once there, he explained that he had flown to Denver on a last-minute emergency and had no reservation.

The receptionist was very understanding, went through the normal check-in procedures, and gave him the key to his room and a map of Denver, and then he was ushered to his room.

Well, here I am, Pickett thought to himself.

He walked over to the desk looking for stationery, pulled out a single sheet, and turned it over. He began to make a list of things he would need to do in the next three days. After that time, he would check out of the hotel, find a cheap motel, bring the car back to the airport rental, take a taxi downtown, rent a different car from a different agency, and begin stalking his next victim. He would have seven days to learn everything he could about the family's movements and routines. By then, he would know where they lived, where the child went for day care or preschool; he would learn timing, schedules, normal daily routines, home security if there was any (surely there would be), and how to gain access to their home.

He would have contingency plans in place and escape routes for the four of them, and just as important, he would have a place to keep the child while the ransom was being collected.

When the ransom was paid, they would split up and again go their separate ways. Only he knew where each of the others lived. Only he knew their real identities. That way, if any of them were ever caught, they could not give up the others to the authorities. They had all used aliases for the first two jobs, and with the new IDs he'd provide them, they still wouldn't know who they were working with.

At the time of their first job, he had provided each of them with sets of false identification papers, a driver's license, and credit cards. These were to be used only when the four of them were together on a job. Each set was upgraded periodically, and the names would change. The old sets of identification would then be destroyed. It had cost him more than thirty thousand dollars so far to provide each of them with new identifications, but it had been worth it. The results were nothing short of perfect. Pickett had found the forger while still with the Special Forces, and their business relationship had grown over the years.

The forger was from Boston, which was convenient for Pickett. After the war, Pickett had moved to Maine so that he could visit his *artist* friend, as he called him, whenever it became necessary. It was the forger who had supplied him with the stationery that he used to communicate with his friends. And it was he who provided Pickett with all manner of false identities that matched Social Security numbers, including the licenses and credit cards he now carried with him. Each name was legitimate, and each credit card was set up with a different bank and held sufficient funds to carry out the various needs of the holder.

Now and over the next week, Pickett would familiarize himself with the city and its surroundings. He had to find an out-of-the-way place to keep the child and provide provisions for her and her babysitters, as well as a vehicle to transport the child; there seemed to be a hundred and one things that needed to be done. Each thing was a challenge, and he loved every minute of it. This was his juice, his rush, his high.

When all these tasks were accomplished, he would fly back to Washington, mail his instructions to the other three players, and then go home to Maine to wait. The actual kidnapping would take place, as always, on July 1. If everything went according to plan, the child would be released on July 4—Independence Day.

The only thing that could undermine his plans was if the family took a vacation. But Pickett had done his homework. The father was hosting a golf tournament that weekend together with a famous local sports figure. That meant the family would be in town.

Pickett got up and stretched his back and legs. He had not exercised since leaving Maine three days ago. The hotel had an exercise room. He promised himself that he would use it.

Pickett picked up his briefcase, sat on the bed, and opened it. Inside were sheets of paper with the words "Washington, DC" printed across the top, and envelopes with identical printing. He removed these along with the yellow legal pad and the other notes that he had written, plus some 9 × 12 envelopes. Then feeling along the bottom side of the briefcase, he found the tiny button that released the false bottom in the case. *Click*, and the bottom popped up, revealing twenty thousand dollars, plus the different licenses and credit cards that his man had prepared for him. Satisfied that all were in order, he closed the secret compartment, closed and locked the briefcase, and placed it between his bed and the nightstand.

He reached for the phone and called the front desk. "Yes. This is Jim Pickett. I noticed that you have an exercise room. Would it be possible for me to purchase some gym shorts and a T-shirt at the hotel?"

A slight pause, then, "Good. Thank you."

Pickett hung up the phone, checked the position of his briefcase, realized that his notes were still on the desk, pulled the briefcase from the floor, opened it, and stuffed his notes inside. He closed and relocked it, but this time he set it on the edge of the desk, the top and left side of it perfectly lined with the desktop. He walked to the door, turned and committed the scene to memory, and left, checking that the door was securely locked. Downstairs, he purchased the shorts and T-shirt and went to the locker room, found his assigned locker, stripped, and put on his gear.

Over the next forty-five minutes, he worked on his legs and lower body, his upper body, and his chest and arms and used the treadmill to work on his stamina.

When he was done, his entire outfit was soaked through with sweat. He retreated to the locker room, stripped and showered, toweled himself off, and redressed. There had been three other men and two women in the exercise room while he worked out and now two of the men entered the locker room. They acknowledged him as they passed, and he nodded in return.

"That was some workout," one of the men offered. "I think I would have died if I had tried to do all that."

Pickett smiled. "You get used to it."

He turned and walked past them and out of the locker room before they could engage him in any more conversation.

They looked at each other, puzzled. "Not very talkative, is he?" one of the men remarked to his friend.

Pickett just kept walking.

Back in his room, Pickett called for room service, and twenty-five minutes later his meal arrived. He had ordered the Rocky Mountain trout with fresh steamed vegetables, a dinner roll, a cup of fresh fruit, and a bottle of Riesling. The waiter opened the bottle of wine and made sure everything was satisfactory, accepted his tip, and left.

Alone, Pickett poured some of the wine and held it up to the light of the late afternoon sun. Its pale, clear color seemed to capture the light and radiated its brilliance in the glass. He sniffed it, took a sip, and let it settle under his tongue.

Sweet, but not too, he thought, *and just dry enough.*

Collecting and sampling good wines had become something of a hobby with him, so much so that he had had a wine cellar built into the old cottage at Ellis Bay.

One of the quirks of his new *profession*, as he liked to call it, was to collect a bottle or two from a victim's home if they were available. Both the oil man and the banker had wine cellars, and Pickett had taken the liberty of helping himself to a few bottles of their finer wines. He sipped his wine and ate his trout and enjoyed his new life. He wondered if Alexander McArthur would have a wine cellar. He'd have to check it out.

CHAPTER 3

Atlanta, Friday, May 25, 4:30 p.m.

The mail was on the dining room table when Tom Owens arrived home. He snatched it up and continued on into the kitchen. He had been anxious for the past two weeks, waiting. He scanned the letters as he walked. Bills, ads—and there it was, the "Washington, DC" envelope. He set the other mail down on the kitchen table and sat down, holding the envelope up to the light as if by doing so he could see inside. He put it down on the table and stared at it. Twice before he had received an envelope like this and twice before he had left Atlanta and returned a whole lot richer.

His wife, Amy, greeted him cheerfully. "Hi, honey."

"Oh hi," he said, sliding the envelope between the other pieces of mail. "What's for dinner?"

"Pot roast. Your favorite. Did you see the mail?"

"Huh? Oh yeah, just some bills and junk stuff," he said, shuffling it all together.

The reason the envelope only had Washington, DC, as a return address was that to many it would appear to be junk mail. He would open it later, after Amy had gone to bed.

"Come here, you sexy little thing," he said, patting his knee.

She giggled, sat on his knee, put her arms around his neck, and kissed him hard on the mouth. Just as quickly, she stood up and turned toward the stove.

"Come on, honey, help me put dinner on."

Tom rose, scooped up the mail, and said, "Okay, I'll just put this mail in the other room. I'll look at it later."

Much later, after Amy was asleep, Tom went down to the dining room and retrieved the letter. He sat at the kitchen table and opened the envelope. Inside were two sheets of paper with continuous rows of letters, single-space from top to bottom.

Each set of communications had been explained by the major verbally before the four conspirators separated at the completion of the previous job. Each one of them would receive two letters. One would come in mid-May and would give each of them a date and location for the upcoming job. That way, they could each make the necessary arrangements to be absent from work and home for the two weeks it would take to complete the job.

The second letter would come in early to mid-June and give them more specifics as to what they needed to bring, how to travel, where to stay, and so on.

Tom rose and went searching for some paper and a pen, then returned to the table and sat down again. He stared at the communication in front of him. This would be their third job, so he counted in three letters and wrote down the letter D. He then skipped two letters and wrote the letter E, skipped three letters and wrote the letter N, then four letters and the letter V, five letters and the letter E, then six letters and the letter R.

When the code was explained to him by the major, it became very simple. Once he spelled out the name of the city, he was to count down three more lines (three for the next job number) and then start again.

As with the first word, he counted in three letters and wrote down the letter J. Again, he skipped two letters and wrote down U. By following the pattern, he eventually spelled out the date: June 22.

That was it. All the rest of the letters meant nothing. Just additional subterfuge.

Tom stared at the message. "Denver, June 22." It seemed like a lot of trouble to go through just to get those few words passed on to him.

Well, he thought, *if the major wants to play games, so be it.* After all, he's lived up to his end of the bargain. Indeed, the major had made Tom and the others lots of money. Tom knew him to be very cautious and thorough. Every step was carefully planned out to the tiniest detail. There were even contingency plans, "plan B" as the major called it, in case something went wrong. But so far, nothing had gone wrong.

Ever since they had teamed up in Vietnam, the major had been putting money in Tom's pocket. The major even showed him how to transfer funds out of Vietnam and into a secret account in the Cayman Islands. Over $800,000 was sitting there now just waiting for him. And before they were through, there would be over a million dollars, tax-free.

So, Tom thought, *if the major has to go through such an elaborate system just to let me know that the next target is to be picked up in Denver in late June, then so be it.*

Tom rose, went to the sink, lit the message and the envelope with his lighter, and watched as the paper burned to ashes. Then he turned on the cold water and rinsed everything down the drain and went back to bed.

Chicago, Friday, May 25, 5:50 p.m.

Cecil Montgomery arrived home from his job at precisely five-fifty every day of the workweek. At four thirty he would punch the time clock at the Chicago National Bank where he was employed as a security guard. He would then walk to the corner and purchase the *Chicago Times.* Then he would walk to his bus stop and ride the bus to his neighborhood. The bus would let him off at the corner of his block, and he would walk to his front gate. He would check his mailbox, scan any mail that might be there, and enter his house.

To the average observer, Cecil lived a relatively simple, if not monotonous life. So on this day, when he scanned his mail and saw the letter from Washington, DC, and rushed into his home, the viewer would have thought that Cecil had won the lottery or something just as exciting.

And perhaps, to Cecil's way of thinking, he had. For Cecil recognized the envelope and knew that its contents could only mean one thing. Another job was coming up, another opportunity to put more money aside for his little family. His heart pounded a little harder with anticipation.

Not since Vietnam had he felt the excitement of danger or the anticipation of doing something that would put him at risk. And as always, with the feelings of excitement, there were also feelings of sadness.

In five minutes, his sister Jalene would bring over his two children. Cecil was a widower, having lost his wife through complications during childbirth. She had died in the delivery room from a cerebral aneurysm almost immediately after giving birth to a daughter. That was nine months ago. Now, his two children, William (not Billy), aged three, and Jasmine, were his life. He was devoted to them, spending all his spare time with them. The two weeks that he would be gone would be hard for him. But the nest egg that he was accumulating would make their future bright.

Cecil put the paper and mail on the kitchen table and went to the refrigerator. He was just opening the door when Jalene came through the back door with his two children.

"Daddy!" his son yelled and ran to the big man's open arms.

Cecil picked him up and tossed him into the air before catching him and hugging the boy to himself. His massive arms almost covered the boy's upper body as he gave William a tight hug.

"Hi," Cecil said to Jalene as he set the boy down on the floor.

"What's for supper?" William asked.

"I don't know yet. Just got home," Cecil answered, tousling the boy's head.

"They give you any trouble?" he asked his sister.

"No. They been good. They is always good."

Cecil reached for his daughter, and she smiled up at him as he cradled her in his arms. For the first few hours of her life, he had hated this little bundle—hated her for taking the life of his beloved wife, Ruby, but he soon realized that nothing could have prevented his wife's death. Love soon replaced those early feelings, and now, along with William, the baby was the most important thing in his life.

"Well, thanks, sis."

"No trouble, see you tomorrow."

"Jalene?" He paused. "Oh, never mind. I'll talk to you later. Say hello to Eugene for me."

"I will. Bye."

She was gone. Cecil stood in the kitchen holding his little daughter. William had run off into the family room. Cecil could hear the TV going on. It was one of those children's shows *Sesame Street*, he thought. Maybe *Electric Company*.

"Well, little girl, let's see what there is for supper."

He would open his mail later, when the children were in bed.

Los Angeles, Friday, May 25, 11:00 p.m.

Jackie Chandler arrived home from the studio exhausted. The filming was just finishing up, maybe one or two more days, and then she would be finished. There had been snags in the production; they had been running behind, but the end was in sight.

Jackie was a makeup artist. This was her second important film, and already people were beginning to take notice of her work. She had labored in the trenches waiting for a break, and maybe this film would be her breakthrough.

She was proud of her work and enjoyed doing it. And she was very good. She had gradually aged the two leading men by over forty years for this film and had received compliments from everyone of importance who was even remotely connected with the film. But it was her ideas on how to make the two men age that was the talk of the set. Her use of latex and cotton was remarkable.

She opened her mailbox, grabbed the fistful of letters and magazines, closed it, keyed the lock of the gated entrance and let herself in, rode the elevator up to the second floor, stepped off the elevator, and walked down the balcony to her apartment. She looked down at the lighted swimming pool as she approached her door. There were two men and two women splashing around in the pool, laughing and playing. Even from her vantage point on the second floor, Jackie could tell that the two women were topless.

"Hi, Jackie!" one of the girls yelled up to her.

"Hi, guys," she called back.

Gretchen, one of the two girls in the pool waved and was immediately pushed under the water by her male friend. She came up to the surface gasping and coughing and splashed him. He laughed and submerged as she yelped with glee.

"Come on in," Bonnie, the other girl, yelled up to her, "the water's wonderful."

"Not tonight, kids, I'm beat!" Jackie called down.

She let herself into her apartment, threw her keys, purse, and mail onto the coffee table, and began undressing as she headed for the bathroom.

Ten minutes later, showered and dried, she came back into the living room, wearing only a white bathrobe. She went into the kitchen, pulled a bottle of wine from the refrigerator, pulled down a wineglass, and retreated to the living room. Settling into a comfortable position, she reached for her mail and began separating it into stacks.

"Bill. Bill. Junk," she said quietly as she went through each piece.

She stopped after the fifth item. In her hand was an innocent-looking white envelope with a return address of only "Washington, DC."

She stared at it, feeling the heat emanating from it while she took another sip of her wine. She held it up to the light from the lamp next to her couch. She turned it over and then back to the front side again. She knew what it was. Her heart raced. Her face flushed.

It's from him, she thought. She knew that it would only give a place and a time, but it was from him! That meant that she would be seeing him again. And soon!

Quickly she used the knife to open the envelope. There it was. Like the two previous times, it contained only the coded pages. She dragged her purse onto the couch and reached inside, retrieving a pen. She circled the letters comprising the message, then wrote the circled letters on the bottom of the page. Like before, only a city and a date showed up.

Jackie mentally calculated. "Good," she said softly, "the movie shooting will be done. I'll be free."

She dropped the pages onto her lap and cried out. "Yes!" she said while raising her fist into the air and pulling it back toward her body. "Yes!"

CHAPTER 4

Denver, Saturday, May 26, 9:10 a.m.

First things first, Picket thought as he walked out of the hotel, the map of Denver in his hand. Let's see where Mr. and Mrs. Alexander McArthur and their precious daughter live.

Climbing behind the wheel of the Pontiac, he opened up the map and checked his notes. He was on Quebec at what? Thirty-Second Avenue? He looked at the index.

"Okay," he said quietly, "if I take this street over to…Monaco, then south to…Hampden, then right to…University."

He followed the route with his finger, making notes as he went. Then south to… *Ah, here it is, Cherry Hills Village.* He found Cherry Hills Farm Drive. Okay, then left to…he tapped his finger on the map. "There it is."

Pickett backed out of his parking spot and proceeded along the route that would take him to the McArthur's home.

It was a beautiful, warm spring morning. Traffic was moderate. It took him thirty-five minutes to find the house. He then drove around the neighborhood. Cherry Hills Farm Drive was square shaped, with other streets cutting through it. Pickett drove around the block and up and down the streets throughout the little community of Cherry Hills Farm. He discovered that there were only two ways to get in and out. Pickett drove around the neighborhood again. The second entrance was a gated entry with a gatehouse in the middle. He drove by the house again and then down the next street. There were no alleys. He recircled the neighborhood and exited out onto University. This time he noticed a white car with the word SECURITY painted on the front bumper. It was backed into a parking spot on the entrance side of the drive. It had not been there before. Pickett added this to his notes. Looked like he would be limited to one way in and one way out, and that way would have a security guard in the car. That didn't make him happy. He would have to find other options or at least figure out how to neutralize or eliminate the guard.

Pickett headed north on University. About a half mile north, he noticed the Cherry Hills City Hall and Cherry Hills Police Station on the right. He had missed that before.

Great, he thought, *police response will be quick.* Oh well, he liked challenges.

Pickett turned left on Hampden and followed it until he came to Sherman. He turned right and found a Safeway parking lot, purchased two more yellow legal pads, some pencils, a bottle of water, and then returned to his car.

Rolling down all the windows to let a breeze flow through, he began making notes of the house's location and the surrounding neighborhood and streets, with observation spots. He wrote in large capital letters, ONLY ONE WAY IN AND OUT! He sketched the neighborhood and described the front and sides of the house. Green hedges bordered the left side of the residence. It would be difficult to climb over without making any noise, but it did offer good cover and privacy.

A circular driveway led up to an entranceway that was covered by a canopied roof. The entranceway itself consisted of two spacious wood and colored stained-glass doors. Across the driveway from the entrance, a large rock garden and fountain partially obscured the front doors. This was good.

On the left side of the house, a patio surrounded by a three-foot-high brick wall bordered with shrubs and flowers invited the visitor to French-style doors entering from the patio to the interior of the house. There had to be a back entrance, but Pickett had not been able to see a way around to the back from his drive through the neighborhood.

To the right of the house a three-car garage faced outward onto the circular drive. The entire house, all two stories, done in gray stone, was covered with Spanish tile that sloped down sharply to a three-foot overhang. It was a beautiful house, and the landscaping around it was perfectly manicured.

The security car wouldn't be too difficult to reproduce, provided he could find one. It was a Chevrolet four-door sedan, all white, probably a 1977 or '78 model. The only distinguishing features were the words SECURITY painted on the front fenders in black letters. Pickett knew he would have to return and scout the security guard's schedule.

He checked his watch. All this had taken only an hour and a half. He looked at his map. There was a road across the street and slightly north of Cherry Hills Farm Drive. Maybe it would be close enough for him to scout the security car's position and thus make note of the guard's schedule.

He added this bit of information to his list. Then he pulled out his list and put a check next to item number one. Item number two would be to find a location where they could hold the child while the ransom was being gathered. The child couldn't stay with them at one of their hotels. Pickett allowed himself two and a half days for this chore. The site had to be secluded, obviously, but it also had to be comfortable. The child and her abductors would be spending several days there.

He scanned the map of the Denver area. He was looking for something out of the way. Something out of the ordinary, something where there was not a lot of housing: maybe something in a warehouse district. Then the idea hit him.

The mountains west of Denver, he thought. *They can't be that far west. I can see them from Hampden. There's got to be houses or cabins up there that are not being used right now.*

He checked his map again. Hampden Avenue, or Highway 285 as it was identified further west in the mountains, led out of Denver and into the mountains. He put the map down and started the car, pulled out of the parking lot, and headed in that direction.

Past Santa Fe, past Federal and Sheridan, past Wadsworth and Kipling, he drove until he entered the foothills west of Denver. He continued on until he found Parmalee Gulch Road.

Denver, Sunday, May 27

Pickett rose early and headed to the exercise room where he went through his usual set of exercises. When he was done, he returned to his room and showered, shaved, and dressed.

After a quick breakfast, he returned to his room, gathered his things, and checked out. He drove to the airport and turned in his car rental. The bus took him back to the terminal where he entered through one set of doors and came out through another. He hailed a cab and instructed the driver to take him to an inexpensive motel somewhere along East Colfax Avenue.

The taxi driver dropped him at a motel where Pickett was able to rent a room with no questions asked. He inquired if there were any car rentals nearby and was told that there was a Rent A Heap car lot down the street.

Pickett put his things in his room, did a visual inspection, moved his bags to the far side of the bed, and then walked the few blocks to the rental lot. The motel room was not as nice as the hotel, but it was clean, and it was on the first floor and afforded him some privacy.

At the car lot, Pickett rented an older Honda Accord. He paid in advance for one week's rental and left a five-hundred-dollar deposit. He returned to the motel and parked in front of his room.

At two o'clock he left the motel and headed south toward the Denver Technical Center. He wanted to see where McArthur worked.

Following Colorado Boulevard south, he found I-25 and turned onto the southbound exit and merged into afternoon traffic. He exited at Belleview and turned east, crossing under the I-25 overpass, then turned right at Syracuse, then wound his way around the Tech Center until he found the building he was looking for. He only lost his way once.

Pickett found a parking spot in front of the building. From his vantage point, he could see the front entrance. The site was actually two separate buildings connected by a huge courtyard. There were enclosed glass walkways that connected each building from the third to the seventh floors. The buildings themselves were made of marble and steel and glass. A black wrought-iron fence with a wide gate stretched from one building to the other, and inside the courtyard, he could see several bronze statues, including a buffalo, a moose, an Indian on a horse descending what appeared to be a steep hill, and a cowboy on a bucking bronco. Each statue was slightly bigger than life-size, and each was placed in such a way that the actual entrances to the two buildings were almost blocked from sight.

Quite impressive, he thought, *I bet they cost a fortune.*

He made some notes on his legal pad and left. He would return tomorrow and get McArthur's itinerary from the man's secretary.

Driving out, he returned to Belleview and followed it west-bound, following the map, until he came to University Boulevard. He passed the guard gate at the south entrance to Cherry Hills Farm. There was a guard at the gatehouse talking to someone in a car that had stopped next to the little building. Pickett turned right on University and headed north, passing the entrance and the security guard parked on the side of the entrance. He was looking for Gaylord Circle and found it right away. He turned left onto Gaylord and followed the circle around until he was again facing University. He stopped the car just short of the corner. Here he had a good view of the entrance down the street without being too obvious.

"Good," he said to himself, "from here we can monitor the guard's movements."

He made more notes on his pad, then sat there for another fifteen minutes before pulling out and turning right, heading south on University. Only two cars had passed him coming out of Gaylord in the whole time he had been parked on the corner.

Checking his map, Pickett turned west on Belleview and drove until he reached Broadway and then turned north, keeping his eyes open for phone booths along the way. This would be the route he would make McArthur drive when the ransom drop-off was made.

Pickett made notes of several locations as he drove north on Broadway and wasn't paying that much attention to the road until he suddenly found himself on Lincoln Street. He pulled over to get his bearings, referring to the map to locate his present position. It was then that he realized the jog he had made onto the one-way street was the end of northbound Broadway. He was in a residential area now, and according to the map, he was only about twenty blocks from downtown Denver.

He looked at the map again. It looked like Sixth Avenue was a freeway running west out of Denver. He traced it westward with his finger until it intersected with Colfax Avenue. He then started again from his present position and followed Lincoln into downtown Denver and found that Colfax ran east-west from far to the east to even beyond the intersection of Sixth Avenue out west.

He put the car in gear and pulled back onto Lincoln and headed north to Colfax. There, he turned left and followed it as it wound its way past the Civic Center. Finally, he was over the viaduct and heading west.

Again, he took notes of the phone booths along the way, adding a star next to the locations that had more than one phone and circling the star if there was a phone within close proximity across the street. He did this until he reached Simms Street in Lakewood.

He checked his odometer. By his calculations he was now approximately seven miles from downtown Denver. The drive from Belleview had been approximately six miles. From McArthur's house to here would be about sixteen miles.

Not enough, he admitted to himself.

He pulled into the 7-Eleven and restudied his map. He wanted more miles from the house to the final phone call. He also wanted more miles to the drop site.

So far, the route had been ideal. It had everything that he wanted: plenty of phone booths, lots of traffic. *Ideal for keeping tabs on the victim.* He would have to increase the distance from the front end and the back end. He looked at the map again. By taking Simms south, he would meet up with Sixth Avenue. He could take that east to Kipling, and then south to… He tapped his finger on the map. He would have to check out the Chatfield Reservoir and Park. It looked like this route might just add enough miles to the drop site.

Pickett pulled out onto Simms and headed south, following the route he had just marked out on the map. He continued to look for phone booths but found none on Kipling until he was almost to Hampden. He turned east and followed it to Wadsworth, turned south, and followed that until he came to the Chatfield Reservoir Park entrance. He turned into the drive and followed it to the guardhouse, paid his visitor's fee, then followed the road around and into the park. He could see the lake through the trees. The road wound around and passed several picnic areas. Pickett pulled into one of the areas and stopped in front of a stone structure holding toilets. He got out of the car and walked around the building. There was a paved walkway leading away from it in a southerly direction.

Pickett followed the path to the crest of a little rise and surveyed as much of the park as he could from that vantage point.

This will do nicely, he thought, *very nicely indeed.*

He returned to the car and made more notes. When he was finished, he had more than five full pages. He was pleased. This seemed to be the ideal place for the drop. It was secluded. There was a way to separate the man from his money and have the money picked up. There was an escape route, and the entire route would let the four partners know if McArthur was being followed by the police or the FBI. McArthur would have driven more than thirty-five miles. The drop was convenient and out in the open. In fact, McArthur could be observed while the drop was being made. Excitement was beginning to spread throughout Pickett's body. The plan was taking shape. He could visualize each step in his mind's eye.

It was after five in the afternoon. Pickett opened his map to check his whereabouts in relation to where he had begun. He wanted to get back to the motel the quickest way possible during rush-hour traffic. It looked like he would have to go back to Hampden and go east to…Colorado Boulevard, then north to Colfax. He followed the route with his finger until he found where his motel was located.

Pickett had little patience with traffic and found himself in the thick of it as he drove back to his motel. He arrived back at six thirty, hot and tired and tense. Once inside, he checked the room for signs of an intruder. Once again, nothing.

He stripped, showered, shaved, and dressed in the last of his clean clothes. He would have to make more purchases in the morning. But for now, these clothes would do.

Pickett found a fast food place and ordered a grilled chicken sandwich—no fries—and a diet cola. He didn't savor his meal, but it was filling. He wanted to get back to the motel, go over his notes, condense them, and destroy what he didn't need. He also wanted to start his second letter to his three friends. This communiqué would be different from the first. This time the letter before and the letter after each *Q* would be used to spell out each word. The *Q* would be randomly placed throughout the letter. Again, a constant series of letters, single-space, would fill up two pages.

Arriving back at the motel at just after eight in the evening, Pickett once again checked the placement of his briefcase to see if it had been tampered with. Satisfied that it had not been, he propped himself up on the bed and began rewriting his notes, putting them in order, making more sense of them.

By ten, he was beginning to doze off. He rose, went to the bathroom, and splashed cold water on his face.

"This is stupid," he said to the reflection in the mirror. "I can finish this tomorrow. Man, this altitude must be getting to me. 'Mile High City.' Must be something to it."

He returned to the bed, scooped up his papers and locked them in his briefcase, removed his shoes, shirt, and pants, threw off the covers, and lay down to sleep.

He was awakened at nine fifteen the next morning by the cleaning lady's knock at the door.

"Senor? Senor?"

He pulled on his trousers and went to the door, looking around the room before opening it. Everything was okay.

"Yes?" he asked, looking through the narrow opening in the door.

Standing in the doorway, a cart full of towels and sheets and assorted cleaning products behind her, was a short, extremely over-weight woman with a full head of black hair piled high on her head.

"I'm sorry, senor," she said, "you want I come back later to clean room?"

She tried to peek around him into the room, but he blocked her view.

"Um, yes," he replied, scratching his head and yawning.

Glancing at his watch, he said, "Give me twenty minutes. I'm sorry, I guess I overslept."

"Si, I come back. Gracias."

With that, she turned and pushed her cart down to the next door and knocked. Pickett closed the door and went into the bathroom.

"Shit!" he said to his reflection. "I wanted to get started before this."

He made a mental note to write this down. *High altitude, less energy.* He would have to advise the others.

Pickett showered and fifteen minutes later was back in his rented Honda and driving out of the parking lot. He found a coffee shop and had a quick breakfast and headed south. He wanted to redrive the route McArthur would have to take to deliver the money and check the miles between each stop and what telephone numbers were at each phone booth.

The entire route would be long, but it would afford them the opportunity to see if McArthur was being followed. To ensure that there were no bugs or homing devices planted in the car, McArthur would have to transfer the money from his own bags to bags that they would provide.

Pickett turned onto Cherry Hills Farm Drive and entered the estates. There was no security car in sight. He turned left past the little island and followed the circular drive around. When he came to McArthur's house, he pushed the odometer button on the dashboard, zeroing out the numbers on his trip meter.

"All right," he mumbled, "let's do it."

He turned the car around just up the street and headed out, resetting the odometer one more time.

Must be accurate, he thought.

Again, there was no security vehicle parked at the entrance. Pickett waited for an opening, pulled out, and turned left onto University, heading south.

"Here we go."

He crossed Belleview this time and continued on south. His first stop was to a Conoco station across from the Southglenn Mall. His first set of instructions, after he left his home, would be typed out and would be taped to the underside of the ledge at the phone booth. They would be simple enough, telling him to proceed to the next stop. There, he would be instructed again and so on and so on until, at one of the stops, he would be instructed to transfer the money to bags left in the trunk of a car, lock his own car, and drive off in the new one.

From there it would just be a matter of following instructions all the way to the drop site. The other members of the team would leapfrog each other along the way, one of them planting the notes under the ledges, one of them keeping McArthur in sight and one of them watching his rear for signs of a tail. Each would change positions as they went along the route.

If it was discovered that McArthur was being followed, the observer was to place an American flag on the antenna of his car and pass the others, honking the horn—one long, two short, and one long—to signal to the others to break off contact with the ransom car.

Each of the three kidnappers would be provided with an extra letter. In case McArthur was being followed, that letter was to be attached to the next drop site, letting McArthur know that his tail had been discovered. A call would also be made to the house telling the police and the FBI that their tail had been spotted. Then plan B would have to go into effect.

Pickett drove the route all the way to its end, stopping several times at places where there was a phone booth and writing down the phone number of each booth. If there was more than one phone at a location, he wrote down these numbers too. He also made note of all additional phones that could be seen from each location. At several locations, there were phone booths located up and down the street, across from each other. The entire route covered thirty-four miles. He estimated it would take McArthur about an hour to an hour and forty-five minutes to make each stop, change cars and bags, and follow all the instructions that had been given to him. They would make sure that he kept moving at a fast pace.

When Pickett reached the end of the route, he made his calculations, wrote them down, and then left the park and headed north on Wadsworth, looking for a place to buy new clothes. He was pleased to discover a shopping mall a few miles to the north.

He purchased slacks and shirts from a J. C. Penney store then went to the Denver Dry. Here he purchased a sport coat, tie, and shoes. He paid cash for everything.

With his purchases in the trunk of the rental, Pickett left the mall and headed back to Cherry Hills once again. The security car was back and parked in its usual spot. Pickett noticed that there were always at least one or two cars parked at the entrance beside the security car. A plan began to take form in his head.

CHAPTER 5

Denver, Tuesday, May 29, 8:15 a.m.

Pickett stood in front of the bathroom mirror and dried his hair. It was much longer now and a darker shade of brown. He took the makeup kit out of his suitcase and placed it on the toilet seat. When he was satisfied his hair was the right shade, he colored his eyebrows to match. To his face he added a fake nose, making sure that the edges blended against his cheeks and under the bridge of his nose, added coloring to his face and down into his neck area, then added a moustache and goatee. He inserted brown colored contact lenses. He blinked a few times to get used to them and looked in the mirror one more time.

The transformation was remarkable. With the cotton added to his mouth later, he would be wholly unrecognizable. He turned his head to the left, to the right, bowed at the neck, then raised his nose in the air.

"Not bad," he said to the reflection in the mirror. "And when Jackie gets here, there will be even more changes."

Putting his makeup kit and the other things away and grabbing his briefcase, he opened the door to his room and looked outside. There was no one around. He quickly hurried to his car and drove off.

This morning his plan was to meet McArthur at his office under the pretext of seeking an interview with him and his wife at their home. Supposedly, he would be doing an article for *Golf World*

Digest on the upcoming tournament, and he wanted to get a different perspective on the story.

Pickett walked through the doors of Inter-Global Tele-Communications at precisely 10:00 a.m. In front of him stood a huge semicircular glass-and-steel counter. Behind it sat an attractive blonde, a headset over her right ear, the mouthpiece in front of a mouth with an alluring shade of red lipstick on it.

Behind her, a curved wall of oak paneling held a raised brass map of the world that highlighted many of the cities of North America, Europe, Africa, and Asia, as well as South America, Japan, and Australia. All these cities were connected to Denver by curved colored wires, and each was lighted by a tiny red light. Above the map, also done in brass was the name INTER-GLOBAL TELE-COMMU-NICATIONS done in block letters, and under it in smaller letters, the phrase *Connecting the World of Today with the World of Tomorrow.* Above all this were clocks that told the time in the different time zones around the world.

The girl at the counter looked up at Pickett as he approached. "Good morning. May I help you?"

"Yes, you can," Pickett said with just the slightest bit of authority in his voice. "My name is Jeffrey Matthews. I'm with *Golf World Digest.* I was wondering, is Mr. McArthur available?"

He reached inside his coat and withdrew a small black leather case, pulled out a card, and handed it to her.

"Well, he's in a meeting right now. What's this all about?" she asked, taking the card.

"Oh, I'm sorry. I should have explained. My magazine is doing an article on the upcoming golf tournament, and I was hoping to get an interview and some pictures of both Mr. and Mrs. McArthur. You know, some background information on the history of the tournament, his philosophy, and so on. It'll only take a minute or two to schedule something with the two of them."

"Well..." She hesitated and looked at her watch. "He should be done with his meeting at ten fifteen. He has another one at ten thirty. Maybe, if you'd like, I can see if he can squeeze you in."

"That would be great, Miss..."

"Jennifer."

"Jennifer. Okay, then, I'll just wait over there." Pickett nodded in the direction of the sofa and chairs.

"No problem." She smiled at him. "Excuse me."

She punched a button on the console in front of her. "Inter-Global Tele-Communications, good morning, how may I direct your call?"

Pickett, now Jeffrey Matthews, walked over to the sofa and sat down. From where he sat, he had an unobstructed view of Jennifer. He also could see the glass double doors that led back to the executive offices.

At eighteen minutes past ten, Alexander McArthur and three Oriental men came through the doors of the executive offices. They stopped in front of the entrance and bowed and shook hands and McArthur said goodbye to each of them.

As he was approaching the counter, he glanced over in the direction of the couch and chairs. He then picked up his messages from a slot in the counter and turned to go.

Jeffrey rose as McArthur was reaching for his messages.

"Mr. McArthur, sir," Jennifer said, "this gentleman here would like to have a word with you. Is that all right?"

McArthur frowned briefly and then turned to look at his visitor.

Holding out his hand, Pickett introduced himself as Jeffrey Matthews from *Golf World Digest.* He explained what he wanted from the man.

"That would be fine," McArthur said, looking at his watch. "Jennifer, call Lisa and have her set it up."

Turning back to Matthews, he said, "You said the Monday or Tuesday evening before the tournament?"

"Yes, sir, and thank you."

Again, Matthews extended his hand. McArthur took it and then said, "I'm sorry, I've got another meeting. I'll be looking forward to seeing you. Goodbye."

McArthur flashed a million-dollar smile at his visitor. Matthews imagined that that smile had probably won over many a deal for the man.

McArthur turned quickly and headed back through the doors and was gone. Jennifer was already on the phone to Mrs. McArthur. She explained the reason for her call, getting details from Matthews as she did so.

It was agreed that Tuesday evening would be best for her and her husband. Matthews and his photographer would arrive at seven thirty. The whole interview shouldn't take more than an hour and a half.

Matthews thanked Jennifer in his most charming manner and turned to leave. "Oh, and one more thing. Could I have his home address? And his home phone number? You know, just in case something comes up. I couldn't find it in the phone book."

She hesitated for just a second. "Well, I don't know, it is unlisted, but..."

Matthews gave her a puppy-dog look.

"I guess it would be all right."

She wrote down the address and the phone number on a business card and handed it to him, standing as she did so. It was then that Matthews had the pleasure of seeing all her for the first time. She was as tall as he was, and the dress she wore flattered her in every way.

"Thank you," he said, "you're a doll."

"You're welcome. If you need anything else, just call."

He looked down at the business card and tapped it against the countertop. "Thanks again." He turned and left.

That was easy, Pickett thought. Get an invite into the old man's home *and* get his unlisted phone number at the same time.

Pickett pulled his briefcase into the front seat and laid it on the passenger seat. He removed his yellow legal pad and jotted down some notes. He included McArthur's home phone number and Lisa's name, then, just for good measure, attached the business card to the top of the page with a paper clip.

Let's see, Pickett thought, running through his checklist. *Things are coming together nicely. I have access to the house, I have his private number, I have the route he will have to follow to deliver the money. I have three possible locations to hold the child while the ransom money is being collected.*

What else? I'll need to rent a mailbox. And I'll have to get hold of a typewriter. We can decide on the best possible holding site when the others get here. Damn, what to do with the security guard? Well, maybe the others will have some ideas.

Finally, he started the car, put it in gear, and drove off. In the afternoon, he rented a mail drop from one of those companies that specialized in shipping and receiving packages.

His next stop was at a Goodwill store where he purchased a used Royal portable typewriter. When all this was done, he returned to the motel.

Pickett hurried into his room, removed his wig and eyebrows, carefully peeled back his rubber nose, being extra careful not to tear it as he took it off, placed it in its container, put his contacts back in their case, and washed the color from his face and neck. He then went in and showered, rinsing the color out of his hair.

Pickett worked into the early morning hours of the next day putting together the three letters that would be sent to his three friends. Each letter would explain in detail what they would have to do before they left for Denver, the things that they would need to send on ahead to the mail drop address in Denver, how they would fly, what they needed to bring with them, and on and on and on. Each letter would also contain twelve one-hundred-dollar bills taped to a blank piece of paper to avoid them from bunching up in the envelope.

When he was done, he placed the encrypted letters in their respective envelopes with the money, placed all his notes in a folder, packed up everything, and went to bed.

CHAPTER 6

Wednesday, May 30

Pickett picked up a box from a grocery store, packed the typewriter, and mailed it to his mailbox. He returned the car to the rental agency, received his change, and walked back to the motel. It was now nine forty on a very warm morning.

Pickett called for a taxi, picked up his things from his room, and checked out. At nine fifty-four a Yellow Cab pulled up in front of the motel.

"Stapleton Airport, please."

The cab driver nodded, and they were off. Pickett sat back in the rear seat and went through the past week's activities in his head. Everything he needed to know was written down on the condensed notes in his briefcase. Everything the others needed to know was written in the coded letters he would send from Washington, DC. Everything else had been burned and flushed down the toilet at the motel.

In three-plus weeks, the exercise would begin.

The cabby pulled up at the airline's drop-off doors and helped Pickett with his suitcase. Pickett presented his ticket, received his boarding pass, and walked down the concourse to his gate. He boarded at twelve eighteen and flew to St. Louis and then on to Washington National.

He had two hours at Washington National before a connecting flight took him back to Boston. During that time, he found a mailbox for the three letters.

He read a newspaper while waiting for his flight. The headlines proclaimed Yeltsin as the new president of Russia after a third round of voting. In sports, the Red Sox were tied with Milwaukee, one game behind the Toronto Blue Jays, who had come from out of nowhere to lead the division.

Damn Red Sox, he swore to himself. *Two games over five hundred heading into June. Shit!*

Pickett boarded his flight to Boston. He arrived there at eight twenty that night. He was tired. The drive to Ellis Bay did not excite him, so he stayed in Boston that night.

Thursday, he returned to Ellis Bay.

CHAPTER 7

Atlanta, Saturday, June 2, 10:35 a.m.

Tom was mowing his lawn when the mailman pulled in front of his house. The two men chatted briefly at the curb, then the mail truck pulled off to make its next delivery.

Tom sorted through the mail as he headed for the house and took the 9 × 12 manila envelope from the major coming to the top as he walked.

Amy was at work. She wouldn't be home for five hours. The house was empty. Tom sat down at the kitchen table, reshuffled the mail, put the major's envelope to one side, and opened the other mail.

When this was done, he picked up the envelope and stared at it. Then he rose, went to the refrigerator, and pulled out a can of beer. He put everything on the kitchen table and sat down facing the window. He would be able to see Amy drive into the back from that angle. She had said she might come home for lunch. He didn't want to be surprised.

Tom opened the can of beer then carefully slit the top of the envelope and pulled out its contents. Taped to the top page were twelve one-hundred-dollar bills. He peeled each one off and removed the tape from their backs and put the bills on the table, then thought better of it, picked them up, folded them, and put them in his pocket. He took another sip of his beer. Taped to another piece of paper were his new identification cards and papers. For this trip, he

49

would become Allen Hodges from Kansas City. The page contained a driver's license and two credit cards, all under Allen's name. Tom wondered how the major was able to come up with all these identification papers. He knew that they would pass muster and would be accepted anywhere. Next came nine pages of single-space rows of letters, typed in capital letters.

"Christ," he muttered.

Tom knew the formula and immediately began to decipher the code. It wasn't difficult. By writing the letter before and after the Q, he was able to pull up the content of the message.

What it asked for was some electronic equipment to tap into the phone lines, at least four bugs that could be planted in the house, four walkie-talkies, and various other electronic devices that might be needed to disable the burglar alarm and to break into the house, plus the additional surveillance equipment they had used on the two previous jobs. Most of these things Tom had stored in the back room at his business address. Tom owned and operated an electronics parts and repair store. What he didn't have in stock, he could manufacture. These items would then be packed and mailed to Denver at separate times over the next two weeks. The plan was to have all these items onsite by the time they all met up.

The second part of the letter gave him instructions on how to get to Denver and where he would be staying. He would be contacted once he was settled in.

The money was to cover expenses. For any additional expenses, he would be reimbursed after the job was completed.

The last part of the letter reemphasized the need for complete secrecy. The major had not been too happy when Tom married just before the second job and had lectured him on the importance of his being able to pick up and move at a moment's notice.

Tom had explained to Amy that he had a top-secret job with the government and that it called for him to be away at times. He could tell her nothing about his job but assured her that it wasn't dangerous. He made her promise that she would never, ever, under any circumstances, reveal this to anyone.

"Amy," he lied, "this is even higher than top secret. If ever I am called away, just tell people that I've gone to an electronics convention."

Tom rose and got himself another beer and returned to the table. He stared down at the encrypted message and at the translation. He then picked up the pages of the letter, went to the sink, lit the pages, and dropped them into the sink. He watched as the flames devoured the paper. When the flames were gone, he rinsed the ashes down the drain.

He then gathered up his translation and reread the words, committing them to memory, then walked to the living room where he touched a secret button in his desk. The false bottom to the lower left drawer popped open. Tom deposited the message, the money, and the false identification papers into the drawer and closed it. He retrieved his beer from the kitchen and went back out front to finish the lawn. It was now two thirty. Amy had not come home for lunch.

Chicago, Saturday, June 2, 11:20 a.m.

Cecil rose late on Saturday, as was his habit. Jalene kept the kids overnight so that he could spend some time with "the boys." Every Friday night, Cecil and two friends would go out to a movie, the bowling alley, or whatever else they had agreed to. All three of them were widowed or divorced single parents. Each week one of them would be responsible for the overnight babysitter. This week just happened to be Cecil's turn; thus, Jalene had his two, plus two others. All three men contributed financially to the arrangement.

Cecil went into the bathroom and stood in front of the mirror. He peered into it, scratched behind his head, and yawned.

"Man oh man," he said into the mirror, "these Friday nights are going to be the death of me."

He stretched, took off his undershorts and tee, and stepped into the shower. When he finished, he looked in the mirror, turned sideways, and patted his stomach. There was a roundness there and a tightness of skin.

"Damn," he said and vowed to lose twenty pounds, starting right now.

He leaned forward and peered into the mirror, ran his hand over his face, and decided not to shave. He'd do that when he had to. That was one advantage of being a single male, he sadly admitted to himself.

In the bedroom, he found clean jeans and a T-shirt and put them on. The jeans were a little snug around the waist, but he managed to get them buttoned. He picked up his watch and put it on, then picked up his wedding ring. He stared at it, turned it around in his fingers, and looked at the inscription on the inside: FOREVER YOURS, C.M.R.W.

He sighed and slipped it on his finger.

There was only one piece of mail in his mailbox, a light-brown 9 × 12 manila envelope with a return address of Washington, DC. Cecil looked up and down the street before reentering the house. He put the envelope on the table and called his sister.

"Hi, it's me. Yah, just got up. Say, listen, could you keep the kids a little while longer? Somethin' I gotta do… Great. I'll call you when I'm done… Thanks, sis."

Cecil hung up, went to the cupboard, and found some cookies. *So much for losing weight today*, he thought.

Returning to the table, Cecil tore open the envelope and removed its contents. Setting the money aside, he picked up the letter. His message was contained in six pages. He reached for a pencil in a cup on the table and, using the back of the envelope, began to transcribe the message.

Cecil would be in charge of the weapons. They would be handguns, preferably small caliber. Cecil would mail them individually over the next two weeks to a drop address in Denver. Of course, each gun would be untraceable. One box of ammunition would accompany each gun. They had never had need of the weapons in the past, but the major insisted that they be available. "Just in case."

Cecil would fly to Denver on June 22 and would stay at the Regency Hotel on Thirty-Ninth Avenue next to the highway. He would have a confirmed reservation under the name Floyd King. His new driver's license, Social Security card, and two major credit cards were included in the envelope. Cecil picked up the fake license and looked at it. It was an Ohio license and looked remarkably authentic. The picture was taken two years ago by the major just for this purpose.

"That man sure do good work," Cecil mused, admiring the forger's work.

The last part of the message cautioned Cecil on the need for secrecy. He reread the entire message, committing it to memory, and burned the letter and envelope in the kitchen sink. He then took the twelve hundred dollars, found an empty envelope, put his fake papers and money in it, and hid it behind the drawer in the dresser. Then he called his sister and said he was coming over.

Los Angeles, Sunday, June 3, 3:30 p.m.

Jackie arrived home exhausted. She had spent the weekend in Las Vegas with Gretchen and Bonnie. The movie shoot was over, and she had some free time on her hands. She told the girls she wanted to celebrate.

Jackie was given a bonus from the studio when the filming was done and talked the two girls into the trip. Her bonus gained her another three hundred and twenty-five dollars in winnings at the slot machines at Caesars. Gretchen had broken even, and Bonnie was behind less than a hundred bucks when they left Vegas. All in all, they agreed, it had been a fun weekend.

Her mailbox was stuffed with mail, most of it junk. There were bills and ads and a 9 × 12 manila envelope. She tossed it all on the couch as she walked by and immediately went into the bedroom where she stripped naked and went into the bathroom and showered.

Stepping out of the shower, she wrapped a towel around her head and put on a bathrobe. She returned to the couch, picked up her mail, and began sorting through it. Exhausted as she was, she decided to open the manila envelope. Her instructions were to ship her makeup materials to Denver to make masks for each of them. This was to be done six days before she left. Her flight and hotel accommodations were included along with her new identity which placed her home in Texas. Her name would be Julie Johnson. She would be thirty-two.

She gathered up the notes, letter, license, and money and put it all back into the envelope. These she brought into her bedroom and slid under the mattress. Then she took off her bathrobe and climbed into bed. It was just after ten in the evening.

She slept until after ten the next morning. The phone woke her. It was Bonnie. Did Jackie want to go shopping? Jackie agreed to meet her in forty-five minutes. She retrieved the envelope from under the mattress and separated its contents, tearing up the letter and notes. These she burned in the sink as she was instructed to do. The money and identification papers went into one of the twenty-two shoeboxes that she kept in the bottom of her closet.

She washed her face, dressed, and met Bonnie thirty minutes later.

CHAPTER 8

Ellis Bay, Maine, Wednesday, June 6, 8:15 a.m.

John Burton, the real name of the planner/major, awoke to a warm and beautiful late spring morning. The sun shone through the window of his cottage and into his face. He stretched, lying in bed, looking at his surroundings, pleased with what he saw.

It was a bachelor's room, cluttered but not messy. There was a desk in the corner with a typewriter on it, and book-lined shelves covered one wall. There was a bathroom off the bedroom and windows that looked out over the back deck to the harbor in the distance.

The rest of the cottage comprised a spacious living room adequate kitchen, small dining room, and one other bedroom, plus another bathroom off the kitchen.

He had purchased the cottage five years ago. It sat at the end of a long driveway that was part of a nine-acre tract of land that jutted out into the bay.

John Burton was a loner. To the townsfolk, he was a writer. He was ex-military. US Army, medically discharged with the rank of major. He had been wounded in battle and had retired with an adequate disability pension from the Army.

Not much was known about him, and this fascinated the townspeople. He had written one published book, a fictional account of the war in Vietnam titled *The Road to Phnom Penh*. It hit the top ten lists almost immediately and quickly rose to become a best seller, where it has remained for nearly sixteen months. He was reportedly working on his second novel, and this, the townspeople assumed, was one of the reasons he was gone for extended periods of time. That and the fact that he visited the VA Hospital in Boston every month.

John rose from his bed and went to the kitchen. He turned on the coffee maker and returned to his bedroom where he stretched out on the floor and took several deep breaths. He then proceeded to do one hundred twenty sit-ups. When he was done, he lay there for one minute, rolled over, and did forty push-ups, twenty with his left arm and twenty with his right. For good measure, he did an additional forty using both arms.

He stopped after counting out his last push-up, rolled over, and lay there with his bare back on the varnished wooden floor. It was cold against his perspiring skin. He waited while his heart rate slowly returned to normal and checked his pulse against the sweep hand of his clock.

"Good," he said, satisfied with his results. The doctors had told him he had the heart of a twenty-five-year-old, and at forty-two, John was determined to take good care of it.

He next stood and began doing deep knee bends, counting each one aloud through one hundred and twenty. To him, these were the hardest, and there was a slight burning sensation in his knees when he was done.

After getting cleaned up, John decided to drive into town for breakfast.

In a single-car garage next to the house, his recently purchased Corvette sat, shined and polished and protected from the elements. John climbed in, took a breath of air into his lungs, and turned the key over. Immediately the car came to life under him. He backed out of the garage and turned it around.

John was off. The top was down. Warm air moved across his face. He was free. He reached the far end of the driveway, pulled to a stop, looked both ways, and gunned the engine, squealing tires as he pulled onto the paved road.

"Freedom!" he shouted to no one and sped on down the road toward the town two miles away.

Ellis Bay had always been a fishing town. Now, though, the fishing was not as good as it had been in the past, and the town had discovered tourism with a vengeance. In early June, activity was light, and the tourists wouldn't start arriving in heavy numbers until later in the month.

This was an exciting time for the residents of the town. New paint covered the old, brass was polished, windows were cleaned, storefronts were repaired, boats were sanded and repainted, and everywhere things were being spruced up, all in anticipation of the summer rush.

John pulled up in front of the Anchor Café and parked. Pulling the emergency brake handle, he opened the door and stepped out. He closed the door and scanned the street in both directions. Everywhere there was last-minute activity in preparation for the anticipated onslaught.

In the café, John was greeted by the owner.

"Morning, John," Annie said pleasantly.

Annie was older than John by maybe twenty years, John had thought to himself when he first met her. He was surprised to learn that she was only fifty-two.

"Morning, Annie," he replied, seating himself at the counter.

She was immediately in front of him, pouring coffee into a mug. "Looks like it's gonna be a hot one," she volunteered.

John looked out the windows and nodded.

"What'll it be this mornin', the usual?"

"Please."

She put his order on the spindle in front of the little window to the kitchen. John put a spoonful of sugar into the cup, poured some cream from his little stainless-steel counter pitcher into it, stirred it, and was just starting to sip it when she turned to face him.

"Missed you last week. I heard you were out of town."

She looked at him, her left eyebrow raised. Annie was the town gossip. No, that wasn't quite right. She wasn't actually a gossip. She was more like the town's unofficial information center. Anything you wanted to know, just ask her. All the news of the town somehow made its way into her café.

So when someone says John was gone for a week or two, Annie felt it was her duty—her obligation—to get all the facts. John had learned this within weeks of moving into this pleasant little town and played along with her prodding.

"Went to Boston. Had to check into the VA again and wanted to do some research," was his standard answer. He said this with the beginnings of that nasal twang that the locals used. It amused him and brought a twinkle to Annie's eyes.

His breakfast finally arrived. When he was through, he tossed some bills on the counter and waved goodbye to Annie and left. Along the row of stores were gift shops, a drugstore, a men's apparel shop, a jewelry shop, two women's clothing stores, and a travel agency.

John looked in the windows of the various shops he passed until he reached the corner. There, he crossed the street diagonally. The post office was on the opposite corner. He entered, went to his post office box, retrieved his mail, and left. John didn't get much mail and only went to the post office once or twice a week. This latest batch of mail consisted of the usual junk, plus his pension check and a letter from his agent. John dropped the junk mail in a wastebasket without even bothering to open it, walked back to his car, tossed the remaining mail on the front seat, and drove off.

He deposited his check at the drive-through at the bank and decided to go home. He knew the contents of the letter from his agent.

"When will you be sending me the synopsis? When will you get a goddamn computer? And most important, when will you get a fuckin' phone installed?"

It was always the same. John didn't need a phone. He was deathly afraid of computers—he still didn't understand them—and his new novel, a saga about the Civil War, was not going as well as the first.

John knew what he wanted to say, knew what the storyline was about, but had had trouble getting started. He had promised Mike, his agent, at least a synopsis by the end of March. Obviously, this had not happened.

All right, John promised himself, *I'll go home and give it some serious attention.*

He raced down the road, feeling the power of the car's engine, feeling the car as it hugged the curves, and flew over the straight-aways. He turned into his driveway and pulled into the garage. One quick rev of the engine and he turned off the key. His hands continued to grip the wheel.

"God, I love this car!"

Back inside John read the letter from his agent. Sure enough, it was just as he had supposed. It also included an invitation to lunch on the eighth of June and a weekend on the Cape if he was free. He made a note on a yellow Post-it to call Mike and accept.

CHAPTER 9

Denver, Wednesday, June 20

The first of the boxes started to arrive by UPS and Federal Express on the eighteenth. They came from Chicago, Atlanta, and Los Angeles. By the twentieth, there were a dozen boxes of various sizes and weights stacked in the back room of the store. All of them were addressed to a Mr. James Pickett.

The boxes were taking up more space in the back than the proprietor had anticipated. Still, the man had paid for six months in advance. And he had agreed to pick them up by the twenty-fifth at the latest.

He hoped that there would not be too many more parcels arriving.

Atlanta, Thursday, June 21

Tom arrived home from work to find Amy in the kitchen. She was drinking. Since they had been married and she had moved in with him, they had only been apart once. That had been two years ago. A week ago, Tom told her of his upcoming trip. He had been vague and told her little about it. She only knew that he would be gone for a couple of weeks, where she did not know, only that it had something to do with the government. Tom had sworn her to secrecy.

"It's those letters from Washington," she accused, "the ones you never talk about."

Tom had nodded but had said nothing more.

Now she sat in the kitchen, a glass of Jack Daniels in her hand, a half-full bottle in front of her, tears in her eyes.

"Oh shit," Tom muttered to himself when he saw her.

"Hi," he said hesitantly.

"Hi," she sobbed.

He grabbed a glass from the cupboard, added some ice and sat down across the table from her. Pouring some of the liquid into his glass, he asked, "So?"

Amy wiped a tear from her cheek with the back of her hand.

"I...I had to leave work early. I started crying and couldn't stop. They all wanted to know what was wrong and I couldn't tell them."

"What did you tell them?"

She sniffed and blew her nose. "Nothing."

Tom pulled his chair closer to the table. Although they were alone, he felt the need for secrecy. He knew this day might come and he had prepared for it.

"Amy," he began, "What I am about to tell you must *never* be repeated. Do you understand?"

She nodded and blew her nose again.

"You remember when I told you that I had been in Special Forces while I was in the Army?"

She nodded again, dabbing her eyes with a hanky.

"Well, in a way, I still am," he lied. "I can't tell you who or what I work for, but sometimes I get instructions by mail telling me of some upcoming mission—job—that I must do.

"When the message comes, I must go. Amy, trust me, someday this will all be over. When it is, we will be rich. That's all I can say.

"You've got to understand, this is all highly secret. You must never breathe a word of this to anyone. If anything about my trips were ever to leak out, I and whoever else is involved could be compromised, and the mission could be destroyed. A lot of lives depend on what I do."

He grasped her hands in his as he said this last part and squeezed them.

"How…how long will this go on?" she asked, settling down somewhat.

"I don't know, maybe one more year, maybe two, maybe as many as four. I just don't know. But I promise you, when it is over we'll be able to do anything we want, go anywhere we want, and we won't have any money worries or anything. And there won't be any more secrets between us. Okay?"

Amy sat up straight in her chair and brushed back the last of her tears.

"I'm sorry," she finally said, "I'm acting like a baby. I'll be okay. It's just that I don't know what you do when you're gone, and I'm afraid that it could be dangerous."

"Trust me, it's not," he said, patting her on the back of her hand. She was nine years younger than him. Sometimes she acted even younger.

"Now, how 'bout I order in a pizza and we go to bed early?" he suggested, standing.

She smiled up at him and nodded, wiping away the last of the tears that were drying on her cheeks.

Later that night Tom and Amy made love three times. In the morning he was exhausted.

Chicago, Thursday, June 21

Jalene helped Cecil pack his bags. The kids were watching television. She knew the drill. Ask no questions, and just take the kids for a while. Cecil would disappear for a couple of weeks and then return. No explanations were given; none were expected. All she knew was that it had something to do with the government. She had seen the mail.

In the morning, she would drive him to the airport and drop him off in front of the United ticket doors. He would thank her for the ride, turn, and walk through the doors, and she would drive off. She had done this before.

"You sho' you'll be okay?" he asked her. "Let me give you some money."

"No, I can manage," she replied as he reached into his wallet and pulled out a hundred-dollar bill, one of many she could see.

"Lord A'mighty!" she exclaimed, "where'd you git all dat money?"

Cecil looked at her as if to say, "Don't ask," and stuck out a bill for her to take.

She took it and slipped it into her jeans.

"Thanks," was all she said.

"Sis," he cautioned her, "not a word to Eugene, okay?"

She winked at him. "I promise."

Los Angeles, Thursday, June 21

Jackie had not worked for almost two weeks, and she was restless. Her bags were packed, and she was ready to go. She had sent everything that she had been asked to send in advance of her arrival. All that was left was her personal belongings.

She told her friends that she was going back east for a two-week visit with some old college friends. No names were mentioned.

Her first stop would be Dallas. There, she would change planes and assume her new identity. From there she would fly to Denver.

Excitement mounted as she thought of the next two weeks. For her, the *mission* was like a drug, a high, a jolt. She knew the risks she was taking, but she didn't care. She was going to see the major again.

They had been lovers once, a long time ago, but their jobs had split them up, and they somehow drifted apart, cards and letters becoming fewer and fewer until they had stopped corresponding all together. And then the jobs had started. Now, when they got together, it was just good sex. She understood this and accepted it. She didn't need a man to complicate her life, and the major asked nothing more of her. She, in turn, put no expectations on him. They were good in bed. Very good. But that was all. Still…

Cleveland, Friday, June 22, 12:35 p.m.

Cecil walked off the plane and into the terminal carrying a briefcase. He followed the signs and found the baggage area. He checked his watch and then went looking for the lockers. He found them and returned to wait for his suitcase.

When his bag arrived, he went back to the lockers. Inserting a quarter in the slot, he put his bag and the briefcase in the locker after first taking an envelope out of the briefcase. He then closed the locker and locked it, looking around the airport casually as he pulled the key from the slot.

Cecil glanced at his watch. He knew that he would have one hour and thirty-five minutes before he would approach another airline's counter as Floyd King, his new identity. He bought a paper from the newsstand and sat down to read it. He found the sports page and checked the ball scores. His Cubs, his beloved Cubs had lost the previous night. He shook his head in disgust. He folded the paper and checked his watch again. He looked around the airport at the other people. He was nervous, and he was sweating. He knew this and yet was powerless to stop it. He looked like someone who had a fear of flying, but just the opposite was true. Cecil loved to fly.

He looked at his watch again. He still had an hour to go. "Fuck!" he said through clenched teeth. He got up and went in search of a bathroom. Finding one, he approached a sink and splashed cold water on his face and then dried it with a paper towel. He then entered a stall and pulled the envelope from his inside coat pocket. He changed the identification from it to his wallet, and his real identification went back into the envelope. Everything else that might identify him had been removed from the wallet the night before. The wallet went back into his hip pocket, and the envelope went back into his coat. He then went back to the sink, splashed more cold water on his face, and left.

Cecil, now with his new identity as Floyd King, returned to his seat. This activity had taken up twelve minutes of his time.

"Goddamn," he swore under his breath. He tapped his right toes against the marble floor.

Picking up his paper again, he started on page one and read the news until his hour was almost up. Rising, he retrieved his bags from the locker, put the envelope back in the briefcase, and got in line at the ticket counter. When it was his turn, he explained his situation to the man behind the counter. There was room on the flight. Did he want an aisle seat or one by the window?

"An aisle seat will be just fine," the big man answered.

His boarding pass was prepared.

"That'll be two hundred eighty-six dollars for a one-way ticket to Denver. How will you—"

Floyd already had the money out of his wallet. He handed the ticket agent three one-hundred-dollar bills.

"Thank you, sir," the ticket agent said, reaching for the money. He counted out the correct change and gave Floyd his boarding pass and his change.

"You'll be leaving from gate C-6. You'll have to hurry. Have a nice flight."

Already, he was looking past Floyd to the lady behind him.

Floyd took the pass, picked up his briefcase, and headed in the direction of gate C-6. He had nine minutes before boarding time, according to his watch.

That's cutting it close, he thought.

Floyd arrived at C-6 just as the gate attendant was announcing the boarding of United flight 286 with stops in Kansas City, Denver, and Los Angeles.

Atlanta, Friday, June 22, 12:45 p.m.

Tom entered the door of the DC 10 and made his way to the back of the airplane. He found his seat and stored his briefcase, sat down, and strapped himself in, then put his head back on the headrest and closed his eyes. He was immediately asleep.

"Ladies and gentlemen," the announcement began, waking Tom from his sleep. He listened as the speech was presented by the pilot. The stewardess in front of the coach section went through her little routine, the bored look of hundreds of such actions on her face. When she was done, he felt a slight lurching movement as the airplane was pushed away from the terminal. He looked at his watch. The plane was only ten minutes behind schedule.

"Not bad," he said to the man seated next to him. "Only ten minutes late this time."

When the plane was in the air, Tom put his seat back and closed his eyes. He thought about last night, and Amy and quickly fell asleep, a smile on his lips. He slept most of the way to Kansas City, waking only once when the man in the seat next to him bumped into him as he returned from the restroom.

Tom switched identities in Kansas City and flew on to Denver as Allen Hodges, arriving at Stapleton at five after five, local time. He hailed a taxi and had the driver drop him off at the Renaissance Hotel across from the airport. When he checked in, there was a message waiting for him. He opened the envelope immediately. It read simply, "Doubletree Hotel, Room 610, 9:05 a.m."

Dallas, Friday, June 22, 10:40 a.m.

Jackie came out of the women's restroom an entirely different woman. Her hair was different now, thanks to the makeup department. She now had long, straight brown hair that fell below her shoulders. She wore glasses. Julie Johnson looked more like a librarian; pretty, in a plain sort of way.

She had no trouble purchasing a ticket on a connecting flight to Denver and arrived at Stapleton at two twenty-seven that afternoon. A taxi took her to the Stapleton Plaza Hotel where she checked in under her new name. There was an envelope waiting for her. It read, "Doubletree Hotel, Room 610, 9:00 a.m."

Floyd arrived at Stapleton and immediately took a taxi to the Regency Hotel. He arrived in his room and put his bag in the closet area before opening up the envelope. Short, to the point: "Doubletree Hotel, Room 610, 9:10 a.m."

CHAPTER 10

Denver, Saturday, June 23, 9:00 a.m.

The first to arrive, as he had planned, was Julie. A gentle knock on the door announced her arrival. John opened the door. She stood there and looked at him and entered when he stepped aside. He opened his arms, and she came to him in a warm embrace. He hugged her, kissed her on her forehead, and stepped back, holding her hands as he examined her.

"You still look good," he said to her. "Come in. I've got coffee and rolls and juice. The other two will be here shortly. Your hair. It looks different from what I remember."

"It's a wig. Thought I'd change my appearance a little when I became Julie Johnson. You like?"

He nodded his approval just as the second knock sounded at the door.

"Excuse me," he said and bowed.

Opening the door, John stuck out his hand and greeted the tall thin man who stood in front of him.

"Welcome, welcome. Come in, come in, please."

The man known as Allen entered, saw Julie, and went to her, holding out his arms.

"Hi," he greeted warmly and gave her a squeeze.

She squeezed him back. "Good to see you again," she said pleasantly.

The three of them made their way over to the cart piled high with sweet rolls and croissants when another knock was heard at the door. It was firm but gentle.

John nodded at his two companions and went to the door just as the knocking began again. Throwing open the door, John was confronted by the huge hulk of the black man standing in the doorway.

"Hey, man, what it is?" Cecil asked, slapping John's hand in greeting, then they both made fists and tapped them together.

John stepped outside and looked both ways after his friend entered, then reentered the suite and closed the door behind him.

After greetings all around, the four of them sat down to coffee, juice, and rolls. John asked how each of their accommodations suited them, and they all answered in the positive. They chatted about what was going on in their lives and what they all had been doing over the past two years. Then the four of them got down to business.

The only rules that John had laid down from the beginning were that they would never reveal their last names to each other and that they would never reveal where they came from. John was at a disadvantage because they all knew who he was, and he accepted this because there was no other way. Other than these two rules, they were free to say whatever they wanted. It had worked well for them in the past. John introduced them to each other by their new identities, stressing that from now on they were to call each other by these names whenever they were together. For his part, he was to be called only by the title major.

At ten o'clock, the coffee and rolls were cleared away, and John invited them over to a circular table. On it were four plain, sealed envelopes. Their assumed names were written on each of them. Inside the envelopes were instructions each of them would need to complete the plan, including a list of the materials each would require. The first order of business was for the major and Allen to pick up all the shipments from the mailbox drop site. They were to be taken to a storage rental unit the major had leased the day before.

Next, the four of them would scout out the three locations the major had picked to hold the child once she was taken. The three of them would have a say in the decision, but Floyd would be the deciding vote. The layout, entrance, and escape routes would be his to decide.

Tom, now Allen, brought up the question, "Could all my equipment be stored there?"

"Good question. We'll check it out when we decide which location to use. Allen, I want you to set up the van like a mobile command center. Julie, how are you at sign painting?"

"Well, it's been a while, but I can still do lettering pretty well."

"Good. Allen, you, and I are going to the house on Tuesday for an interview with the parents. I'll need to have pictures of the inside of the house and also their security system."

Allen looked at the major, surprise showing on his face.

"It's okay, it's all set up. I'll explain later."

The major made some notes on his yellow pad. He then reached into his briefcase and pulled out three stacks of bills of varying denominations.

"Here," he said nonchalantly, tossing a stack to each of them. "There's two thousand dollars each. You'll need it for incidentals."

They reached for the money, checking the amounts. Each stack contained twenties, fifties, and one-hundred-dollar bills. Almost simultaneously, they set the money down in front of them, clasped their hands, their arms and hands encircling the money, and looked at their benefactor.

The major thought, *That's why I picked these people. They think and act so much alike.*

"Okay, any questions so far?"

He looked at them and they looked at each other, and then their eyes all came back to him. There were no questions.

"Good. I want each of you to study the plans and timetables. I expect each of you to meet the deadlines outlined in your folders. If you have a problem with something, I need to know immediately. Is that clear?"

He looked at each one of them as he said this, his eyes meeting theirs. Each of them looked back at him, confidence and trust showing in their expressions, but nothing was said.

"Good!" he said, slapping his hands on the table. "We'll meet back here at four o'clock tomorrow afternoon. By then I want your input on each of the items I've outlined. Once you've committed my instructions to memory, I want them destroyed. Again, he looked around the table. "Understood?"

They nodded and rose.

"Allen, I've got a van parked downstairs. It's in the third row on the side of the hotel. White. License number AKT 435. Here are the keys. I'll meet you in ten minutes. Just move it to the side of the entranceway and pick me up when I come out."

Allen took the keys from the major and left.

Floyd looked at Julie and then at their leader. He looked at his watch.

"I'll go first," he said, rose, went to the door, looked back at the two remaining members, winked, and went out.

Julie continued to stand next to the major, tension rising inside her.

"John," she said, just as he turned and said her name.

They both laughed, breaking the tension. She looked up into his eyes. He reached for her, wrapping his arms around her, holding her against him. He smelled the fresh scent of her hair and squeezed her lightly against him.

"Later," he whispered, "Allen's waiting."

"Right," she managed to say and pulled herself away. "I'd better be going."

He nodded and kissed her lightly on the lips.

"Good luck."

"Good luck to you too," she replied, and she too was suddenly gone.

Alone in his suite, the major picked up his notes and put them in his briefcase, locked it, and put it next to the couch. He then went through the room, picking up anything that might reveal his visitors' presence and threw it in the trash. Next, he wiped down the top of the table they had been sitting at and then the chairs. He didn't want their prints or his to be found together. He made a mental note to purchase some latex surgical gloves for each of them. He then took the bag of trash, found a janitor's closet down the hall from his room, and deposited it in a trash can. Then he went down to the lobby.

Walking through the lobby, casually searching for the unusual, and seeing none, John walked out into the sunshine. Almost immediately, Allen arrived with the van, and the major climbed into the passenger side.

Allen put the van into gear and drove off, following the directions the major was giving to him. John explained about the upcoming interview with the McArthurs and what he needed to do. Allen nodded his understanding as his instructions were given to him.

"I just hope Julie has my face disguise done in time."

"She will. That's why you go in for makeup first. She'll be ready for you when we're finished. You're going straight over there when we're done at the storage unit."

Again, Allen nodded.

He drove in front of the mailbox drop store and parked.

"I'll just be a minute," the major said and let himself out of the van. He walked across the parking lot and into the store.

Allen sat behind the wheel and watched the man as he entered the store. They had been through a lot together while still in the army. It was because of the major that he was still alive. Allen had often said that he would follow the major into hell if he had to.

And so, here I am.

Five minutes later the major reappeared and walked directly to the van and got in.

"Let's go around to the back. We'll pick up the stuff back there."

Allen started the van and drove to the end of the strip mall and around to the back.

"There's quite a bit of stuff, especially from you, Allen. The owner was a little upset about having to store it all. It took up more room than either he or I imagined."

"Well, there's a lot of stuff I'm going to need. I didn't want to have to purchase too much out here for fear of setting off some alarms."

John nodded in understanding as they pulled up by the rear door of the store. The owner was leaning against the open door waiting for them.

Allen and the major jumped down from the van and followed the man inside where they were given a dolly. John introduced Allen to the store manager, and together the three of them hauled the boxes and cartons out to the back of the van. In ten minutes, the van was loaded.

The major thanked the manager for all the trouble and inconvenience and offered him a fifty-dollar bill. The man took the offering and thanked his customer.

"There will be more things coming in about two weeks," the major lied, "but it shouldn't be as much or as big as this load. Thanks again. I'm sorry all this took up so much room. I really hadn't expected so many boxes in so short a time."

They shook hands, and the major climbed into the van. They drove off. It was now two o'clock. At two forty-five the equipment was safely inside the storage rental unit.

"I'd better check on my equipment before we leave it, if you don't mind," Allen said. "I'd hate to have to repair or replace something now."

The major looked at his watch. "Sure."

Allen opened each box and inspected the items, explaining what each one was for.

There was surveillance equipment, sweepers to weed out bugging devices, telephone equipment to tap into phone lines, and most important—to the major anyway—walkie-talkies that would allow them to keep in touch with each other. Allen handed one to the major.

"Cobra hand-held CB 5-watt two-way radios. One mile per linear amp. I've boosted it a little, should be able to reach between five and six miles. Big question is, will they work in the mountains? I assume you're going to hide the kid up there?"

Allen jerked his head in the direction of the mountains to the west. "I think we'll be all right. I'd like to check them out, though."

The major smiled. Allen was smart, and he was thorough.

"Oh," Allen continued, "remember to use channel 5. Five can't be heard by anyone but the four of us. I've already confirmed that. This is a closed system channel. Channel 9 is for emergencies, and 19 is open to truckers. They all use it to talk to each other. Sometimes you hear some pretty weird things on that channel. Sure wouldn't want them listening in on us though."

When Allen was finished explaining these things to his boss, he took back the radio, packed it with the others, closed up the boxes, and stacked them separately from the others. He numbered each one according to its importance and use.

One of Julie's boxes was marked with the number 1. They found it and took it with them to be delivered to Julie in her room.

"Okay, let's get out of here."

The van pulled up in front of the Radisson and Allen got out. He retrieved the box from the back and walked into the hotel. The major drove off.

Inside the hotel, Allen walked up to the counter and placed the box on top of it.

"May I help you?" the girl behind the counter asked.

"Delivery for a Miss..." He paused and looked at the address label. "Miss Julie Johnson."

The girl checked her listings and dialed Julie's room. It was answered on the second ring.

"Yes?"

"There's a delivery down here in the lobby. Do you want me to sign for it?"

"No, no, ah, could you have him bring it on up? I've been expecting it."

"No problem."

The hotel clerk hung up and said, "She wants you to bring it up. Room 312."

"Thanks," Allen said, trying to show some exasperation. He picked up the box and headed off toward the elevators.

The door to her room was open when Allen arrived. She let him in, looked up and down the hall, and closed the door behind her. It was now three fifteen.

"Any trouble?" she asked.

"No."

"Let's get started then."

Allen put the box down on the table next to the bed.

"Sit here," she instructed, pulling up a chair in front of the mirror.

Allen sat as she opened the box and spread its contents over the table and bed. She sorted through the various things spread out in front of her and lined up what she would need.

She started by molding his head with sheets of latex, careful to leave room for his eyes, nose, mouth, and ears. Her fingers were gentle and quick. Tom started to doze off, and she let him. She hummed a little tune as she worked, and by five fifteen, the first part of her work was done. Julie had a rough mask that she would work with. She woke her subject up and carefully removed the mask from his head and put it on a dummy head.

Allen wiped his face with his hands. "What's next?" he asked.

"Now I become creative. How pretty do you want to look?"

"Pretty?"

She laughed. "Just kidding. I can make you blonde, I can make you...Latino, Italian, Oriental, Jewish...what would you like?"

"How 'bout..." Allen remembered his upcoming interview with McArthur and reminded Julie.

"Okay, you're a thirty-eight-year-old post-hippie type with a beard and moustache. How's that."

"Suits me."

"Good. It'll be ready Monday morning."

"Thanks, Jackie, um, Julie," he corrected. "I'll see you later then."

The major arrived back at his hotel, parked the van at the far end of the lot and returned to his suite. He called down for room service and a bottle of bourbon, a six-pack of 7-Up and some snacks to be brought up. When it arrived, he fixed himself a drink and sat in an easy chair that he had pulled to the window.

The ringing of the phone woke him. It was Julie.
"Hi."
"Hi yourself."
"Did I wake you? You sound like you were sleeping."
"Um, well…"
"Sorry."
Silence, then…
"Can I come over?"
The major looked at his watch. It was eight twenty.
"How's the mask coming?"
"Good."
"Good."
"Well?"
"Oh. Sure."
"Did you eat?"
"No. You?"
"No."
"I'll order in. What do you want?"
"Sandwich will be fine. I don't know. Anything. Surprise me."
"Okay. See you when you get here. And, Julie?"
"I know. Try not to be seen."
The major hung up. She would be here in fifteen minutes. He quickly went into the bedroom, stripped, and showered. He was dressed and pouring himself another drink when there was a light tapping on the door.

He opened it. Julie was wearing a pair of jeans that must have been painted on and a white silk blouse. The top three buttons were undone. She wasn't wearing anything under it. It pressed hard against her breasts, and the points of her nipples stood out prominently.

John stepped aside and let her enter. He looked up and down the hall. It was empty. Closing the door, John watched as she walked into the room—glided would have been a better description. She had a gentle sway to her that always turned him on. For years he had been in love with her but had never told her.

He wrestled with this problem from time to time. His biggest fear in life was commitment. Jackie never asked him for anything, never made demands on him. He liked that. He often thought that when this was all over, they could go away together.

She turned to face him, a wicked smile on her lips. She picked up the bottle of bourbon.

"May I?"

"Help yourself."

She put some of the melting ice in a glass, poured herself a glass of 7-Up and added a splash of bourbon. She swirled the mixture around with her finger, licked the liquid from her finger, and took a sip.

John walked over to her, took the glass from her hand, and kissed her.

"You taste good," he whispered in her ear.

She eagerly fell into his embrace. She looked up into his eyes and saw the lust there. She reached up and pulled his head down to hers and kissed him hard, her tongue darting in and out of his mouth.

There was a knock at the door.

"Shit," she muttered and laughed.

John went to the door, looked through the peephole and then opened it and said a few words to the person outside, then wheeled a cart into the room.

"Hungry?"

"You mean for food?"

"You've got to eat," he said, lifting a silver cover off one of the plates and revealing a Monte Cristo sandwich. Next to it were two of the biggest, reddest strawberries she had ever seen.

John removed the other cover. He was having the same thing. A bottle of Riesling wine and two glasses, along with two glasses of iced water, completed the tray's contents.

"Looks good," she said as she sat at the table.

John served her. "Eat up, we've got some unfinished business to take care of."

She giggled.

John sat down and cut into his sandwich. His knee brushed hers, sending an electrical current through his body. They talked about her success in Hollywood and ate their sandwiches and drank their wine. They felt comfortable with each other; the mood was relaxed and easy.

"Here," he said, pouring the last of the wine into her glass.

"What are you trying to do, kind sir," she asked, putting her hand to her chest, "get me drunk?"

"Why no, fair lady, nothing of the kind."

With that, he took her glass and his and stood, motioning her to follow him over to the couch. She sat next to him and accepted the offered glass. She sipped some wine, all the while looking over the rim of her glass at him, a slight smile on her lips.

He could stand it no longer. Putting down his glass and taking hers, he drew her to him and kissed her full on the mouth. She responded with an ardor she had shared with few others.

"Oh, God," she said at last, taking a deep breath. "It's been so long."

John rose and led her into the bedroom where he turned and faced her. Her hands moved quickly to the buttons on his shirt. He helped her and pulled her blouse out of her jeans and unbuttoned it, pulling it off behind her. They embraced, their hot skin sending charges through each other's bodies.

Julie pushed him down onto the bed and came down on top of him, her tongue searching for his. His hands were everywhere, and so were hers. She giggled as he tried to remove her jeans and finally had to stand to get them off. She wore no panties.

John removed his slacks and shorts, and she came to him, her mouth hot and wet on his. They made love atop the bedcovers. When it was over, they lay next to each other, not saying anything, just staring up at the ceiling. The quiet hum of the air-conditioning system was the only sound.

John put his arm under her head, and she moved closer to him, entwining her fingers with his. The smell of her hair was sweet in his nostrils. She snuggled up next to him and buried her face in his neck. Her breathing became lighter and more regular. He held her to him. After a while, John looked at her. She was asleep. Smiling, he lay back and closed his eyes.

At 2:00 a.m., he awoke, chilled. She was gone. He got up, went to the bathroom, and washed. Putting on shorts and a T-shirt, he went out into the living room. Jackie was curled up on the couch, wearing his hotel bathrobe.

"Hi."

"Hi."

He sat next to her, and she curled up in his arm, her head on his shoulder.

"That was nice," she whispered.

He squeezed her gently, said nothing.

"I've been looking forward to this ever since I got your first message."

He squeezed her again.

Jackie took a deep breath and went silent.

She woke at three fifteen. John was asleep next to her; his head slumped down on his chest. She took off the bathrobe and covered him, then bent and gently kissed his forehead. He stirred slightly but did not wake. She smiled down at him and went off to find her clothes.

She took them into the bathroom, splashed water on her face and put on fresh lipstick. Back in the living room she found a piece of hotel stationery and jotted down a quick message. She let herself out.

Jackie decided to walk the short distance from his hotel to hers. Even with the lateness, she walked with a light step and a smile on her face.

At 6:00 a.m., John woke on the couch. She was gone. He rose and went looking for her. She was nowhere to be found. On the table was a handwritten message. It merely said, "Thanks," with a smiley face, written in lipstick.

CHAPTER 11

Julie was working on Allen's mask when Floyd called.

"You got time for me this afternoon?"

"I should be done with Allen's mask at, oh, say three, maybe three thirty. Why don't you come by then?"

"Three thirty is good. See you then."

The next call was from the major.

"Hi."

"Hi."

"What time did you leave?"

"About three thirty."

"Anybody see you leave?"

"Just the bellhop. I think he thought I was a pro." She snickered.

"Did you walk?"

"Uh-huh."

There was a pause. Then, "Jackie?"

"Yes?"

"Thanks."

She smiled. "You're welcome. And, John?"

"Yes?"

"Thank you."

He laughed into the phone.

"So how's the mask coming?"

"Pretty good, I think. I'm just about done. Floyd is coming by later. I'll start his this afternoon. What about you?"

"I think I'm going to go with what I have. McArthur's seen me…well, he's seen what I want him to see anyway. I'll be all right."

"Suit yourself, but I still think you should have a backup disguise, just in case."

"I'll think about it. I'm picking Floyd up at eleven. I'll drop him off at your place later."

"Okay."

She held the phone to her ear even after he had hung up. The dial tone finally brought her back to reality.

"Oh, that man," she said into the receiver and then hung it up and returned to her work.

Floyd was waiting out front when the major drove up in the van. He stepped off the curb as the van stopped and climbed into the passenger side. The major quickly pulled away.

"So where to?" the big man asked.

"I thought we'd check out the house and the security guards. I want your input on the guards."

"Sounds good to me. Let's get it done."

They drove south on I-25 to Hampden and exited westbound. The major turned left on University Boulevard and continued south to Gilpin. Turning right, he drove around the circle and gave Floyd all the particulars from his past observations. Floyd asked a few questions and then sat back to watch.

Ten minutes went by before the security car turned around at the entrance to the drive and backed into the space. Both men looked at their watches.

"Looks like he makes his rounds on a regular basis, based on the times you've noted," Floyd commented, flipping through the notes the major had given him.

The major nodded.

"Let's sit here and wait until the next time he makes his rounds. My bet, it'll be in an hour."

The major agreed and sank down in his seat, trying to get comfortable. Floyd rolled down the side window and stuck his elbow out.

"When we goin' to get the guns out of storage?"

"I thought we'd leave them until the day we pick up the little girl. We really don't need them before then."

"Guess you're right."

"What did you bring us?"

"I got two nine-millimeter Glocks, one Beretta nine-millimeter, and one Smith and Wesson."

"Sounds good. Untraceable, I hope."

"Yes. I made sure all the serials were filed off. Even used a little acid myself on the serial numbers, just to be sure. Ran a carbon check. There's no trace. FBI finds 'em they got nothing. They all work. They all clean."

The major nodded. He knew that Floyd was thorough. "Good."

The two men settled in and waited. They could see the guard sitting in his car. He appeared to be writing on something. Every so often, he would look up and then return to what he was doing. Cars entered and left at various times, and the guard waved his acknowledgment when he recognized the occupants.

Floyd commented, "Fool's probably got himself a crossword puzzle to keep him occupied."

An hour later, the security guard put down what he was doing, pulled out, and began his rounds again.

The major made a note. "Just like clockwork," he said. "I want you to come back here and log his movements each night this week between the hours of 6:00 and 9:00 p.m. Then I want you to follow him. I need to know what time he passes the McArthur house each night. Any questions?"

Floyd shook his head.

The major started the van and pulled out onto University, crossing and turning into Cherry Hills. He turned left and followed the road around until the McArthur residence came into view.

He pointed. "There it is."

"Man, sho' is big," Floyd remarked.

"There's nothing behind it but landscaping. No back road or alley. There is sort of a ravine about seventy or eighty yards from the back of the house. No fence. I couldn't determine where the back door is located. Looks like the only way in is through the front from what I can see. I know there had to be a back way in. I need you to find out how and where. I also need you to find out what kind of security they have outside. Allen'll need this info by Thursday morning. He and I will be inside on Tuesday night, and he'll find out what's on the inside."

Floyd nodded.

The major continued around the drive. As they came to the first stop sign on the circle, he stopped the car.

"See if you can figure out what this little street does." He suggested to Floyd, pointing to a dead-end street to the left.

The major continued on, making the loop around the neighborhood.

"There's the gate I mentioned in my notes. It empties out onto Belleview. I want you to check it out as a secondary escape route. I'm thinking the way we came in is the way we leave, but I need to know if the gatehouse is occupied at night or if the gate is blocked. Let me know, will you?"

Again, Floyd nodded.

Continuing around the drive, the major turned north, passing the security guard who was traveling in the opposite direction. He waved at the guard, and the guard returned it.

"Security seems pretty lax to me," Floyd observed.

"That's what I'm thinking too. Could be different at night, though."

The major turned left and exited onto University, heading south. At the intersection of Belleview and University, he turned left.

"Up ahead is the gate," he volunteered.

He slowed as he passed the gate. The security car was parked in the exit drive, the gate guard leaning on the car door talking into the open window.

When the major could turn around, he drove by the gate again. The security car was gone. He turned right on University and headed north, passing the entrance. The security car was parked in its usual spot.

"Yep, just like clockwork. Shame on them."

Up ahead, the major pointed out the police station.

"Couldn't have the police any closer, could you?" Floyd joked.

"Comes with the territory," the major responded. "Little added pressure keeps the blood flowing."

"Yeah," Floyd responded, laughing lightly.

"I'll drop you off at Julie's hotel. I understand she's doing you this afternoon."

"Kind of curious what she's got in mind for me this time. Should be interesting."

"It always is, Floyd, it always is."

They both laughed. It was now two thirty.

The major dropped Floyd in front of Julie's hotel.

"Tell Allen I'll be…no, better yet tell them I'll be right up."

Floyd nodded and disappeared into the lobby. Five minutes later the major entered and headed up to Julie's room.

She was fitting the finished mask on Allen's head when Floyd let the major in. Allen had been transformed into a younger, broad-er-faced, long-haired, and bearded man—a photographer. His appearance was completely changed, even down to the change of the color of his eyes, brown now, from his new contact lenses.

"Okay, that'll do it. Walk around a little bit, move your head around, see how it feels."

Allen rose and went to the mirror. "Jesus Christ!" he said. "You're good. You're really good."

Julie looked at the major and smiled.

"I know. That's why they pay me the big bucks."

They all laughed.

"Shh," the major cautioned.

"How does it fit?" Julie asked, approaching him.

"Fine. A little rubbing down here. He touched the left side of his neck under his jaw bone. But otherwise, it feels fine."

Julie felt around his face with her fingertips.

RICHARD LIPPARD

"That should be no problem to fix. Okay, let's take it off."

She showed him how to remove it so as to avoid damage, then placed it back on the Styrofoam head.

Turning to Floyd, she said, "You're next."

"Could you make me look like Mel Gibson?"

"You're too big."

The major said, "Come on, Allen, you, and I are going for a ride. Julie, Floyd, see you later."

They left separately, the major first, and when Allen climbed into the van, he asked, "Where to?"

"We're going to the storage unit. I want you to start setting up the equipment, and I want to check out the radios. How far is the range of these things again?"

Allen explained the radios' usefulness to him.

"We could take them into the mountains and try them out if you want," he offered.

"I'll think about it," was the answer.

At the storage unit, Allen carefully unboxed his equipment by number. In this way, he was able to set up a sequence for the installation of the equipment into the van without too much of it being exposed to prying eyes. Unfortunately, this all had to be done out in the open.

First out came the stand the equipment would be secured to. By drilling six holes in the bottom of the van, he was able to secure the base of the stand to the floor. The major climbed under the van and secured the bolts that Allen fed him through the floor.

Next, Allen and the major assembled the rest of the stand. It fit snuggly against the driver's side of the van. When that was done, Allen unpacked his receivers and radio equipment and fastened them to the stand. Next, he fastened a small antenna to the outside of the rear door and ran a wire back to his equipment.

The major watched in amazement as Allen put it all together. Allen was fast, and he was meticulous. But then, this was his specialty.

"Okay," Allen said at last, "let me run a connector to the battery, and we'll see if this stuff works."

Allen ran a wire from the junction box through an adapter, then taped it to the floor, running it forward and under the driver's seat and then up to the firewall. After drilling a hole through the firewall, he fed the cable through to the major.

"Okay, I've got it," he said as he pulled on the wire.

"Good."

Allen was out of the van and quickly attached the cable to the battery.

"Now, let's see if this little puppy works."

Allen reentered the rear of the van and turned on some switches. Little red and green lights immediately lit up on the various pieces of equipment on the stand.

"Good," Allen remarked to the admiring major. "Take one of the bugs down to the end of the aisle and go behind one of those buildings, then call me."

The major did what he was told. In two minutes, Allen heard his call. He adjusted a few knobs and waited for the major to return. When he didn't return, Allen moved up front and gave the horn a two-second beep.

The major returned to the van and handed Allen the bug.

"Is it a go?"

"It's a go."

"Good. Let's get this area picked up and get out of here."

Allen turned off the switches and jumped down from the rear of the van. The two of them picked up the empty cases and put them back in the storage unit, bagged up all the loose pieces of junk they had cut and snipped, tossed it into the storage unit, and closed it. Allen took one last look around and found two small pieces of wire cuttings. He picked these up and put them in his pocket. The major started the van, and they were off.

"I'll be able to receive transmission up to a thousand yards away with this stuff. We'll just have to find a safe place to park the van."

"Floyd's working on that. It should be no problem."

"Good. Then we're all set. When do you want the bugs installed?"

"I was thinking the night we pick up the kid. There's less chance of somebody stumbling over them that way."

"Sounds good to me. How many do you want?"

"I was thinking four: for the living room, the dining room, the kitchen, and the bedroom. What do you think?"

"Maybe we should put two of them in the living room. That's where they will be spending the most time. If one of the bugs fails, we've still got a backup."

This time the major nodded.

"You want TV surveillance? I could hide a camera or two?"

"Bugs'll be fine."

Allen pursed his lips and gave a quick nod.

It was now 7:40 p.m.

Monday, June 25, 10:00 a.m.

As arranged, they met at the Safeway Store parking lot on Fourteenth and Krameria. Today they would scout the three locations the major had found in the hills west of Denver. It was crucial for them to have a safe, out-of-the-way location to hold the child while the ransom money was collected. The major wanted her and her guardians to at least be comfortable while they waited.

"Oh, and by the way," he said as they were finally all settled in his rental car, "divide these up among you."

He handed Floyd a box containing latex surgical gloves.

"I want each of us to wear these whenever we are together from now on. I don't mean in public, but well, you know. I just don't want there to be any way for us to be connected. Understand?"

They all nodded.

"We've been lucky in the past. That's because we've been careful. In and out. No trace. Clean. Neat."

They headed south on Colorado Boulevard until they reached Hampden, then headed west. It was a beautiful, warm June morning, the air was dry, and the breeze coming through the open windows was refreshing.

Soon Denver was behind them, and they crossed under the new C-470 overpass. To the north and south, nature had created an incredible bit of landscaping, for the land lifted into a ridge that Coloradoans called the hogback. This natural phenomenon, created millions of years before, was caused by the shifting of the earth's plates during the forming of the Rocky Mountains. This was indeed the gateway to the Rockies.

The car was climbing in altitude now, and great rock formations could be seen on either side of the road. The plains were no longer visible. It was as if they had, in five minutes time, entered a whole new region.

He turned to Julie riding next to him. "Beautiful, isn't it."

"Wow! This is incredible!"

The major turned off the highway onto Parmalee Gulch Road and followed it for about a mile. Abruptly he turned onto what was nothing more than two ruts heading into the woods. About two hundred yards from the road, he stopped. In front of them was an old log cabin.

"Location number one," he said to his three passengers.

They got out and walked to the cabin. The door was boarded up, as were the windows on each side of it. There was a space between the boards and Julie peered into the window to the left of the door.

"Looks like nobody's home," she joked.

They walked around to the back of the cabin. There were a porch and a back door. There were no boards blocking the doorway.

"Come on," the major implored his fellow conspirators, "the door's open."

They followed him up the steps. He turned the handle and the door opened. He turned to the others and smiled knowingly.

"Credit card," he explained. "Opened it last time I was here."

They entered, Floyd last. He looked around, checking the woods behind the cabin and the path he had just taken. He could see nothing but trees around the house. The road they had just turned off of was nowhere to be seen. There were no other cabins or houses in sight. He listened and heard nothing.

There was just enough light coming through the boarded-up windows and back door for them to see as they made their way through the dwelling. It was obvious that no one had been here for quite some time; dust and cobwebs were everywhere.

"I found a newspaper in the other room when I first found this place. It was dated August 14, 1972."

"Kitchen, living room, two bedrooms. Bathroom's out back. Sort of old-fashioned if you know what I mean. No electricity or running water, but the place is secluded. Can't see it from the road and we can hide the vehicles in the trees."

They each followed the major from room to room as he guided them through the cabin. The living room had a couch and two matching chairs and a coffee table. The two bedrooms had twin beds and dressers.

"Kendra can stay in this room," the major said, pointing to the smaller of the two bedrooms. "A little cleaning and some blankets and sheets, and it could do just fine. What do you think?"

Floyd was the first to speak. "It's got possibilities. Sho' seems private enough."

"That's why I brought you here first. The other two are more comfortable but not quite as secluded. More chance of being discovered."

The major went on to describe the other two locations to them as they walked around the cabin. When they were back in the kitchen again, the three companions looked at each other, then turned to their leader.

Floyd spoke for all of them. "This place'll do jus' fine. Let's get to cleanin' it up. Make it kind of homey for the little one. Okay with you guys?"

They all agreed.

"We'll need some things," Julie interjected. "Let's make a list. Who's going to be staying with her once she's here?"

"I figured you and Floyd could take turns. And Floyd's had experience with kids. Allen and I will be monitoring McArthur's house. What do you two need.?"

Julie and Floyd made a list that included sheets and blankets to food and water and a radio.

"Oh, and cleaning supplies and toilet paper," she added. "That was an outhouse I saw out back, wasn't it?"

"Don't forget flashlights and lanterns," Floyd said. "And a kerosene stove. I think that stove has seen better days."

He stated sheepishly, "One more thing. M&Ms. The kind with nuts. Couple of big bags? Oh, and, uh, some Oreo cookies. Kids love Oreo cookies."

John nodded. "Anything else?" he asked them. When there were no more suggestions, he continued. "All right then. That should do it. Why don't the three of you start putting this place in order. I'll go and get what you need and be back later. Floyd, walk me to the car, will you?"

The two men walked out the back and around the cabin.

"Leave the outside of the cabin as it is," the major advised as they walked toward the car. "Don't take down any of the boards covering the windows or door."

Floyd nodded.

"Come on, ride with me to the end of the driveway. I want you to keep an eye open for traffic. I don't want anyone to see me pulling out of here."

The two men climbed into the major's sedan, and the car backed around and headed up the driveway. The major stopped about fifteen yards from the road. It was just visible through the trees. Floyd climbed out of the car and walked the remaining distance to the edge of the road. When he saw no one was coming, he motioned for the major to pull out, waving as he passed. He turned and walked back to the cabin scouting the area all around the building as he did so.

It was now close to noon.

The major returned at 4:00 p.m. with most of the things on the list. The rest of the items could be picked up later. He brought sandwiches and beer with him also.

The three workers tore into the sandwiches and drank the beer with gusto. The major apologized for not getting back sooner, explaining that he couldn't find a store for the longest time. He was pleased with the work that they had done. The place looked livable now.

"We'll need something to cover the windows at night, maybe some blankets," Floyd offered. "I walked the perimeter. You got yourself a pretty nice little hideaway, Major. Nothing to give us away unless someone stumbles in here by accident."

"How'd you find this place?" Allen asked.

"Completely by accident. You won't believe this, but I swerved to avoid hitting a deer and braked right at the entrance to this place. Something about it struck me. I don't know, it just didn't look quite natural. I got out of the car and discovered the driveway. I almost missed it. Anyway, I followed the driveway, and *voila!*" he said, spreading his arms.

"Well, I'm impressed, even if the bathroom is an outhouse. Ugh!" It was Julie speaking. "But we should be able to keep the kid safely hidden up here. Maybe even go out for walks in the daytime?"

She looked at the three men for agreement. They all nodded.

At six thirty, they put their cleaning equipment and supplies away, packed up, and drove down the mountain. That problem was solved.

The major pulled into the Safeway parking lot a little after seven. Each accomplice was given the next set of instructions. Floyd would scout the neighborhood and the security at the McArthur house, Julie would finish Floyd's mask, and Allen would work on the bugs to be planted in the house. It was suggested that one be placed in the McArthur's car if possible, just in case he was wired during the drop. Allen would have to figure out how to hide it, and where.

"What if the FBI plants a homing device and finds the bug?" Julie asked.

The major turned. "Allen?"

"It's got to be somewhere that it can pick up any conversation he may have but not be obvious. I'll work on it."

"Good. See what you can come up with."

The major wished them good luck, and then they separated. Julie was the last to go.

"You know, you really should have a mask, at least for the final phase. Let me see what I can do."

John nodded.

She reached through the open window and gently touched his shoulder. "Later?"

"I'll come by," he promised.

Alone in his car, he sat with his hands on the steering wheel, pleased with himself. He watched as each car pulled out of the parking lot and thought about the day. It had gone well. He was especially pleased with their acceptance of the cabin in the woods. And he thought, *Jackie and I seem to have picked up right where we left off in Detroit.*

He thought about her and the others. This might be their last job together. He had to get on with his life, and they had their lives to live. He didn't want to press his or their luck.

Tuesday, June 26

At 10:00 a.m., the major put in a call to the McArthur residence. A woman answered. "Mrs. McArthur?"

"Yes?"

"Hi, Mrs. McArthur. Jeffrey Matthews here. *Golf World Digest?* I'm calling to confirm tonight's interview?"

"Oh yes. Yes, Mr. Matthews, we're set for seven thirty. Now, will you be needing anything? Do we have to do anything?"

"No, just be yourselves. This shouldn't take more than an hour, hour and a half at the most. Oh, and I'm bringing along my photographer, Charlie Harris. I hope that's all right."

"That's fine. We'll see you at seven thirty then."

"Thank you."

The major hung up and called Allen at his hotel with the news.

"Good. I'll need to get the camera equipment from storage."

"I'll pick you up in an hour."

The next call was to Floyd.

"Yo!"

"Yo yourself, big guy! How's it going?"

"Okay, if we get the same guy. It's automatic. Just like clock-work. Same time, same route as before. I'm going back tonight and tomorrow. My bet is that whoever makes the rounds is consistent. I've got a few ideas about how to neutralize the guard if we have to. Let's discuss them at your convenience.

"Works for me. Allen and I are on for tonight. We're going to pick up the camera equipment in an hour. You feel up to joining us?"

"Fine by me."

"Later."

They hung up, and the major went back into the bedroom. Julie was just beginning to stir.

"Come on, Sleeping Beauty, time to rise and shine," he urged, slapping her gently on the hip.

He threw open the curtains, and the room was flooded with sunlight. Julie squinted and shaded her eyes with her hand as she turned to face him.

"Good morning."

"Good morning," she answered, sitting up, the sheet falling away from her and exposing her upper body to him.

He bent down and kissed her. Her arms went around his neck, and he lost his balance, falling onto the bed. They both laughed as she rolled over, and he became entangled in the sheets. He kissed her on the mouth, and she responded, her body aching for him.

They made love. It was quick and intense. When it was over, they broke away from each other and lay back breathing heavily.

"Umm," she murmured, "that was good."

He smiled, kissed her on the end of her nose, rose, and headed for the bathroom.

"Nice buns!" she yelled after him as he disappeared.

John turned on the shower just as Julie opened the door. Together they stepped under the water and washed each other. It had been a long time since they had done this, and he enjoyed it. When there was nothing left to wash, nothing left to caress, they embraced and let the cascading waters wash over their bodies, rinsing away the sex and the soap and the weariness of the past twelve hours.

The two of them toweled each other off, and John walked back into the bedroom, a towel wrapped around his waist. He picked up his watch and checked the time.

"Damn," he mumbled and picked up the phone and dialed Allen's hotel.

"Allen, it's me. I'm running a little behind. Better plan on twelve o'clock."

"That's fine."

"Oh, and call Floyd. Let him know. He's coming with us."

"Makes sense to me. It's his equipment."

"Right. See you at noon."

John hung up the phone just as Julie wrapped her arms around him from the back.

"Come on," he said, turning to face her. "We've got to get a move on."

A quick squeeze and she let go of him. She was wearing a white towel, wrapped tightly around her. It accentuated the color of her skin, tanned by the California sun. John could have spent the entire morning alone with this woman, but he had things to do.

When they were both dressed, he kissed her lightly on the lips and promised to meet her at the hotel later in the day. He had finally agreed to let her do a mask for him. He gathered his things and left. In five minutes, he was in his car and heading for Allen's hotel.

Julie went down to the coffee shop and had a late breakfast. She thought about what was happening between John and her. It was intense when they were together. The sex was great. She knew that she loved him, but what did she really know about him? He was from back east. His parents were dead, as was his twin brother, the victim of a tragic auto accident when he was sixteen. That was basically it. And yet she loved him. And not knowing who he was intrigued her. She sighed and bit into the last of her strawberries.

The major picked Allen up at noon and headed over to the Regency to pick up Floyd.

"You guys hungry?" he asked as Floyd climbed into the back seat.

"I am," Floyd immediately volunteered.

Allen smiled. "I'm always hungry."

"Good. Let's get some lunch first. Floyd, do we need to get film and flashbulbs or anything for the camera?"

"Film. I didn't pack any."

"Film it is then."

During lunch, the three men kept their conversation to a minimum. They did talk about sports, the Red Sox, the Cubs, and the Braves, each singing the praises and woes of their respective teams. When the check came, the major automatically picked it up and paid for it. Allen and Floyd knew that there was no arguing with him.

Back in the car, he asked, "You guys still okay with your money? You need anything?"

They both said they were fine.

The major pulled up to the gate of the storage units and punched in his code. The chain-link fence gate moved across the entrance, and they passed through. Stopping in front of the unit, the major looked in the rearview mirror. The gate was not visible from the car. There were no other vehicles in sight. He looked down the row of storage units.

"Okay, let's get to it. As long as we're here, I want to look at the weapons. That okay with you two?"

"Suits me," Allen replied.

"I think you'll like them," Floyd offered.

He found the boxes that the guns, and the camera equipment were shipped in and set them on the floor in the middle of the unit.

"Camera equipment's in that one," Floyd said, pointing to the largest of the five boxes. "Guns are in those."

Allen went to the camera box and opened it. Inside was a Nikon thirty-five-millimeter camera stored inside a black canvas bag. Also included were three different lenses: close-up, wide-angle, and a long telescopic lens for distance shooting. There was also a flash attachment and a box of flashbulbs. He put the flash attachment into its slot, screwed the close-up lens into the front of the camera, and hefted it in his hands, getting a feel for the thing.

"I'll show you how to use it later," Floyd remarked. "Little tricks that'll make it easier for you to use."

Floyd turned to the major. "Ready?"

The major nodded.

"I thought this one would be for you," Floyd explained as he opened the first box. In it was a black Glock nine-millimeter pistol. It also held two cartridge clips wrapped in bubble wrap, each clip fully loaded.

"And, Allen, this one's for you," he said, presenting him with another box; it was the other Glock. "Julie can have this one," he said, opening the third box and showing it to them. It was a blue metal Beretta. "And this little baby," he said, pulling out the Smith and Wesson, "this one's for me."

The major took his gun and inspected it, hefting it in his hands. It felt comfortable. He was impressed. He said so. Floyd beamed.

CHAPTER 12

Tuesday, June 26, 7:30 p.m.

The major and Allen arrived at the McArthur residence at precisely seven thirty. Allen was wearing the mask that Julie had made. For good measure, she had painted a black leopard on his right arm just above the wrist to resemble a tattoo at least five years old.

The major had again put on his nose, moustache, and beard, put in his contacts, and colored his hair so as to become Jeffrey Matthews.

"Hi," Lisa McArthur greeted as she opened the door.

"Good evening. I'm Jeffrey Matthews. This is my photographer, Charlie Harris."

"Come in, come in. Alex will be down in a minute. Can I offer you anything? Coffee? Iced tea? A soda perhaps?"

"No thanks. Maybe later. Thank you though."

Lisa led them to the study.

"Please. Be seated," she said, gesturing.

Both of the men took a seat on the couch, Charlie setting his camera bag down next to him. Lisa took up a position opposite them in an overstuffed chair.

She was an attractive woman, slim and statuesque. For this evening's interview, she had dressed in pale-green slacks and a white sleeveless V-neck cotton pullover. A diamond pendant hung from a silver chain around her neck. Her dark-brown hair was done up in the back, and her eyes and mouth were carefully painted.

The major guessed that she had spent the better part of the day at the beauty parlor. If he had asked, she would have had to admit it.

Alex's footsteps could be heard on the stairs and on the polished stone landing as he approached. Both men rose when he entered the room. Alex walked past his wife and lightly caressed her neck before extending his hand.

"Hi, he said as he shook hands with the journalist and his associate.

"This is Charlie Harris," the major offered and nodded toward his partner. "He'll be taking pictures while we talk."

"Nice to meet you," Alex said. "Well, let's get started. I assume Lisa's offered you something to drink?"

"Yes, thank you," the major responded, "maybe later."

Alex took a chair next to his wife, sat, and crossed one leg over the other, smoothing the fabric of his pants as he did so. "What would you like to know?"

If you only knew, the major thought to himself.

He reached into his inside coat pocket and pulled out a note pad containing a series of questions. He also produced a small tape recorder which he set on the coffee table between them.

"Do you mind if I tape all this?" he asked the couple.

Alex and Lisa looked at each other and gave him permission to tape.

"Okay, to begin with, you and Brett Ellsworth started the tournament three years ago. Tell me, how did the two of you get the idea and how did it come to be?"

"Well," Alex began, leaning forward in his chair, "we were on the golf course together, opposites in a foursome..."

He went on and on, warming to the subject. All the while, Charlie took pictures of him, of them, of the three of them from different angles. He was everywhere, and before long, he became a nonentity.

Alex launched into his story with such excitement and animation that he completely controlled the interview. He had told this story before, and each time it became more embellished and full of detail. The major encouraged him to continue, asking questions to clarify points in his narrative.

Finally, Lisa interrupted and offered to get them all drinks. Charlie volunteered to help and followed her into the kitchen.

"Do you have any children?" he asked casually while helping her get glasses down from the cabinet.

"Yes, a little daughter," Lisa replied.

"How old is she?"

"Kendra is five. She'll be six in September."

"Is she awake? I mean, if she is, maybe I could get a few pictures of her with the two of you, you know, for the magazine."

"Well, we put her down just before you arrived, but…tell you what. Let's sneak upstairs and see if she's still awake."

"You sure Alex won't mind?"

"Oh, he's so wrapped up in his charity tournament that he won't even notice. Come on," she said, a hint of conspiracy in her voice, "follow me."

Charlie followed her up the back stairs and down the hall to the little girl's room. She opened the door and peeked in, then withdrew.

"She's asleep," she whispered. She shrugged as if to say sorry and closed the door.

Lisa and Charlie went back down the stairs and returned to the kitchen. She gathered up the drinks, and snacks and the two of them reentered the study.

"Here we are," she said, smiling graciously.

She set the tray on the table between the men and sat down again. Charlie took another picture of Alex and winked at Lisa. They now had a secret to share.

The major took this opportunity to ask Lisa questions about the family, and at eight fifteen, he announced that he was through. He asked Charlie if he had enough pictures, and Charlie said that he had plenty. He did, though, ask if it would be all right to come back during the day to take a few pictures of the outside of the house.

"This is quite a beautiful home you have, Mr. McArthur. Thank you so much for your time. I'll let you know when the article will be published."

He put out his hand and Alex took it.

"Would you like to see the rest of the house?" Alex asked.

"Well, I…"

"Oh, come on, at least see the main floor and the basement. Nothing but bedrooms upstairs anyway. Come on."

The major looked at Charlie and Charlie said, "I'd love to see it. Do you mind if I take pictures?"

"That would be fine. Come on, follow me."

Alex took them through the main floor, showing the elegance and majesty of the house. Large arched windows dominated all the rooms.

"You've got to see the basement," Lisa said. "Alex has his own driving range down there, plus we have a theater that can seat up to twenty-four people."

The two men followed Alex and Lisa down to the basement. Sure enough, Alex had set up a computerized driving range in one end of a long room. He explained that it could measure the lengths and accuracy of his drives by means of tiny little sensors on the back of the screen.

"I've got six of the country's top golf courses set into the computer. Each fairway and green is laid out exactly to specifications. I've even got Saint Andrews in there. Let me show you."

He touched a switch, and the screen suddenly showed a beautifully manicured fairway. Above the scene in the left-hand corner were the words Pebble Beach and the number of the hole. Alex set a ball on a tee. A quiet beep sounded. He took out his number one driver. Addressing the ball, he adjusted his stance, took a practice swing, and then hit the ball toward the padded screen. In the upper-right-hand corner, the number 235 yards registered with the words, *Slight hook to the left. Ball on fairway.* A small picture of the fairway showed him where the ball would have landed on the real course.

"Not bad," he bragged. "You want to try?"

The major said that he hadn't been near a golf club in nine months but took the driver anyway. He took off his coat and handed it to Charlie. He loosened his tie, felt the balance of the club in his hands, took a ball from Alex, and placed it on the tee. The beep sounded again. He stepped in, looked down, then to the screen, and then back at the ball. He took a practice swing, then another, and stepped up to the ball. He adjusted his feet slightly and took a mighty swing. It hit the screen square in the middle and dropped to the floor. Immediately the screen lit up—*193 yards. Ball in the middle of the fairway*—and showed him where the ball would have landed in real life.

The major turned and handed the driver back to Alex, who took it and admitted, "Nice drive. We'll have to play a round sometime."

"I'd like that," the major said. "Maybe after the tournament."

"You got it. Come on, let me show you some of my other toys."

They entered another room that was set up as a theater with four rows of high-back cushioned chairs, six to a row, and a big screen against the far wall. Alex pushed a button on the wall by the door, and the screen rose up to the ceiling, revealing two magnificent billiard tables. But it was the wall behind the tables at the far end of the room that caught the major's eye. Built along the whole length of the back wall from floor to ceiling were wine racks, each section shaped like a diamond, with bottles stacked in each one. The whole wall was covered by cut glass doors.

"And this," Alex said, leading his guests to the doors, "this is my pride and joy."

His arm swept the area of the wine racks. Some of the best wines in the world.

"Very nice," the major said, but inwardly he was thinking, *I couldn't have asked for more.*

To Alex he asked, "How many bottles of wine do you have here?"

"Couple of hundred, I'd guess," he answered. "Got them divided into the reds, whites, blushes, champagnes, and so on. Some of them are quite rare. It's all climate controlled. It's a hobby of mine, collecting fine wines. Some of the labels are quite unique."

The major nodded. "I'm impressed. Do you mind if Charlie takes a few pictures? We can add this all to the article?"

"I guess it'll be all right. I keep it locked up tight. Sure."

"And may I mention your golf course and movie theater?"

Alex nodded.

The major looked at Charlie, who began snapping shot after shot of all that they had seen.

The major looked at his watch. "Well then, I guess we'd better be going. Thank you so much for your time and hospitality. Charlie will be back sometime during the day to take some exterior pictures. I'll be in touch."

Alex and Lisa led the two men to the front door where they said their goodbyes. Walking back to the car, the major asked, "Did you find out what you needed to know?"

Allen nodded. "Very simple security system. Control box in the front entrance and one in the kitchen. Kitchen door leads to the backyard. Should be a piece of cake. No cameras or sensing devices that I could see. By the way. Where'd you learn to drive a ball like that?"

"I didn't."

"What?"

"I never hit a golf ball in my life before tonight."

"But how?"

"Simple. Just watched what Alex did. Figured it couldn't be all that hard. Besides, if I'd screwed up, I could have blamed it on not knowing his club or not having swung a club in a while."

"You got balls, sir," Allen said, shaking his head.

They climbed into the car. Somewhere off in the distance a dog barked. As they drove out, the security guard was parked in his usual spot. The major pulled up and parked next to him.

"Hi. Jeffrey Matthews. *Golf World Digest.* I just did an interview at the McArthur residence. I didn't see you when I drove in. I may be back again. Should I check in with you before I go in?"

"That's the usual procedure," the guard said smugly. "I like to know who's coming and going. Looks good to the company."

"All right then, thank you, Officer."

The major put the car in reverse. The guard sat up a little taller in his seat after being addressed as "officer" and gave a quick two-fingered salute to the two men as they backed out of the parking spot next to his. Then he hunkered down in his seat again and turned the radio back up.

"You don't miss a thing, do you?" Allen said.

"I try not to, Tom, I try not to."

The major dropped his passenger off at his hotel and headed over to Julie's. It was now nine fifteen.

The knock on the door startled her.

"Yes?" she asked. "Who is it?"

"It's me."

She went to the door, doing a double take when she saw his face.

"Hi," he said.

"Hi, yourself. Nice disguise."

He looked up and down the hall and entered. They hugged, and the major walked over to the table. On it were drawings of faces.

"See anything you like?"

He picked up one in particular and stared at it. "This one."

"That's you."

"Well, okay, let's get started."

The major sat at the chair by the table and removed his own disguise and put it aside. Julie then began making a mold of his face. They talked about the events of the coming week while she worked. When she started to work on his lower face, she told him to be quiet.

He stared up at her, amazed at the concentration she possessed. She worked quickly, her fingers and thumbs creating magic as they pressed and pinched and folded the material onto his face.

He hadn't noticed the crow's feet around her eyes until now but thought, *She sure is one good-looking woman.*

"There," she finally said, holding up the mirror, "what do you think?"

The major stared into the mirror and saw a much older man, a man with a much fuller face, a man with bushy gray eyebrows, with a scar on his cheek, running down toward his chin.

"Nice." He nodded, turning his head from side to side. "Very nice."

"Don't touch it just yet. We need to give it a few more minutes. I've got a wig in the box that should be just right."

She retrieved the wig, put it on his head, and adjusted it. He now looked like a sixty-year-old man.

"Incredible!" he exclaimed. "You're really good, you know that?"

"I know. I'm getting more recognition and more work on important pictures."

"You really enjoy this, don't you?"

"Yes, I do. It's fun. You know, some people paint, some write, some sculpt. Me? I create new faces. It's challenging. And my faces and bodies are seen by millions of people."

As tired as she was, she beamed.

"Well, I'm impressed."

She helped him remove the mask and put it on the only remaining dummy head. Next to it were Floyd's mask and one of a much younger woman. Allen still had his with him.

The major looked at his watch. It was three fifteen in the morning.

"I'd better be going. You look exhausted."

"Believe it or not, I am," she said wearily. "Do you mind?"

"'Course not."

He kissed her lightly on the cheek and left.

Jackie picked up her makeup box and put it away. She then put his mask and the others in the big box the dummies had been shipped in and put it in the closet also. She cleaned up the mess. Then she washed her face, took her makeup off with cold cream, and went to bed. It was four in the morning.

Wednesday, June 27, 9:15 a.m.

The call woke John from a deep sleep. In his sleep, he had dreamed he and Jackie were on a beach somewhere. They were being served drinks by a houseboy as they relaxed on chaise lounges.

He picked up the receiver and mumbled, "Hello?"

"Floyd here. Did I wake you?"

"Um, that's okay. I need to be up anyway. What's up?"

"Thought I'd fill you in on last night. I'm downstairs."

"Great. Give me ten minutes, then come up. You eat yet?"

"Just coffee and an English muffin."

"Tell you what. Meet me in the coffee shop. Order me two eggs over easy, ham, hash browns, wheat toast, orange juice, and coffee, black. Order what you want. I'll be down shortly."

Floyd repeated the order and then said, "You got it."

The major hung up the phone and went to shower. Twenty minutes later, he walked into the coffee shop and spotted Floyd. The waitress was just setting down their breakfast. He sat down across from the big man and picked up his napkin.

"Morning."

"Mornin'."

"Looks good, what is that?" he asked, pointing to Floyd's plate.

"Belgian waffles."

Before him, Floyd had a plate of eggs, sausages, bacon, hash browns, toast, juice, coffee, and those Belgian waffles.

"That's quite a breakfast."

Floyd smiled as he stuffed a big bite of the waffles into his mouth.

"First off," Floyd began between mouthfuls, "I found a place for you to park the van."

He pulled out a pen and began drawing on a napkin.

"Here is Cherry Hills Farms Drive," he said, drawing the road in a circular pattern. Here's University, and here's Belleview. Okay, to the north is another street. Cherryridge Road. Here."

He drew the street on the map.

"More private homes. No security, though. I figure Allen can park the van here."

He hastily drew a grove of trees between two of the houses on the street onto the napkin and tapped them with his pen.

"Room enough between the houses so's he's not parked close to any of them. That puts him in range of the target's house without being seen."

The major nodded. "Sounds good."

"Now. I checked the areas around the house. There's this dead-end street you asked me about. It comes up behind like this."

He drew an L-shaped line on the map leading off the McArthurs' street. "It dead ends about here." He pointed to where the van could be parked. "If we came in from the back, we'd need to circle around the end of this street. Problem is, they got this big dog at this house."

He pointed to the house at the end of the street. "Damned dog barks his head off."

The major listened to all this while he chewed on his breakfast. He remembered the dog barking when Allen and he had left the house last night.

Floyd put down his pen and picked up his fork. "What do you think?"

The major stared at the map and thought while he took a sip of his coffee. "What if we just come in through the front door?"

"Say what?"

"What if we come through the front door? Listen. Suppose we neutralize the security guard, drive up to the front door, overpower the babysitter, and just take the kid?"

"That's crazy," Floyd said. And then he grinned that big toothy smile of his. "That's so crazy it just might work. But how we goin' to overpower the guard?"

The major leaned forward. "All right. The guard is pretty sloppy. Let's say we drive up under the guise of delivering something. Julie can drive up while you sneak around the van. The two of you can tie him up and lock him in the trunk of his car. Then you simply drive up to the house, pretend you are delivering something, say flowers, and tie her up and put her in the closet. Then you can snatch the kid. By the way, her name is Kendra. You leave a note and be out of there in ten minutes. Allen and I can plant the bugs and do whatever else needs to be done. Wham, bam, in and out. Allen'll give you the layout of the house."

Floyd thought about it. He rubbed his chin and looked at his boss, putting the last bit of sausage into his mouth.

"How we going to get a delivery van?"

"Already got one. We use the white van. Julie can do some lettering on the side."

"Mind if I think about this a little?"

"Go ahead. We've got to run it by the others anyway."

Floyd grinned again. "By God, it just might work."

"Let's get the others together, pick up the rest of the stuff we'll need, and go to the cabin."

They agreed to meet at the Safeway parking lot at 2:00 p.m. It was now ten forty-five.

Up in his room, the major put in calls to Allen and Julie. He asked them each for a list of anything they might have forgotten yesterday. He would go shopping for the rest of the supplies and anything else that they could think of. It was agreed that no food or beverage would be brought to the cabin until after the child was safely back there.

The major stopped at the Target store on South Colorado Boulevard and purchased sheets, blankets, and camping supplies. At 2:00 p.m., he drove into the Safeway parking lot. All three were waiting. They climbed into his car.

"Trunk's full of stuff. Might as well be comfortable while we wait."

During the drive to the cabin, the major and Floyd explained the layout of the neighborhood to the other two, and then the major told them of his plan. They liked it.

"Julie, do you think you could somehow letter the side of the van with something?"

"No problem. Get me some white butcher block paper, and I can do wonders."

"Butcher block paper?"

"Sure. Use it all the time on the sets. If you need a sign painted on a van fast, you use butcher block paper. Turn it over shiny side out, and it can blend right in with the painted van. Butcher block paper and some tape and *voila!* You've got yourself a sign. At night it's hard to tell the difference from the real thing."

"All right," the major continued, "we need to brainstorm the night of the kidnapping."

For the next half hour, the four threw out ideas. By the time they reached the turnoff to the cabin, a plan had been worked out that was agreeable to all.

The major continued on past the turnoff and drove to the next street. There was a car behind them. He turned around and drove back to the turnoff. When he was sure no one could see him, he turned into the drive and pulled up to the cabin. They sat in the car for a moment, each of them searching for some sign of an intruder.

"Okay, let's get these things into the cabin."

The major popped the trunk lid, and they all grabbed something and carried it inside.

"Floyd, come outside with me," the major instructed. "I want to take another walk around the perimeter."

They left Allen and Julie to put the purchases away and went outside.

"How difficult would it be to put some kind of trip wire or sensing devices around the perimeter? You know, give us an idea if someone intrudes upon our little haven."

"That's not the problem. Here, look."

Floyd squatted down and pointed to some deer droppings.

"You've got large animals traipsing through the property. Deer, maybe even elk. Who knows what else. Any one of them could trip an alarm. No, I'm afraid we're going to have to pass on that."

The major frowned. "What would you suggest?"

"Nothing we can do when no one's here. Post a sentry when we're here would be the only thing I can think of."

"So there's no way we can tell if this place is ever compromised?"

"Not unless they disturb something. I can set up the usual traps: hair across the door, those types of things, but no, somebody walking through the area would be hard to spot. From the looks of this place, nobody's been around here for a long, long time. Somebody might wander by, but I doubt it."

"All right. I guess we're stuck with what we've got. Come on, let's get back."

CHAPTER 13

Friday, June 29, 10:00 a.m.

The major stared out of his window at the rain. It had been raining off and on since eight that morning. Weather reports said it would last for another two to three hours. Right now, it was raining heavily. Unusual for this time of year.

He sipped his coffee and went over his notes once again. Everything was in place. All the planning, all the details, everything was ready. Julie was working on the signs for the van. Allen had all his surveillance gear tested and working. The bugs worked. The radios worked.

Waiting. That was the hard part. He had wanted the four of them to do a practice run this morning, each of them leapfrogging the victim's vehicle as they drove the drop route. The rain had spoiled that. They decided they would wait for the weather to change; otherwise, they would be soaked climbing in and out of their cars delivering the various notes and envelopes.

Maybe this afternoon, John thought. *There's still time.*

He looked at his watch. There was a news conference scheduled for seven o'clock tonight. All the pros and celebrities were going to be there. At that time, the pairings for the upcoming tournament would be announced. There would be the usual question-and-answer period, followed by autograph signings and then a cocktail party.

The major felt that he should make an appearance as Jeffery Matthews but knew that he couldn't. He was on the list of reporters with privileges, thanks to Jennifer's help, but would call her later today and apologize for not being able to appear. He'd use some excuse about an emergency back home.

At eleven o'clock, the rains stopped and the sun came out. He called the others. They agreed to meet at the Southglenn Mall at 1:00 p.m.

The plan was for Allen to drive the van and act the part of McArthur. The other three would flip-flop their way along the route. They would converse with each other over the Cobra CB radios that each one had in their vehicles.

The major was the first to arrive. He double checked the time from the Estates to the mall. It took him three minutes longer this time. He had hit all the red lights. Next to arrive was Floyd, then Allen. The three men gathered in the major's rental and waited for Julie. At twenty past the hour she arrived. She'd gotten lost.

The major was annoyed. He didn't like mistakes, and he especially didn't like schedules to be messed up. He said so.

"I'm sorry," she said, exasperation evident in her voice. "I got lost. It happens."

"It had better not happen again."

The major looked at her, his eyes cold, menacing. Just as quickly, the look disappeared.

"Okay, listen, all of you." He looked at each one of them as he continued. "This is not a game. Everything that we do from now on has a reason. Everything we do is important, and everything we do has a specific purpose. We can't afford any screw-ups. Our timing is critical."

He looked at them again. "Understand?"

They nodded.

"I'm sorry," Julie mumbled, a tear forming at the corner of her eye. "I promise, it won't happen again."

"Good. Allen, give them their radios."

Allen opened the box in his lap and handed each of them a radio.

"Now," he began, "these are Cobra CB radios. This is how they work."

He showed each of them the various buttons and the purpose for each. "You want to keep your radio set on channel 5. Make sure you don't switch to any other channel. We could be picked up by other radios if you do. You can speak to each other like this."

He demonstrated how to talk and listen on his radio. When he was done, he asked, "Any questions?"

There were none.

Allen watched them study their instruments. "Good."

The major spoke. "Okay, Allen, you drive the van. The first phone booth is over there."

He pointed in the direction of the Conoco station and the phone booth next to it.

"Floyd, you find a spot to watch for his arrival. The first set of directions will be taped to the underside of the ledge on that phone stand. Once he picks it up, I want you to follow him to location two. I'll back you up from here. Make sure he's not being followed. If he is, I'll alert each of you to fall back.

"Julie, if we do have to cease operation, you're to put the alternate envelope under the next drop site ledge. That goes for each of us, depending on if and when we spot a tail. Understood?"

There were no questions.

"Good. The rest of the run will go just like it has in the past. Allen monitors the house. If he even suspects that something's wrong, he will call me, and we will back off and go to plan B. If everything's okay, then we flip-flop our way along the route until he reaches the drop site. I'll be there to see that he makes the drop. I'll pick up the money and meet you all at the cabin. We divide up the money if you want. Otherwise, I'll take the money back to the hotel and make sure it reaches your individual accounts on the island. We release the child, split up, and go our separate ways."

The major concluded, "Each of you will put in a verification call to the bank three days after we split up, if you choose to leave the money with me, and that's it. Any questions?"

There were none. They had done variations of this before. The money always showed up in their accounts. There was no reason not to trust their leader or to doubt that the plan would not work.

Allen spoke for all of them. "Sounds like a plan to me. It's worked in the past. Let's do it."

"Good, let's get started."

With their radios in hand, each of the conspirators got out and headed to their respective cars. On the major's signal, Allen pulled up to the booth. Each of them had a watch, and they synchronized them at the major's command.

"Let's do it."

Allen got out of the van, walked to the phone booth, retrieved the imaginary envelope, returned to the van, pretended to read it, started his vehicle, and drove off.

Floyd pulled out behind him, leaving about a block's worth of distance between them. The major waited for one minute, and then he too pulled out. Julie left and went west on Arapahoe to set up the next drop site.

Following the directions the major had already mapped out, the four vehicles proceeded along the route. The major made notes of the times and distances and checked them against his previous notes. They were all in line with one another.

Two hours and twenty minutes later, the van pulled into the parking lot at the reservoir and parked. The major jotted down the time. Allen's arrival time was thirteen minutes later than he had accounted for but was still within the parameters of the plan. The major was pleased. Shortly afterward, the others pulled up. They spotted Allen and the major at a picnic table and walked over to the two men.

"Good job," was the greeting they received when they took their places next to the two men.

Allen spoke as the others were approaching. "That was one hell of a ride. You didn't leave much time for me to catch my breath."

"You weren't supposed to."

"Oh, Floyd, I spotted you in my rearview mirror once, between Franklin and Clarkson on Dry Creek. Didn't see you after that. I don't know if McArthur will be sharp enough to pick up on any of you but thought you ought to know."

"Thanks, Allen." It was the major speaking. "Floyd?"

"It won't happen again, boss."

"Good. That whole exercise took two hours and thirty-five minutes. A little longer than I planned but still okay. I'd like to shave some time off of the run, though, what can we do?"

They each threw in suggestions, and with only minor adjustments, an alternative plan was devised.

"Good job, everybody. Any questions?"

He looked at each of them. There were no more questions.

In less than twenty-eight hours their plan would be put into motion.

He turned to Julie. "How are the side panels coming?" he asked her.

"They'll be done by morning."

The major raised an eyebrow.

"I'll be putting the finishing touches on them tonight. They'll be dry by morning."

"Excellent."

"When do we put them on?" Allen asked.

"Tomorrow night, just before the pickup."

Allen nodded.

"Guns? Floyd?"

"Same. We don't need them before then."

"Let's hope we don't need them at all," Julie added.

"You've each got your schedules, you know what to do. This should be pretty simple. Good luck."

They rose in unison and walked back to their cars. One by one they drove out of the park and onto Wadsworth and headed north. The major, as was his custom, was the last to leave. He was pleased with what had been accomplished so far and felt good about the plan and the players. It was now just past 6:00 p.m. Twenty-six hours until kickoff.

Back at his suite, the major sorted through his notes, burning those he no longer needed in the bathroom sink. The rest he put in order and placed them in his briefcase. At nine thirty his phone rang.

"Hello?"

"Hi."

"Hi."

"Can I come up? I'm downstairs in the lobby."

"Sure."

He heard the click as she hung up. Three minutes later, there was a soft knock at the door. He opened it and let her in, once again checking the corridor. As she passed, he caught a light whiff of her perfume. It was delicious. He closed the door and turned just as she swung and hit him solidly in the stomach. He grunted and doubled over.

"You son of a bitch!" she yelled at him. "You arrogant son of a bitch!"

She swung again, attempting to slap him across the face, but he caught her wrist in his hand. He turned it down and twisted it behind her and drew her close to him.

"How dare you call me down like that in front of the others! How dare—"

"Easy," he interrupted. "Easy."

He looked down at the defiance in her eyes. "God, you're beautiful when you're angry."

She struggled to get loose but could not.

"I had to do that. They've got to understand who's in charge and how important schedules are. I had no other choice. If it had been Allen or Floyd, I'd have done the same thing. And besides, you *were* late."

He kissed her then, loosening his grip. Her arms went up and circled his neck. She squeezed him to her, pressing her body against his, feeling his manliness against her.

He pulled back and, in the same motion, lifted her off the floor and carried her into the bedroom, placing her on the bed. He lay beside her and kissed her hard on the mouth again, his tongue searching for hers.

She giggled and pushed him away.

"Smells like a fire in here, and I don't mean you. You burning something?"

"Just some notes. In the bathroom.

Jackie stood and removed her blouse, kicked off her shoes, took off her slacks, and stood spread-eagled in front of him wearing only a pair of black lace panties.

"Well?"

"Well, what?"

"Well…aren't you going to get undressed?"

"Oh," he said.

He stood and slowly unbuttoned his shirt, teasing her with his movements.

After they made love, she sighed and wiggled close to him.

"Still mad at me?"

She snuggled in his arm. "Uh-uh," she breathed into his ear. "How could anyone stay mad after that?"

They lay silent, awash in the glow of the moment.

"John?"

"Um?"

"John?" She paused. "Oh, never mind."

"What?"

She hesitated, trying to find the right words.

John waited.

Finally, she rolled over onto her stomach, her elbows under her and looked at him.

"John," she began tentatively, "have you ever thought about us?"

"Yes," he replied. "We're pretty good together, aren't we?"

"No, you dufus, I mean *us*. You and me. Together. Not just when we have a job to do, I mean…together. You know. You come home, I'm there. I come home, you're there."

John knew that this conversation would come up sooner or later. "What? You mean marriage?" he blurted out.

"No, I don't mean marriage necessarily. I mean you and me together. Living together. Growing old together."

"As it is, we see each other every two years. We get together, we have sex. We do a job together, and then we separate. Don't you want more? I know you do."

"I think about you a lot, Jackie," he said. "I look forward to our getting together, and yes, the sex is great. But I'm a forty-two-year-old man. Pretty set in my ways. And you, you're what? Thirty-four? Thirty-five?"

"I'm almost forty but thank you."

"Oh!" he said. "Well, anyway, I've always been a loner. I've—"

"That's the point, you big galoot. You need someone. I want to be that someone. I love you. Don't you know that?"

She bent down and kissed him before he could answer.

"Well, I…I know you liked me," he teased.

"Oh, you…" she said as she grabbed a pillow and hit him with it.

Suddenly she was off the bed and heading for the shower.

"Think about it," she said over her shoulder as she closed the door.

John lay there thinking about what she had said. He did love her. He enjoyed her company. And the sex *was* great. But what would happen when the sex ran down? And besides, could she live in a little town in Maine? Would they have to leave the country? What if this was the last job?

A hundred and one questions ran through his head. There were no answers to any of them. Except…except, he did love her. Of that he was certain.

He heard the water being turned off and heard the shower door slide open and shut. He could hear her humming through the closed door.

It would be nice to hear that more often, he thought.

She opened the door and stood in the doorway, a bath towel wrapped around her body and another wrapped around her head.

"John?"

"Yes?"

"I'm sorry, I didn't mean to push you."

"Honey, it's okay. And you're right. I do need to think about it. Tell you what. When this is over, let's say you and I go away for a while. Just the two of us. You don't have any other commitments, do you?"

"I'd like that," she said and turned and closed the door behind her.

Again, he could hear her humming behind the door.

When he awoke, she was gone. She had covered him with a blanket. There was a note propped up against the light on the nightstand. It read, "I love you."

CHAPTER 14

Lisa sat in front of her vanity mirror and applied lipstick. She leaned back and looked admiringly at her reflection.

"Darling? Would you be so kind as to call the Emerys? Darlene should have been here by now."

"Sure," Alex called from downstairs.

He picked up the phone in the hall and dialed.

"Hi, this is Alex, has Darlene left yet?"

Just then the doorbell sounded.

"Oh, never mind. I think she's at the front door now. No, no, it's all right. Yes, thank you. Bye."

Alex went to the front door and greeted their fourteen-year-old babysitter.

"I'm sorry, Mr. McArthur. I couldn't find my sneakers."

"That's okay, Darlene, come in. Kendra's in the playroom. If you'll excuse me, I've got to finish getting ready."

Darlene went off to look for Kendra and Alex climbed the stairs.

"She's here," he said as he passed his wife.

"Good. I'm just about done. Would you zip me up?"

Lisa stepped into the dress and wiggled it up over her body. She turned and offered her back to him.

"You look lovely, my dear," he said, bending to kiss the back of her neck as he zipped up the gown.

"Thank you. You like it?"

She twirled around with her arms held out and then faced him with a smile.

"Exquisite," he replied.

"You're not so bad yourself. Now go, put on your coat and let's get out of here. We're going to be late if we don't hurry up."

Alex took his dinner jacket from the back of a chair and slipped it on. He stepped up behind her and admired the two of them in the full-length mirror covering the sliding closet doors.

"Damned good-looking couple, if you ask me," he bragged.

She smiled and put her arm through his.

"Shall we go, my prince?"

She retrieved a little matching purse from her vanity and joined him at the door.

"Darlene?" she called as they descended the stairs.

"Yes, Mrs. McArthur?" Darlene answered, holding Kendra's hand in the entranceway.

"There's dinner for both of you in the refrigerator. She's to be in bed by seven thirty. We'll be home by midnight."

"Yes, Mrs. McArthur. You two sure look nice."

"Why, thank you, Darlene." Alex bowed to her as they reached the bottom step. "Lock the door and set the alarm when we're gone."

"I will. And have fun."

They went through the kitchen and out to the garage. Darlene could hear the Mercedes start as the garage doors lifted. She and Kendra watched as the car pulled out of the driveway, turned, and headed off down the road.

"Come on, let's go play," she said to her charge. "We can eat later. Okay?"

"Okay," said the little one with a big smile on her face.

Saturday, 5:30 p.m.

The major picked up the arrangements from the florist and headed to the storage unit. Julie, Floyd, and Allen were already there.

The weather was perfect. Tonight would be mild and cloudless, temperatures in the midseventies.

He drove through the gates and headed for his unit. The van was parked in front. On the side was a sign that said Citywide Florists Delivery Service. Under it was an address and a phone number. To anyone who knew the city well, the address would put the business just north of the Denver Zoo, in the City Park Municipal Golf Course. Part of the phone number seemed to be missing. Along the left side of the sign was a profusion of painted flowers. Julie had made them look like the paint was fading. From a distance, the sign looked authentic. The major was pleased. On the front fenders, she had added PUC and some numbers.

"Very professional," he said as he pulled up next to the van.

She smiled at him.

"Very nice," he said again. "I especially like the way you faded the flowers."

"Little trick I learned on the set."

"Okay, the plan is for the three of you to pick me up across the street on Gilpin at eight thirty. Then we take care of the guard, deliver the flowers, grab the kid, plant the bugs, and leave. We switch the kid to the car and Floyd and Julie head for the hills. Allen and I bring the van back here, remove the signs, and go to the surveillance site. Then it's everything by the numbers. Any questions?"

As usual, there were none.

"Good."

The major extended his right hand in front of him, palm down, and one by one the others added their own to his.

"Good, then let's go get something to eat. My treat, I'm starving."

They had a quiet dinner. Each of the four was lost in his own private thoughts, and each could feel the tension mounting as the minutes ticked off. At seven thirty, they left the restaurant.

"You all got your gloves?" the major asked as they walked to the car.

They produced several pairs of gloves.

"Good."

They rode back to the storage unit in silence. Once there, each of them put on their disguises.

Julie examined the others. Everything fit. For herself, she had chosen a red wig, pulled back in a ponytail, and a much younger cheerleader-like face with freckles across her nose. She had picked up a brown blazer at a Goodwill Store and, with a white cotton blouse and tie, looked like a fresh and bouncy young delivery girl.

The major was wearing the older-man mask and a wig that gave him a balding pate. His face was rounder, and the gold tooth that Julie produced make him look quite eccentric.

Allen wore the mask he had worn during the interview, with one major difference; Julie had removed the beard and moustache.

Floyd's nose was much broader, and he had a thin moustache and a single strip of goatee running from his lower lip to his chin. He had thick, bushy eyebrows and a shiny bald head. On the left side of his head, Julie created a two-inch scar that ran from front to back.

Each of the four kidnappers had at least one distinguishing feature on his or her person that would be noticed and passed on to the police when their descriptions were given.

"Nice touches," the major remarked to Julie when she was finished with her inspection. "Now, let's get this show on the road."

8:20 p.m.

The van pulled up next to the security guard's car. The guard sat slumped behind the wheel working on a crossword puzzle. He sat up as the van pulled up next to him.

Julie pulled up so that her window was just behind his. He would have to look a little behind him to talk to her. This would make him have to get out of his car.

"Hi," she said, a broad sexy smile beaming back at him.

"Hello," he responded.

"Could you help me? I've got a delivery for—"

Julie dropped her clipboard onto the ground. Immediately the guard was out of his door and offering to help. He picked up the clipboard and handed it back to her through the window.

"Oh, dear, what a klutz," she said, flashing a broad smile at him. "I'm sorry, I'm looking for—"

The cold metal of the gun's barrel against the back of his neck made the guard stiffen.

"Oh, shit!" he muttered.

"Don't move," came the deep voice from behind. "Put your hands behind your back. And not a sound, you understand?"

The guard nodded slowly.

Julie gave him one of those "Sorry, do as he says" looks and opened the door.

Floyd wrapped his hands with the duct tape. He worked swiftly, securing them behind the man's back. He tested the bindings, and when he was satisfied that they would hold, he grabbed the guard's arms and pulled him away from the door.

"What the hell!"

"Shut up and don't say a word," Floyd warned. He spoke to the man with an accent that came from the Caribbean.

To Julie the black man said, "Pop the trunk."

"Oh, Jesus," the guard moaned, and a dark spot appeared in the crotch of his khaki pants.

They walked around to the back of the car just as the trunk lid lifted. Floyd placed a strip of duct tape over the guard's mouth and pressed hard. The guard stared into Floyd's face, his eyes wide with fear.

"What you lookin' at, homey? Get in there."

He motioned for the guard to climb into the trunk.

The guard stepped into the trunk, and Floyd forced him down. He then wrapped the guard's ankles and legs with tape and bound them together with the man's hands. When he was sure the guard was secured, he closed the trunk lid. He heard the man mumble and begin to cry.

"Wimp!" Floyd said through the closed trunk lid.

Julie threw the keys into the bushes, closed the door, and climbed back into the van. Floyd quickly moved around the van and climbed into the passenger side. No one saw what had transpired. The whole episode took less than three minutes.

Julie backed up the van and headed into the Estates.

"Well done. Two minutes and forty seconds from start to finish. Beat your old time by almost twenty seconds," the major said from the back. He was referring to a clandestine kidnapping by the Special Forces back in the seventies.

Floyd turned and grinned at the passenger in the back.

"And the accent. Nice touch."

Julie pulled into the circle in front of the McArthur's house. The front porch light lit up as the van approached. The rooms in front were dark. A faint light showed through the windows on the left.

"Showtime," the major stated.

Julie and Floyd climbed out of the cab and walked around to the back of the van. Floyd opened the doors, reached in and pulled out one of the arrangements, and handed it to Julie. He reached in and winked at the two men as he withdrew the other one. Together they walked up the steps. Julie pushed the doorbell and waited.

"Yes?" came a young female voice.

"Delivery for Mrs. McArthur. Mrs. Alexander McArthur?"

"Can you leave it on the porch?"

"No, ma'am, somebody's got to sign for it."

"Just a minute."

They heard her footsteps recede, then return. This time there were two sets of footsteps. One set sounded too heavy to belong to Kendra.

"Shit," Floyd whispered to Julie, "there's two of 'em."

The door opened slightly, and a cute little teenager peered through the crack. Julie stepped in front so the girl could only see her. She smiled at the girl behind the door.

"Hi. Citywide Delivery. We have some flowers for your mom."

"She's not my mom. I'm the sitter. They're not home right now."

"Will they be home soon?"

"I don't know. Um, maybe."

"Darn, this is my last delivery. I'd hate to have to wait long. Got a date."

The girl hesitated. Julie could hear whispering in the background.

"It's okay," Julie thought she heard, "I'm here."

Darlene turned and whispered something to the unseen voice and turned back to Julie.

"I guess it would be all right. She closed the door and slid off the chain and opened it again. "Come in."

Julie stepped back as Darlene opened the screen door. A pimple-faced young boy, roughly Darlene's age, stepped out from behind the door.

He can't be much older than her, Julie thought as she stepped past them into the entranceway.

Floyd appeared and followed her in and looked around. "Nice house," he commented with just the slightest hint of an accent.

Julie asked, "Where can we put these? They're pretty heavy."

Darlene pointed to a long table against the far wall.

"Over there, I guess."

Julie and Floyd put the flowers on the table and turned to face the kids. They had moved away from the door. It was still open. Floyd reached behind him and drew his pistol.

"Don't either of you move. And don't make a sound. If you do as I say, no one will get hurt. Understand?"

The boy stepped in front of Darlene.

"What do you want? We don't have any money."

"Never mind what we want, just do as I say, and you won't get hurt."

Floyd went around them and closed the door. The boy realized what he had done, and his shoulders sagged slightly.

"You." He pointed to Darlene. "Put your arms out."

Darlene, now sobbing, extended her hands, and Julie wrapped her wrists with the duct tape.

"What's your name?"

"Darlene."

"Now, Darlene, I'm going to cover your mouth with this tape. It'll be all right. Just don't want you making too much noise now, do we?"

Tears were running down Darlene's cheeks. Her eyes were wide with fear.

Julie turned to the boy when she was done with Darlene.

"What's your name?"

"Josh."

"Well, Josh, I guess it's your turn."

"You won't hurt us, will you?"

"No, Josh, we won't hurt you. Just do as we say."

Josh extended his arms, and she wrapped them with the tape. She checked them when she was through. They would hold. She tore off another piece of tape and covered his mouth.

"There, now, that didn't hurt, did it?"

Josh's eyes were slits of hatred. Floyd put his gun away and found a closet.

"Come here," he said to Darlene. "Get in there and sit down."

By now, Darlene was crying openly. She did as she was told and sat down. Floyd wrapped duct tape around her legs and secured her hands and legs together. He stood and closed the door, turning to Josh.

Josh glared at him, but he came to Floyd when he was told to. Floyd put his hand behind the boy's neck and directed him down the hall until he found a room with a closet.

"You know the drill, kid. Get in and sit down."

Josh did as he was told, and Floyd secured him the same way he had done with Darlene.

"You might as well just be quiet until the folks come home. No one can hear you anyway."

Floyd closed the door and walked back to the entranceway. Julie had opened the door, and the two men were just coming through it when he arrived.

"Okay, you get the kid ready," the major instructed Julie. "Make sure she's got some clothes and toys."

He turned to Floyd and Allen. "You two okay with the bugs?"

They both nodded.

"Good. I've got a little wine collecting to do in the basement."

They laughed and split up.

John went down to the basement and found the wine cellar. He opened the closet and quickly scanned the wine selection, finally deciding on a Merlot and a Pinot Noir.

Allen and Floyd hid the bugs: one taped securely under the coffee table, one behind the picture over the fireplace, one in the study up under the desk, one in the kitchen, and one up in the master bedroom. The letter instructing the parents what to do to get their daughter back was left with the flowers.

Julie went upstairs and found Kendra's bedroom. Quietly she gathered three changes of clothes, socks, tennis sneakers, underwear, and a sweater from the bureau and the closet. These she put into a plastic garbage sack. She looked around the room to see if she was missing anything. Kendra's room had its own bathroom, and Julie retrieved a toothbrush, toothpaste, two washcloths, two bath towels, and a comb. She returned to a still sleeping Kendra and gently woke her up.

"Kendra. Kendra, honey, wake up. Come on, honey, open your eyes."

The little girl rolled over and opened her eyes. When she saw the strange lady sitting down on the bed next to her, she sat up and rubbed her eyes.

"Where's Mommy?" she asked. "Where's Darlene?"

"Mommy's not home, and Darlene had to leave."

"I want Mommy."

"Kendra. My name is Julie. Aunt Julie," she said soothingly. "Would you like me to take you to see your Mommy?"

"Yes," the little girl answered, rubbing her eyes with her fists.

Kendra held out her arms. Julie bent down and picked her up, holding her tenderly against her.

"Where's Darlene? How come she's not here?"

"Darlene had to go home. That's why I'm here. Come on, we've got to go now. Are there any toys or animals you'd like to take with you?"

"Only my bunny." Kenny pointed to the light-pink bunny she had been sleeping with.

"Okay, bunny it is," Julie said. She gave the bunny to Kendra, grabbed the sack of clothes, and walked down the stairs. The other three were already in the van.

Julie took one last look around before leaving. She thought she heard sobbing from the closet. She looked at Kendra and smiled. Kendra had not heard anything.

Julie went to the rear of the van. The doors opened, and Allen quickly grabbed the child from her. Julie climbed in behind them and slammed the door shut. The scream that came from the little girl was piercing. Allen covered her mouth with his hand. She fought him, squirming and kicking and screaming.

"Easy, Kendra, take it easy. I'm not going to hurt you."

"Give her to me," Julie offered.

Allen handed her to Julie, glad to be free of her.

"Mercy," he muttered.

"I want my mommy, I want my mommy!" Kendra screamed.

"Shh," Julie whispered, "it's going to be all right, shh."

The van pulled out of the driveway and headed down the street. Floyd was driving, the major next to him.

"Easy, Floyd, not too fast."

They passed the neighbor's house. The major noticed a face in the front window. In the back of the van, Julie finally got Kendra to quiet down. The child was sobbing quietly in Julie's arms. Julie rocked her back and forth, talking quietly all the while.

"All right. When you drop me at the car, we need to yank the signs off the van. I think we were spotted by the neighbors." He said this quietly so that Kendra could not hear. He looked over his shoulder and saw her cradled in Julie's arms, her back to the front of the vehicle.

"Roger."

The van pulled onto University. The security car was still parked where they had left it. Turning into Gilpin, Floyd made a U-turn and pulled up behind the parked rental. Immediately Allen and the major jumped out of the van and tore the signs from the sides of it, then they moved forward and removed the PUC numbers from the front fenders. Floyd and Julie took Kendra and her belongings and climbed into the sedan.

Throwing the papers in before him, Allen climbed into the passenger side of the van and closed the door. The major ran around to the driver's side and climbed in. He waved to Floyd and the two vehicles took off, heading north on University. Floyd continued on, heading for the cabin. The major and Allen turned on Cherrydale and finally parked the van in the surveillance area that Floyd had found for them.

It was now 8:53 p.m. The whole operation from start to finish had taken thirty-three minutes.

CHAPTER 15

The Mark Hotel, Downtown Denver, 9:15 p.m.

Lisa had been bored all evening. Alex had pretty much left her to fend for herself while he rubbed elbows with the golf pros and celebrities at the party.

Now she was really bored, bored and restless. She had traded stories with some of her friends: Kendra did this, Kendra said that, and smiled at all the right times when the other mothers bragged about their kids.

There were reporters and photographers everywhere. The local TV news crews from channels 4, 7, and 9 were there, along with staff from the *News* and *Post*. She had hoped to see that nice Jeffrey Matthews and his charming photographer, what was his name? Oh, yes, Charlie Harris. But Jennifer said that Matthews had been called away on an emergency. She guessed that was why Charlie wasn't there either.

"Oh, well, at least Alex is having a good time." She put down her glass of wine—her third since dinner—and walked over to Alex just as he finished telling a small group of men an amusing story. They all burst into laughter just as she arrived.

"Darling," she interrupted, "do you have change? I want to phone home and check up on the baby, and I left my phone at home."

"Sure, honey."

He reached into his pocket for some change.

"You remember Jack and Arnie?" he said, giving her a handful of change. "And this is Hale, and this is Lee. Gentlemen, I'd like you to meet one of the three things that make my life worth living. Gentlemen," he said, holding up his glass of scotch. "I present you my wife, Lisa."

He bowed in her direction, lifted his glass to his lips, and sipped. Lisa blushed as she was introduced but managed a big smile and acknowledged each of the four golfers in turn. Accepting the change her husband offered, she bowed to the group, turned, and walked away, feeling the stares of the men on her back.

"Excuse me, where might I find a phone?" she asked one of the waiters.

"Go out those doors, turn right, go down the hall to the restrooms, and turn left. They're next to the palm plants," the waiter said, pointing to the doors across the room.

"Thank you."

She threaded her way through the groupings of people, smiling and nodding as she went, and finally was through the doors and heading down the hall.

Lisa found the bank of phones and deposited her coins. She punched in her home phone number and waited. After eight rings, she hung up, retrieved her coins, and tried again. When it wasn't answered on the second try, she began to worry. She tried one more time. There was still no answer. She sat there and stared at the phone in her hand, put it up to her ear once again, and listened to the ringing sound. She hung up and dialed Darlene's mother.

"Hi, Anne, it's Lisa. Are Darlene and Kendra over there?"

Darlene would sometimes bring Kendra over to her house to play with her doll collection, though never this late.

"No, why would they be?"

"I just called the house. There was no answer. Would you mind checking on them? I'll stay here by the phone."

She gave her neighbor the phone number and hung up. Lisa looked at her watch. It was just past ten o'clock. She so wanted to have a cigarette but didn't dare leave the phone. Five minutes went by and then ten. The waiting was becoming unbearable. Lisa was imagining all kinds of things. Fifteen minutes later the phone rang. Lisa was startled back to reality.

"Hello?"

"It's Anne. I went by the house. All the doors and windows are locked. I could hear the television in the day room but couldn't get Darlene to open the door. I couldn't see her anywhere. I've called 911. I'm going back over there now. Something's wrong. You'd better get back home as soon as you can."

"Thank you, Anne, we're on our way."

Lisa ran back to the banquet room. She threw open the doors in a panic and started yelling for her husband.

"Alex! Alex! Where are you?" she screamed.

A hush fell over the ballroom, and all eyes turned in her direction.

"Here!" he exclaimed. "What is it? What's wrong?" he asked, rushing up to his wife.

"Something's wrong at home," she sobbed. "Kendra, Darlene, and Kendra. Something's wrong. We've got to go!"

"Hold on, now," he said, trying to calm her. "Tell me, what is it?"

She took a deep breath, trying to stop herself from shaking. Between sobs and gasps, she told him about her conversation with Anne.

"Please, let's just go," she begged.

By now a large crowd had gathered around them. News cameras were rolling. Flashbulbs were going off. Alex looked around. He found his vice president.

"Bob, take care of things here, will you?"

He put his arms around his wife and quickly walked her out of the room, followed by reporters and cameramen.

"I'm sure everything's fine," he said, trying to calm her. "Maybe Darlene fell asleep and didn't hear anything. I bet when we get there everything will be fine."

"I hope so," she sobbed, gulping in breaths of air.

Alex gave the valet his ticket, and the couple waited for their car to arrive. By now the entranceway was filled with reporters, cameramen, and curious onlookers.

People shouted at them, asking questions, demanding answers.

"No comment," was all Alex said.

They left downtown Denver and headed south. Behind him a caravan of cars and vans followed closely. They rode in silence. At ten thirty-five, they drove up to the house. There were two police cars already there, the red and blue lights on their roofs flashing. Alex was out of the car and around to let his wife out when a uniformed officer approached.

"Mr. McArthur?"

"Yes?"

"Officer Richard Huard. We were just about to break down the front door. We can't seem to get any response from inside the house. Mrs. Emery"—he pointed to the lady on the front porch—"called it in. She said there's a daughter inside babysitting your child?"

"Yes, that's right," he replied, directing his wife and the officer to the front porch.

"Anne," he acknowledged as he climbed the steps.

He had his key in the lock as he spoke, pushed the door open, and dashed into the house. The alarm did not go off.

Strange, Alex thought.

Lisa, Anne, and the officers followed him in. Outside, other vehicles came to a halt in front of the house.

"Darlene! Darlene! Kendra!"

He heard thumping coming from the closet and ran to it, throwing open the door. There, on the floor, her hands and feet tied, was the sitter.

"Oh my God!" Lisa screamed and ran up the stairs.

Alex helped Darlene to her feet and carefully removed the tape from her mouth.

"I'm sorry, Mr. McArthur," she cried, gulping for breath, "I'm sorry! I'm so sorry!"

"What is it? What happened?" he asked.

The scream that came from upstairs filled the entire house. Alex's face went white. Lisa screamed again and came running down the stairs.

"She's gone! My baby! She's gone!" Lisa screamed at her husband.

Alex turned and ran up the stairs, passing Lisa midway, and ran into the baby's room. He came out and walked down the stairs where his wife was standing. He was in a daze.

"Josh! Josh is here somewhere!" Darlene screamed.

They heard a door being kicked and found him in a closet off the dining room, hands and feet bound just like Darlene's.

A police officer unbound Josh and escorted him into the entranceway. He walked up and stood next to Darlene.

"Alex? Alex? Where did those flowers come from?" Lisa asked as she noticed the two bouquets of flowers on the table along the wall.

"They brought them," Darlene said quickly. "They said that they were for you. She said this was her last delivery and that she couldn't wait, and she needed for me to sign for them. That's why I let her in. There was a man with her. I didn't see him until I opened the door."

She began to cry again. Her mother moved to comfort her. Alex walked over to the flowers and reached for the note.

"Don't touch that!" officer Huard warned as he saw Alex approaching the table.

"But—"

"I've got a call into the Denver police headquarters. There should be a detective here any minute. In the meantime, let's not touch anything. Come on, let's see what the kids have to say."

Together, the three adults, the two police officers, and the children went into the living room. Darlene and Josh were holding hands. They were terrified. Anne sat next to Darlene, her arm around the girl's shoulders. Josh sat down on the other side of Darlene.

Officer Huard approached them and knelt before the two kids.

"There'll be a detective here in a few minutes. He'll want to ask you some questions. Do you think you'll be able to answer them?"

The two both nodded.

"Good. In the meantime, would you like some water? A soda?" He looked at Alex and Lisa.

"I'll get them some soda," Lisa said and went off to the kitchen.

"For God's sake, man," Alex demanded of the officer, "shouldn't you be on the phone or something?"

"I've already called headquarters. There's nothing we can do until the detective and the lab people get here. In the meantime, let's just keep calm and try to figure out what happened."

"Shit! We know what's happened! Someone's taken our little girl."

"Alex," Lisa admonished, nodding at the two kids on the couch as she returned with two cans of soda.

"Sorry," he said to them.

Just then two plainclothes policemen entered the room, followed by a crime-lab team.

"Don," the officer said acknowledging one of the detectives. "Bob," he said and nodded to the other. "Mr. and Mrs. Alexander McArthur. He nodded to the two parents. "And this is Darlene and Josh. Looks like we've got a kidnapping. The baby's missing and there's a note on the table in the entranceway. Crime scene's secured."

"Thanks, Dick. You the first on scene?"

The officer nodded.

Don turned to the lab crew. "Do the note first."

One of the lab people set his kit on the coffee table, opened it, and took out a pair of latex gloves. He went back into the entranceway, retrieved the note, and brought it back into the living room and set it on the table. He took his fingerprinting kit out of the bag and dusted the envelope for prints. There were none. He then opened it and withdrew the single sheet of paper and dusted it too. Again, he came up empty.

The single sheet of typewritten paper was then handed to Alex. He took it and read it. Then he read it again out loud for the others to hear:

Dear Mr. and Mrs. McArthur,

> *By now you've discovered that we have Kendra. And by now, the police are there with you.*
> *Please be assured that we are taking every precaution to ensure that she is safe and unharmed. Nothing is going to happen to her as long as you follow these instructions:*

You are to collect two million dollars in unmarked, nonsequential bills, nothing smaller than fifty-dollar denominations. You will be given until Monday night to collect the money. At 8:00 a.m., Tuesday morning, you will receive a phone call giving you further instructions.

There is to be no police involvement and no media play.

If you want to see your daughter alive, you will follow these instructions exactly. Otherwise...

Alex stopped reading. There was nothing else. He turned the letter over, hoping for more. He looked at Lisa and then looked up at the detective.

"What do we do now?" he asked.

"We begin by dusting for prints," the one called Don answered. It was apparent that he was the senior detective. "And we question these two."

"Mr. McArthur?" Josh said hesitantly.

"Yes, Josh?"

"They wore gloves like that man over there."

"What?"

"They wore rubber gloves. I saw them. The black man had trouble with the tape because of the gloves. She wore them too."

The detectives and the police looked at each other. Don raised his eyebrows in an "Oh well" sort of way. "Let's see what we've got anyway."

"What about all those people out there, the press and the TV and radio people?"

The lead detective looked at Officer Huard. "Go outside and tell them it was a false alarm or something, will you, Dick?"

The policeman left.

In the van, Allen and the major heard every word.

Don approached Darlene and squatted down so that he was eye to eye with her across from the coffee table.

"Sweetheart," he began, "it's very important to us that you remember everything that happened here tonight—what they looked like, what they said, how many of them there were, everything. Do you think you could do that?"

Darlene nodded. She looked at Josh.

"I'll help," he offered.

Don stood and pulled his note pad from his sport coat.

"First off," he began, "tell us what happened. You know, how they got in and so on. Don't leave anything out. Even the smallest details. Even if you think they aren't important. Do you understand?"

Darlene nodded. She began at the beginning and told them everything that happened until the time she was put in the closet.

"I think there were more than two of them, though," she concluded.

"Oh?" Don asked.

"Yes. It sounded like there was at least one more voice, maybe two. I couldn't hear what they said, but I think there were more voices. And laughter. I heard laughter. Yes, I'm sure of it. I remember someone—not the lady or the black man—said something and I heard laughter. I don't know, maybe three or four people were here."

The other detective wrote on his pad.

"Okay. Now I want you to describe the two people that you did see. Everything you can remember. Don't leave anything out."

Darlene began with the lady. She described a pretty young redhead with freckles across the bridge of her nose. With Josh's help, the two teens described a woman exactly like Julie wanted them to.

They next described a black man: bald, with a scar on the side of his head. Josh filled in the details: moustache, thin beard, big space between his teeth. Accent. In the end, they had described Julie's and the black man's creations to a tee.

The major, listening to the whole conversation, was proud.

"I'm going to bring in a police sketch artist. Do you think you could do that again, Darlene?"

She nodded to the detective.

"Good. Mrs....?" He looked at Darlene's mother.

"Emery. Anne. Call me Anne."

"I hope you don't mind us doing this tonight, while everything's still fresh in their minds."

"No, it's okay."

Don was interrupted by the two security guards entering the room, escorted by Officer Huard.

"Yes?"

"Thought you might be interested," the officer interjected. "This is Bubba—Larry Watson. He was the security guard on duty tonight. Bubba, why don't you tell these detectives what you told me."

Bubba looked at the other security man. It was obvious that he was Bubba's supervisor.

Bubba began at the beginning and described the van, the girl, the black man, and his eventual confinement in the trunk of the car. His description of the perpetrators matched those of Darlene and Josh. The one additional piece of information was the name on the side of the delivery van: Citywide Florists Delivery Service.

"Bob?" Don asked, looking at his partner.

Bob looked at Alex. "Phone?"

Alex took him to the phone in the study and returned to the living room.

The two security people were just finishing up with the lead detective when Bob returned. He heard Bubba agree to help with the artist's drawings.

"There's no such company listed in the phone book, but we'll keep on checking," he said to his partner.

Don turned to Alex. "I'm sorry, sir, but I've got to ask. Can you raise two million dollars by Monday night?"

Alex was embarrassed. "It'll take some doing, but yes, I can get the money."

"Good."

The major looked at Allen. The grin on Allen's face was huge.

"Yes!" he yelled.

The major clapped his hands and rubbed them together. "We're in business."

CHAPTER 16

10:00 p.m.

Floyd and Julie pulled up to the cabin and stopped. Floyd reached across and pulled a flashlight out of the glove box. He switched off the dome light and opened the door. He stepped out and closed it behind him. The sound woke the little girl. She stirred in Julie's arms and opened her eyes.

"Is Mommy here?"

"Not yet, honey, but she will be."

Kendra snuggled back into Julie's arms and fell back to sleep.

Floyd opened the door for them, and Julie carefully got out of the back seat. Following the band of light from Floyd's flashlight, they made their way around to the rear of the cabin and entered. Floyd led them to the smaller of the two bedrooms, and Julie laid the little girl down on the bed. She stirred once but did not open her eyes. Julie covered her with a blanket and bent down and kissed her softly on the forehead. Kendra moved on the bed, settling deeper into its comfort.

They left her there and went back to the kitchen where Floyd lit one of the kerosene lanterns. The glow from the flame dimly lit the kitchen.

"I'll go get the kid's things," he said and left.

Julie sat down at the kitchen table, the excitement of the last two hours finally subsiding. She could hear Floyd walking around outside. His footsteps were heavy on the wooden porch steps. He came back carrying the sack. In his left arm was the bunny. Julie laughed when she saw him.

"What?" he asked.

"I'm sorry," she giggled, "you look so cute carrying that pink bunny in your arm."

She laughed even louder. This made Floyd laugh. Their laughing woke Kendra.

"Mommy! Mommy!" Kendra began crying.

"Shit," Floyd muttered.

Julie was on her feet and heading for the bedroom, lantern in hand.

"Mommy?"

"Shh, it's okay, I'm here," Julie said, handing the little girl her bunny. She reached over and caressed away a loose strand of hair from Kendra's face, and then she picked her up and walked around the room.

"Where are we?" the little girl asked.

Thinking quickly, Julie said, "We're up in the mountains, camping. Didn't your Mommy and Daddy tell you about this place?"

Kendra stopped crying. "No."

"Well then, maybe I shouldn't say anything more. It's supposed to be a surprise. Are you sure they didn't say anything?"

Kendra looked her in the eyes and slowly shook her head.

"Well, Kendra, it's really late and you've got a big day ahead of you tomorrow." She put the child back down on the bed and covered her up. "Would you like me to leave a light on in your room?"

Kendra smiled. "Yes, please."

"Floyd!" Julie called, using Cecil's alias. "Could you bring me another lantern for Kendra?"

She heard footsteps and saw the light of the lantern illuminating the doorway as Floyd entered the room.

"Kendra, this is Floyd. He's here to watch over us and keep us safe."

Kendra looked up from the bed. "Keep us safe from what, Aunt Julie?"

Julie thought for a moment, not sure what to say. "Well, maybe there are bears up here. Anyway, with Floyd around, nothing can hurt us. Isn't that right, Floyd?"

"That's right, Miss Julie."

He gave Kendra a big toothy smile and said good night and left.

"Good night, Kendra. Oh. Do you need to go to the bathroom? They don't have a real bathroom up here. We need to go outside to the outhouse. Do you know what an outhouse is?"

Kendra shook her head.

"Well, if you need to go later, you call me, okay? I'll take you. I'm just going to be in the next room."

She bent down and gently smoothed the child's hair. "Good night now."

She kissed the little girl on the forehead and left.

"She's sure one brave little girl," Julie said to her companion as she came back into the kitchen. "If it'd been me who'd been snatched out of my bed by complete strangers, I'd probably still be screaming my head off."

"You want me to take the first watch?"

"No, she's used to me. I'll stay up with her in case she gets up during the night."

"Suit yourself. Wake me at four. Good night."

"Good night."

Floyd lit another lamp and carried it into the other bedroom. Julie sat at the table, the flame of her lantern casting dancing shadows around the room.

She was awakened by a gentle tugging on her arm. She sat up with a start. Kendra was standing next to her.

"I have to go to the bathroom," she whispered.

Julie looked at her watch. It was a little before five. She should have woken Floyd before this. She yawned. "Okay, honey, come on. Let me introduce you to the outhouse."

She put a sweater on the little girl, took the flashlight and a roll of toilet paper off the counter, grasped Kendra's hand, and started for the door.

Julie led the little girl out the back door and down the path to the outhouse.

"This is going to be a new experience for you, honey," Julie said. "There's no running water. You sit over a hole and go. It's called 'roughing it.' You ever rough it before?"

"No," Kendra said hesitantly.

The night was chilly. Julie and Kendra both felt it as they walked to the outhouse.

"Here we are," Julie said, pointing the flashlight at the door. She opened it, and Kendra walked in.

"Do you want me to come in with you?"

"No thank you."

"Do you want the flashlight?"

"Yes, please."

Julie closed the door. She rubbed the chill off her arms and paced back and forth in front of the outhouse door.

After a few minutes, she asked, "You okay in there?"

"I can't go."

"You can't go?"

"No."

Damn! Julie thought. "Well, keep trying."

She could see the flashlight beam bouncing off the walls through the cracks in the wooden slats. Five minutes went by.

"Kendra?"

"Yes?"

"Did you go yet?"

"No."

"Do you still have to go?"

"No."

"Do you want to come out?"

"Yes."

"Okay. Do you need any help?"

"No."

The door opened, and Kendra appeared.

"Sure is messy in there. There's a big, deep hole under the seat. Lots of yucky stuff down in that hole."

"I know. You sure you're all right?"

Kendra looked up at Julie. "I went pee. But I couldn't poop."

She took Julie's hand. Together they walked back to the cabin. The first streaks of light were beginning to appear in the sky.

"I don't like that place."

"Neither do I, honey, neither do I."

The major had wiped down the two vases that the flowers had come in, so they weren't a problem. The gloves meant fingerprints weren't a problem. The bugs were sterile; they would present no problems if they were found. He was sure they would be eventually. He just hoped that eventually meant after the four of them were gone.

"Not much going on. I'll take the first shift if you want," Allen said.

"I don't expect any more activity for a while. You go. I'll keep an ear open. I've got some things to do anyway. Pass me a bottle of water, will you?"

Allen retrieved water from the cooler and passed it to the major. There was an army cot set up in the van. Allen lay down, covered his eyes with his arm, and fell asleep. The major stared at the equipment in front of him. It was pitch-black in the van save for the little red and green lights on the equipment which gave off a faint glow, illuminating his face.

He twisted off the cap and took a long drink from the bottle.

All in all, things have gone pretty well so far.

He knew that the police would contact the FBI. He knew that the McArthur's phone lines would be tapped. He knew that McArthur would probably be wearing a wire when he made the drop. And he knew that there would probably be a homing device hidden in the money bag. He also knew that McArthur would be followed on Tuesday morning.

He had taken all these things into account and had made the necessary plans to counteract anything the police and the FBI might try to do.

Still, there might be something they could do that he hadn't thought of. He sat in the dim light of the equipment going over all the possible scenarios. He could think of nothing that they could do that he hadn't anticipated. Satisfied, he adjusted the earphones to his head, leaned back in his chair, and listened to the quiet humming in his ears.

Alex and Lisa had already gone to bed. He switched the receiver to listen in on any conversation they might be having. He could hear a quiet, steady snoring coming from the bug in the bedroom. He could also hear a soft sobbing sound. Lisa was crying.

Sitting in the van, listening to the sounds of the mother, the major was touched. He had no children, had, in fact, never really wanted any, so he couldn't imagine the loss and the fear she must be feeling. He reached up and turned down the volume on the receiver.

Am I getting sentimental in my old age?

Behind him, Allen started to snore. "Great," he said softly.

CHAPTER 17

Washington, DC, Sunday, July 1

The call came into the offices of the FBI in DC at 1:00 p.m. local time. It was immediately routed through to Inspector Jack Donovan's home number in Arlington, Virginia.

"Hello? Yes, this is Jack Donovan. What...? When?"

He listened to the voice on the other end of the line. It was his station chief in Denver. There had been a kidnapping the night before. The Denver police had notified the Denver office earlier that morning, a courtesy call they had said. The Denver chief was just calling to alert Jack. Jack's office headed up the national division that was involved with kidnappings and abductions.

Jack listened and took some notes. The details were sketchy, but the job was obviously done by professionals. He hung up. He thought about what his station chief had said, and immediately the kidnappings in Houston and Detroit came to mind: the professionalism involved in those two, and now this one. Could they be all be related?

Through the kitchen window, he could see his wife in the garden.

"Honey," he called to her through the open window. "I got a call."

She knew what he meant and immediately put down her trowel, rose, wiped her hands on her jeans, and came into the kitchen.

"Where to this time?" she asked as the screen door slammed behind her.

"Denver. I'm going to the office to pick up some things, and then I'll fly out."

"I'll pack."

"Thanks, honey."

He kissed her on the forehead and headed for the bedroom. She followed him up the stairs and pulled the suitcase down from the closet shelf while he went into the bathroom. When he came out, his bag was packed, and his suit and a clean shirt and tie were lying on the bed. They had done this before. He quickly changed. She helped him knot his tie.

"Say goodbye to the kids for me, will you?"

She nodded and walked down the stairs with him.

"Call Sally and have her meet me at the office. Tell her to call and have a plane ready by two thirty."

He kissed her, checked his pockets for his wallet, keys, glasses, and money, and walked out the front door.

At his office, Jack gathered his files and put them in his briefcase. On a hunch, he withdrew one and scanned it, reading the notes quickly. He then pulled out another one and read it too.

"Damn," he muttered.

Picking up the phone, he called the Denver station.

"Pete? Jack Donovan. Yeah, I'm leaving Washington around two thirty local time. Should be there sometime early this evening. Listen, Pete, was anything else taken?"

He listened to the reply. There didn't appear to be.

"I don't mean jewelry—anything like that. Check and see if McArthur had a wine cellar or at least a wine collection of some sort. And if he does, have him check and see if he's missing any bottles of wine…

"Yes, I know it sounds crazy, but check it out, will you?"

Sally arrived just as he was hanging up the phone.

"What's up? Sue said we're going to Denver."

"Another kidnapping. I'm betting it's the same group that did the Houston and Detroit grabs. You all packed?"

"Ready to go."

"Good. I'll fill you in on the way to the airport. Did you eat?"

"Just breakfast a couple of hours ago."

"All right, we'll grab a bite downstairs. Where are your bags?"

"In my car. I packed for four days. That enough?"

"I hope so. If this is the same group that I think it is, the kid'll be released on the Fourth of July."

"How ironic," she quipped.

"I know."

The two agents took the elevator down and walked to the cafeteria.

Inspector Jack Donovan was forty-six years old. He was in his twenty-fourth year with the bureau, having been recruited right out of college. Special Agent Sally Martin was four years removed from the academy. Eight months ago, Jack had requested that she be assigned to his office, based on her qualifications. Reluctantly she had accepted. She had wanted to be assigned to a more exciting branch of the bureau, but Jack was quite convincing.

These, then, were the two people who would be taking on the kidnappers. For Sally, this would be her first time going up against this particular group of perpetrators.

Denver, Sunday afternoon

Jack and Sally were met at the airport by Pete Jordan, Denver's special agent in charge (SAC).

"Sorry to call you out on a Sunday," he apologized. "Figured you'd want to be brought up to speed as soon as possible. I've got you booked into the Marriot downtown. It's only a few blocks from the office.

"Incidentally, you were right. There were two bottles of wine missing. A Merlot and a Pinot Noir. McArthur said the kidnapper knew his wines. They were worth a couple of bills apiece. Not the most expensive of his collection but good. And they're untraceable."

"I think that it's part of his signature," Jack explained. "I think he wants us to know that it's him. He's left nothing in the way of evidence—no prints or anything else to tie him to these crimes, but in each case, there has been this link—the wine."

Jack and Sally were riding in the back of the company sedan. Pete turned and looked over his shoulder.

"You think this is a signature?" he asked. "You know this guy?"

"I think so. At least I think it's the same people who hit Houston and Detroit. The wine thing has never been publicized."

He referred to his notes. "This is their third job that we know about. Successful first two times. Two million each time. Always kidnaps the child at the end of June. Always releases the kid on the Fourth of July. It's got to be his signature.

"My notes say there are as few as two and as many as four or five of them. They're good. Never leave anything behind. In and out. Quick, neat, no clues. They do each job differently, and yet, each is similar. The good thing so far is that they haven't hurt any of the children. In fact, both kids, Houston and Detroit, reported liking the woman who took care of them. In both cases, the father is much older than his wife. Both kids were only children of the parents."

"Sounds like this case. McArthur's much older than his wife. Kid, Kendra's her name, is an only child. Damn! Serial kidnappers. If that don't beat all."

"I want to see the parents tonight. Can you swing it?"

"Already done."

"Good."

The sedan pulled up to the Marriot. A young man in a long red coat and black top hat opened the door, and Sally climbed out. Jack got out the other side.

"Wait for us. We'll check in, drop our bags and be back down ASAP."

Pete pulled into a space in front of the entrance and waited. Fifteen minutes later, the two agents came through the revolving door, spotted Pete's sedan, walked over, and climbed in.

"Tell us about the family," Jack asked.

Pete gave a background sketch on the two parents. Both were very rich. His earned, hers inherited. Both well thought of and well liked in the community. Charities, fund-raisers. Society people.

"And the ransom?"

"Two million. He can get it. Nothing smaller than fifty-dollar bills. Unmarked, nonsequential, et cetera, et cetera, et cetera. The kidnappers will call Tuesday morning with instructions."

"Phone tap?"

"Tomorrow."

"Any way we can mark the bills?"

"Not much time. If McArthur gets it all together, we still have to write down the serial numbers. It's the nonsequential that takes time. With enough people, we could maybe do a quarter mil. Maybe a half to a full million, but two? I don't see how. Course, if we get some of them recorded, and they turn up later, that's something."

"No, we'd better rule that out. Too risky. If we bring in too many people and they spot them, we're up shit creek. Sorry, Sally."

"What about a tracking device in with the money? Or maybe a wire for him?" she asked.

"We've thought of that," Pete responded. "Wire's a good idea, but if McArthur gets separated from the money, then we've lost it. Homing device in the suitcase might work but requires the use of a van and additional manpower. I've got two men away on emergency leaves and two on vacation. I could call them back if you really need them.

The car entered the circular drive. Alex opened the door and welcomed them into his home. They went immediately to the living room where a table had been set up with plates of sliced meats and cheeses, pickles and chips, and three different kinds of breads.

"We figured you hadn't had time to eat. Help yourselves," Alex offered.

"That's awful nice of you, Mr. McArthur, it's been a long flight. We came straight here after dropping our things at the hotel."

"Alex. You can call me Alex."

"And I'm Lisa," his wife said as she entered, carrying a tray of tea, ice, and glasses.

Pete explained the purpose of the two agents visit and their involvement in the case. Jack gave a brief history of the other two kidnappings and the possibility that this was the work of the same people. He assured the McArthurs that so far, none of the children had been hurt and promised that they would do everything in their power to get little Kendra back and catch the people responsible for these kidnappings. He went on to explain what the police and the FBI would be doing over the next two days, setting up phone taps, preparing Alex's car with a homing device, and so on. He then asked them to tell him and his associate all about Kendra.

"Was she on any kind of medication? Was she a happy child? How did she do with strangers? Anything and everything the two of you can tell us about her will be helpful."

Jack asked them to tell him what had gone on the night of the kidnapping, taking notes all the while. Sally sat next to him and watched. Pete sat back and listened.

Jack looked at his watch. It was after ten in the evening.

"Well," he said, closing his notebook, "that's it for tonight. Thank you both for your help."

Turning to Pete, he asked, "Pete, you'll have your people in place by...?"

"Eight tomorrow. That okay with you two?" Pete asked, looking at Alex and Lisa.

"Fine," the husband agreed. "Oh, one thing. The papers and the TV people. The first night was an absolute circus. We've requested that they stay away, allow us some privacy. Can that be done?"

"They could be a big help if we can get a picture of Kendra to them."

"I don't want them involved," Alex said sternly. "Lisa and I have discussed this, and we want this kept private, for Kendra's sake. The ransom note said no media. We want it that way."

"If you insist. I'll meet you at your bank at 9:00 a.m.," Jack said.

"Nine it is."

When they were back in the car, Jack told Pete what he would be needing over the next few days, including a car and maps of Denver and its surrounding areas.

"I'll get right on it. We can get the car from the pool."

In the van, Allen and the major heard every word. The major took notes.

"Well, Jack Donovan, nice to meet you," he said as the meeting broke up. "You've been doing your homework. That's good. Allen, can we put a bug in McArthur's car?"

"We could, but it wouldn't do much good. I'd have to follow him, or he'd get too far from the receiver and we'd lose audio.

"Good, then they can't do it either. The only way they could would be if they followed him too."

"Right."

"What about the homing device?"

"Well, that'd have a much broader range, but they'd still have to keep the car within a specified range."

"So how far back do you think they will be?"

"Safe guess? No more than ten blocks. About a mile to be effective and still not be seen."

The major did some mental notes. "So we get McArthur to lose the mike. Then we have him change cars."

"That'd work," Allen replied. With a puzzled look, he asked, "How do we do that?"

"Leave it up to me."

"You're the boss."

"One more question. You've got a scanner in your little bag of tricks? Something that would find a homing device, don't you?"

"That's two questions," Allen said, "and yes, I've got one. Why?"

"Suppose we find the homer after Mac switches vehicles. We take it out of his car and put it into another. They're going to follow the car by signal, not by sight, right?"

"Right. And they'll—"

"Follow the other vehicle wherever it goes."

"But how do we get into his car to find it?"

149

"Simple, we tell him to leave it unlocked and leave the keys on the floor."

Allen hesitated, and then it all became clear in his mind. "All right!" he exclaimed. "I like it!"

Monday, July 2, 9:00 a.m.

Alex was waiting for the doors to open when Jack Donovan arrived. It was two minutes past nine when the guard unlocked the doors, and a small group of people pushed their way into the bank's lobby.

Before arriving at the bank, Alex had called the bank president at home and asked that the president meet with him when the bank opened for business. He told the man that it was extremely urgent that they meet but would say no more over the phone. The president was a little irritated but agreed to meet with Alex when the bank opened. He would rearrange his schedule. After all, Alex, his wife, and his company were responsible for over two hundred million dollars of the bank's assets. Yes, he would rearrange his schedule.

Alex and Jack walked up to the receptionist's desk. She recognized Alex immediately and told him to go on up. Mr. Collins was expecting him. When the elevator doors opened, Patrick Collins was waiting.

"Alex," he greeted cheerfully, "it's been a while."

He took Alex's hand and patted him on the shoulder with his other hand. Then he glanced at the other visitor, a questioning look on his face.

"Pat, I'd like you to meet Jack Donovan. Jack. Pat Collins."

Pleasantries were exchanged, and the three men headed for the bank president's office.

"Alice, no interruptions, please," he instructed his secretary.

She nodded. "Yes, Mr. Collins."

Once inside his office, Collins turned to Alex.

"What's this all about, Alex? I hope you're not planning to—"

"Close the door and sit down, Pat, please."

Collins did, then sat behind his desk.

"Pat." Alex took a deep breath. "I need two million dollars. I need it in denominations of one-hundred-dollar bills. If you don't have that much, then make up the balance in fifties. Nothing smaller. They are to be used bills. They are to be nonsequential. And I need them by closing time tonight."

Pat sat back in his chair and laughed. "My God, man," he joked, "you sound like you need ransom money."

He looked at the two men in front of him. They were not laughing.

"Oh God! You're serious, aren't you?"

For the first time since the kidnapping, tears came to Alex's eyes. He said nothing.

Pat looked at Jack. "And just what do you have to do with this, sir?"

Jack reached inside his coat pocket and produced his badge and identification.

"Inspector Jack Donovan, FBI. I've flown in from Washington to lead the investigation into the kidnapping of Alex's daughter, Kendra."

Pat turned to Alex. "Alex, I'm so sorry. What happened?"

Alex told his friend about the kidnapping and the ransom note. Jack had briefed him to say nothing more. "So you see, I need the money by tonight if I want to see Kendra again."

Patrick leaned forward and turned on his computer. He punched some keys, wrote something on a note pad, punched more keys and wrote again. He did this several times. He rubbed his chin and punched still more keys.

"You said used and unmarked? Two million, right? There's no other way?" he asked, looking at Jack.

"I wish there were, Mr. Collins, I wish there were."

Patrick hit a computer key one more time and almost immediately a printer produced a sheet of paper. He removed it and looked at it. He looked at Alex and at Jack and then picked up his phone.

"Alice? Get Paul in here right away."

He hung up, then looked at the paper again and then up at his two visitors.

"Four o'clock okay?"

Jack could sense Alex's shoulders relax in the chair next to him. He had been watching Patrick Collins the whole time. Now he turned to Alex just as the man wiped his eyes with the palms of his hands.

"One more thing," Jack cautioned, addressing the banker, "it goes without saying that this is to be done in the strictest of confidence."

"You can count on that," the banker agreed.

There was a knock at the door. Paul Romano entered.

"Paul, you know Alex McArthur? This is Jack Donovan. Close the door."

Paul closed the door, walked over, and stood next to the two visitors, shaking hands with each of them. The two visitors sat back down, and Paul remained next to them waiting for his boss to speak.

Collins said, "Paul, what you are about to hear is said in the strictest confidence, do you understand?"

"Yes, Mr. Collins."

The banker explained the situation to him and gave him the sheet of paper.

"I want you to handle this for me, and I want it all here in my office by four o'clock this afternoon. Any questions?"

Paul looked at the piece of paper in his hands. On it was a list of branch banks that he would have to contact to get the remainder of the cash.

"No, sir."

To his visitors Collins asked, "How do you propose to transport this money?"

"Two suitcases, probably," Jack responded.

They rose.

"Thanks, Pat, I won't forget this."

"Let's hope your little girl's safe, that's all," he responded, standing up and walking around the desk.

Alex, Jack, Paul, and Patrick Collins left the office. Paul continued on while the other three stopped at Alice's desk. She noticed the somber faces on the men.

The three shook hands again, and Patrick Collins watched them as they headed for the elevators. He walked back to his office.

"Mr. Collins?"

He did not respond but closed the door behind him. Five minutes later, he picked up his phone.

"Alice, I'll be here all day, but cancel all my afternoon appointments. I will take calls though. And get me some coffee."

"Yes, Mr. Collins."

CHAPTER 18

Jack walked the few blocks back to the Marriot after saying goodbye to Alex. He called up to Sally's room from the lobby.

"Good morning. You ready for the day ahead?"

"Yes, I've been ready. Where are you?"

"Downstairs in the lobby."

"How did the meeting at the bank go?"

"Good. Money will be here by four."

"We going back to the house?"

"Yes. Pete's having a car sent over. Should be here any minute."

"I'm on my way."

She walked into the lobby wearing a navy-blue suit coat and matching slacks. A white silk blouse and multi-colored scarf completed the outfit. She was wearing navy-blue shoes with raised heels. Under her left arm was a slightly noticeable bulge.

Jack spotted her first. She was attractive, he had to admit.

When she saw him, her face lit up and she waved. Jack watched the stares of a group of men as she crossed the lobby.

Eat your hearts out, he silently said to the four men as she approached.

"Hi," she said as he stood.

"Let's grab a quick bite and get out of here. Car's not here yet. I'll leave word at the front desk."

They walked down the circular stairs to the restaurant, found a small table and sat down.

"So tell me about your trip to the bank?"

Jack described the meeting in the banker's office.

"You know, it never ceases to amaze me how some people can ask for two million dollars, or one for that matter, and bingo, it's theirs."

"Pity the rich," she joked.

They were just finishing their coffee and bagels when a man in a gray suit approached.

"Mr. Donovan? Jack?"

"Yes?"

"Tom Richards. The concierge said I'd find you here. Your car's here."

"Oh, good. Sally?"

They stood. Jack left some money on the table, and the two agents followed Richards up the stairs.

Outside, Tom reached inside his suit coat and removed a pair of standard-issue aviator sunglasses.

Oh shit, Jack thought, *FBI stereotype.*

"I'll drive, sir, if you don't mind. Pete—Agent Jordan—wants me at the house."

Jack nodded, waited for him to unlock the doors, and opened the rear door for Sally.

"Why, thank you, sir," she said.

Jack noticed the look from Agent Richards as she climbed into the back seat.

Letch, he thought. *I bet he's wondering if we're doing it.*

They drove to the house in silence. Jack knew that Tom was bursting with questions and enjoyed giving him the silent treatment. He didn't particularly like this man, and they had only just met. Jack had a feeling for people. They were going to have to work together, but that didn't mean he'd have to like it.

There were no news vans or reporters parked at the entrance to the Estates, and there was only one car parked in front of the house when they pulled up.

Lisa opened the door before they reached the top step. Jack could see that she had been crying. Her eyes were red and puffy, and she had dark circles under her eyes.

Last night had not gone well, he guessed.

By now, feelings of helplessness and guilt would have set in, followed by feelings of regret. She would begin to blame herself. Jack called this the "if only" stage.

"Good morning," he said to her with as much cheerfulness in his voice as he could muster.

"Hello," she said.

The three agents passed her and went into the living room. Two other men were there. A table was set up next to the phone stand, and several pieces of equipment were spread out on it. Two sets of Mickey Mouse earphones lay next to it.

Tom Richards introduced the two men to Jack and Sally.

"We're just about done," the one named Cal said.

"Good."

Jack and Sally spent the rest of the morning going over the routine with Lisa. He explained that the agents would stay with her until Kendra was returned. He apologized for any inconvenience this might cause her and her husband.

Lisa said that it would be all right. She then told them that Alex had just called. He was going to the office. He told Lisa that he felt it best for him to keep busy now. There was nothing he could do at this time. He begged her forgiveness and understanding and told her he would be home when the money was ready.

Lisa told him that she understood, and yes, it would be okay for him to be at the office. Inwardly, she resented him for not being with her.

Now would come the waiting time. Now, tempers would get short, the parents would become agitated, and agents would get bored. He'd been through this too many times before. The smart thing for him to do now would be to leave.

"Tom? You gonna be all right here? Sally and I have some things to do."

"Uh, sure. I guess. I can ride back to the office with one of these guys."

"Okay then. See you later. Come on, Sally."

Sally gave him a questioning look and stood up.

"Mrs. McArthur," Jack said as she walked them to the door, "we'll find your daughter. And don't blame yourself for what's happened. This was not your fault."

"Thank you, Mr. Donovan." She smiled weakly.

"We'll be back. And please, call me Jack."

In the car, Sally asked, "Where are we going?"

"You and I, young lady, are going to the zoo."

"The zoo!"

"That's right. Between now and the time they call tomorrow morning, there's absolutely nothing more we can do. The police are on the case, and the equipment's set up; nothing to do now but wait. I don't want to be around Lisa McArthur. She's going to become a basket case. And I certainly don't want to be around Tom Richards, that arrogant SOB. So we're going to the zoo. Those shoes comfortable enough to walk in?"

"Uh-huh."

"Good."

Floyd replaced the major and Allen in the van at ten thirty, same as he had done on Sunday morning. He would monitor the house for the next four hours. He didn't particularly like being in the van; he'd rather be up at the cabin, but duty was duty. The cabin was cooler, the air was fresh, and he could move around. It was like an oven in the van, and the quarters were cramped.

He had to admit, the little girl really wasn't much of a problem. She and Julie got along famously. Even Floyd had fun playing with them. They had gone for a walk yesterday afternoon, and Floyd had taught her about the woods.

Kendra was a quick learner, quite smart for her age really, and when Floyd spotted a deer and pointed it out to the little girl, she was ecstatic.

Now, alone in the van, headset covering his ears, sweat pouring off his head, Floyd thought about his own kids. He decided that this would be his last job. He would have over a million dollars when this was over, more than enough to take care of them all. He'd bide his time and eventually move. It would be hard on Jalene and her family, but they could keep in touch.

Floyd settled into the chair and listened. The three agents arrived. Cecil noted the time and entered it on the log. He listened in on the conversation and made more notes.

"Man, this is boring," he said to the equipment.

He had brought fresh ice, more bottles of water, and his M&Ms. He took out a bottle and opened a bag of candy.

Two of the agents left. He made another note. One of the agents was named Sally. This too he wrote down.

There were several magazines on the floor. Floyd picked up each one and skimmed through it. *People Magazine* interested him the most, and he read it from cover to cover.

At two thirty, Allen and the major returned. Floyd had a few words with them, gave them his notes, and left. Both the major and Allen had showered, changed, and eaten a decent meal. They looked refreshed.

Floyd was going to offer to trade places with one of them but decided against it. Kendra wasn't all that bad. He drove back to the cabin. Julie and Kendra were waiting for him as he drove up.

"She wants you to take her for another walk. She wants to see the deer again."

Floyd laughed, bent down, picked up the little girl, and tossed her into the air. She squealed with delight as he caught her.

"So my little Queenie wants to see some deer. Well, I can't promise anything, but let's go see if there are any around."

With Floyd in one hand and Julie in the other, Kendra led them off into the woods.

When the trees grew thicker, she let go of them and let Floyd lead the way. They walked about two hundred yards further into the woods when Floyd stopped and knelt down.

"Kendra," he whispered. "Come here."

She snuck up beside him. He pointed to the ground.

"Do you remember what this is?"

"Deer poop."

"Right. And how long has it been here?"

She squatted down, her hands on her knees, and studied it. "It looks new," she whispered.

"That's right. And what does that tell you?"

Kendra whispered in his ear, "There's deer here."

"Right, so we've got to be real quiet, huh."

He stood and took her hand. She looked for Julie and took her hand also. Together the three explorers crept through the woods, looking all around them for their quarry.

"Look, there's more," Kendra said.

Little dark-brown pea-sized mounds of animal droppings littered the path in front of them. Floyd stopped. Off to his right, about twenty yards away, stood a magnificent buck. Floyd knelt and pulled Kendra to him.

"Shh," he whispered into the little girl's ear. "Over there, see him?"

She looked into the woods and nodded. Julie saw the animal and knelt also. The three continued to stare at the male. It was staring back at them. The animal stood perfectly still, his ears pointed straight up, twitching in the air.

Floyd counted seven points on each antler. "Magnificent," he whispered.

The buck took a few hesitant steps and turned to look at them again. On the ground, three feet from him, under the shade of a tree, two does were resting, their heads up and alert, their ears flicking this way and that, listening for signs of danger.

The three humans did not move but continued to stare at the three animals.

"They're beautiful," Julie whispered.

The male moved away from the two does as if he was trying to lure the humans away from the others. The two does continued to watch the humans. After about a minute, one and then the other stood and quickly walked over to where the male stood. Together, the three turned and trotted away from the intruders.

"They were pretty, weren't they?" Kendra said.

"Yes, Queenie, they were," Floyd responded. "Come on, now, we'd better get back."

"But I want to walk more."

Floyd looked at Julie. She looked at her watch.

"Fine by me," she said.

"Okay, but just for a little while."

Kendra grinned and took the big man's hand in hers.

"Come on, Aunt Julie, let's go."

It was now after four in the afternoon.

Alex, Jack, and Sally returned to the bank at four thirty. They went directly up to Patrick's office.

Alice greeted them and then buzzed her boss.

"They're here," she said into the phone. Turning to the three, she said, "Go on in."

Alex opened the door. Pat was standing behind his desk. All his personal items had been removed and put on the credenza behind the desk. Piled neatly on top of the desk were stacks of bills, all banded with the total amount of cash in each bundle clearly printed on the side of each one.

"It's all here," he said, sweeping his arm. "Two million dollars."

Jack had seen this much money before, but the size and amount of the stacks of bills still impressed him. Sally was mesmerized. She just stared.

"Sally?"

"Oh, I'm sorry. I've never seen this much money before."

"Impressive, isn't it?" Collins stated.

She smiled at him sheepishly.

"Oh," Alex said. "Pat, this is Special Agent Sally Martin. Sally, Patrick Collins, president of the bank."

"How do you do?" she asked, extending her hand.

"Pleasure to meet you."

The three visitors gathered around the desk. Alex had with him two Samsonite suitcases. He placed one on each chair and opened them. The four stacked the bundles of money into each of the suitcases and closed them.

Jack picked one up. It was heavy.

"You want security to help with them?" Pat offered.

"No. The less attention we draw, the better," Jack answered.

"You don't think you'll draw any attention carrying two heavy suitcases out of here?" Collins asked.

"You're probably right. How many people know about this?"

"The money you mean?"

"Yes."

"Well," the banker began, "there's Alice, the four branch managers who helped get all this here, the security people, of course Paul, and"—he thought for a moment—"two of the tellers on the main floor. I think that's all. At least all that I know about. But each of them only knows about his or her part, not the total picture, and not what the money's to be used for."

"That's a lot of people," Jack responded, looking at Sally, "but I guess it can't be helped."

He checked his service revolver. Sally checked hers. Collins was surprised when the lady pulled it from her holster.

"You ready?" Jack asked Sally and Alex.

"Let's go," the father nodded.

Turning to Pat Collins, Alex extended his hand. "Thanks again, Pat. I won't forget this."

Pat took the man's hand in his two hands and held on.

"Good luck, Alex, I hope you get your daughter back safely."

He turned to Jack and Sally. "Catch those bastards, will you?"

"We're certainly going to try, sir," Sally responded.

"Okay, let's go." Jack nodded to the others. Collins shook hands with the agents and walked them to his door.

Each of the men picked up a suitcase and headed for the door. Sally followed, her revolver inside her coat but readily available. Patrick Collins followed behind.

The three rode the elevator to the first floor. A security guard met them as the doors slid open. They all walked through the lobby and out to the parking lot. Pete was waiting for them. He popped the trunk lid, and the two suitcases were placed inside.

Alex closed the lid and turned to the security guard. "Thank you."

"No problem."

Jack and Sally scanned the lot and climbed into the car, Jack in front, Alex and Sally in back, and pulled out of the lot. When they turned onto Curtis, another car pulled out from a spot on the street and pulled in behind them. This car would remain behind them all the way to the McArthur residence.

CHAPTER 19

Monday afternoon, July 2, 5:30 p.m.

When Alex and the three FBI agents arrived at the McArthur home, there were two vehicles parked in the circular drive. Down the street, an unmarked police car with two detectives was parked facing the direction of the house. The car that had followed Pete's Ford sedan stopped three houses away. The driver and his partner stayed in the vehicle.

Pete pulled his car into the drive and stopped.

"Looks kind of crowded, doesn't it?" Pete asked.

All the way back to the house Jack had been instructing Alex on what to expect on Tuesday. Alex was full of questions, and Jack tried to answer them. He kept prefacing each answer by saying this would probably happen, or that they could expect that to happen.

"After all," he explained, "we really don't know what to expect. Most of the time, certain things take place. It's almost like a pattern, like a chess game."

"When we're all together we'll go over the procedures that the two of you will need to know."

They parked by the front door. Pete opened the trunk lid as he climbed out of the car. Immediately, three men came outside. One stood just outside by the front door; the other two walked to the rear of the car. Each of them scanned the street and neighboring yards for signs of anything out of the ordinary. Jack and Alex pulled the two suitcases from the trunk and carried them into the house. Jack was not pleased.

"This is beginning to look like a circus," he muttered over his shoulder to Sally as he climbed the steps.

The man at the door heard him. Anger and resentment showed on his face. Jack caught the look as he passed him.

"Where can we put these?" Jack asked as he set his suitcase down inside the entranceway.

"How 'bout the closet in the study?" Alex suggested.

"You sure that's safe enough?" It was the man from the front door.

Alex looked at Jack.

"He's right. I don't want these bags out of our sight. Let's put them next to the couch.

The man from the doorway approached.

"My name is Tony De Marco." He showed Alex his detective sergeant's badge. "And these two are Robert Cotto and Kevin McNally. We've been assigned to assist the FBI in any way we can. There are two unmarked cars parked down the street. We'll be with you throughout the night. We'll try to keep out of your way."

"Thank you, Detective De Marco," Jack responded. He turned and introduced Sally and Pete to the three men.

"We know Pete," the detective informed Jack.

"Well, good. It's nice to have you on board, Detective. We can use all the help we can get."

He took the detective's hand and shook it. Jack could feel the resentment through the man's grip. It was always the same, the resentment from the locals to the FBI's interference in their investigations.

Lisa walked into the room. "I didn't know what else to do, so I'm ordering pizzas. Is that all right with you?"

Nods of agreement came from all around.

It was too late for Jack to reduce the number of bodies on hand. If the kidnappers happened to drive by, they would notice all the activity and know that the locals and the FBI were involved.

In the van, two observers heard the arrival of Alex and the FBI and heard them talking about the money.

"Two million dollars!" Allen said to the major. "Two million freakin' dollars! And it's all ours!"

"Not yet, my friend, but soon."

"Too bad we couldn't just waltz in there and take it. Man, wouldn't that be somethin'. Two million green freaking dollars!"

"Let's not spend it yet. We've still got a long way to go."

"Yes, sir. Like I said, you're the boss."

"Okay," the major said, trying to bring him back to reality. "What do we know so far?"

His companion thought for a moment. "Well, we know they have the money. And we know that both the locals and the Feds are now involved. Those are the obvious things."

"What else?"

"The money's in two suitcases. We'll have to get something large enough to switch it into."

"Go on."

"With that many people there, I count six badges plus the technician inside, and at least two, maybe four outside. They aren't keeping it much of a secret. They probably figure we know about them."

"And?" Allen thought some more. He looked at the major's face for a clue. The face was blank.

"And…there's going to be quite a caravan of vehicles on the road tomorrow."

"Good. That means we've got to scare them off somehow."

"How do we do that?"

The major explained his idea to his friend.

"I like it. It makes sense."

"Only problem is, it'll probably compromise our listening devices."

"Well, I didn't expect to be able to walk back in there and get them back anyway. So it's no great loss to me."

"Tom," the major used his given name, "is there any way—any possible way—that the bugs could be traced back to you?"

Tom didn't hesitate. "No way, man. I bought the components from several different wholesalers throughout the south. Each part by itself wouldn't be enough to identify what the sum total was, and

I made modifications to them. No, Major, there's no way they can be traced."

"Okay then, when the time comes, they're going to know that the house is bugged. And when that happens, you are to hightail it out of here in a hurry. You understand?"

"Yes, sir."

"Good. You head for the cabin. We'll meet up there. And wear your face," he said, gesturing to the mask on the floor. "One more thing. The voice alternator, where is it?"

"Right here," Tom said, opening his toolbox.

Inside was a small box. The major opened it. The box held an electronic device that could hook onto the phone. The major closed it and gave it back to Tom.

Eight pizzas arrived, and Alex helped Lisa carry them in. After they were eaten, Jack gathered everybody together in the living room.

"All right. Nothing's going to happen until the phone call tomorrow morning. Alex, Lisa, whichever of you answers the telephone, I want you to keep them on the line for as long as possible. Maybe we'll get lucky on a trace.

"We'll be listening. Do whatever they say but try to stall as long as possible. If they give you instructions, ask them to repeat them. Then you repeat them back to the caller. Anything you can think of to keep them on the line. Got it?"

The parents nodded. Lisa turned to Alex. "Honey, I think you'd better take the call. I'm afraid I might not be able to handle it."

Alex took her hands and looked directly into her eyes. "It's going to be all right. We're going to get Kendra back safely," he said.

"I hope so," she said. And then she sobbed.

Alex looked at the men in the room and apologized. "Come on," he said to his wife, "let me take you upstairs. Excuse us, gentlemen."

The sound of a mother crying moved the major slightly. Up to now, he had never met the parents of his victims. This was the first time, and he really liked the two of them. They were not what he expected.

The woman's sobbing moved him enough that his eyes watered. Tom noticed but said nothing. His eyes were also moist.

Back in the living room, the detectives and the FBI waited for Alex to return.

"God, I hate this part," Detective De Marco said. "Those bastards."

Alex entered the room and took a seat.

"I gave her a mild sedative, I hope that's all right."

"Fine," Jack answered.

"All right. Tell me what I can expect tomorrow?" He looked from one detective to another.

"Go ahead, it's your show, you're the boss," Tony said. "You tell him."

"No, it's not my show!" Jack fired back. "It's *our* show. Yours, mine, his, his, hers, all of us have a part in this. We're here because we were called in to be here. Not because you can't do the job."

"Gentlemen, gentlemen," Pete interrupted. "Please, let's not fly off the handle here. Jack's right. We all have a job to do. I realize tempers are a little short right now, but let's work together. Come on now."

Jack looked at Tony De Marco. "He's right. I'm sorry. I guess we're all a little on edge.

"Sorry," Tony said.

Alex stepped in. "If you guys are done fighting your territorial games, I'd like to know how I'm going to get my daughter back."

"Jack?" Tony said.

"Well, we think this is the same group that kidnapped the children in Detroit and Houston. I say we *think* because there are too many similarities, although the manner of the kidnappings is different.

"Anyway, what can we expect?"

Jack explained what he thought would happen, beginning with the phone call, then the drive to the drop-off where the ransom would be paid. In both Houston and Detroit, the children were returned in good health. Happy even."

"Then I want to do what they say. I don't want you to follow. I give them the money, they give me back my little girl. They can keep the goddamn money."

"Alex," Jack interrupted, "if we do that then they truly have won. And they'll go on and do it again. Only, one of these times, the child might not be so lucky. Do you want that on your conscience?"

"I just want my daughter back."

"Then trust me," Jack said. He looked at the other detectives and agents in the room before continuing.

"As I was saying, they'll lead you on a wild chase around town until they think they've lost us, then they'll tell you to go to a drop site where you'll leave the money. Then you'll have to pray that they return your child unharmed."

"So what do you do while I'm driving God knows where?"

"We're going to rig you with a wire. Someone will always be close enough. Each time you get a message to your next location, we send someone on ahead. At one of these locations, you'll be told to leave the money. We watch and follow."

"But what happens if we lose contact?"

"Then we have a backup. We'll insert a tiny homing device into each of the suitcases. One of the backup vehicles will have a receiver in his car. That car will be following the suitcases wherever they go. Either way, when they pick up the money, we will be there. We just follow them back to where they have Kendra. Bingo. We grab them, rescue Kendra, retrieve the money, case closed."

"Bingo! Case closed!" the major mimicked. "Only one thing, Inspector Jack Donovan. It isn't that simple. We know your plans, but you don't know ours."

Floyd arrived back at the cabin at eight forty-five after going back to his hotel to shower and change clothes. Julie was waiting for him when he drove up. Kendra was nowhere to be seen.

"Am I glad to see you," she said, walking up to his car. "Don't slam the door, she's just gone down to sleep."

"What's up?"

"This afternoon's been the day from hell. Ever since you left, she's been a little witch. She wanted to know when her mommy and daddy were coming. She wanted to go home. She didn't like this. She didn't like that. 'How come Uncle Floyd can go but I can't?' she asked when you left. She wouldn't eat. She wet her pants. I'll have to wash her clothes, nothing's clean. She won't wear yesterday's clothes. And it took forever just to get her to go to bed."

"It's almost over. Don't give up. Tomorrow—"

"Tomorrow! Tomorrow we tie her up and leave her here all alone!"

Floyd shrugged. "I'll make sure she's comfortable."

"I'll make sure she's comfortable," she repeated. "The poor child's scared. She'll be a basket case by the time we get back here tomorrow."

"You got a better idea?"

"No, dammit, I don't! I just don't like it, that's all."

Floyd put his hands on her shoulders. She looked up at him. There were tears in her eyes.

"Kid's gotten to you, hasn't she?"

She sniffed, wiped her nose with the back of her hand, and nodded.

"Got to you a little too, didn't she?"

Floyd grinned.

"Come on, tell you what. Why don't you go in and go to bed? I'll take your watch tonight."

"No, I'll be all okay."

The two walked to the cabin and entered.

"What if we gave her a sleeping pill or something?" Julie asked. "Something that would keep her out for five or six hours. Maybe we could be gone and back before she woke up. Then she'd never know."

Floyd pondered it. "Kind of risky, her bein' so small and all."

"I've got some sleeping pills in my purse. If we cut it in half…"

"Let me think on it. It sure would make life easier. I mean, not having to worry about her being tied up while we're gone."

"She probably should be tied up anyway, just in case she was to wake up. But we tie her to the bed, and she sleeps through the whole thing, then what's the harm?"

Julie pulled the pills from her purse and handed them to Floyd.

"They really work for you?"

"Sleep like a baby. And there are no aftereffects."

"Okay, let's cut one in half. We'll give it to her in her juice tomorrow."

"Thanks, Floyd. I feel better already."

Julie checked in on Kendra and came back out to the back porch with two cans of Coke. She gave one to Floyd and took a seat next to him on the porch. They stared into the woods as darkness fell on them.

In hushed tones, the two talked about their plans for the future. Julie was unsure what she was going to do. There were factors that she was unsure of. Floyd guessed that the major was somehow involved but kept his mouth shut. Instead, he talked about his kids and his dead wife and how he was going to move somewhere else and start a new life.

It was completely dark when they stood to go inside. The sky was filled with stars. Both Floyd and Julie were awed by the sheer numbers of stars in the sky. Life in the city never afforded them the openness of the night sky.

"Beautiful, ain't it," Floyd remarked.

"Oh look!" Julie whispered.

A shooting star raced across the sky and disappeared.

"Floyd smiled. "My mother used to say that if you ever saw a shooting star, then all your dreams would come true."

"Wouldn't that be nice," she remarked.

He held the door for her and took one last look at the sky and the woods before closing it behind him. Julie found the lantern and lit it.

"I'll take the first watch," she said. "You get some rest. Tomorrow's going to be a busy day."

Floyd agreed, washed his face in the basin in the kitchen, and went off to the bedroom. Julie grabbed another Coke from the cooler and went out to the back porch again.

She thought about Kendra and what was going to happen tomorrow. The kid had made an impression on her, unlike the two previous children. Something about Kendra touched her.

She wondered if she would be in any danger if she were given a small dose of the pills? Probably not.

Julie decided it would be okay to give it to Kendra in her juice at breakfast time. She was still on the porch forty minutes later when the first of eleven deer quietly moved through the backyard. Julie was mesmerized as the herd slowly moved by, stopping to nibble at the vegetation, ever alert for signs of danger.

Julie sat up, scarcely daring to breathe. She could almost reach out and touch them; they were that close. The leader was a huge buck. She counted the points on his antlers.

How many had they seen on the other buck? Fourteen? This one had sixteen. He was magnificent! They should see this, she thought, wanting to run into the cabin and wake the two of them. Instead, she sat there and watched until the herd moved on and were out of sight.

She picked up the empty Coke can and went inside, tossing the can in the trash bag as she passed. She picked up the lantern and looked in on Kendra, then went to the couch and sat down. Wrapping a blanket around her, she curled up at the end of the couch and stared into the flame of the lantern.

It was now eleven thirty.

CHAPTER 20

July 3, dawn

The sun was just above the horizon when the major drove up to the cabin. He sat behind the wheel of his rental car and listened to the noises in the woods. Birds chirped and filled the air with their songs. Off to his left, a squirrel barked. A flash of orange in the trees next to the cabin caught his attention. Chickadees sang. A Steller's jay shrieked. The orange flew out of the trees; it was a northern oriole. Another followed it as it disappeared behind the car. On the ground, two squirrels chased each other in and out and up and down a tree.

It was peaceful here, cool and peaceful. The major checked his watch. Five twenty-four a.m. Time to get this show on the road. Floyd met the major as he was rounding the corner of the cabin.

"Mornin', Major," he greeted.

"Floyd."

"Fine mornin' looks like."

The major looked up at the eastern sky.

"Good morning for making money. How's it been for the two of you?"

"I guess it was a little rough on Julie yesterday, but she's fine. You and Allen?"

"Allen's fine."

"Come on in."

Julie was pouring coffee as the two men entered. She flashed a big smile at the major as he entered. He was wearing the mask that she had made him. They sat at the table. The major studied the two of them. The masks that they had been wearing since the kidnapping still looked like the real thing.

"Kendra's still sleeping," Julie said in a hushed tone as she sat down with the two men.

The three went over their plans for the day. The major brought his map and spread it on the table. He gave a duplicate map to each of them and proceeded to show the route that McArthur would be driving, and the changes that he had come up with since they had driven it last. On each of the three maps, he highlighted the stops that each of them would be responsible for: his in red, Floyd's in blue, and Julie's in yellow. He gave them each the notes and envelopes they would be dropping off as well as the note that would warn McArthur they had spotted his tail. He pointed out where that note would be used if it was needed.

They discussed all the options that were available to them and all the things that could go wrong and what to do if anything was to go wrong. It was agreed that they would all meet back at the cabin when this was over.

The major explained about the change in plans and how Allen would probably beat them back to the cabin. They agreed that the major and Julie would be responsible for getting Kendra back to her parents when it was over. Just how they would do it wasn't clear yet, but the major had some ideas.

Julie brought up the idea of the sleeping pills. The major didn't like the idea, but Julie and Floyd were quite persuasive. In the end, he agreed.

He drew a diagram of the layout at Southglenn Mall and the Conoco station across the street.

"Floyd," he said, putting an X on the drawing. "I'll want you parked here."

He turned to Julie. "And I want you parked on the other side of the bank." He put an X next to the bank's square.

"I'll make the phone call from this phone booth," he said, pointing to the phone booth at the Conoco station. "That's where I'm going to leave the note. Then I'll cross the street and park here." He placed an *X* between the other two *X*s. "After McArthur arrives and receives his first envelope, Julie, I want you to head west on Arapahoe here and set up across from the Conoco at Broadway and Grant Way.

"Floyd, you'll follow McArthur from here to here," he said, pointing to the corner of Broadway and Grant. "Then you'll continue to the next spot. Then we just play hopscotch until we get there. You park your car in this lot, and I'll pick you up. This is where we make the switch."

The major continued to review the plan. "I want both of you in place by eight this morning. Any questions?"

There were none.

"Good. I'm leaving now. You two get Kendra up and give her some breakfast. Be careful with those sleeping pills. Good luck."

He rose and left the two of them drinking their coffee. It was now six fifteen. Driving back down the mountain into the morning sun was brutal.

McArthur residence, July 3, 7:00 a.m.

Alex opened the door for Jack and Sally. His eyes were red, and he had bags from a long and sleepless night. Jack nodded to the man as he passed. Sally gave him a smile of encouragement.

The three of them walked into the living room. They were met by Tony De Marco, his two detectives, Lisa, the phone technician, and Pete and his two agents. It was crowded: nine officers and agents and parents.

At seven fifteen Jack called them all together.

"Tony? Your men in position?"

Tony unfolded a map of the area and spread it across the coffee table.

"I've got a car here," he said, pointing to the intersection of University and Belleview, "and one here." He pointed to Quincy and University. "In case Alex goes either direction, we've got it covered. The van you saw outside? That's where the tracker is located."

"Good. Sally will coordinate everything from here. We'll keep in constant radio contact with each other. Pete? The map I asked for?"

"Right here."

He produced a large map of the entire metro region. It was attached to a Styrofoam backing. This he placed on a stand.

"I brought some pins to use to identify each stop. These little red flags may help us to determine a pattern or route they might use. Maybe we can anticipate them."

"Excellent," Tony remarked.

Jack looked at his watch. They still had twenty minutes before the phone call would come in.

"Anything else?" he asked.

No one spoke.

"Mr. and Mrs. McArthur? Alex? Lisa?"

Jack turned to the parents. "When the call comes in, remember, keep them on the line. Keep them talking."

The technician helped Alex with his wire while the other people in the room found their own little groups, cops to cops, agents to agents, talking in hushed tones. Lisa went off to the kitchen and returned several minutes later with more coffee which she poured into the urn.

"Help yourselves, please," she insisted.

Several of the men, including Jack, poured more coffee. Sally went over to where Lisa had seated herself and squatted down next to her, trying to start a conversation.

"You can't be comfortable," Lisa observed. "Come on, let's go into the kitchen."

Excusing themselves, the two women retreated to the kitchen.

In the van, Allen adjusted the knobs on his receiver. He could switch from the living room to the kitchen and back by simply switching channels on his receiver.

The major stood. "Okay. We know what they're planning. We'll need to neutralize their wire and get rid of the homing devices. Allen, I need you to pay close attention to what they say after my call. If we're lucky, they will remove the wires, but I doubt it. Call me in two minutes after I hang up. I need to know what they are going to do."

"You got it, Major."

"Okay then, this is it. Good luck."

The call came precisely at 8:00 a.m. Alex looked at Jack before picking it up. On the fourth ring, Jack nodded to him.

"Hello?"

"Good morning, Mr. McArthur. May I call you Alex? It will make everything so much easier. Oh, always answer the phone, 'Alex here.' Understand?"

The voice on the phone was electronically altered. Alex tried to place it, but he couldn't. The technician turned a dial, and the phone voice filled the room so that the others could hear too.

"Yes, I understand."

"Good. Now listen carefully because I won't repeat this. You've probably got the FBI and the police listening as we speak. Don't deny it. I'd be disappointed if they weren't there.

"You've got ten minutes to load up your car and get to the Conoco station across from Joslin's at the Southglenn Mall. There's a phone booth there. Taped to the underside of the ledge you'll find your first set of instructions. And, Alex, if you want to see your daughter alive, you'd better tell the police not to follow you. Otherwise, we'll just run you around in circles for a while, and you'll never see your daughter again. Do you understand?"

"Yes. Wait!" Alex yelled just as he heard the dial tone on the other end.

The entire conversation lasted thirty-eight seconds.

"Did you get that?" Jack asked the technician.

The look on the man's face told Jack that he hadn't.

"Damn!" he looked at Tony. "Get your men over to the Conoco station and set up. I want to be in the van when Alex leaves the station. Alex, are you ready?"

"Yes."

Tony checked the man's wire one last time and wished him good luck.

"Remember, we'll be behind you the whole time. Each time you get new instructions get back into the car before you tell us where you're going next. That way they can't see you talking to us if they have their own tails."

Alex looked quizzically at the detective.

"It happens."

"Let's get going. You've got less than nine minutes," Jack urged.

Together the two men carried the bags out to the Mercedes, which had been brought around to the front of the house.

Sally and Lisa followed them out along with the rest of the police and the FBI. The two women would remain behind with the technician and one of the FBI agents.

The two suitcases were loaded into the trunk, and Alex drove off. Two minutes later, the FBI and the detectives followed. Jack rode with Tony and his two detectives, much to Pete's disappointment.

After the major hung up, he placed the envelope under the ledge, got into his car and drove across the street to the parking lot by Joslin's. The others were in position. He parked his car so that he could see across the street and watched for the Mercedes to arrive.

Allen called the major as the bags were being loaded into the car.

"Looks like two cars and a van in position and two cars from the house. Um, wait a minute."

There was a pause. The major looked at his watch. Five minutes after eight.

"Sorry about that. Looks like the lady cop is staying at the house with Lisa and the tech. I don't hear any more voices."

"Good. Sit tight. Remember, first sign of trouble, you get the hell out of there."

"Roger that."

Each of the others heard Allen's communication and were alerted to the arrival of the police. The first to arrive was a dark-blue Ford sedan with two detectives. It parked two spaces away from Julie. The driver turned off his engine. He could see the Conoco station across the street.

Julie looked over at the two men and flashed them a big smile. Then she opened her purse and withdrew her lipstick, blush, and eyeliner. She could feel their eyes on her as she applied the blush to her cheeks, did her eyes, and finally applied lipstick to her mouth. She was her real self now, not the young redhead who had been at the house.

A maroon Ford pulled up at the Conoco station with two more detectives. The driver parked next to the building, leaving the engine running. The driver lit a cigarette while his partner went inside, returning shortly with two cups of coffee.

Julie was blotting her lipstick on a tissue when Alex arrived. He waited for an opening in traffic and then quickly crossed University and pulled next to the phone booth. He looked around before getting out of his car and approaching the booth. He spotted the detectives immediately. The driver saluted him casually with his cup of coffee.

Under the ledge was the envelope. Alex removed the envelope and quickly opened it. A single sheet of white paper with a set of instructions and a Polaroid picture of Kendra holding the morning edition of the *Rocky Mountain News* was inside.

Alex looked at the picture and shuddered. Her hair was done up in pigtails and she was wearing a pink jersey. She was holding the newspaper in front of her. He could see the front page. It was today's newspaper. She seemed to be in good spirits. In fact, she had a grin and looked healthy and unharmed. Alex put the picture back in the envelope and read the typed message next:

Conoco station. Broadway and Grant Way. Ten minutes. Phone Instructions. Don't be late.

Alex turned the page over. There was nothing else. He looked at his watch. Eight twelve. He looked over at the detectives. He perceived the slightest nod from the driver.

Alex climbed back into his car, started the engine, and pulled out onto southbound University Boulevard, nearly getting struck by two northbound moving vehicles as he crossed into the southbound lane. The two detectives at the Conoco station weren't so lucky. They had to wait through a red light before traffic would allow them to cross onto southbound University.

Julie left the parking lot and headed west on Arapahoe. She would park across from the second Conoco station and make the next phone call.

On the road, Alex spoke into his wire. "They told me to go to the Conoco station at Broadway and Grant Way. They said they'd phone me from there. They've given me ten minutes. They also gave me a picture of Kendra holding today's issue of the *News*. She's alive, thank God."

The phone was ringing when Alex pulled up next to it. He threw open the door and nearly fell as he raced up to it.

"Hello? I mean, Alex here."

"You're late." It was a female voice. "Don't be late again."

"I'm…I'm sorry."

"There's a Total station at the corner of Broadway and Tuft's. Phone booth in front. You've got ten minutes."

"But—"

The phone went dead.

"Shit!" Alex yelled into the receiver. He slammed it on its hook and climbed back into his car, repeated the message to the authorities and headed north on Broadway.

The major was parked at the 7-Eleven diagonally across the street from the Total station when Alex drove up.

Alex ran to the phone and picked up on the second ring. "Alex here," he said, beads of sweat beginning to appear on his forehead.

"Alex. We seem to have a problem here."

It was the same voice he had heard at his home.

"You haven't been completely honest with me, have you?"

"What do you mean?"

"I mean, you've been leading a parade of police and FBI cars around town, haven't you?"

"I don't… What… How…"

"Never mind how," the voice interrupted, "now listen up. I want you to call home and ask for Sally. You know who Sally is, don't you? Put her on the phone and tell her that the four cars that have been following you have been spotted. Tell her to call them off. Do you understand? Have her get in touch with Jack and have all four of their vehicles fall back and return to the house. And after you've done that, I want you to remove your wire and throw it in the trash. Do you understand?"

"Yes."

"Fine, Alex. I'll call you back at this number in ten minutes. When I'm sure you've done these things, and the cops and the FBI are gone, I will give you our next set of instructions. If you want to see Kendra again, you'd best do as I say."

The line went dead. Alex continued to stare at the phone in his hand, the shock of what he had just heard beginning to sink in. He turned and looked up and down Broadway. He spotted the blue Ford sedan with the two detectives parked about one-half block to the south.

Jesus! If I can spot them, no wonder they can. Shit!

He picked up the phone and dialed his home.

"Hello?" It was Lisa.

"Lisa? Don't ask any questions, just put Sally on, will you please?"

Lisa looked at Sally and handed her the phone.

"This is Sally."

"Sally, listen. They know. I just got off the phone with them. They know about the four cars. They know about the wire. Sally, they even told me to ask for you. They know your name. How did they know your name? They even told me to have you call Jack and have everybody back off. How did they know this? How could they know?"

"I don't know, I...oh my God!" A light went off inside her head.

"What is it, Sally?" Alex asked desperately.

"Listen, Alex, do exactly what they tell you to do. I'll call Jack and relay the message. Everything's going to be just fine. I promise."

Sally hung up the phone.

"What is it? What happened?" Lisa asked.

Sally held up her finger to her lips, signaling for Lisa to be quiet. She retrieved a piece of paper and a pen from the radio table and began to write something down. While she was doing this, she told Lisa what Alex had said.

She finished writing and handed the note to the FBI agent. The note read, "We're being bugged."

The FBI agent read the note and handed it to the technician and motioned for him to be quiet. All the while Sally kept talking calmly to Lisa while she moved about the room looking for bugs.

"Lisa, I've got to call Jack now. Would you mind getting me a glass of water?"

"No, I want to stay right here, I want to hear everything," she said hysterically.

"All right."

Sally dialed Jack's cell phone. He answered on the first ring.

"Jack, it's Sally. Alex just called—"

"I know. I'm in the van. Have you found—"

"I'm looking," she said.

She repeated Alex's message to her boss, all the while continuing to search for the bugs in the room. The tech and the other agent joined in. They found the two bugs in the living room. She motioned for the two men to leave them where they were. While she talked to Jack, it was agreed that the four cars would return to the house.

"After all, the van wasn't mentioned. Maybe they didn't know about it. And besides, the suitcases had the signals in them. They could still track the money." It was Tony speaking. He was with Jack in the van.

In the surveillance van, Allen heard the entire conversation from the minute the phone rang. He picked up his radio and called the major, relaying the entire message to his superior.

"Guess it's time for me to go," he said as he finished. "See you back at the rendezvous spot."

The major put the radio under the seat of the car and adjusted his rearview mirror to better see his target across the street. Alex was walking back and forth in front of the phone booth. He had removed the wire he was wearing and had thrown it into the trash bin next to the row of phones.

The major exited his car and went inside the 7-Eleven to get change. He could see Alex across the street as he put the change in his pocket. The major stood inside watching the man for several minutes before going back outside. He went to the row of phones in front and dialed. The sound of the phone ringing startled Alex even as he expected it to ring.

"Alex here."

"Good. You called home. The cops are backing off. I've got to assume you're not wearing the wire anymore. You've got ten minutes. Next stop is 2160 South Broadway across from the EMW Furniture Warehouse. There's a 7-Eleven there. Next phone call. Get moving."

The phone went dead. Alex turned around and looked up and down Broadway. The blue Ford sedan was gone. He got into his car and headed north.

Floyd pulled up and parked in the restaurant parking lot on the corner of South Broadway and Warren and walked to the phone booth attached to the side of the building. From there he could see the phone booth up the street. By standing around the corner of the building, he could not be seen.

At eight forty-seven, Alex drove into the 7-Eleven and parked his car. The phone was ringing. He raced for it and grabbed the receiver from its cradle, dropping it as he did so he grabbed the wire and pulled the phone up and put it to his ear.

"Alex," he said breathlessly.

A different voice came through the line, the voice of a black man, a voice deep and low, with the slightest hint of a Caribbean accent. The man spoke softly.

"Good morning, Mr. McArthur. I trust you're having a good morning.

Alex waited. He was not amused.

"Your next stop is at the corner of West Colfax and Wolff. There's a phone booth there. Under the ledge, you'll find your next set of instructions. You've got twenty minutes. Talk to you later."

The man hung up.

Oh God! Alex screamed to himself. *What did he say? West Colfax and Wolff? Yes, that was it. But how far west on Colfax? What alphabet was Wolff in? He decided to drive north on Broadway and then go west on Colfax. That way he'd be sure to find it.*

Jack and Tony were the last to arrive back at the McArthur's residence. The conversation between the two men had been brief during the ride back to the house.

Sally met them at the door.

"We found four of them," she said as she followed the two men into the living room, "two in the living room, one in the study and one in the kitchen. Those bastards! They've known everything from the beginning."

Lisa was sitting on the couch, a box of tissues next to her, a small pile of used ones on the coffee table in front of her.

"What will happen now?" she asked as Jack came and sat down opposite the grief-stricken wife and mother.

"We've still got the van tracking the money. We're not getting anything from Alex, so we've got to assume that he's lost the wire. All we can do now is wait until something develops.

"I'm sorry, Lisa, none of us expected this. These people are high-tech and they're clever. They've thought this whole thing out down to the smallest details. They caught us off guard."

"I just want my baby back," she blurted out and started to cry again.

Sally came over and sat down next to her, taking her hands in her own. "We'll get Kendra back. I promise."

Just then the phone rang. Lisa looked up at Sally and then at Jack.

"Let me talk to Jack," the voice demanded.

"This is Jack Donovan speaking."

"Jack? Hello, Jack," the disguised voice said. "I see you've found some of our bugs. Congratulations. Tell Sally I'm impressed she figured it out. Just one thing, Jack. It's about the van. Dump the van, will you, Jack. I don't want to be a nuisance. Know what I mean? Having to drive all around town and all? Talk to you later."

The phone went dead.

The frown on Jack's face caused Sally to ask. "Was that him?"

Jack nodded.

She waited for more.

Jack stood and walked over to the bay window and stared out to the manicured lawn in front of the house. Quickly he turned and crossed the room.

"Come with me. All of you."

They followed him out of the kitchen, through the sliding doors and into the backyard. When he was in the middle of the yard, he turned, stopping to look at Sally.

"Are you sure you got all the bugs?"

"Pretty sure. Pete'll be back with the sweeper. We'll know for sure then."

"I think there may be more. That was the disguised voice. He wants us to pull the van back in. Not only do we have to worry about Alex and the money, now he's got us wondering about more bugs. Son of a bitch!"

He looked at the others. "Well then." He paused and looked at each of them again. "Tell me, what do we know so far?"

"Not much." It was Detective McNally.

Tony spoke up. "They're well organized. They're high-tech. It's almost like this is a military operation."

"Exactly!" Jack cut in. "Sally, I want you to call Washington. See if we can get any type of tie-in to any military-type acts of criminal behavior. Especially abductions. Look for anything that involved the use of listening devices. I know it's a long shot, but… You know what I want."

He looked at the others. "What else?"

"Right now, we've got Alex heading north toward downtown. It's highly unlikely that he'll be making the drop there. Too many people. Too few safe places to leave the money. Unless…"

"Yes, go on," Jack instructed.

"Unless he's leaving it at the bus station or the train station."

"Good thinking. Tony, get some men to cover both of those locations. Maybe Kevin's right. What else?"

Sally spoke up. "If we didn't find all the bugs, then someone's still listening. And if he's still listening, then he has to be in the neighborhood. He'll probably be in a van—"

"Precisely. Tony? I want a helicopter in the air, crisscrossing the neighborhood. Look for a van or some type of vehicle that doesn't belong. This is too nice a neighborhood for vans to be parked without a good reason. I'm guessing it will have antennae sticking up from the back. What else?"

Jack looked around at his team.

"Okay," he said at last. "I don't want to lose our van. It's our only link with Alex. Tony? What's the maximum distance the van can follow at and still be effective?"

Tony thought and quickly responded. "Maybe a mile and a half. I wouldn't want to go any further away. Too many things could happen."

"Right. Have your men drop back to maximum distance and remain steady. Sally, call Washington. Have them also cross-check our kidnappers against any possible terrorist activity. Anything. Everything. Get going."

"Tony, if Alex is heading north on Broadway, and into downtown, where would he go?"

"Well, assuming he gets into downtown but not into ground zero, he could go east or west on any number of streets, the most obvious being Sixth Avenue, Eighth Avenue, Thirteenth, Fourteenth, Colfax, or he could go through downtown and—"

"I don't think he'll do that. Let's assume that he doesn't go through the city itself. If they're following him too, then they could stand a good chance of losing him in traffic. No, I think Alex'll change directions before he reaches downtown proper. Could we position our police cars on the larger side streets to see if Alex drives by?"

"That would take too long to set up, and you're asking for dozens of patrol cars. We don't even know if he's going all the way downtown. Our last contact with him was on Evans. He could have gone east or west from there. From a logistical point, it just wouldn't work."

"Can you have your patrol cars be on the lookout for Alex's car and radio in its location if he is spotted?"

"That might work."

"All right then, let's do that. Now. Let's assume the house is still bugged. Until Pete gets here, we do all our talking and planning out here as it pertains to the case. Agreed?"

All agreed.

Alex turned west on Colfax from Lincoln and fought his way through traffic and the lights. The police were no longer behind him. He hoped the van still was. He suddenly felt alone. And desperate.

Floyd left the phone booth one minute after Alex pulled out of the 7-Eleven. There had been no police cars following him. He took Broadway north to I-25 and took it north as far as Sixth Avenue where he turned off and headed west to Federal, then north to Colfax and west to Wolff. The plan was for him to meet up with the major, leave his car in the back of the VFW lot across the street from the 7-Eleven and watch Alex make the transfer.

The major was parked in the VFW lot when Floyd arrived. He told Floyd to park in a backed-in position at the back of the lot. Floyd did, locked the car, and left one of its keys on top of the passenger-side front wheel.

"Good," the major said as Floyd climbed into his car. He pulled out of the lot and drove a half block north on Wolff, parked the car, adjusted the mirror, looked at his watch, and said, "Five minutes."

It was ten minutes past the hour when Alex turned into the 7-Eleven parking lot. The phone booth was right on the corner of Colfax and Wolff. He pulled up to it and got out, looked in the direction he had come from and then looked west on Colfax before reaching under the ledge to retrieve the envelope. He studied it, turning it over and over in his hands, before getting back into his car.

The note told him to look for a silver Chevrolet Cavalier parked across the street in the back row of the VFW parking lot. Alex looked up. There it was, along the back row, backed in against the fence. His heart raced faster. The note instructed Alex to back up next to the car and transfer the money from the suitcases to the duffel bag he would find in the trunk. He would find the keys on top of the passenger side front wheel. When the transfer was complete, he was to put the duffel bag in the trunk of the Cavalier and get into the Cavalier where he would find his next set of instructions in the glove box.

Alex did as he was told, backing the Mercedes up next to the Cavalier. He sat in his car and looked around. There was a Ford pickup and a Chevy pickup and an older model Chevy Nova parked in the lot; otherwise, he was alone with the Cavalier. Across the street, there were several cars in the 7-Eleven lot. He watched for anything suspicious. There was nothing that caused him any concern. He looked over his shoulder and spotted several cars parked northbound and southbound on Wolff, but they appeared to be empty. Nothing looked unusual or out of the ordinary. He continued to sit there looking at his surroundings, looking for something, anything that shouldn't be.

"What the fuck's he doin'?" Floyd asked from his scrunched-down position.

"He's looking around, probably knows he's going to lose his last contact with the police," the major replied.

In the police van, the same questions were being raised. When Alex pulled into the parking lot, the van was just crossing the Colfax viaduct. It turned right onto Irving Street and parked when it saw that the Mercedes wasn't moving. They didn't dare get any closer, and so they parked and waited. They didn't notice the change of positions on their screen when Alex crossed over to the VFW parking lot and parked.

Special Agent Tom Richards finally spoke. "He's been there more than five minutes. What's going on?"

The cop at the screen shrugged. "Don't know. Should we move closer?"

"How far are we from him now?"

"'Bout a mile, maybe a little less."

"Let's give it another five."

Alex finally opened the door to his car and got out. He found the keys to the Cavalier and walked to the back of the car where he opened the trunk lid. Inside was a large blue duffel bag. He pulled it out and examined it. He went to his car, opened the trunk, and set the bag down inside, opening it as he did so. He then opened the first of the suitcases and transferred the straps of bills into the duffel bag. When he had emptied the first of the suitcases, he opened the second one and did the same. When he was finished, he lifted the duffel bag. He quickly put it down. It was too heavy for him to take out of the trunk. He swore under his breath and emptied half of the contents onto the floor of the trunk. He put the bag into the trunk of the Cavalier and proceeded to transfer the rest of the money from his Mercedes to the Cavalier. He looked up each time he moved some of the money to make sure no one was watching.

By the time he was done, he was soaked through with perspiration. He closed the trunks of both cars, locked his car, and climbed behind the wheel of the Cavalier.

Reaching over, he opened the door to the glove box and retrieved the envelope. He opened it quickly, tearing it.

"Shit!" he yelled. "Okay, okay, calm down. Relax."

He put the pieces together and read the words typed on the page. They instructed him to leave the keys to the Mercedes on the passenger side front wheel. He complied with this instruction and drove off in the Cavalier, heading west on Colfax.

The note told him to drive west to the phone booth in front of the 7-Eleven at Colfax and Simms.

Julie found the motel next to the Ford dealership and pulled up to the phone. From there she could see the 7-Eleven down the street from where she was parked. She checked her watch. Nine fifteen. Alex would be coming up the street any minute now.

She got out of the car and walked to the phone. A small Hispanic housekeeper came out of the office and approached the phone at the same time. She smiled at the younger woman and grabbed the phone before Julie could reach it. Julie nodded and turned to look up the street for the Cavalier. The woman dialed a number and waited.

Julie looked at her watch again. Nine eighteen.

The woman spoke into the receiver and listened. She spoke again, this time louder. Julie could not understand what was being said, but from the sound of the woman's voice, she knew that the woman was arguing with someone else on the other end of the line.

Julie looked at her watch again, 9:22.

Damn!

The woman continued to argue with the person on the other end. Julie looked back up onto Colfax just as Alex passed. He pulled into the 7-Eleven. There were no spots available in front of the store for him to park in. He pulled around to the side.

The woman continued to argue into the phone. Alex appeared from around the corner and walked to the bank of phones in front of the store. He looked around the parking lot and then felt under each of the phones. The note said he would be contacted. Maybe there would be another note. But no, there was nothing.

Alex stood there staring at the phones, his hands on his hips. Finally, he reached out and picked up one and then another of the phones and put them to his ear until he had tested all four of them. They all appeared to be in working order. He hung up the last of the phones and turned around. He looked at his watch and turned to the phones again.

Julie glared at the woman on the phone who said something into the phone and slammed the receiver down onto its cradle, glared back at the much taller white woman, and stormed off.

Julie picked up the receiver, dropped some coins into the slot, and quickly dialed the number.

Alex scrambled to the ringing phone. "Alex here!"

"You're late," Julie scolded.

"I've been…I'm sorry," he responded weakly.

"There's a phone at the Diamond Shamrock convenience store at thirteenth and Wadsworth. You've got ten minutes." She pushed down the cradle and the line disconnected.

Julie would wait the required ten minutes and then call the number at the convenience store. Then she would be done. She would then reapply her disguise, drive to the park, and wait for them all to show up.

The phone was ringing when Alex pulled up in front of the convenience store. He slammed the car door shut and raced to the phone.

"Hello? I mean, this is Alex," he said in a near panic, breathing heavily.

The female voice was back. "There's a 7-Eleven at Yale and Wadsworth. There's a phone in front. Envelope will be under the ledge. You've got fifteen minutes. And um…Alex?"

"Yes?"

"Don't be late."

The phone went dead. Alex hurried back to the Cavalier, backed it up headed east again, and then headed south on Wadsworth. He looked at his watch. It was nine thirty-two. He'd been chasing around all over Denver, and it had only taken a little more than an hour and a half.

"Damn," he said to no one, "how long is this going to take?"

Back at the van Tom Richards made his decision. "Something's wrong. Alex's been there too long. We've got to check it out. Let's go."

The van circled back onto Colfax. Tom spotted the Mercedes in the VFW lot, and the van pulled in. Alex's car was parked along the back row on the lot. Alex was nowhere to be found. They found the keys on top of the right front wheel where Alex had left them.

"Son of a bitch!" Tom yelled, spinning around as he punched one hand against the other. "Son. Of. A. Bitch!"

He climbed into the back of the van. "Shit! Shit! Shit!"

He picked up the van's phone and called Jack. "We've lost them," he said to the inspector when Jack came on the line. "They switched cars. The Mercedes is parked in a lot on West Colfax."

He listened to the inspector's instructions and clicked off. "We're to go back to the house. Nothing more we can do here."

The driver pulled back onto Colfax and headed east.

Floyd and the major were waiting when Alex drove up. They watched from their car as he pulled to a stop in front of the 7-Eleven. He was just returning to his car with the envelope in his hand when the two men pulled out onto Yale, turned left, turned left again, and headed south on Wadsworth. This was it. Next stop would be Chatfield State Park and the drop. Fourteen miles. The two men smiled at each other. All the planning, all the time, all the money spent, all the preparations would soon pay off.

Alex closed the door and settled himself into the seat of his car before opening the envelope. It read,

> *Go south on Wadsworth to Chatfield State Park. Once you enter the Park and go through the gate, bear around to the right until you come to a turnoff marked **Fox Run**. Turn in there and go to the far end of the parking lot. There you will find a small stone building with men and women's restrooms. Inside the men's restroom, taped to the back of the second toilet, you will find your next set of instructions. If you want to see your daughter again, you will not try to contact anyone. You have been watched each time you stopped, and you are being watched now. You've got twenty minutes to get to the next stop.*

Alex threw the message onto the front seat and started the engine.

Twenty minutes to the next stop… You're being watched…

The words kept going through his mind. He was getting close. He felt more alert. And he felt more anger than he had ever felt in his life.

They've been watching me. They had to be near. Those sons a' bitches!

He looked all around, checked his rearview mirror to see if he was even now being watched.

"Shit!" he yelled, pounding his fist against the steering wheel. *Why couldn't I have paid more attention to what was going on around me? Of course! Each phone call. They waited for me to arrive so that I would be the one who answered the phone. They had to be watching me! And the notes. They had to plant them just before I arrived, and they had to watch to make sure I was the one who found them! Fuck! They've been following me and watching me the whole time!*

"God damn it!" he yelled out loud.

Well, if that's the case, they will probably be watching me when I get to the park. Maybe I can spot them.

Julie was the first to arrive. She drove past the turnoff to Fox Run and found the next turnoff, called Catfish Flats, approximately one-half mile to the south. She turned in and made a U-turn and headed back to Fox Run. She turned into the lot, spotted an empty table, parked her car, and walked up the short rise to one of the tables and sat down.

At ten minutes after ten, the major and Floyd arrived. They parked their car among the others that were beginning to fill up the lot and joined Julie at her table. There were four other park tables spaced about the area. All of them were being used by other people. From their vantage point, the major, Julie, and Floyd could watch cars coming and going. They also had a good view of the stone restrooms building at the end of the parking lot.

At ten twenty, Alex turned into Fox Run and followed the road around to the parking lot. He spotted the stone building at the far end of the area and drove to it.

"Damn," he said to himself, "there's a lot of people here."

At one table, he spotted a family of five: Mom, Dad, and three young children. The next table had three adults, two men and a woman. They were drinking coffee or something. The next table had two men. They looked like construction workers. Next were four adults: two men and two women. The last bunch, the one closest to the building was a group of teenagers.

He scanned the tables again. Could the kidnappers be in this group? Each group looked like they belonged. And yet, what was it?

Something was gnawing at him. Something wasn't quite right.

Alex parked in front of the restrooms. He looked at the note again and then tossed it on the seat next to him. Once again, he scanned the picnic tables, opened the door, looked at the cars and trucks in the parking lot, closed and locked the door, and followed the path into the men's room. There, taped to the commode, was the envelope. Alex retrieved it and tore it open. The note began,

> *Good job so far, Alex. This is your next to last set of instructions. If you want Kendra back alive, you will follow these instructions exactly as they are written.*
>
> *Walk out of the restroom and follow the path that leads south away from the parking lot. This path will take you to the next parking area, a half mile to the south. This lot is called **Catfish Flats**. There you will find several picnic tables.*
>
> *Go to the last table. Under the bench seat, you will find a note. This note will tell you where to leave the money. It will also tell you how to get your daughter back.*
>
> *Good luck and thank you.*

Alex almost smiled as he read the last five words. He hurried out of the men's room. Searching the parking lot and picnic area, Alex turned and, walking at a quick pace, started down the path to the next lot.

An attractive young woman in black jogging clothes with white stripes along the sides approached him from the south and smiled as she passed. She had earphones on and a small radio attached to her right arm.

Alex studied her as she approached and turned to watch as she passed him by. He committed her image to memory just in case. He continued on down the path. An elderly couple, walking hand in hand, blocked his way and he had to step round them, excusing himself and muttering under his breath. Two more young women in shorts and T-shirts approached from the south and divided so that he could pass. Alex studied each of these people as he passed.

Could any of these people be the kidnappers?

He looked at his watch. It was now ten forty. Off in the distance, he could see the parking lot. He quickened his pace until he was jogging. Sweat was forming inside his shirt and under his arms.

Alex worked out, but by the time, he reached the parking lot he was short of breath, and his shirt was drenched clear through. Still, he continued at a fast pace until he reached the table.

"Shit!" he exclaimed.

The last table was occupied. A family had spread a tablecloth and set out food.

Alex approached.

"Excuse me," he said to the father. "I know this sounds crazy, but may I look under the benches at your table?"

"¿Cómo?"

"I need to…" Alex stopped, realizing that the man probably didn't speak English.

"Tú hablas ingles?"

"No, Señor."

He tried to explain what he wanted to do, but the man did not understand.

"Maria!"

A young girl of ten or so years came running up to the table. The father said something to her, and she turned to Alex.

"May I help you?" she asked.

"Thank God," Alex said. "Yes. I need to look under these two benches. Will you tell this man this?"

"Sí…Padre," she said, turning to her father. She explained what the strange man wanted.

Her father smiled brightly. "Ah. Sí, sí," he said and gestured with his arm toward the table.

Alex got down on his hands and knees and looked under one and then the other of the benches. There was nothing there! He looked under the table. Nothing! He looked under the benches again. He stood and read the note from the men's room again.

It said, last bench, and this was the last bench. Fear began to set in. "Those sons a' bitches," he said through clenched teeth.

To Maria's father and the rest of the family he said, "Gracias."

He started back toward Fox Run.

"Of course! How stupid of me. The rest stop is the drop sight. Get me away from the car. Lead me off on a wild goose chase. Well, if I hurry, maybe I can still spot them. Shit!" he muttered through clenched teeth.

He turned and headed back up the path as fast as his legs could carry him.

The major and Julie watched as Alex parked the car in front of the restrooms. Floyd sat with his back to the parking lot.

"What's he doin'?" Floyd asked.

"Just looking around…there, he's going in."

Less than two minutes later, they saw him come out of the restroom, look around the parking lot and up at the tables, and then turn south on the path.

"Give me a minute to scan the car, then, Floyd, you take my car. I'll transfer the bag to the car, and you head back to the cabin. We'll meet you there."

Floyd nodded and rose with the major, taking his keys from him. The major walked down to the Cavalier and circled it, his sweeper in his hand. The device was strong enough to pick up the tiniest of signals. There were no alarms, no homing devices, no electrical impulses. He circled it one more time to be sure, then went to the trunk and opened with the second set of keys. He inspected its contents, sweeping his electronic device over the bag for good measure. He then stood and waved to Floyd. His hands were shaking. He looked at his watch. By now, Alex would just about be reaching the next picnic area.

Floyd walked to the major's car, got in, and drove over to where the major was standing. The two men transferred the money into the trunk, and Floyd drove off. Julie walked down the hill, got into her car, and was waiting while the two men made the transfer. When she saw Floyd get into the car, she drove over and stopped. The major opened the passenger side door and slid in. The whole operation had taken less than six minutes.

"We did it!" she exclaimed as he reached around to fasten his seat belt. "We damn well did it!"

"Don't be celebrating it just yet, we're not out of the woods by any means," he said, though finally breathing easier.

Allen arrived back at the cabin at eleven fifteen. He parked the van in the back and went into the cabin. He checked in on Kendra, expecting her to scream when he came through the bedroom door. She was tied to the bed, sleeping. He went over to her and gently untied the harness that held her to the bed. She didn't wake up. He felt her forehead. It was cool to the touch. Still, the little girl slept.

Quietly, Allen exited the room and returned to the kitchen. There he found a Coke and some cookies. He sat at the table and finished off the whole bag as he sipped his Coke. He looked at his watch. Eleven thirty.

If all goes well, he thought, *they should be back here with the money in about two hours. I could take a nap.*

He left the empty Coke can and the empty Oreos package on the table, returned to the couch in the living room, stretched out, and was soon snoring.

Alex returned to the parking lot of the Fox Run picnic area. The Cavalier was still parked in front of the restroom. He looked around at the tables. They were all occupied. He opened the trunk and discovered what he feared. It was empty. He quickly turned and searched the parking lot.

How long have I been gone? Ten? Fifteen minutes? In that time, they got it. They got it all.

He slammed down the trunk lid and looked at the picnic area again.

"What is it?" he asked. "What's different?"

He ran the scene through his mind again. *First table, family. Okay. Still there. Second, four people. Third, construction workers...*

His eyes returned to the second table. Four people—two men and two women. Young. All white. *There had been two men and a woman before. And the one with his back to the parking lot had been black. He was sure of that.*

Alex closed his eyes tight and tried to remember. *The white man seemed much older than the girl sitting next to him. From that distance, he couldn't be sure, but he appeared to have between in his early, maybe midsixties. Probably not much younger than that.*

The girl? What was it about her? Oh yes, red hair! Darlene had said that the girl had red hair. And the black man. "Big," she had said. The black man at the table had been big.

Of course! That was them! It had to be! They fit the descriptions. Why didn't I see it before?

He ran up to the table where the four people were seated.

"Excuse me," he said excitedly, "did you happen to see the people who were sitting here before you?"

"No," one of the men replied, "the table was empty when we arrived."

"Thanks," Alex said. He looked around the lot again, then ran down the hill to the Cavalier and got in, started the engine, and sped out of the lot. When he reached the gate, he slammed on his brakes and ran to the window.

"Did a car with an old man, a black man, and a redheaded woman just pass through here?"

The park ranger looked up at him. "I didn't see a car with three people come through here, no," she said.

"You're sure? Old man, black man, redhead? Must have come through here less than five minutes ago, probably no more than ten."

"I didn't see no—"

"Is there another way out of here?"

"No, sir, this here's the only way in or out."

"I need to use your phone! Quick! Please! It's an emergency!"

"I'm sorry, sir—"

"Please," he interrupted, "it's an emergency, damn it!"

He glared at the female park ranger.

"Phone's only for official business."

"God damn it! My daughter's been kidnapped. Give me the fuckin' phone!"

The ranger's eyes opened wide. She stammered. "Okay, but I'll have to dial the number."

She handed the receiver to Alex, and he gave her the number to his home phone. It was answered on the first ring.

"Hello?" It was Lisa.

"Lisa, is Jack there?"

"Yes, what's—"

"Give me, Jack."

"Just a minute," she answered.

"Jack Donovan."

"Jack, they've got the money! I'm down here at Chatfield State Park. I saw them. Jack—"

"Hold on, Alex, calm down."

"I tell you, Jack, I saw them! There were three of them. They tricked me into leaving the car then they took the money. But I saw them, Jack. Redhead, black man, and another much older man."

"What were they driving?" Jack asked, pulling his note pad from his pocket.

"I don't know. I didn't see them leave, but I know it was them. Just a minute."

He looked at the park ranger. "You sure you didn't see them leave?"

She shook her head. "I'm sorry."

"Damn!" he said.

"All right, Alex. Get back here as soon as you can. We found your car. Lab boys are dusting it for prints right now. Get back here and tell us what happened."

"I'm on my way."

Jack turned to Tony. "The drop was made at Chatfield State Park. Get a crew down there ASAP. Maybe somebody will have something. Maybe they can give us a description of them, the car, something."

Tony was immediately on the phone and giving instructions.

Jack turned to Lisa and explained what had happened.

"The ball's in their court now," he admitted.

Alex apologized to the park ranger for his rudeness, climbed back into the Cavalier, and headed for the house. Tears flowed freely down his cheeks. They still had his little daughter, and now they had the money too. He prayed to God that they would give him back his little girl unharmed.

How could they have done it? he asked himself. Those bastards had outsmarted him. They had outsmarted the police. Shit, they had even outsmarted the FBI. *And I still don't know where my daughter is. And what about the van? What had happened to the police van that was supposed to be following me?*

CHAPTER 21

The cabin, 11:30 a.m.

Allen heard the car door close and was immediately alert. He went to the window and peered through the slats. Relief flowed through his body. It was Floyd. He went to the back room and checked on Kendra. She was still sleeping. He looked at his watch. It was eleven thirty-five. He thought it was strange and checked her cheek again. She was breathing lightly and felt cool to the touch. He shrugged and went to the back door just as Floyd entered, dragging the heavy blue duffel bag behind him.

"Let me help you with that," Allen offered.

The two men managed to carry the bag into the living room and set it down in the corner.

"It's done," the big man said, grinning at his partner. "Julie and the major should be here any minute. Man, it went so slick—"

Allen looked up. Kendra was standing in the doorway, rubbing her eyes, a big yawn on her face.

Allen looked at Floyd and jerked his head.

Floyd saw the little girl and grinned broadly.

"How's my little explorer doin'?" he asked as he moved over and swooped her off her feet. "You been asleep a long time."

She giggled. "I'm hungry."

"You hungry? Well, Uncle Allen, what have you been doin'? Dis here little girl's hungry. Man oh man, I can't leave you alone for nuttin'! Come on, missy, let's see what we can find."

Turning to Allen, he said, "Put that bag away, will you?"

The major arrived with Julie twenty minutes later. Floyd and Kendra were just cleaning up their plates. Kendra complained of a headache and wanted to go back to bed. Julie took her into the bedroom and lay down beside her until Kendra was sleeping. She then rose and joined the three men on the back porch. They were discussing the final stages of the operation.

All their eating and drinking had been done with disposable containers. The trash they had accumulated over the past few days now filled several bags, piled up on the porch. They were discussing the removal of the trash when she arrived. It was decided that each of them would split up the bags and leave them in different dumpsters at various locations when they left in the morning.

Allen and the major would return to the storage unit, break down the electronic equipment, repack it and ship it back to Atlanta.

Floyd had no use for the guns, and so they would be broken down, and the parts would be disposed of at different locations. Julie's makeup box would also be packed up and sent back to her California address. Each of their disguises would be burned.

The money, as in the last two jobs, would be taken to an unnamed New Orleans bank where it would be electronically transferred to four separate account numbers on the Cayman Islands. For this project, a fairly substantial bribe would need to be paid. Each of the members agreed.

Kendra would be taken to a shopping mall in the morning and be dropped off. A call would be made to the McArthurs, telling them where to find her and then the four conspirators would go their separate ways, each returning to their home cities by the same route they had used to come to Denver. When they arrived at their homes, they were to destroy all the identifications that they had used for this job. It was important for them to understand that. *All* the identifications *had* to be destroyed.

The major told each of his team that this was the last job they would do together. There were things happening in his life that would make it impossible for him to continue. He looked at each of them as he said this, stopping a little longer when his eyes met Julie's.

For a brief moment, her heart raced. She didn't know if he was saying goodbye to her or if she was to be included in his plans.

Floyd was the first to speak. "Well, it's been a ride. I sho' gonna miss you all. This was going to be my last job anyway, so I'm glad it's ending this way. Gonna take my kids and relocate somewhere."

He reached over and took the major's hand in his. "Thanks, Major. Thanks for everything."

Allen reached out his hand, took the major's and said, "Likewise."

Julie looked at the three men, tears in her eyes, and said, "You guys."

They all stood and moved together to form one group and hugged each other, no one wanting to be the first to let go. Finally, the major spoke. "Come on, Allen, let's get your equipment packed.

It was decided that Floyd should lose the disassembled weapons parts in different locations between the cabin and the hotel. The major's only request was that Floyd make sure they were wiped clean.

When the four people disengaged, there were tears in their eyes. The major turned away from them so that they couldn't see his.

Alex drove up to the front of his house and stopped. Immediately he was joined by Lisa, the police, and the FBI. Before Jack said hello to Alex, he turned and gave instructions to the police.

"I want this car gone over completely. Dust for prints, look for hair, fibers, anything and everything. Alex, how are you?"

He gritted his teeth and shrugged. "They got the money. Have they called yet?"

"No, we haven't heard anything yet. My guess is, we won't hear anything today. Their pattern is to release the children on the Fourth.

Lisa stepped up beside her husband and put her arm around his waist.

"I'm sorry, sweetheart," he said softly, "they were too good. They knew. It's like they were everywhere I was. They were watching everything I did."

"Let's go inside," Jack cut in. "There are some things we need to discuss." To the forensic team, he said, "Don't miss a thing."

The house had been swept by Pete's team. They found the other bugs from the kitchen, study, and bedroom. Jack told Alex what they had found and how the kidnappers had managed to stay one step ahead of them.

"Those bastards!" Alex yelled.

"All right, Alex," Jack said. "I want you to start at the beginning and tell us everything that you can remember from the time you left here until now. Don't leave anything out. Give us locations, people, cars, anything you can think of. Sally will take notes. Remember, even the smallest details could be important."

"I need some coffee first. Lisa?"

"There's some over here," she said, motioning to the table in the corner.

Alex sat down on the La-Z-Boy, puffed up his cheeks, blew air through his mouth, and started his story. Sally wrote feverishly. Jack only interrupted a couple of times to clarify certain points in the narration.

Alex is good, Jack thought as the narrative continued. *He has a good recollection of events and surrounding scenery. He makes for a good witness.*

Sally filled page after page with notes, finally finishing up when Alex described the two men and the woman at the park. His description of them closely matched Darlene's description of the two intruders from the first night. When Alex was done, he just sort of relaxed and formed himself into his chair. He was exhausted.

Jack thanked him and turned to Tony. "When your crime team is done with their prelim, I want that car brought downtown. I want every inch of it gone over. Find something for me, Tony. Find something. Call the rental agencies until you find out which one rented this car, then get any info you can."

"Already on it," Tony replied.

"We still have a chance," he explained to the nervous couple. "They will be calling tomorrow. Maybe we'll be lucky. Alex, I told you, we found your car. It's being dusted. It'll probably come up clean, but we've got to give it a shot. We're checking the paper and envelopes, usual stuff. I'm afraid we'll have to hold your car for a few days."

"No problem."

Allen and the major arrived at the storage unit at two thirty. It took them only an hour to disassemble and repack the equipment into the boxes at the unit. They said little. There was little to say.

Allen wanted to take his share of the money with him when he left, but the major talked him out of it. The major did agree to let him take a small portion of it, though, and Allen was satisfied.

The major's reasoning was that too much money at one time might draw unwanted attention. Plus, they still weren't sure if some or all the serial numbers had been recorded. By laundering the money through the bank in New Orleans, the funds would be immediately available through the bank on Grand Cayman. And those funds would be clean.

When everything was packed, the two men drove to a Pak Mail and had the equipment shipped back to Atlanta. Then it was back to Allen's hotel. Allen picked up his rental car and followed the major to a car wash where the two men cleaned the van inside and out, removing all traces of their activities over the past few days. They filled it with gas, then drove it back to the rental agency where the major turned it in and paid cash for the charges.

The rental agency salesgirl did a cursory walk-around inspection and was satisfied with the condition of the van. She did not notice the holes Allen had drilled through the floor in the back of the van. She thanked them for cleaning it before returning it.

"You'd be surprised at the condition some people leave these vehicles," she said, smiling at Allen.

Allen drove the major back to the cabin. On the way back, Allen decided that he would leave the money in the major's hands. He really didn't need any of it right now.

"You're right," Allen said. "I guess, with all that loot lying around I got a little greedy."

"Wise choice," the major said.

Floyd took Kendra by the hand. "Come on, missy, let's go for a walk."

"Will we see any deer?"

"Don't know. Maybe. Maybe not. Deer's funny animals. They let you see them if they want. If they don't want you to see them, then they hide."

"I like deer."

"I know. And they like you, little princess. Come on, let's go find them."

"Bye, Aunt Julie. Uncle Floyd and I are going to go find the deer."

"Goodbye, Kendra. Good luck."

Julie watched the two walk into the woods. She was glad to have them gone. There was a lot of work to do. All the trash, supplies, and equipment had to be gathered. They would be gone from here in the morning, and there had to be nothing left behind.

She thought about what John had said. She had not talked with him since he'd said this was the last job and wondered if she were indeed a part of his plans. If she was, what would she do about her job, her apartment, her life in California?

So many unanswered questions, and yet, she knew that if he asked her, she would follow him anywhere.

"Uncle Floyd?"

"Yes, missy?"

"When am I going to see my mommy and daddy?"

They had just inspected some fresh deer droppings that Floyd had spotted and knew that some deer had been close.

Floyd picked up his little charge in his massive arms. "For sho', tomorrow, little one. For sho' you'll see them tomorrow. I promise you that."

"I miss my mommy and daddy."

"I'm sho' you do. I hope you been havin' fun up here at the camp. Yo' mommy and daddy be mad at us if you not been havin' fun. You like it here?"

She looked at him and wrinkled her nose. "It's been okay. I like it when you're here. Most times I like Aunt Julie too, but sometimes she's mean."

"Mean? How you mean 'she's mean'?" He laughed and sang. "Mean, mean, how you mean, mean?"

She laughed at him. "You know, she makes me do things. Like work things. Mommy doesn't make me clean my room and pick up. And the toilet! *I hate* the toilet! She calls it an outhouse. It smells. And you can't flush it. *Ew!* It's awful!"

"I know, baby. I don't like it either. But you know what?"

"What?" she asked, looking him straight in the eyes.

"That's all part of camping. I been places where there wasn't even an outhouse. Makes you appreciate your real home, though, doesn't it?"

"Yeah. I like my real home. And I like my own bed, and I like my own bathroom too. I want to take a bath when I go home. Aunt Julie washed me with paper towels. They were scratchy." She gave him a funny look.

He grinned. "I know. Real baths and real showers and real toilets are so much better." He scrunched up his face and rolled his head.

Kendra laughed at his silliness.

Floyd put her down on the ground, and the two walked further into the woods. They did not see any deer, but they did spot rabbits and several squirrels, and though not sure, they thought they saw a fox.

When Allen's car pulled into the drive, Julie was just carrying the last of the trash out to the back.

"Hi," she said brightly.

"Hi yourself," the major said. "Floyd around?"

"He and Kendra are walking in the woods."

"Good. How's she holding up?"

"Pretty good. She sure likes it when Floyd's here. She calls him Uncle Floyd, you know."

All three adults went into the cabin. The major was carrying a twelve-pack of Miller Genuine Draft Beer. He was wearing the older man's mask again.

"Have a beer," he offered.

"Thanks," she said, grateful for something cold to drink.

She opened the can and took a long draw and smacked her lips.

"How'd it go? Did you turn in the van?"

"Yup. No problems. The salesgirl didn't even notice the holes in the floor. We shipped everything off to Allen's home town. We'll send your stuff back later."

"Okay. What about—"

She was about to ask about the money when Floyd and Kendra came through the door.

"Hey, man," Floyd greeted.

"Floyd," the major said. "Hello, Kendra."

"Hello," she answered shyly and positioned herself behind Floyd's leg, her arm around it for protection.

"Have you been behaving yourself?" the major asked the little girl.

She nodded slowly and looked at Julie.

"It's all right, Kendra," Julie said. "These two men are friends of your daddy. They just came to tell me that you're going home tomorrow. Isn't that great?"

A big smile appeared on the little girl's face. She looked up at Floyd. "You were right, Uncle Floyd. I'm going to see my mommy and daddy tomorrow."

Floyd grinned. "See. Uncle Floyd knows."

He bent down and picked her up, tossing her into the air. She squealed with joy.

"Do it again," she begged.

He tossed her one more time and put her down on the floor. She rushed off to her bedroom and returned carrying her pink bunny.

"I told bunny that we were going home tomorrow. She said that was great."

Kendra turned and ran back into the bedroom.

By three o'clock, Fox Run was crawling with police. They interviewed everybody. No, no one had seen anything. Most of the visitors had arrived after the kidnappers were gone. One couple did remember seeing someone take a bag out of one car and put it into another.

They couldn't remember anything about the other car except that it was maroon in color. Maroon, or red, or maybe it was brown. They couldn't be sure.

Business cards were left with everyone with instructions to call the police if they remembered even the slightest thing. The police were frustrated. Everywhere they turned was another blind alley. After more than an hour, they gave up. Even the park ranger at the gate could not help. One more dead end.

Tony received the phone call, talked to the lead detective on the scene for a few minutes, and hung up the phone, rather forcefully, Jack noticed. The police detective looked at him.

"Nothing. Not a damned thing. One couple thought they saw the transfer but couldn't remember the color or make of the car."

Jack went over to where Alex sat. He sighed heavily. "I'm sorry. On the plus side, though, you should get your daughter back tomorrow. That's been their pattern."

Tony spoke. "What about all this equipment? Should we keep it up or start taking it apart?"

"Leave it up until we hear from them. Maybe they'll get careless, and we can trace their call tomorrow."

To Sally, he said, "Come on, there's nothing more we can do here today. Alex, Lisa, we'll be back in the morning."

Sally picked up her notes and purse, smiled weakly at Lisa, nodded to Alex, and followed Jack to the door. Peter rose and followed along behind them.

"Pete, take us downtown," Jack ordered.

Sally and Pete hurried to keep up as Jack approached the car.

"Damn!" Jack said, slamming his fist on top of the SAC's car. "Damn! Damn! Damn!"

"It's not your fault," Pete offered. "These guys are good."

Jack looked at him. "Yes, but we're supposed to be better."

He paused before continuing. "I want a conference room. Get me an easel and a large artist's drawing pad. In fact, get several. And some colored markers. Black. Red. Blue. Yellow. And some masking tape.

"Sally, we've got a lot of work to do. Pete? Call your wife. It's going to be a long night. And order in some sandwiches or something."

At the cabin, the same conversation about food was going on.

"Kendra?" the older man asked. "This is going to be our last night together. What would you like to have for dinner?"

The little girl thought for a minute. "Are we all going to eat together?"

The adults looked at each other, then faced the child.

"Yes," Julie replied, "we'll all be here to celebrate with you. It'll be like a party. You can have anything you like."

Kendra pursed her lips and frowned. She thought and thought. Finally, she said, "I want chicken. Can we have chicken? Chicken nuggets?"

"Kentucky Fried Chicken?" Julie asked.

"Yes," Kendra replied, nodding. "Kentucky Fried Chicken. And dessert. Can we have dessert too, please?"

"You sure can, honey," Julie replied.

"That okay with you, Floyd?" the major asked with a big smile.

"Um-um, sho' is," Floyd agreed emphatically. The others laughed.

The order was written and the major left to get their food. When he returned, the sun was low in the sky. Shadows covered the backyard and the trees. The other three adults, with Kendra's help, had set up the table on the back porch. The major set the bags on the table and went back to his car, returning with beer and wine and root beer.

CHAPTER 22

FBI headquarters, Denver, 4:45 p.m.

The conference room was set up when the three FBI agents arrived. The easel with a large white pad was standing next to the end of the table.

"Let's get started," Jack said, taking off his coat and rolling up his sleeves. "Sally, give me the details of Alex's trip."

Sally began with his first stop and reviewed all his stops until he arrived back at the house. Jack wrote down notes on the large pad on the easel. As each page filled, he tore it off and taped it to the wall. When Sally was done, he had seven large poster-sized pages taped to the wall. He walked around to the other side of the table and stared at the various sheets of paper before him.

"All right," he said to them, "what do you see?"

Sally and Pete stared at the pages. There was silence.

"Come on, people," Jack said, "what do you see?"

Sally spoke first, "Phone calls and envelopes. Sometimes phone calls and sometimes not."

"Exactly. Why?"

Pete spoke up. "Maybe they called from phones close by. Maybe they couldn't sometimes."

"Good. Pete, call Tony. Have his people check all these locations, the ones where Alex used the phone. See if there are phones nearby to each of them. If there are, I want prints. Then tell him to have his people canvas the neighborhoods. Maybe somebody saw something."

He paused and studied the pages on the wall again and then asked. "What else?"

Sally answered, "All the stops were visible from the street."

"Exactly. Okay," he said, making more notes, "let's assume that Alex was followed. Based on what he told us, it's a good probability. He said that there were three different voices on the phone, and he said he saw three people at the park. Let's assume that there was at least one more person to cover the conversations at the house with the bugs. Then there had to be someone to watch Kendra. That's five people."

Jack wrote furiously on the pad. "Now, each one of them had to be driving a vehicle of some sort at one time or another. Let's assume that they flew in from out of state. If it's the same group as before, then they are from out of state. That means they'd have to rent cars. That means rental car agencies. That means they could have used credit cards. Maybe they even took pictures of their licenses. We could get lucky there.

"Pete, have every rental car agency in town screened. Go back two, no, three weeks if you have to. I want a list of every car rental made over that time for every person that could possibly resemble our kidnappers. And I want the names of every renter and their identifications sent to Washington. And vans and trucks too. I want them all included."

He tore off another sheet and hung it on the wall, stepped around the table, and reviewed them all again.

A secretary stuck her head in the door. "Food's here."

Jack tossed his marker on the table. "All right, people, let's take a break."

Sally approached Jack as they were finishing their meal. "The bugs?" she asked.

"Huh?" Jack asked.

"The bugs," she repeated. "What about the bugs?"

"Damn!" he exploded. "The bugs! Of course! I'd forgotten about them. Yes, have them sent to Washington. We should be able to track where they were manufactured. Thanks, Sally. If we can find that out, then we can find out who they were sent to."

He made more notes on his pad.

Pete returned after calling his wife, and the three FBI people picked up where they left off.

"Sally's going to send the listening devices off to Washington for manufacture identification," Jack informed Pete as the head of the Denver office took his place at the table.

Pete nodded. "Good idea. Maybe they could do prints too."

Jack made another note.

"Everything all right at home?" Jack asked, turning back to his SAC.

"I told her it would probably be another late night. She's used to it."

The three agents were interrupted by a call from Tony De Marco. Jack put it on speakerphone.

"Thought you ought to know. The investigation at the park didn't turn up anything new. No one saw anything, no one heard anything. I think we need to interview Alex some more. Maybe he saw something, heard something, something he's just not remembering now."

"I'd like to give him some time with his daughter," Jack suggested. "I'll bet some time to relax with her will help refresh his memory."

"You're probably right. See you tomorrow. You going to be at the house?"

"Sally and I will both be there."

He looked at Pete who nodded.

"Pete'll be there too."

"Later then." Tony hung up.

Jack looked at his two subordinates. "Not much help from that end of the investigation, but Tony's right. Maybe Alex'll remember something else tomorrow."

The three agents walked through the entire kidnapping from start to finish, going until almost ten thirty. They agreed that although they did have a wealth of information, they really didn't have much to go on—four, maybe five accomplices. One, a woman. One black. All or probably most of them from out of town. At least one was an expert with electronics. At least one had to be familiar with weapons. Darlene and the security guard had both said there were weapons involved. Descriptions had obvious characteristics: tattoos, scars, the red hair, to mention a few.

The plan had been well thought out. Whoever was in charge obviously knew the city. This could mean that he lived here, had lived here, or had come in early to scout the locations needed to carry out the job. This last thing was what probably happened. The two previous kidnappings had been in different cities, far away. Maybe one of the crew lived in each of these cities. If there were four or five people involved, it was possible that there could be one or two more kidnappings in the works. Jack didn't want to wait two more years to find out.

All these things were written down on the various large papers taped to the wall.

"Pete, call the airport. Alert security to be on the lookout for excess baggage, especially new suitcases. Look for extra heavy duffel bags. X-ray anything suspicious. If they try to move the money through Stapleton, we may get lucky."

Another note.

"What are we missing?" Jack said to the paper on the wall. "What are we not seeing?"

He looked over each sheet with the other two agents, listening, checking, cross-checking the notes, talking, questioning.

"Call the railroad station and the bus station. Tell them—tell them—shit! What do we tell them? Look out for suitcases? Look for a—what was it?" Jack referred to the note. "A blue duffel bag? And what if they mail the money out of town? Or send it FedEx or UPS? Drive out of town with it in the trunk of a car? What do we have to do? Put up roadblocks? Stop every suspicious person on the road?

"Christ!" he said, slamming his fist onto the table.

His sudden movement and the sound of his fist hitting the table startled Sally and Pete.

"Sorry," he apologized. "Look, it's nearly ten forty-five. Let's call it a night. Pete? Sally and I will drive down in the morning. If you need time with Angie, come down later."

"Thanks. I'll be there."

"I want to leave this stuff up if that's okay with your people."

"Fine by me."

"Sally? I'm going to walk back to the hotel. Care to join me?"

She nodded to her boss as she stood, hanging her purse over her shoulder.

The cabin, 9:30 p.m.

"If you two guys want to go back to your hotels for the night, you're welcome to," the major said. "It might be nice to sleep in a real bed again."

Floyd and Allen looked at each other. Allen spoke first. "You don't need to ask me twice."

"Me neither," Floyd said, standing quickly.

When they were sure that the little girl was asleep, they finalized their plans.

Julie and the major would deliver Kendra back to her parents. Floyd and Allen would stay in town until the fifth of July. They would deliver their rentals back to their agencies at the airport and fly back to their homes the same way they had arrived, using their false identifications.

"Can I call Amy?" Allen asked.

"It'd be better if you didn't," the major reminded him. "Let's just do as we have in the past. No changes, no surprises. No way for anyone to trace you to Denver."

"And what about us?" Jackie asked after the two men had left.

"Us?" John asked teasingly. "Us? You mean as in you and me?"

She nodded.

"Actually, I've been giving it considerable thought. I thought that *we* as in *us* should make plans for the future." He dragged the words out. He continued: "At least we ought to spend some time together to see if we do have a future. I mean, the sex is great, but what do we really know about each other? I've got to get this money down to New Orleans. I thought maybe you'd like to join me later. You could fly back to LA and finish up any business you may have there. Then you could join me, say in a week or two. They maybe we could drive up the coast, and you could see what I do with my life when I'm not kidnapping little children."

"Oh, John, I'd love to!" she exclaimed.

"Shh," he cautioned. "There's a child asleep inside."

"I'm sorry. Do you mean it? You. Me? Together?"

He smiled. "Yes, I think it would be fun."

She rose from her seat on the porch and came over to sit on his lap. They talked about the things they would do, the places they would see and the life that lay ahead of them. Finally…

"Jackie?"

"Yes?" she asked dreamily.

"You need to get up. I think my legs are dead."

She laughed and punched him on the arm as she rose.

"Wait here," she whispered and went into the cabin. She returned a few minutes later with a blanket and two pillows.

"Kendra's sleeping like a baby. Come on."

She took his hand and led him off the porch and into the trees. She found a spot under a pine, gave the pillows to John, and spread the blanket on the ground. John threw the pillows down onto the blanket. Jackie was already kneeling on it, facing up at him. He knelt down in front of her and took her in his arms.

She giggled as she said, "I've never made love to someone this old. Your mask going to be able to handle this?"

He laughed and removed his mask. She removed hers.

Under the stars, John and Jackie make love in the woods. Then they slept. It was after two when the chill of the night woke Jackie, and she in turn woke her lover. Together, still naked, they picked up their things and hurried back to the cabin.

Once inside, they put their disguises back on and dressed. John pulled two beers from the cooler, and they went back out on the porch, two lovers sharing the night in a cabin in the woods, neither wanting it to end. They sat in their chairs and sipped their beers and stared at the stars. It was peaceful.

"Floyd and I sat here under the stars the other night. We saw a shooting star. Floyd told me that if you saw a shooting star and wished upon it, you wish would come true. I wished, and it did."

She looked over at John and smiled.

Sally and Jack walked the few short blocks from the offices of the FBI to the hotel.

"Care to join me for a drink?" he asked as they entered the lobby.

She looked at her watch. It was approaching eleven o'clock. "All right, but just one. It's getting late."

They found the bar and a waitress seated them at a booth in the corner.

Jack ordered a rum and Coke and Sally a white wine.

"You look exhausted, Jack," she observed in the dim light of an overhead lamp.

He removed his glasses and rubbed his eyes with the heels of his hands, then pinched the bridge of his nose.

"I am," he admitted as he opened his eyes wide and refocused. "There's something about this case that we're missing, and I can't put my finger on it. It's almost like I know these people, and yet I don't." He held his palms up.

Sally understood the frustration. She was feeling it too.

"You've been chasing these people for, what, six years? It's got to be frustrating. But you know so much more now than you did a week ago, Jack. It's only a matter of time."

The waitress arrived with their drinks.

They sipped and talked small talk until the waitress said, "Last call."

Jack told her about himself and his family—things she didn't know. She told him about her life outside the bureau.

"There's really not much to talk about," she said. "The bureau has been my life for the last four years. Oh, I've had dates, but most men feel threatened when they discover that I'm a Fed." She shrugged. "They just seem to stop coming around."

Jack reached over and patted her hand. "You'll find him some-day, Sally. You're too special, and you deserve happiness."

"Oh, don't get me wrong. I am happy. Sometimes I feel like I'm living in a dream. I love what I do, and sometimes I—we—do make a difference. And besides, I'm learning from the best."

She smiled at him. He blushed.

"We'll find these people, Jack. Somehow, some way, we *will* find them."

She smiled broadly at her superior and rose. "Goodness, it's nearly two. I need my beauty rest."

They rode the elevator up to their floor, and Jack said good night to her at her door. When he entered his room, he put in a call to his wife.

"Hi," he said when she picked up the phone. "Sorry to wake you, I just needed to hear your voice."

They talked for twenty minutes, and then Jack hung up.

CHAPTER 23

July 4, 6:00 a.m.

John woke first. He moved in his chair. The effort was painful. He looked over at Jackie. She was stretched out in her chair, her legs straight in front of her. She still held a can of beer between her legs.

He stood and stretched the kinks out of his body, bent down, straightened, and twisted left and right. He moaned low. Jackie opened her eyes. She sat up straight.

"Morning," he said.

"Good morning," she replied.

"Oh," she moaned as well, arching her back and stretching her arms out in front of her. She stood and twisted her body into different positions. And then she yawned.

"What time is it?"

"Little after six."

"Umm. Want some coffee?" she asked.

"Love some."

They brought their coffee back onto the porch. Birds chirped, squirrels chattered, and a slight breeze rustled the leaves on the trees.

"Let's go over the plan for Kendra's pickup," John suggested.

Jackie nodded.

"We're going to do it at the Villa Italia Mall."

He drew a diagram. "There's a fountain in the middle of the mall. Here's Penney's. Across by the entrance is a bank of phones. And down here is where the restrooms are."

"I figure we've got five minutes max from the time I call until security finds her. I'll watch her from…from here." He put an X down the corridor from the fountains. "After you change, join me there. If all goes well, she'll be back home safely, and we'll be out of here."

She agreed. "But what if somebody tried something funny while she's alone?"

"We'll just have to hope that nothing happens. I know that those five minutes are critical, but we'll be watching."

"If you say so."

"You've kind of grown attached to that little girl, haven't you?" John observed.

Jackie smiled sheepishly. "It's kind of hard not to. She's so precocious. She's just so smart for her age. And she's been such a trooper. She's hardly complained at all about being away from her parents and home. I really think she's had fun here."

Denver, 6:30 a.m.

A ringing phone woke Jack from uneasy sleep.

"Hello?"

A recorded voice stated the wakeup time.

Jack hung up and called Sally's room. She answered on the second ring.

"Good morning. Are you moving?"

"Yes," she replied, "just drying my hair."

"Good. Meet me at the elevator in twenty minutes."

Jack rose and looked at himself in the mirror. He had slept in his clothes, and they looked like it. He stripped and showered, then shaved and went to the closet to pick out something to wear. To his dismay, all his shirts had been worn. He would have to put on a shirt that was not fresh. How could he hide the fact that he was not wearing a clean shirt?

That's when it hit him. "Son of a bitch!" he yelled at his reflection in the mirror. He dressed then raced to the elevator. Sally was there when he arrived.

"Well, you're certainly in a big hurry," she said. "Breakfast isn't all that good."

The elevator doors opened, and they stepped in.

"Remember last night when I said I was missing something? Oh, and please excuse the clothes. I, uh, slept in them. Anyway, it came to me this morning as I was looking for something fresh to wear."

The doors closed behind them, and they started down.

"Yes?" she said expectantly.

He pushed his glasses back up onto the bridge of his nose.

"Follow me on this. What do we know about the kidnappers? I mean, tell me what they look like."

Sally began with the girl, then the black man, then the older man. All the time Jack nodded but said nothing. When she was finished, she looked at him, waiting for an answer.

He crossed his arms and leaned against the back of the elevator. His grin was huge.

"Jack?" she said staring at him. Slowly her thought processes caught up with his.

The look of pleasure and excitement she saw in his eyes confirmed what she was thinking.

"Precisely, my dear Sally. We saw what they wanted us to see. Right from the very beginning. I mean, think of it. Darlene described a redhead and a big black man. Alex sees a redhead and a big black man *and* an older man with a cane.

"It's too easy. Either they've got to be very careless, which they are not, or they are even smarter than we gave them credit for."

The agents stepped out of the elevator.

"So…if this is true," Sally ventured, "then we really don't know what they look like, do we? All we've got is their physical sizes, and one of them is black."

Jack squeezed his lips together and nodded.

It was just after 10:00 a.m. when the major pulled into the front of the mall. He told Kendra that they would do a little shopping and maybe get a new outfit for her before she went home. John brought his briefcase. Jackie had two empty Ward's shopping bags folded in her purse. She also had a dress and a pair of shoes.

He found a spot not too far from the front entrance to the mall, and the three of them walked hand in hand into the mall. He noticed the bank of phones to his left as he walked through the second set of doors and nodded their location to Jackie.

The two adults had talked about buying clothes for Kendra but decided that this might cause a problem. They didn't want to be with her for too long. She might be recognized. As they approached the front of J. C. Penney, the major stopped and knelt in front of Kendra, using his cane to help steady himself.

"Honey," he said to her. "I've got to find a few things for myself. Why don't you and Aunt Julie wait here by the fountain. When I come back, we'll go and find you some new outfits. Okay?"

He winked at her. She smiled back at him.

He watched them walk over to the fountain and smiled as Jackie lifted her up and sat her down on the edge. Turning, he hurried down the corridor, using his cane to affect the limp of an older man. He turned right and walked down the long corridor to the men's room.

He checked under each stall and confirmed that he was alone. Quickly he entered a stall and removed his mask. Next, he removed his shirt and pants and exchanged them with the clothes in his briefcase, putting the mask in the briefcase with them. He changed from loafers to sneakers and put them into his briefcase also. His cane folded, and he laid this on top of his clothes and closed the briefcase.

No one had entered the bathroom while he was changing, so he opened the stall door and walked to the sink at the end of the row, placed his briefcase on the counter, and removed the residue of the mask from his face. He washed his face and hands, combed his hair, checked his appearance, and walked out of the bathroom just as three juveniles came down the hall.

The three boys stepped aside to let him pass and one said something in Spanish, causing the other two to burst out laughing. They continued on their way and entered the bathroom. The major continued down the hallway and entered the mall corridor, crossed over and passed Jackie and Kendra from the other side of the hall.

Kendra didn't notice him, but Jackie did. She checked her watch. In two minutes, she would excuse herself.

The major approached the phone bank and quickly dialed the number for the McArthur residence. He did not have the voice scrambler with him, so he had to improvise.

"Hello?" the male voice on the other end answered.

"Hello, Alex," the major said with a very heavy British accent, "and congratulations."

"Who is this?" Alex demanded.

"No time for that, old chap. I just called to tell you that your daughter is alive and safe. In fact, if you call security at the Villa Italia Mall, they'll find her at the fountain in front of Penney's. I'll bet they will probably have her safely tucked away by the time you arrive. She'll be wearing a pink top and blue jeans, and her hair is done up in pigtails. Oh, and Alex?"

"Yes, you son of a bitch?"

"Come on, old boy, let's not get nasty. I just wanted to say thank you. You've got a lovely daughter. She was quite delightful. Actually, she was no trouble at all. Goodbye."

The major wiped the phone clean with his handkerchief and hung it on the cradle. Next, he used the cloth to rub each of the buttons on the face of the phone. Then he turned and nodded to Jackie who was watching him from the fountain.

Alex hung up and turned to Jack. "She's at the Villa." He told the agent what the caller had said.

Jack immediately picked the phone up and called information, writing down the number on a scrap of paper. He dialed the number.

"Villa Italia Mall, good morning."

"Security please, this is an emergency."

There was a pause as the call went through.

"Security, Graham."

"Listen, there's a little girl down by the fountain in front of Penney's. She's wearing a pink top and blue jeans. She has brown hair done up in pigtails. She's probably alone. She was kidnapped and was just dropped off there. Her name is Kendra. Kendra McArthur. My name is Jack Donovan. I'm with the FBI. Get to her immediately and bring her to your office. Do you understand?"

The security guard repeated back the description and location to Jack. "I'm on it, sir."

"Good. Hold her there until we arrive."

Jack hung up the phone. Quickly, he, Alex, Sally, Pete, and Lisa headed for the door.

Tony was on the phone to headquarters. They would notify the Lakewood Police Department, who would be the first to arrive at the scene.

When Jackie saw the major's nod from the bank of phones, she turned to Kendra.

"Honey," she said, "Aunt Julie has to go to the bathroom. I need you to wait right here until I get back. Can you do that for me, sweetie? Can you wait right here?"

Kendra nodded hesitantly.

Jackie pulled an envelope out of her purse and gave it to Kendra. "Take this and don't lose it, okay? Aunt Julie will be right back. And, Kendra, don't talk to anyone that might say hello to you. Only if they are wearing a police uniform and ask you why you are all alone. Then you can tell them that you are waiting for me. Okay? I'll be right back."

She stood, patted Kendra on the knee, and hurried into Penney's. From the directions the major had given her, she knew there was a restroom on the second floor. She hurried up the escalator and retreated to the back of the store. She entered the ladies' room. There were several women inside. She had to wait for a stall to become vacant.

Damn, she thought, looking at her watch.

Finally, a stall became available and she hurried into it, closing the door with a loud bang. She removed her wig as she sat down, then pulled out her hand mirror and began removing her makeup, freckles first, then eye makeup, contact lenses, lipstick, and everything else that made her look twenty years younger.

When she was done, she stopped to listen. The other women were gone. Jackie bent down and looked under the walls of the stall. There was only one pair of legs visible in the bathroom now, these from a stall two doors down.

Quickly she stood and began removing her clothes. She had picked this dress to change into because it fit into her purse and because it was nearly wrinkle-proof. Simple but classy. She pulled the dress over her head, straightening her pantyhose just before it slipped down over her body. Next, she removed her tennis shoes and put on a pair of white flats.

The toilet flushed two stalls down, and she heard the woman open the door and walk over to the sinks. The sound of running water, then the sound of the hot-air dryer and then the sound of the woman's shoes echoing off the tile walls as she left the bathroom.

Jackie listened and looked under the stall again. Stuffing her clothes into the shopping bag, she hastily put on a blond wig, stepped out of the stall, and approached the sinks. She looked at her watch again. She had less than two minutes to put on a new face and get out of there. Quickly she applied new lipstick. A touch of blush and eyeliner to finish the job and, in less than two minutes, she walked out of the ladies' room, carefully shielding her face as she moved through the upstairs area. She rode the escalator down to the main floor.

There was a big commotion going on in front of J. C. Penney. Several policemen and a policewoman and two security guards were clustered around Kendra. She looked scared and confused. In her hand, she held the white envelope. She was afraid to give it up.

Jackie hovered around the jewelry counter, watching the proceedings while she pretended to look at the various types of watches in the case.

"Can I help you find something?" the clerk asked her.

Jackie looked at her. "No, thanks. I'm just looking for some ideas for my sister. She's real hard to shop for."

The clerk smiled and moved on down the counter to help an elderly woman. Jackie circled the counter, keeping her eyes on the front entrance. In the background, she could see the major watching the proceedings. He looked up, saw her, and shook his head. She casually retreated back into the store, looking at various items on display as she moved farther away from the entrance.

The major worked his way through the crowd that had gathered and entered the department store. He found Jackie in the back by the sporting goods.

"Let's give it a few minutes," he whispered in her ear. "Come, follow me."

He led her to the escalator, and the two of them rode up. On the second floor, they found the mall entrance and walked to the elevator on the west side of the mall in front of Ward's. They waited for it to arrive and rode it back to the first floor.

He took Jackie's hand and walked back toward the front entrance. By now the crowd was breaking up. The police and security people were gone. So was Kendra.

They made their way through the dispersing crowd and out the front doors. There were three police cars parked in front, their lights flashing. Casually strolling past the police cars, they walked to their car, passing another car that was just pulling into a handicapped spot. He looked at the driver and the back-seat passengers.

When they were away from the mall and heading south on Wadsworth Boulevard, Jackie let out a big whoop. We did it!" she yelled. "We friggin' did it!"

The major looked at her and smiled. The rush of excitement finally got to him, and he let it out.

"Fuckin' A!"

He pounded his hands on the steering wheel and let out a loud "Yes!"

PART II

The Chase

CHAPTER 24

Villa Italia Mall, 10:30 a.m.

Pete arrived at the mall and pulled into a handicapped spot in front, narrowly missing a couple walking back to their car. The male pedestrian glanced in at the driver and at the tall, slender man with glasses who sat next to him. The passenger reminded the pedestrian of a much taller version of Woody Allen. In the back were two attractive women and a man. The pedestrian recognized two of the passengers immediately.

When the car stopped, the five people got out and headed toward the entrance, obviously in a hurry. The blonde from the back seat gave the major the once over as she hurried to catch up with the tall, slender man in the dark suit.

The five headed through the doors. Inside, they found a policeman. Jack flashed his badge and was directed to the security offices. He and the others hurried up the escalator. He found the administrative offices, and the security office and entered, his badge held high in his open hand.

"Jack Donovan, FBI. These are the parents," he said, motioning to the couple just coming through the doors. "Where is she?"

The female guard stood and motioned for him to go through a closed door.

"Thanks," he said, leading his party into the office. Kendra was sitting on a couch, her eyes wide with fear. All around her, people were talking and asking questions. She looked up as Jack and the others entered and spotted her parents.

"Mommy! Daddy!"

She flew off the couch and ran to her mother who scooped her up in her arms. Tears ran down Lisa's cheeks. Then both of them were crying. Alex wrapped his arms around them and buried his face in Kendra's hair.

"Baby, baby," was all he could say.

Amid this scene, Jack asked, "Who's in charge?"

"I am," a uniformed officer said, stepping between the mass of bodies in the small room.

"Lakewood Police Agent Richard Meade."

"Jack Donovan. FBI. I'm heading up the investigation into this little girl's abduction. This is Special Agent Peter Jordan, head of the Denver division, and this is Special Agent Sally Martin."

He looked around at the crowd. "Can we clear this room? Agent Meade, you can stay, and I'd like the security guard who found Kendra to stay, but please, there are too many people in here. Kendra's probably scared to death."

Agent Meade did as he was asked. When they were gone and it was quiet, Jack approached Kendra.

"Hello, Kendra. My name is Jack. How are you doing?" he asked softly.

"Fine," she said timidly, holding tightly to her mother's neck.

"Good. Do you want anything? Water? A pop? Something to eat?"

"No thank you."

Jack reached up and gently pushed a loose strand of hair from her face and wiped away a tear.

"Would you like to go home?" he asked, again talking softly to her.

She relaxed her grip on her mother's neck and nodded slowly.

Jack turned to Agent Meade. "We all came in one car. Would you...could you drive us back to their house? I'd like for the three of them to drive back in our car, alone. I think they need that right now. Is that all right with you Pete?"

Pete nodded.

He turned to Alex. "Don't press her with questions right away, okay?"

Alex nodded and took Kendra from Lisa.

"Let's go home, honey."

Pete gave Alex his car keys as Alex passed him.

"We'll be along shortly," Jack said to them as they passed. "Bye, Kendra. See you at home."

"Bye," she mumbled.

"Agent Meade, have someone get the names of everyone involved: the guards, the police who answered the call, any witnesses you can round up. I'll want to talk to them later. Right now, though, I want to go back to the house and talk to Kendra. Agent Meade, you can fill us in on the way.

"Oh, and have the surveillance tapes rounded up. We'll need to look at them," he said to the security guard.

Outside, in the security guards' front office, the other police and security people were milling about, unsure as to what they should be doing. Agent Meade gave his people instructions and walked out, the three FBI agents right behind him.

"This one's mine," he said over his shoulder as he walked to the unmarked white car parked in front of the doors.

When the four were inside the car, he called dispatch and informed them of his plans. His car was immediately taken out of service.

Looking in the rearview mirror at Jack he said, "Where to?"

The cabin, 11:15 a.m.

"How'd it go?" Allen asked as he opened Julie's door.

She jumped out of the car and threw her arms around him. Jumping up and down like a child, she exclaimed, "We did it! She's all right! We're rich! We did it!"

Floyd came around the corner of the cabin to see the three others patting each other on the back and laughing.

"Man, ain't that a sight," he said as he joined them. "You three're noisier than a barroom full of drunks on a Friday night. But you know you can't be makin' all that noise. Sound carries up here. Come on now."

"Floyd's right," the major said. "Let's keep the celebration down to a quiet roar."

They walked to the back of the cabin. The trash was gone. The porch looked like it had when the four of them first arrived four days earlier.

"Everything's in the back of my car," Allen said. "Inside's done too. Surfaces wiped down for prints. Nobody'd know we've been here except there's no dust."

The major walked through the cabin and inspected each room. Like Allen had said, everything looked like it had when they had first arrived. Except for the dust. He theorized that in two to three weeks a film of dust would cover everything. All traces of their having been there would be gone.

"Fine, fine," he said as he returned to the kitchen. "What about the outhouse?"

Floyd beamed. "Outhouse done too, Major, 'cept I ain't crawlin' down in that hole."

"Good." He slapped his hands together. All right, people, this is it. I'll be in New Orleans by Friday or Saturday. I'm driving. By Monday morning at 10:00 a.m. local time, the transfer should be done." He looked at each of them as he spoke. "Good luck to each of you and God bless. It's been a good run. And it's been fun. You've all been a great team, and I'm proud of each one of you. You are true professionals.

"Remember, don't try to get in contact with each other or me. Go back to your daily routines. Give it at least another year before you make any kind of life change. I'd recommend relocation somewhere else if you are going to change your lifestyles. If you start throwing money around, people are going to notice. The less obvious you are, the more successful you will be. Any questions?"

They looked at one another, then back to the major.

"Well then, this is it. Goodbye and good luck."

Hands were shaken, hugs and kisses were exchanged, and one by one, each of them left. The money was hidden under the porch until the major could return for it with a different car later. That would be the last thing he did before leaving town.

McArthur residence, 12:30 p.m.

Agent Meade dropped his three passengers in front of the house and called in his location. Jack thanked him for his help and said goodbye, straightened, and walked up the steps behind the other agents.

Alex was standing by the open door waiting for them.

"She's amazing," he said as they entered the house. "She said she wasn't scared or anything. She kept saying that Aunt Julie and Uncle Floyd were fun. She talked about deer and how to find them and about rabbits and squirrels. She said it was fun."

"Where is she now?" Jack asked.

"Having lunch in the kitchen with Lisa. She looks kind of tired. Must you begin right away?"

"We'll play it by ear."

"Hello, Kendra," Jack said to the little girl as he entered the kitchen. Mm, that looks good. Peanut butter and grape jelly?"

She smiled through a mouth full of sandwich and nodded. "My favorite," she mumbled.

"Kendra, we don't talk with our mouths full, do we?" her mother chided.

Kendra looked at her mother and shook her head. She looked back at her visitors and smiled again.

When Kendra was through with her lunch, Jack sat at the table and said, "Kendra? I'd like to ask you some questions. Is that okay?"

Kendra looked at her mother and father. They nodded.

"Okay."

"Would you like to go into the other room, or would you like to stay here?"

She looked around at all the people and said, "Other room."

233

They all retreated to the living room and found seats. Kendra sat on the couch between her parents. Each of them held one of her hands tightly.

"Do you mind if Sally takes notes of what we say?"

Kendra shook her head.

Lisa said, "Just tell these people what you know, honey, okay?"

"Oh, I almost forgot," Alex interrupted, jumping up from the couch. He left the room and returned carrying the envelope Kendra had held on to through the whole time at the Villa.

"I opened it when we got home," he apologized.

Jack took the note and read it.

To whom it may concern:

My name is Kendra McArthur. My father's name is Alexander McArthur.

Her name and address and phone number were given. It continued:

If you read this, please contact him or the police. I have been kidnapped. The people who took me have dropped me off here. Please call my daddy or the police. Thank you.

"Probably won't do any good to dust for prints, but we'll try," Jack said as he handed the note to Pete. "Take care of that, would you?"

He turned to Kendra and began asking her questions. He took her through the whole ordeal from the minute she was taken until the time the security guard found her by the fountain. He went slowly and led her from one event to the next.

Kendra was quite helpful for a child so young; her recollection of events was impressive. She repeatedly referred to Aunt Julie and Uncle Floyd and also to Uncle Allen and an older man with a cane who was a friend of her daddy.

She gave descriptions of each of them, and these were consistent with what they already had. Jack knew that these would be of little value, but he did not let the parents know.

At three in the afternoon, they took a break. Lisa insisted on feeding her visitors, and they were grateful. Alex walked Kendra to her bedroom where she lay down to take a nap. It was then that she realized her bunny was missing.

"I left it in the car," she cried to her daddy.

"We'll try to find it, honey, I promise. Now, lie down and take a nap. Daddy and Mommy will be right here if you need us."

He helped her take off her shoes and covered her with a light blanket, kissed her on the cheek, and stroked her head.

"I love you, baby," he said as he rose.

He turned and left the room, closing the door behind him.

"Daddy?" she called.

"Yes?"

"Can you leave the door open?"

"Sure, honey. We'll be right downstairs. Sleep tight. Don't let the bed bugs bite."

Downstairs, the three agents were just sitting down to lunch when Alex walked in. "She went right down," he offered. "Though she did ask that I leave the door open. She's never done that before."

"She's a remarkable little girl," Sally remarked. "This whole thing doesn't seem to have affected her much at all."

"Thank God," Lisa piped in.

"I'm amazed at her recollection of events and her description of the kidnappers," Jack added.

"What's next?" Alex inquired.

"I want to know about where she was taken. She mentioned deer and other woodland animals. It sounds like she was free to roam about while she was held."

Alex looked at Lisa. "Kendra left Bunny in their car. She was upset that it was gone."

Jack looked up. "Who's Bunny?"

"Her little bunny," Alex explained. Her favorite stuffed animal. It was pink with a white nose and fuzzy white tail."

"Sally?"

"I've got it, Jack," she said, adding another note to her rapidly filling notebook.

Jack asked, "How long do you think she'll sleep?"

Lisa said, "She usually naps for an hour to an hour and a half. I don't know. Might be four, four thirty before she gets up.

"Well then, I don't want to take up any more of your time today. Can we come by in the morning, say about ten?"

"We'll be here."

John and Jackie had agreed to meet later in the afternoon. They would check out of their hotels and check into a hotel together downtown as husband and wife. It would be easier that way. Jackie would turn in her car at the hotel. John would pick her up.

When John showed up at her door, she had everything packed and on the bed. They agreed to get rid of her makeup materials. This would be done at various locations in town. It would be easier than packing everything up and shipping it back to LA. It just made sense. It also made his life easier.

John looked in the phone book and found a hotel downtown. He booked the two of them into a honeymoon suite. When asked for a credit card, he gave her the info but explained that he would be paying cash.

"It would be just for the night," he explained.

Driving toward the downtown area, they found an alley where dumpsters were set out behind various buildings. They chose several of them along a four-block area and tossed parts of her stuff into each. When everything was disposed of, they drove downtown.

John had chosen the Brown Palace Hotel to stay at and drove up to the front entrance. The valet opened the door for him and helped him with his bags. John kept his briefcase with him and pointed to one bag for himself and Jackie also picked one out.

They would be staying in the old section of the hotel, and he was directed to the front desk. John asked for Marianne, and she appeared from a door behind the counter.

"Yes?" she inquired of the couple.

"Marianne? Hi. John Parks. We talked on the phone earlier?"

"Oh yes, Mr. Parks. And Mrs. Parks?" she asked, looking at Jackie. "Welcome to the Brown Palace. If you'd please fill this out," she said, handing him the registration form.

John filled out the form as requested and pulled a wad of bills from his pocket.

"I'd like to pay in advance."

She figured the bill, including a bottle of Mum's champagne to be sent to his room later, and handed it to him. He counted out some bills, including an extra twenty and told her to keep the change.

The bellhop arrived almost immediately and led them to the elevator.

The Brown Palace was a beautiful old brownstone with a huge lobby. The lobby atrium rose eight floors, and each level had a balcony that opened onto the lobby below.

"It's beautiful," Jackie whispered to John as they rode the elevator up to their floor. The bellhop turned left off the elevator and walked down the open corridor. Both John and Jackie looked down at the lobby and marveled at the sight below them. It had all been done up in celebration of the Fourth of July, and the colors were dazzling.

When the bellhop arrived at their door, he set the two bags down and unlocked the door for them. John, briefcase in hand, grabbed Jackie and lifted her into his arms and carried her across the threshold. She hollered at his unexpected action and laughed as he carried her into the room.

"This is exquisite," Jackie gushed when the bellhop was finally gone.

"Come on, let's get the car business over with and then we can relax."

When they drove up to the Brown Palace, John had noticed a Budget Rent-A-Car across the street. They walked over and had no trouble renting a Buick. John parked it on the street in front of the Navarro. This building had once been a brothel. Now it contained offices. It was as old as the Brown, maybe older. They retrieved John's first rental car and transferred their remaining bags from it to the trunk of the Buick before turning it in.

Allen and Floyd would be shipping everything out from the storage unit, and except for picking up the ransom money, the last remaining detail from the kidnapping was now done. John and Jackie could now enjoy each other and their future.

Pete drove Jack and Sally back to their hotel and dropped them off. Jack asked about a nice place to eat, and Pete recommended a cozy little restaurant called the Ship's Tavern.

"It's just down the street. You can walk to it if you want. It's Angie's and my favorite place," he added. "I can make reservations for you if you want."

"That would be great. Ship's Tavern it is, then," Jack agreed. "Sally, how 'bout you meet me in the lobby at, say, six thirty?"

They each went to their separate rooms. Sally to nap and Jack to review the notes she had given him. Jack took off his coat and loosened his tie. He sat down at his desk and called the hotel's laundry service and requested a pickup. He would buy some new clothes as well.

Jack checked his watch. Four thirty. He had time to shop and be back in time to shower before meeting Sally. He arranged her notes on the desk and gathered his dirty clothes.

Jack waited, and in five minutes, there was a knock at the door. He opened the door to a member of the hotel staff who took his laundry and assured him that they would be returned within the next two hours.

Jack closed the door behind him and followed the man down the hall, taking the elevator down to the lobby. He asked directions to the nearest clothing store and was directed to an establishment across the street.

He found what he was looking for and returned to his room, his arms full of clothes bags. He stripped and went in to shower. When he returned, the message light was blinking on his phone. He quickly dialed the front desk while drying his hair.

"This is room 2410. I have a message?"

"Yes, sir, just a minute."

Jack waited and looked over the clothes on the bed. He decided on a powder-blue Polo shirt and tan slacks.

The voice came back on the line. "It's from a Tony De Marco. Want me to read it?"

"Yes, please."

"Nothing yet on the rental cars. Hope to have something tomorrow. Going home to family barbeque. Call me if you need me. My home number is 303-555-3968."

Jack wrote it on the corner of one of Sally's notes.

"That's it," the voice said. "Want me to save it?"

"Um, yes, could you put it in my box?"

"Certainly."

Jack shaved, added cologne, and applied deodorant, then dressed.

It was just after six. He had time before meeting with Sally, so he picked up her notes and brought them to the chair by the window. He opened the curtains and sat down to review them.

He read and reread Sally's notes on Kendra's interrogation and was again amazed at how articulate the little girl was. Apparently, she truly believed that this Julie person was her aunt and that Floyd was her uncle. At least they had been kind to her and had treated her well. The fact that she was able to get out and about in the woods was in itself amazing. He made a note to pursue this in the morning.

Jack looked at his watch. It was six forty. "Damn," he said and quickly rose. He checked his image in the mirror one more time and rushed for the door, notes still in his hand. He turned, tossed the notes on the bed, and exited his room.

She was sitting on a couch in the lobby when he stepped off the elevator and stood when he approached. She was wearing a black dress, cut low in the front, the hem a few inches above her knees. Her blond hair was done up on top of her head. Around her neck a single string of pearls hung, the curve of the string resting nicely against her skin. Two matching pearls hung from delicate silver chains attached to her ears. Her beauty took his breath away.

"Oh my God," she said as he approached. "I thought...I..."

He laughed, appreciating the humor of the situation.

"You look great, Sally," he said.

"But..."

"But nothing. I didn't have anything to wear. I gave everything to the laundry service, so I bought these. I'd be honored to take you out looking like that if you don't mind me dressed like this."

She burst out laughing. "I'd be proud to have dinner with you," she said and offered him her arm. Jack took it, and they walked out into the evening air.

They walked the few blocks to the Brown Palace and entered the Ship's Tavern. Jack noticed the model ships right away. Large models of clipper ships, galleons, steamers, and sloops were strategically placed around the room.

A worn hardwood floor, highly polished, accepted the wooden tables that were spread throughout the room. It was rustic. It was old. It was perfect.

The waiter led them to a table under one of the clipper ships in the corner. They sat. He stared at her, a blush of embarrassment on his face.

"What?"

"What?" he repeated. "I'm sorry. I can't help myself. Doesn't it bother you to be stared at like that? All the men lustful and the women jealous?"

He quickly looked around the room and returned his attention to her.

"I bet every man in this room just took you to bed in their minds."

She blushed. "Jack!"

"I'm sorry. I didn't mean—" His face red again.

"It's all right. It used to bother me. There were times, especially in college when I would do whatever I could to make myself look plain. I thought this was a curse."

She motioned to herself with her hands. "I was self-conscious. I was afraid boys only wanted to go out with me because of my looks. I think that's part of the reason I studied so hard. I guess I just got tired of all the boys hitting on me.

"Anyway, my mom and I had a long talk one day during Christmas break in my junior year. 'Call it a curse or call it a blessing,' she said, 'but what you got, you got. Live with it, enjoy it. Just be yourself. Be natural. Be honest. Above all, don't be ashamed or self-conscious. Someday you'll be thankful for what God has given you.'

"I always remember those words," she continued. "Now," she said and paused. Now I accept it. Sometimes it's even fun. If a guy gets out of line, I just tell him to kiss off."

She blushed again. "My dates sure get off on it."

She looked at Jack, her eyes teasing him.

"Well, sure, I mean, I know I do. It's kind of nice being seen with you."

The waiter appeared and poured their water.

"Can I get you something from the bar?"

Jack looked at Sally.

"White Zin," she asked the waiter, "with a side of club soda."

"And you, sir?"

"Rum Coke with a twist of lime."

"Thank you. Would you like an appetizer?"

Again, Jack looked at Sally, his eyes questioning.

"Let's be adventurous," she teased. She looked at the waiter. "Rocky Mountain oysters?"

"Yes, ma'am," he said. He looked at Jack who only nodded.

Jack sat back. He was relaxing. Sally was good company. She was easy to talk to, she was witty, and God, she was gorgeous.

Jackie was the first to shower. It was all John could do to stay out of the shower with her, but he managed. Instead he turned on the television to Channel 9 News. They were carrying a blurb about Kendra McArthur being found at the Villa.

"Details are sketchy," the news reporter was saying. "but it appears she was kidnapped and then dropped off here."

The fountain was behind the reporter, and he turned slightly to acknowledge it.

"This might explain why Alex McArthur, one of the cofounders, was so conspicuously absent from his own golf tournament. We hope to have more information available as it comes in. Back to you, Paula."

The coverage switched back to the studio where the anchor moved on to the latest update on the new C-470 corridor that was being built.

John switched off the television and looked through the blinds at the city below.

Not a bad place to live, he thought to himself.

Jackie came out of the bathroom with a towel wrapped around her; another was wrapped around her head like a turban. John spotted her crossing the room.

"We don't have to go out," he teased.

"I'm starved," she called out.

She came to the French doors. "Should we dress up or go casual?"

"Casual's okay with me," John answered. "In fact, if you want to just go naked, I won't mind at all."

"You animal." She threw her body towel at him, stuck out her tongue, wiggled her bottom and quickly retreated to the bathroom, shutting the door behind her.

John wandered over to the bed and lay down on it. He imagined life with Jackie and thought it would be fun. His imagination was in full swing when she came out of the bathroom wearing a black bra and the briefest of panties.

"It's all yours, my love," she said, drying her hair with the towel. "Should I go natural, or should I go as a blonde?"

John thought for a moment. "Blonde," he finally decided.

"Blonde it is then," she said, dancing around the bed.

John rose, patted her rear, and headed for the shower.

At seven thirty they rode the elevator down to the main floor. John inquired at the front desk and was told that there was immediate seating in the Ship's Tavern. He took Jackie by the arm and walked over to the entrance where a waiter greeted them and led them to a table.

John held the chair for Jackie as she sat down. She smiled and gave a demure nod to him as he pushed the chair in for her. Walking around the table, John scanned the crowd until his eyes came to rest on Sally. His memory clicked in. He had seen her before, he knew it. When he sat down opposite Jackie, he had a clear view of Sally and her companion. Jackie was talking, but he didn't hear her. His mind was racing.

How do I know her? he asked himself. *Is she a movie star?*

Her companion shifted in his chair, and John got a better look at him.

And then he remembered. The flash of recognition caused his face to drain of color. Jackie noticed.

"What is it, John?" she asked. "You look like you've seen a ghost."

She started to turn around to see what had caused him to go pale.

"Don't turn around," he said sharply.

She stopped turning and froze.

"Look at me," he commanded.

"What is it?" she asked again. "What's wrong?"

He leaned forward and bent slightly. In this position, the table in the corner was obscured from his view. He looked into Jackie's eyes.

"You'll never believe who is sitting in the corner over there."

She started to turn.

"Don't turn around."

"Who?" she questioned.

"The FBI!"

"The—"

"Shh," he interrupted. "I think that it's Jack. And I'm pretty sure that's his assistant. We saw them this morning when we left the

243

mall, remember? That's him, I know it. Shit, the whole goddamn town and he has to pick this place to dine in."

"What should we do?"

"Let me think."

Jackie reached into her purse and withdrew her makeup mirror and held it up, pretending to be touching up her hair. She found the couple's reflection and stared at them.

"It's them," she whispered. "I remember her sitting in the back seat of the car. She was behind the driver."

"All right," he decided, "we are going to order dinner and enjoy each other's company. To hell with them. They are not going to spoil our evening.

"Besides," he continued, "I think it's kind of exciting."

Jackie smiled nervously. "But what if they recognize us?"

"What? A couple in the parking lot at the mall? Besides, you're a blonde now, remember?"

"But you recognized them."

"I recognized Alex and Lisa in the car. They were just there with them. I figured they had to be FBI."

Across the room, Sally ordered trout and Jack ordered the prime rib. Jack asked the waiter about the ships on the walls. The waiter explained that they were all part of the Boettcher Foundation and were on permanent loan to the restaurant, and no, they weren't for sale. He went on to explain their history and how they came to be in Denver.

Dinner was exquisite, and the time passed quickly. For the time being, the kidnapping and subsequent recovery of Kendra was forgotten.

Jack relaxed and enjoyed the company of this totally delightful young woman. She seemed to enjoy his company as well. In all the time that they had worked together, they never had the opportunity to just relax and be themselves. It had always been business. It had always been meetings, discussions about current cases, chasing leads, following up on leads, and reading reports. Business! And now, here they were, just two people having dinner together.

When their plates were removed, they continued talking over after-dinner drinks. Their conversation passed back and forth; he talked about his family, she her life before the bureau.

When he finally looked around, the restaurant had thinned considerably. Only three other tables were occupied. One was a party of six elderly people, one was two women, possibly mother and daughter, and one was a man and a woman.

He looked at his watch. "Oh, mercy," he said. "It's nine thirty already. We probably should be going. I want to go over your notes some more before I call it a night. I have a feeling tomorrow's going to be a long day."

He signaled for the check.

"Well, young lady," he said, "I can't tell you how long it's been since I've enjoyed myself more. Thank you for a most enjoyable and relaxing evening."

They walked toward the exit. The man seated with the blonde woman looked up at him as he passed, and Jack nodded to him. The man nodded back and went back to his conversation with the woman. Jack noticed that he was also having the prime rib. On an impulse, he looked at the woman's plate. Sure enough, she was having the trout smothered with almond slices.

On the way back to their hotel, Sally volunteered to help Jack review his notes.

"I could change and come over," she offered.

"No, Sally," he said, "you get some rest. I'm just going to read through them again before I turn in."

"Okay," she conceded, "but call me if you have any questions."

"Thanks, I will."

They stepped off the elevator, and Jack walked her to her door, thanking her again for a lovely evening. She thanked him too.

"It's nice to go out to dinner without worrying if my date is going to hit on me afterward," she said to him as she put her key into the door. "Good night."

He smiled, touched his finger to his forehead in a salute, bowed, turned, and walked back to his room, his step light. He didn't review her notes. He did call Sue, and they talked for twenty minutes.

CHAPTER 25

"Well, that went well," John said after Jack and Sally walked out of the restaurant.

"What a beautiful woman," Jackie remarked. "You don't think they're doing it together, do you?"

"Just like a woman. You all love to imagine. I suppose that's where gossip comes from."

"Do you think he recognized you?"

"I don't think so. I didn't see it in his eyes. Besides, I think he was more interested in her back than he was in us."

"Well, I hope so."

They finished their dinner and discussed how and when they would meet. New Orleans was out. Not enough time for her to finish up all the things she needed to do, including packing up her belongings and moving out of her apartment. And what would she do with all her furniture and things? Store them? Sell them?

She would store them for the time being. She could always dispose of them at a later date. She would mail the keys to Gretchen and have her take care of things.

They finally decided to meet in Washington, DC, in two weeks. John would make the money transfer in New Orleans as planned and then drive east to US 95 and head north to DC. There he would wait for her, and they would then drive up into New York City, then through Boston and on to Maine where he lived.

She was surprised that he would live in Maine.

"I was too. Wait until you see the place, then you'll understand."

"I'm so excited."

"I'm looking forward to it."

Outside the restaurant, on the wall by the entrance, was a map showing the Denver Aquifer. They stopped to study it.

John was fascinated. "There's a lot of water under us. Look at this."

He pointed out various parts of the shaded area to Jackie. The water table stretched all the way into Kansas and Nebraska.

"Amazing," he said as the two of them walked away.

"What would you like to do?" he asked her as they entered the lobby. "The night is still young?"

"Let's take a walk. In all the time I've been here, I've not seen downtown."

He nodded. "Walk it is. Oh, wait here. I just need to do one thing first."

John walked over to the front desk and said something to the night clerk and returned.

"Let's go."

They walked across the street and headed toward Sixteenth Street. Once there they turned right and, hand in hand, walked the entire length of the downtown mall, looking in windows, listening to the sounds and smelling the smells of the city, finally ending up on Larimer Street. All the while, the two people shared their past, openly, freely. John learned things about her that only helped to strengthen his feelings for her. She, in turn, learned about his hopes and dreams and aspirations. She was surprised to learn that he was a published author. She had heard about the book but had never dreamed that he was the author. They found a book store, and he bought her a copy, signing it, "With love, John Burton."

And then they headed back to the hotel, walking slowly. The entire walk took about an hour and a half.

Inside their suite a table had been set up. On it was a silver bucket with a magnum of champagne, two long-stemmed glass flutes, and a single rose.

"Oh, John," Jackie cooed, "what a lovely thought."

"I thought we could celebrate our success and our future together, my pet."

"I'd like that."

John opened the bottle and filled each glass with the bubbly liquid and offered one to her. He picked up the other one and held it up to her.

"Thank you," she said as she took the glass from him.

"To us," he began. "To tonight and to all the nights we will share. And to tomorrow and all the tomorrows that life gives us."

They both sipped from their flutes, eyes locked on each other.

He gently kissed her lips, took her glass from her, and set it down on the table along with his. He looked into her eyes again and read the love and the passion that was there. Scooping her off her feet, John carried her into the bedroom.

CHAPTER 26

Denver, Thursday, July 5

The three agents discussed the case while Pete drove them south to Cherry Hills. Jack had condensed Sally's notes to one page and reviewed these with his companions.

"The thing that still gets me is how the kidnappers managed to gain little Kendra's trust. She didn't seem to be afraid at all. It's like it was a vacation for her."

Sally spoke up. "The older man said he was a friend of her dad's. He must have known something about the family that helped gain her trust. He must have said something."

"Good point," Jack remarked. "Let's pursue that angle with the McArthurs when we get there. Maybe it's somebody new in their lives…an acquaintance, a business associate. Someone who entered their lives in the past, let's say, six months.

The FBI car pulled up in front of the McArthur residence just after ten o'clock. Lisa greeted them at the door and explained that Alex had to go to the office on some unexpected problem but would try to get back as soon as possible.

Kendra was up in her room playing.

"How's she doing?" Jack asked.

"She seems to be doing just fine. She even renamed two of her stuffed animals. Julie and Floyd. Alex is furious, but of course, he would never say anything to Kendra about it."

"Maybe that's good."

"Good?"

"Sure. If Kendra doesn't realize that she was kidnapped, maybe she won't have any of the post-abduction trauma that some kids have to live with."

Lisa thought it over and agreed.

"Tell me," Jack asked, "have either you or Alex met anyone new in the past six months or so? Anybody new in your lives? Friends? Business acquaintances?"

Lisa thought for a moment. "No," she said finally, "at least nobody on the home front. Of course, Alex is always meeting new people at work. You might ask him. Why? Do you think it might be somebody we know?"

"Just a hunch," Jack answered.

He looked upward. "May we talk to her now?"

Lisa smiled and called upstairs for Kendra. The little girl appeared at the top of the curved staircase and saw her visitors.

"Hello," she said.

"Hello, Kendra. We've come to talk to you again. That is, if you're up to it."

She shrugged. "Okay."

Dragging a stuffed bear behind her by its leg, she slowly came down the stairs and walked into the living room with them. They all took seats, Kendra sitting on her mother's lap, the three agents on the couch opposite.

Jack turned his focus on the little girl who was holding her bear loosely in front of her.

"Kendra, remember yesterday when we asked you about the people who took you?"

She nodded. "You mean Aunt Julie and Uncle Floyd and the other two men?"

"That's right. Now, Kendra, I want you to think real hard. What can you tell me about the other two men? Do you remember their names?"

She nodded. "My dad's friend? He had two names."

Jack looked at Lisa and then back to the little girl.

"Two names?"

"Uh-huh. Sometimes they called him major. And once, when they were in the kitchen, I heard Aunt Julie call him John. He was the older man."

Jack looked over at Sally. She had a pen in hand and was taking notes.

"And the other man? Was he an older man?"

"Nope. He was younger, like Uncle Floyd."

"And did he have a name?"

"I heard the major call him Allen. And he even called him Charlie once."

Lisa sat straight up on the couch. "Oh my God!" she exclaimed.

"What is it, Lisa?" Jack asked.

"Charlie! But it can't be! He was so nice!"

She had Jack's attention. "Go on," he urged.

Lisa told them the story of the golf reporter who had visited on the Tuesday evening before the kidnapping. She remembered the reporter's questions centered more on their family life than on golf or business.

"But it can't be them," she said. "Neither of them was old, and besides, the reporter had a beard and a moustache. And, Charlie? He had a scraggly beard and moustache and long hair. Kind of hippie looking."

"Mommy! That's him! That's Charlie. He had a beard and a moustache! I remember Mommy."

"What color was his hair?" Jack asked Lisa.

"Um, dirty blond, I think. Maybe light brown. I think his beard had just a hint of red."

Kendra yelled, "That's Charlie, Mommy!"

"His eyes?"

Both mother and daughter thought and answered simultaneously, "Blue!"

Jack looked over. "Sally?"

"Got it," she answered.

Jack asked the mother and then the daughter to tell them everything they could about the two men. The only thing the two McArthur females could agree on with regards to the major / golf reporter was his approximate size. Lisa had seen a man in his late thirties or early forties. Kendra had seen an older man, possibly in his early sixties. A man with a limp who walked with a cane. But Charlie! They were both in agreement about him.

"Okay, now, Kendra," Jack continued, "I want you to tell me everything you can about where you stayed. The camp, I think you called it."

She went deep in thought. She brought the bear up and held it against her chest.

"Well," she began, "it was old."

"Old?"

"Like a log cabin. You remember, Mommy? Like the one Abe Lincoln lived in?"

"Yes, dear," Lisa answered, patting her daughter's head gently.

She looked at Jack. "One of her books has a picture of Lincoln's log cabin.

"Oh," Jack said. "Go on," he urged.

Kendra went on to describe the cabin in the woods. No, there were no other houses or cabins nearby. She described the walks she and Floyd and Aunt Julie took and the animals they saw and how you could tell if deer had been near. She even talked about the little brown house out back that they all used for a bathroom.

"I didn't like it," she said, "but I got used to it. It had a big hole, and I had to hold myself up when I sat down. It smelled really, really bad."

"Can you tell me how you got to the cabin?"

"In a van," she said matter-of-factly.

They waited for more. She just looked at them blankly. There was silence.

Jack smiled at this precocious little child. *Of course*, he thought. *You ask a simple question, you get a simple answer.*

"Do you remember seeing anything outside?"

"Nope. It was dark. And besides, there were no windows."

"Oh!" she suddenly remembered. "The cabin? All the windows had boards over them. It was always kind of dark inside. And I remember when I was inside the van. It had these boxes on the wall. And they had little red and green and yellow lights on them."

"Could they have been radio equipment?" Jack asked.

Kendra shrugged.

"That's okay, Kendra. You're doing great. Now, can you tell us about yesterday? You know. When you left the cabin? When they brought you to the mall? What do you remember about the ride to the mall from the cabin?"

She thought for a moment before she spoke. "It was long. We rode in a car."

"We?"

"Aunt Julie and the older man. The major. And me."

"Okay, so you rode in a car. What color was the car?"

She thought briefly. "Kind of brownish red."

"Good. What do you remember seeing while you were in the car? Close your eyes and try to picture everything you can from the time you got into the car until the time you arrived at the mall."

She closed her eyes and thought. Opening them again, she said, "We drove down a long driveway. It was more of a path for a car really. It was dirt. And it had two paths that the wheels rode on. And sometimes little bushes grew in the middle."

"You couldn't see the main road from the cabin?"

"Nope."

"Go on."

"I remember when we got to the road we turned left."

"Left?" Jack asked.

"I'm left-handed," Kendra said proudly. She held up her left arm. "We turned left, see? We turned this way."

"Good. And then what?"

"The road was really windy."

"Windy? You mean like curves?"

"Yes. And then we came to a bigger road with lots of cars and trucks, and we turned left again. We drove faster on the big road."

"What did you see on the big road?"

Kendra closed her eyes again. Her lips tightened together. She jerked her head up and opened them. "It was windy too. There were lots of trees and rocks. We were going downhill."

"Can you see anything on the side of the road? Signs? Houses?"

"Nope. Just trees and rocks and things, but there was a fence in the middle of the road."

"A fence?"

"You know. A metal fence to keep cars from crashing into you."

Again, Jack looked at Sally who nodded. She was writing furiously.

"And then what?"

"I remember just before we got to the bottom, I saw some red rocks on this side," she said, raising her right arm. "They were kind of flat. And then a kind of hill that we drove through, and then we weren't in the mountains anymore.

"And then we drove for a while until we came to a bridge. We turned off the road and turned left again. We went under the bridge and passed some stores. We drove up a hill and then we got to the mall."

"The road took you straight to the mall?"

"Yes."

"Wadsworth," Pete explained. It has to be Wadsworth. The hill would put them just north of Hampden. They had to have come down Highway 285."

"Kendra?" Pete asked, "do you think if we tried to go back there, you could show us the way?"

"I don't know."

By now, she was beginning to show more attention to her bear than to her visitors. Jack stopped the interrogation. It was now almost eleven.

"Thank you, Kendra, you've been a big help."

He rose and gave her a pat on the head. Turning to Lisa, he said, "You've got a remarkable daughter."

"We know," Lisa beamed. "Thank God she's safe."

"I think we're done here for now. Kendra?"

"Yes?"

"Can we come back again and visit with you?"

Kendra looked up at her mother who smiled and nodded.

"Uh-huh."

Turning back to Lisa, Jack said, "Thank you so much for your time and hospitality. We may be back with more questions. Pete's idea of retracing her route might be an option. At any rate, thank you again.

Lisa walked them to the door.

"One more thing, Mrs. McArthur," Jack added. "Tell Alex we are sorry we missed him and that I'd like to ride along with him over the entire route he drove the other day when he dropped off the money. That is, if it's convenient for him. You've got my card."

"I'll tell him."

"Bye, Kendra!" Jack yelled as he walked out the door.

They left and drove back downtown. Pete called his office and told them to expect the three of them by noon.

"Have lunch brought in for the three of us," he ordered.

He hung up. "There's a message from Tony. Wants us to call him ASAP. Says it's important."

Pete punched in the numbers, and the phone rang.

"Tony? Pete Jordan here. Just got your message. What's up?"

"I think we just got our first break in the case. Got a call from a car rental out by the airport. Seems they found a pink bunny stuffed between the cushions in the back seat of a rental. Matches the description of the little girl's rabbit. I'm on my way out there now."

"Great. We'll meet you there." He called his office back and canceled lunch.

Tony was waiting for them when they drove up.

"What have we got?" Jack asked as Tony approached their vehicle.

Tony turned and pointed out the vehicle. "It's been washed, but they haven't done the interior yet. Car was dropped off here late yesterday afternoon. They found the animal and called us this morning. Nobody saw our fax about the rentals until the car was already washed. I've got a tow truck coming for it. Should be here any time."

"Let's go inside and question the salespeople."

"I've already done that. The sales rep who logged it in was off yesterday. Office was closed. Said they just left it in front."

"How 'bout the rep who signed it out?"

"Off. We're trying to track him down."

"Damn! Anything else in the car?"

"Nope."

"Where's the bunny?"

"In my car."

Jack and Sally walked around the Cavalier. They bent down and looked inside the windows.

"Anybody else touch this car?" Sally asked Tony as they completed their circle of the car.

"Except for the guy who logged it in and the guy who washed it, no. Don't expect we'll find anything on the outside, but maybe we'll be lucky on the inside."

"Good work, Tony. Let us know as soon as you find anything. We're going back to the office. You're welcome to join us. We may have a lead."

"Oh?"

"Golf interview on the Tuesday before the kidnapping. Might be bogus. Descriptions of the two match two of our suspects though."

"Let me finish up here and I'll follow you back. Give me a minute."

He went back inside the rental office and said something to his partner and hurried back.

"Can I ride with you? Kevin can finish up here and meet me at your office."

"Sure. Hop in."

He retrieved the stuffed bunny and slid in the back seat next to Sally.

Driving back into town, Jack brought him up to speed with Kendra's interview.

"She may be able to take us back to the cabin. It's a long shot, I'm sure, but you wouldn't believe how much that little girl remembers. She'd make quite a witness."

Pete spoke. "From the description, it sounds like it's in the hills west of Denver, off 285."

"That so?" Tony said. "My wife's brother and his wife have a summer cabin up that way. Maybe we can help."

"I'm open to anything," Jack confessed.

CHAPTER 27

Brown Palace

At five minutes past eight, the door to the honeymoon suite opened and closed. John was immediately alert. His body stiffened, causing Jackie to waken.

"Yes?" he questioned the intruder as the footsteps came closer to the French doors.

"Maid service. I'm sorry," the voice said. "I didn't know you were still here. I'll just leave and come back later. Sorry to have bothered you."

John's heart was pounding. Behind him, Jackie's hand gripped his shoulder, her nails digging into his skin. He listened as the footsteps retreated and then he heard the sound of the door opening and closing.

"Maid service," Jackie mimicked. "I don't think you need maid service. Come here."

Later John spoke, "We should be moving. You've got a plane to catch. Besides, the maid will be in shortly."

"Oh, you," she said, hitting him over the head with a pillow.

She pushed herself off of him and headed for the bathroom. John lay there, his hands cupped behind his head, a feeling of contentment sweeping over him.

I could get used to this, he thought.

The car pulled up in front of the United Airlines drop-off point and parked. John and Jackie got out of the Buick and walked to the rear of the car and removed her suitcases. She was dressed like a businesswoman.

They kissed goodbye at the curb, and she walked through the doors without looking back, the sky cop following closely behind her.

Jackie approached the United ticket counter. There were several people in line. When her turn came, she smiled at the ticket attendant.

"Hi. Christine Burton. You're holding a ticket for me?"

"Oh yes. Burton, you say?"

The attendant punched in the last name. A puzzled look appeared on her face. She punched in the name again. Her eyebrows came together in a frown.

"I'm sorry, you said Burton? Was that with a *u* or an *e?*"

"*B-u-r-t-o-n,*" Jackie spelled out to the girl at the counter. She turned around. As they had planned, there was now a long line behind her. She turned and faced the attendant again.

"I'm sorry, your name doesn't appear on our manifest. Are you sure—"

"But my company made the reservation on the third of July," Jackie cut in, acting a little panicky.

"Look again. Try Christine with a *c*, Burton with a *u*, please."

The attendant tried all the combinations she could think of but with no luck. "I'm sorry," she apologized again. "This is United Airlines. Are you sure you are at the right counter?"

"Of course I am. Oh, God, what am I going to do? I've got to be in Dallas by three thirty this afternoon. I was there when they made the reservation. Flight 405 to Dallas, confirmed. There's got to be some mistake."

The agent gave her one of those I-can't-help-you looks.

Is there someone I can talk to? I've just got to get on that plane."

"Just a minute."

The agent looked at the long line behind this woman and made a decision. She punched some more keys on her keyboard. "I've got a seat available in coach. It's on the aisle."

"Oh, thank you," Jackie said. "I'll take it."

The attendant told Jackie the price.

"Oh dear, the office was supposed to put it on their account. Can I write a check?"

A look of exasperation flashed across the young woman's face. "Well—"

"Oh, never mind. I'll pay cash. The company can reimburse me later."

She pulled some cash out of her wallet, counted out the correct amount to the nearest dollar and laid it on the counter.

"Thank you *so* much," she said as she scooped up her ticket and her change.

Jackie lifted her two bags onto the scale and accepted the tag receipts. Turning, she bumped into the man behind her, apologized, and headed for the C Concourse. When she arrived at her gate, they were just beginning to board. She handed her boarding pass to the attendant at the gate and walked down the tunnel and onto the plane. She found her seat, placed her purse under it and sat down.

Well, that was easy, she thought. *I didn't even have to produce any identification. Security sure is lax out here. That would never have happened back home.*

She put her head on the headrest and closed her eyes. An elderly woman interrupted her thoughts, and Jackie stood to let her in. The woman sat in the middle seat. A man in a bright-yellow Hawaiian flowered shirt excused himself and stepped over the two women before Jackie could stand again. The older woman gave him a stern look and then smiled at Jackie.

Jackie gave her a quick smile and closed her eyes, resting her head on the back of the seat again. The announcements were made, the plane backed away from the terminal and Jackie could finally relax.

"You'd better buckle up, dearie," the elderly woman whispered, "the stewardess is coming."

Jackie opened her eyes, reached down, found the straps, and clasped them together.

"Thank you," she whispered back to the woman.

She could tell the woman wanted to talk, but she didn't, so Jackie just closed her eyes again.

She slept until her dream was interrupted by the pilot's voice. "We're beginning our final approach into Dallas/Fort Worth Airport. Please put your seats back in their upright positions and store your loose bags under your seats. Once again, thank you for choosing United."

There was the usual commotion as people prepared themselves for landing.

John watched Jackie walk through the doors and into the terminal. Through his front windshield, he could see a uniformed officer approaching and pulled out into traffic. If Jackie followed his instructions, she would be all right.

He smiled. This had turned out to be quite a trip. He was richer, and he was in love. The thought of those words had a calming effect. He had never been in love before. At least, not like this. He'd never said those words to anyone, not when he was in high school, or college, or the years since then. Even when he'd known Jackie back at Fort Bragg, and they had had their affair, he had not even thought about love. She had been convenient, and she had been exciting, and she had certainly been willing.

He pulled into the Budget rental on Broadway and inquired about taking a car as far as St. Louis. He was told it was against company policy to rent a car that would cross state lines.

"Where can I buy a car then?" John asked the agent.

The Budget agent said, "Well, as a matter of fact, my brother-in-law owns a used car dealership on south Broadway. It's a small lot, but the cars are clean and reliable. And they're reasonably priced."

The agent called a cab for John and gave him one of his cards. The cab arrived within five minutes, and twenty minutes later John was let off in front of the dealership.

An hour later, John drove off the lot in a silver 1986 Honda two-door coupe.

CHAPTER 28

Nashville, Tennessee, July 5, 2:10 p.m.

Tom arrived in Nashville without incident. He walked out of the airport terminal at two thirty and caught a cab into downtown Nashville. The driver dropped him at the bus terminal.

Tom stored his bags in a locker and purchased a one-way ticket to Atlanta. From Nashville, the bus would take him through the Cumberland Plateau, and over the majestic Appalachians, down through the Blue Ridge mountains and into Atlanta. That would put him there around midnight. Tom took his ticket and walked over to a bench and sat down. Twice he walked over to the bank of phones to call Amy and each time he returned to the bench without making the call.

He paced. He bought a copy of People Magazine from the newsstand and quickly thumbed through it. He looked at his watch. Time dragged. He went over to the lunch counter and ordered a cheeseburger with onions and ketchup, a side of fries and a large chocolate milkshake. When he finished, he returned to the bench and sat down, stretching his legs. He looked at his watch again. Two minutes before five.

At five minutes after five, they announced the boarding of his bus to Atlanta, with intermediate stops at various locations along the way. He proceeded to the boarding area. Tom handed his ticket to the driver and climbed aboard the big silver Greyhound bus.

He found a seat next to the window, put his head against the headrest and closed his eyes. He'd be home soon and back in the arms of his lovely Amy. The thought brought the slightest of smiles to his lips. She would be asleep when he arrived. He would take a taxi home and surprise her.

The bus pulled out of Nashville and headed south on US 75. It was only about one-third full. The seat next to his was empty. With the late afternoon sun shining through the tinted windows of the bus, Tom now had a chance to review the past thirteen days.

The mental checklist he had developed over the years to review his actions was a great help to him now. Every move he made since he left home was reviewed. Each action taken, like the moves on a chessboard, was scrutinized and analyzed. Had he done everything that he could to erase all possible signs that he had been in Denver?

One by one, he eliminated each step from his trip until, at last, he was up to the present time, riding on the bus. He felt good. He was happy. There seemed to be nothing that could place Tom Owens in Denver. Pleased with his assessment, he nodded off.

In Manchester, the bus picked up additional passengers, and the seat next to him was taken by an army corporal on his way home to Atlanta and then on to Fort Benning. Tom listened absently while the soldier prattled on about army life and nodded at all the right times, but his mind was on his home and the girl who would be there when he arrived.

The sunset over the Appalachians and Tom excused himself from the soldier's conversation, begging exhaustion. The corporal apologized for talking so much, excused himself, and headed for the bathroom at the rear of the bus.

Tom was asleep when the soldier returned.

Indianapolis, Indiana, July 5

Cecil chose his return route through Indianapolis. He could catch a bus north to Chicago and be home by 5:00 p.m.

The thought of seeing William and Jasmine again made him giddy. They were his life, the reason he rose every morning and lived each day. He changed identities in the men's room at the airport and headed for the bus station.

Soon he was headed north, the skyline of Indianapolis on the horizon behind him. This, he promised himself, was his last time away from his children.

He now had over a million dollars stashed away (or soon would have) and he could look forward to a new life with the kids in the suburbs somewhere. He had a year to think about this, and he would choose wisely. The only thing that was written in stone was that he would remain close to Chicago. He could not leave his beloved Cubs, nor could he leave his Bulls or the Bears. He had already decided he would buy season tickets to each team's games.

Schools were important; he vowed after the Houston job that they would go to only the best schools and receive the education that he wasn't able to get.

He put his seat back, cupped his massive hands behind his head and turned to look at the acres of farmland that passed before him.

"Yes," he promised himself, "my kids, they gonna have the best."

Soon the skyline of Chicago appeared. He was home.

Dallas/Fort Worth Airport, 1:55 p.m.

Jackie entered the terminal as a blonde, just as she had left it thirteen days ago. She wore dark glasses. As she stepped out of the dimness of the tunnel and into the light of the waiting room area, she scanned the many faces there. Panic momentarily took her breath away. Standing together by one of the building's support columns were two men who were obviously plainclothes cops, or worse, FBI men. They wore gray suits and aviator sunglasses. They were watching the arrivals coming through the doors. They were obviously looking for someone.

No! They *couldn't have tracked me down this fast.*

There was a slight hesitation in her step when she first spotted them, and then she stiffened and walked past. They didn't appear to notice her. She was determined not to look back, and the effort was excruciating. She found a water fountain bent over, held her hair away from her face and took a drink. She turned slightly and glanced in their direction. One was holding what must have been a picture cupped in his hand. He looked at it and then up at the people who were still coming through the door.

Suddenly the one with the picture elbowed the other, and the two men moved forward. Jackie looked in the direction of the doors and saw a dark-skinned man with black-rimmed glasses hesitate and then turn and bolt through the emergency door next to the tunnel entrance.

Immediately one of the two FBI agents (by now Jackie was sure that they were) pulled a walkie-talkie from his coat pocket and began talking into it. The two men ran for the door, bumping and yelling at people to get out of the way. Jackie noticed that the man with the picture had drawn his revolver. Then they were through the doors, their footsteps clanging on the metal stairs as they descended to the tarmac below.

Jackie straightened, wiped her mouth with the back of her hand, breathed a sigh of relief and headed for the ladies' room where she removed her wig, changed her appearance, and exited as Jackie Chandler.

She would catch another flight into LAX, and return home to settle up, move out and begin her new life.

Denver, July 5, 4:30 p.m.

John finally was clear of Denver and heading east on I-70, the money safely stashed in the trunk of the Honda. He had removed it from under the porch where it had been buried. He checked the area once more and, satisfied that all was well, drove away from the cabin after brushing the tracks of his Honda from the dirt drive with a pine branch.

He did not feel completely comfortable until he passed southbound I-225, then, he relaxed. His first stop would be Burlington, Colorado, out on the eastern plains. From there he would drive to St. Louis. Then he would turn south on Interstate 55 and, with a little luck, be in New Orleans by Saturday night.

He looked in his rearview mirror for one last glance at the Rocky Mountains. Several of the peaks to the west still had caps of snow, even in early July.

Onward he drove until there was nothing but open space and fields of corn, their straight, neat rows of stalks waving in the late-day breeze. The drive became monotonous, and John had a chance to think about the future. He hoped Jackie would be happy in Maine. In time, he would ask her to marry him. He imagined the two of them sitting on his back porch watching the boats sail in and out of the harbor, both of them growing old together.

It was dark when John pulled into a Best Western Motel on the business loop in Burlington and checked in. He paid cash for one night, telling the night clerk that he would be leaving early. The clerk recommended the Western Sizzler for a good steak dinner. John took his advice.

At six thirty in the morning, he was up and moving. He ate breakfast, gassed up the Honda, checked his fluids and was on the road by eight.

Atlanta, Friday, July 6, 12:30 a.m.

Tom arrived home and paid the cab fare. He walked to the front door. All the lights were off. Amy's car was not in the driveway.

Maybe she pulled it around back to wash it, he thought. Sometimes she did that. She loved her old Mustang and kept it well-serviced and clean.

He quietly unlocked the door and let himself in, put his bags down and climbed the stairs to the bedroom. He had thought of this moment all the way from the bus station and had decided to strip naked and quietly climb into bed next to her.

He was removing articles of clothing from the time he put his foot on the bottom step. By the time he reached the bedroom door, he was completely naked. The door was open, and he stepped in. The light from the moon fell across the bed. It was empty.

Tom looked over at the clock on the nightstand. The little red numbers read twelve thirty-five.

Damn, he thought to himself, feeling foolish with his nakedness, *she must be working a double or something.* He went in and showered and put on some clean shorts, then went and retrieved his clothes from the stairs. He brought his suitcase upstairs and unpacked it. At 2:00 a.m., he called the hospital.

"Fifth-floor nurses' station," the woman's voice answered. Frieda Hansen."

"Frieda, it's Tom Owens. Is Amy there?"

"No, she and Doctor…excuse me a minute Tom."

She put Tom on hold and was back on the line in less than a minute.

"I'm sorry Tom, she checked out at ten. Said she was going straight home."

Tom thanked her and hung up. His stomach was in knots. "*She and Doctor…*"

Tom went down to the kitchen, pulled a beer from the refrigerator, and brought it into the living room where he sat in the dark and waited.

The lights of her car shining through the window as she turned into the driveway brought him back to full wakefulness. He heard her open the back door and close it, heard her keys hit the counter as she dropped them, heard her turn on the water and fill a glass, set the glass down and walk down the hall and climb the stairs. Her steps were slow and deliberate.

When Tom saw the light go on in the bedroom, he rose and quietly walked up the stairs. She was removing her makeup when he appeared behind her. His reflection in the mirror startled her and she gasped, then turned and threw her arms around him.

"Tom! You're home!" she shouted as she hugged him to her. "What…when did you get in?"

"'Bout twelve thirty. Unpacked, showered, and grabbed a beer. Must have fallen asleep. What time is it?"

She looked at her watch. "Four thirty. You look tired. How was your trip?"

Tom shrugged. "Okay. Did you work a double?"

"Uh-huh. Karen called in. One of her kids has strep. I covered for her."

"Kind of late, isn't it?"

She turned away and faced the mirror. "It was busy. We had five births tonight after ten."

"Oh," Tom said as he walked back into the bedroom. "Well, I'm exhausted. I'm going to bed. Wake me at eight, will you, hon?"

"Okay. Good night."

"Good night."

He threw off the bedcovers and lay down, his back to the middle of the bed. She joined him, her hand brushing his shoulder. He could feel her breath on the back of his neck.

"Honey," he apologized, "it's too hot. Good night."

"Good night," she said. "I love you."

How could she say that?

Amy rolled over, pulled the sheet up to cover herself and lay still next to him. Outside, a gentle breeze rustled the leaves on the tree next to the window. A dog barked. The sound of the milkman's clinking bottles being delivered across the street could be heard. Tom lay watching the minutes on his digital alarm clock change as the night wore relentlessly on. Amy's breathing was regular. She was asleep.

CHAPTER 29

Baton Rouge, Saturday, July 7, 8:00 p.m.

John pulled into Baton Rouge and found a small motel. He was now within eighty miles of New Orleans. Using his James Pickett alias, he signed in. He would stay until Wednesday morning. By the time he was checked in, had something to eat in the restaurant and returned to his room, it was almost ten. He decided to wait until morning to make the call.

Sunday morning came quickly for John. The exhaustion from two days of constant driving had caught up with him, and it was almost 10:00 a.m. when he awoke to the noises outside.

The first thing he did was check his car from the shuttered windows in his room. No problem. He glanced across the parking lot at the pool. It was already full of screaming happy children and parents. He showered and walked next door to the café.

When breakfast was over, he asked for several dollars' worth of change and walked to a phone booth outside the motel. He pulled the banker's home phone number from his wallet and dialed the number.

A woman answered. "Hello?"

"Um, yes, is this the Cyr residence?"

"Yes?"

"Is Frank home?"

"Yes, who's calling?"

"Just say it's…the major. He'll know."

"Just a minute."

John held the phone loosely to his ear and surveyed his surroundings. The only way out of the parking lot was the way he had entered. A heavy wire cable attached to cement pilings blocked any exit from the rear of the property. Across the street was a used car lot. Hundreds of colored plastic flags hung from wires and radio antennae. They were all flapping gently to the slight breeze that did little to cool the air. It was hot. Damned hot. John's shirt felt damp under the arms and on his back.

"Major!" the man bellowed into the phone. "This is a surprise. Where are you? How are you, you old son of a gun?"

"Hi, Frank. I'm in the area. Thought you and I might get together this afternoon. Maybe talk a little business."

"Um, sure. Can you come by the house? We can do a barbecue."

"You're sure Ellen won't mind?"

"Heck no, it'll be great. Come by about two, two thirty."

"That sounds good to me."

John heard the click on the other end of the line and hung up. It was now eleven fifteen. Figuring an hour's drive to Frank's house, that still gave him two hours. He would drive to New Orleans, find a shopping mall, park the car in plain sight, and take a taxi to Frank's house.

He trusted Frank, but two million dollars can do funny things to a man, so John was not quite ready to give up the location of all that money. That would come later when arrangements had been made to move the money.

John arrived by cab at two ten—not too early, but not late by any means. Frank was in the front yard watering his roses.

"John Burton!" the banker exclaimed as John climbed out of the cab. He dropped the hose on the grass and hurried to the edge of the lawn as John started up the embankment.

The house was a sprawling ranch-style brick with a Spanish tile roof. Two columns supported a peaked covering over the front door, and Frank's roses grew up the column. A black Jaguar was parked in the driveway.

"Hi, Frank," John greeted and held out his hand. Looking around, he said, "Nice yard."

"Yes, but it's a lot of work, believe me." He took John's hand in a firm grip, put his arm around the visitor's shoulders and led him toward the house.

"Come on in. We've got shrimp and crab legs."

Frank was tied to John the same way Tom was. Frank owed John his life. It had been on a search and reconnaissance mission that Frank had been wounded and the rest of his squad killed. A rescue mission was launched but was unsuccessful in bringing him out. That's when John and his radioman went in after him. Twenty hours later, John, a medic, and his radioman walked out of the jungle carrying the officer on a makeshift stretcher. Frank's left leg was in bad shape, and several surgeries would be required to fix it, but he was alive.

He was sent back to the States, while John and the others received the Bronze Star. The two Special Forces officers met up again at Fort Bragg. It was then that John recruited him. It was easy.

"Ellen! John's here!" he shouted to his wife as they entered the home.

Ellen came through the dining room door wiping her hands on her apron and saw her guest.

"John!" she said. They hugged. "It's so good to see you again. What brings you to New Orleans? How long are you staying? What—"

"Whoa, darlin'" her husband interrupted. "All in good time. All in good time."

"Well, you two men go on out back. Bertha and I are just about through in the kitchen. I'll join you in a minute. Bertha! He's here!"

"Yes, ma-am," a voice called back from the kitchen.

"Come on, John, beer's on ice."

The three friends spent the afternoon recounting fond memories of things past. John brought them up to date on his life as a writer living the easy life in Maine. He mentioned Jackie briefly, and that brought on more memories.

"We sort of keep in touch," John explained. "I was in LA recently and looked her up. She's still single and working as a makeup artist in the movie business. We dated, and as Frank likes to say, "One thing led to another…"

Finally, it was time for serious matters, and Ellen excused herself to help the housekeeper clean up the dishes.

"How much this time?"

"Two million, less your fees. Hundreds and fifties. Nothing smaller. All unmarked. All nonsequential. Same as before."

"Jesus."

"What do you think?"

Frank let out a big puff of air. "I think I need another beer. You?"

"Please."

Frank retrieved two more cans of beer, the third for each of them, and sat down at the table again. "Two million? Fuck, partner, you don't fool around, do you?"

"I try not to," John answered seriously.

"I'm not going to ask how you got it, so long as you didn't kill somebody for it…"

John was silent.

"You didn't…did you?"

John shook his head.

"Drugs? You know how I feel about that. It's not drugs is it?"

Again, John shook his head. "Let's just say no one was killed or injured. There were no drugs involved, nothing was stolen, well, nothing of any real value anyway, and no banks were robbed. And, Frank, if I keep denying all the possible ways there are, you will eventually figure it out. So I'm going to do something I never thought I would. I'm going to tell you. Sort of…"

John hesitated, took a draw of his beer, and leaned forward. He looked Frank straight in the eyes. With a twinkle in his eyes, he said, "I built a better mousetrap."

"Shit, man!" Frank exploded. "Come on--

"Shh," John whispered, trying hard not to laugh. "Ellen will hear us."

Frank dabbed at the spilled beer on his shirt with a paper napkin.

"You son of a gun, now you've got to tell me."

"Let's just say I'm sort of a modern-day Robin Hood. The money comes from those who can afford it and then it is distributed fairly to those who deserve it and need it."

Frank sat back in his chair and drained his can of beer. He burped loud and long. He looked at his friend, eye to eye.

Suddenly: "You're a fuckin' kidnapper! That's all that's left. You're a fuckin' child snatcher!"

John stared blankly at his friend.

"Cool, man!" Frank exclaimed.

He raised his can in salute and realized it was empty. "Shit. You want another?"

"No thanks, and you'd better slow down on the beer too."

Frank burped again. "Oh, right. Shh."

He looked back at the house. Ellen was through in the kitchen. The lights were off.

"Come on, John, let's go for a walk."

"Ellen! John and I will be back in a while," he yelled through the open screen door. "We're going to walk off some of this food."

"Okay!

The two men rose, walked to the side of the house, and let themselves out through the gate. As with the rest of the yard, rose bushes covered the fence next to it.

The sun was low in the sky when the two men turned and headed down the street, their bodies casting long shadows in front of them. They walked at a leisurely pace, Frank greeting the neighbors who were out walking their dogs.

"Been a lot of changes in the banking industry since we last did business," Frank began. "Heard about a bank bust over in Biloxi couple months back. Money coming in from Atlantic City and then out to the Caymans. Feds caught up with them. Big investigation. Opened up the bank's books goin' back ten years. Over four hundred million passed through that bank alone in those ten years.

"Now the Feds are looking into all the banks down here. We've been lucky. Nobody's noticed anything yet."

John stopped and turned to his friend. "Frank, if you don't think—"

"I didn't say that. It's just that it might take some time to transfer that much money and have it not be noticed.

"How much time?"

The two men continued on. He was silent, and John did not interrupt his thoughts. They crossed over a street and began walking down another. When they reached the next corner, Frank turned right. John kept up with him. Neither had spoken a word for the whole block.

"It could take up to two years," the banker said, finally breaking the silence.

"Two years?"

"To do it right, we'd need to set up several different dummy companies. Unless we use the same ones you used the last time. How many we looking at this time?"

"Same four as last time."

"Okay, let's say the same four dummy corporations. You're still the major shareholder I assume. Same account numbers?"

"Same numbers."

"Okay then. Four companies. Then we'd have to deposit a small sum into each account every month or so. We can stagger the amounts between them, sometimes more to one or two, sometimes none at all. The amounts varying from month to month.

"The money can be transferred that same day. Problem is the amounts. Banking Commission's been looking really close to large cash balance transactions, especially large deposits. We don't want to send up any red flags."

Frank fell silent for a minute before continuing. "Two years. I can't see any other way. If you want it done right. And I've got to cover my ass *and* the tellers' asses."

Frank fell silent again, walking along with his friend. They turned another corner and were walking into the late evening sun. In a minute it would disappear under the horizon. Now it was just the top half of a big red ball. John put on his sunglasses. Frank just squinted. They reached the corner and crossed over before John spoke.

"And there's no other way?"

"Nothing safe. Damn computer generation. Everything happens so fast now. Feds know right away. They'd be down here faster'n flies on shit."

John was thinking, "Well, I guess I'll have to figure something else out."

He was silent again. They turned right again as the last of the sun disappeared beyond the trees and houses to the west.

"What if I were to fly down to the islands and deposit it directly? Would I have any problems doing that?"

"Probably not. Course, that much money will be sure to cause some notoriety. Cayman banks don't report the names of their depositors to the US of A. At least the government hasn't put any pressure on them yet. I suppose you could do that, but how are you going to fly that much money down in a commercial airplane? It'd weigh, well, you know, you're probably carrying it around...it'd weigh too much for a couple of ordinary suitcases. That is, unless, of course, you were to bring several of them with you. Problem is, there is too many suitcases is sure to draw attention to yourself and invite a search of your belongings."

"Maybe I could hire a private charter."

"That might work, except you'd be leaving a trail for the Feds. Plus, you'd have to clear customs on the Caymans.

"I could sail it down."

"Sail?"

"Just a thought. Anyway, now I've got to figure this out. My, ah, partners expect the money to be there by Monday noon at the latest. I kind of figured we could get this all done by then. They're going to call in their numbers for confirmation."

"Is that a problem?"

"Not if I can contact them beforehand."

"You're welcome to use my phone."

"I've never contacted them by phone before. It's always been an unwritten rule. Less chance of being connected that way."

"You've got this all pretty well worked out, haven't you?" the banker asked.

"It's worked perfectly well three times because we are careful."

"God damn! And the victims? They're okay?"

John nodded.

They approached the house. Ellen had parked the Jag in the garage.

"Where are you staying?"

"Baton Rouge."

"Why don't you come on down here and stay with us for a while? You're in no hurry, are you?"

"Well, I—"

"Good. I'll have Bertha make up the guest room. You'll stay there."

"But—"

"No buts about it. Tomorrow you can call your, ah, friends and let them know what's going on."

John sighed. "Okay, if you insist."

"I do."

Frank looked around. "You didn't take a taxi all the way from Baton Rouge, did you?"

"No," John answered sheepishly.

"Well, where's your car?"

"In a parking lot."

"In a parking lot!" Frank said loudly.

John grinned. "Call it paranoia. I've been driving around with two million dollars in the trunk all the way from...well, let's just say I've put a lot of miles on the car these past few days."

"And now it's parked in a fucking parking lot?"

"Why not? It's safe. It's open. Nobody's gonna break into it."

"I think we need to get you back to your car."

The two men went in and told Ellen that they were going for a drive and would be back shortly. Frank informed his wife that John would be staying the night, and as the two men were leaving, John thanked her for her hospitality.

John hugged Ellen and extended his hand to Bertha. "And thank you for your fabulous cooking. It was delicious."

Bertha wiped her hands on her apron, smiled and took his hand. When she felt his hand in hers, a slight frown appeared on her face and quickly disappeared. Ellen noticed her expression but said nothing.

"Ellen tol' me how the three of you met while we wuz in the kitch'n. How you's ol' friends 'n all. Nice ta meet cha."

John nodded, turned, and followed Frank out to the garage. Frank backed the big Jaguar out of the garage and John climbed in next to him.

"What parking lot?"

"The one at the mall. It's in front of the entrance on the west side."

They drove off in silence. It was Frank who spoke first.

"Jackie's involved in this, isn't she?"

John looked over at his friend but said nothing.

"Oh, come on, John. Makes sense. You said it yourself, you and she—"

"You know I can't say—"

"You don't have to. It's written all over your face. I believe the saying is, 'You can't con a con man.'"

"Well, let's just say she's been a great help to my career."

"I bet she has," Frank said.

They found John's car and pulled into a space next to it.

"I think I'll head back to Baton Rouge tonight," John apologized. "There's too many things I have to do. Tell Ellen it was good to see her again, and that I'm sorry I couldn't stay. I'll see you tomorrow."

The two men shook hands and John got out of the Jag. Frank pulled out of the lot. John climbed into his car, pulled out of the parking lot, and headed back to Baton Rouge. He had a problem. He had hoped to be rid of the money by tomorrow morning at the latest, and now he was stuck with it. What bothered him more was that his friends would be calling in for confirmation and would be told nothing had been deposited into their accounts. A loose end that had to be fixed.

He would call them in the morning. All the way back to Baton Rouge he worked on this problem, and when he arrived at his motel, he had come to a decision.

He would call Cecil first and explain the situation. Cecil would have three options. First, John could take the chance and ship his portion via UPS. Second, John could keep it with him and hold it in Maine until Cecil came for it. Or third, John could deposit it directly on the island at some later time.

Next would be Tom. John decided one possibility would be to drive through Atlanta on his way north and drop Tom's share off with him. That appeared to be the best solution for Tom's share.

Lastly, he would call Jackie. They would be together soon so that would be the least of his problems.

He reached his motel in Baton Rouge and backed the Honda up to the front door to his room, locked it, checked the trunk, and went inside. It was after eleven o'clock.

Frank arrived back at the house and pulled the car into the garage. When he entered the kitchen, Ellen and Bertha were sitting at the kitchen table, drinking coffee. It was obvious they had been waiting for him.

"Hi," he greeted, going to the refrigerator for something cold to drink. "Um, John's gone back to Baton Rouge. He said he had too many things that needed to be done and asked me to tell you he's sorry he won't be staying over."

He looked at both women and sensed something was wrong.

"What's the matter?" he asked innocently.

Ellen looked at Bertha. "You tell him."

Bertha crossed her arms in front of her. "Mr. Cyr, sir, dat man's trouble."

Frank stiffened instinctively. Bertha sensed things. He sat down at the table and asked the two women to explain themselves.

"Go on," he said warily.

Bertha shrugged, leaned back, and stretched her legs out before her.

"I don' know, Mr. Cyr, sir. I just touched him, you know, shook his hand? And I felt it."

"Felt it?"

"Yes, suh. Good things is goin' ta happ'n ta him, but bad things is goin' ta happ'n too. Dat man goin' to see much sadness."

"How? How is he going to see this sadness?" Frank asked.

She started rocking back and forth, crossing her arms in front of her, holding her sides tightly; her eyes closed.

"I don' know. Just is. Dat's all I see'd," she finally said, opening her eyes and cupping her hands around her coffee cup. "Dat's all I know'd."

The three of them sat there. Finally, Ellen spoke. "What should we do? Should we tell him?"

Frank stood. "I don't know. He'll be here in the morning. Let's sleep on it. Will you be here tomorrow?"

Bertha shook her head. No, Mr. Cyr, sir. Tomorrow, me and my kids is goin' down to Delacroix to be with my sister. She be givin' birth soon. Miss Ellen say it be okay."

Frank looked at his wife who nodded.

"Well, we need to get you two together again. Maybe you can see something else. Maybe—"

"Don' know 'bout dat, Mr. Cyr. Sir. Maybe see somethin', maybe not. Anyway, I best be getting' on. It's late. I got a bus to catch. Gotta be home fo' Maurice go to work."

"Let me drive you home, Bertha," Ellen insisted.

"You sho' it won't be no trouble?" Bertha asked.

"Don't be silly. Frank, I'll be back in a while."

Frank was asleep when she got back.

The sound of voices in the next room woke John at seven in the morning. He rose, showered, shaved, packed his things, and loaded them into his car.

He walked over to the diner and ordered a light breakfast, checked out and drove off, looking for a phone booth along the way. He found one and called information and had the phone company put the call through to Chicago. He caught Cecil just as the big man was leaving for work.

"Cecil! Glad I caught you. It's the major."

Cecil tensed. The major had never called before. The rule had always been: no direct contact.

"Yes, sir?" he asked tentatively.

"Sorry to call this early, but there's been a slight change in plans. My contact was not able to accept delivery of the parcel," John went on, "that leaves me with a little problem."

"Go on," Cecil said anxiously.

"Three options: UPS it to you, you pick it up at a later date, or three, I deliver it to its destination at a later date by other means."

Cecil pondered the three options. "What happened?"

"Let's just say things aren't as easy as they used to be and leave it at that."

"Shit man, what am I goin' to do with—"

"I'll call you back tonight for your answer. If you decide on option one, I'll send along instructions in a few days in the usual way explaining how you can take care of it."

"Okay. I've got a bus to catch. Talk to you later."

John hung up first. Cecil gently put the phone down and stared at it. His two kids looked up at him from the kitchen table.

"Come on, kids, we got to be movin'. Daddy's got a bus to catch."

He dialed Jalene's number, and she answered.

"I'm on my way over."

Cecil turned the kids over to his sister and hurried for the bus stop. The bus was already there when he arrived.

He nodded thanks for waiting to the bus driver, dropped his token into the slot and found a seat.

Damn, he thought, *what the fuck I goin' to do with all that money? I ain't ready yet.*

John got back to his car and headed for another phone booth along the way. He would call Tom from there. He stopped in Gonzales, Louisiana and placed his call.

"Hello?" It was a woman who sounded as though she had been crying.

"Hello, is Tom there?"

"No, he's already left for work. Can I help you?"

"Could I have his work number please?"

The woman gave him the number. John wrote it down on the corner of the phone book and hung up.

That must have been Amy, he thought, and she didn't sound happy.

That bothered him as he dialed the number she had given him.

"Tom's Electronics."

"Tom, this is the major."

"Major!" Alarms went off in Tom's head.

"Sorry to bother you, but I've got a little problem."

John explained what had happened in the same cryptic sentences and gave Tom the options. When he was done, Tom spoke quickly.

"By all means, deliver the package in person. It'll be great seeing you again. You can deliver it here to the store. I'll give you the address."

John fumbled for something to write on and finally tore part of a page from the phone book.

"Go ahead."

Tom gave him the address and John said to expect him in a couple of days.

John wanted to ask him if there was a problem with Amy but decided against it. If Tom wanted to divulge anything, he would do so when they met. John hung up.

CHAPTER 30

Denver, Monday, July 9

Jack was up and moving by 6:00 a.m. He left a message at the front desk for Sally. She could meet him at Pete's office. He had things to verify and questions to ask. Yesterday, he and Alex had driven the entire route. Jack had made notes and taken Polaroid pictures of the areas around each of Alex's stops.

His hunch was right. Each time Alex received a phone call, there was another phone within sight of his phone. When there was a written message, there was no phone nearby. He ordered all the phones he could see to be dusted for prints and Tony De Marco had his detectives canvas the neighborhoods and question anyone who might have seen anything.

There was the question of Jeffrey Matthews of *Golf World Digest.* He'd know about that today. He wanted to interview Alex's recep-tionist. Maybe she could add something more to Alex's story. He also wanted to take Kendra up into the hills. Maybe they'd get lucky. It was asking an awful lot from a five-year-old to remember where she was kept, but then, Kendra was proving to be an extraordinary child.

The kidnappers had kept her for four nights and more than three days. There had to be something that the kidnappers had left behind. No one was that careful. No one was that good.

Jack walked the short distance to the offices of the FBI, arriving at just after seven.

"Morning, Thelma," he greeted as he entered the waiting room.

"Good morning, Mr. Donovan."

She buzzed him in and led him to the conference room. "Pete's inside."

Pete was sitting across the room, staring at the many sheets of paper taped to the walls.

"Pete."

"Jack."

Jack walked up behind Pete and stared at the wall.

Pete said, "I've been looking at this for almost twenty minutes now. It's amazing. Each move they've made, each step along the way, so precise, so calculated. It's like a military operation. Like a chess match. Sally was right. These guys are good."

"Tell me about it," Jack agreed. "I've been following these guys for six years now. In Houston, they picked up the kid at a day center. Rigged the phone lines from a block away. When the day care people called to verify release of the kid to a well-dressed man, it was rerouted to a female voice claiming to be the father's secretary, and she said it was okay to release the boy to him.

"In Detroit, they snatched a little girl from right under her dad's eyes at a ball game. Right in front of twenty-eight thousand fans in the stands, if you can believe that, and no one saw a thing.

"The dates of the kidnappings, the obvious coincidence with the kid's releases on the Fourth—it's like they're sending us a message." He patted Pete on the shoulder and walked around the table.

"Okay, let's put today's game plan together. I want Sally to interview Jennifer, the receptionist. I think you and I should take Kendra into the hills if she's up for it. And her mother should go along."

Sally arrived at seven thirty.

"Sally. I want you to interview the receptionist this morning. Maybe she can shed some light on this so-called Jeffrey Matthews character."

Jack turned to Pete. "Have we heard anything about his magazine?"

"Should hear pretty soon. Washington's two hours ahead of us. Thelma will put the call through to us when it comes.

Pete put the call through to Lisa McArthur. She agreed to bring Kendra and go with them to search for the cabin. She put Alex on the line, and he gave Sally permission to talk to Jennifer, saying he'd call ahead to set it up.

Pete assigned one of his agents to go along with Sally. They'd meet back at the office at four in the afternoon.

Sally arrived at Global at nine fifteen. Jennifer was expecting her. Sally and Bob, the other agent, followed Jennifer into the spacious conference room. It was bright and spacious. Through the windows, Sally could see a golf course fairway.

Jennifer invited the two FBI agents to sit. "I don't know what more I can tell you," she began. "I told everything I can remember to the police."

Sally removed her notebook from her purse. "I know. This is just for our records," she said, looking at her fellow agent and then back at Jennifer. "Anything you can remember about the man will be a big help. What he looked like, how he walked, how he talked. Did he have an accent? You know. Sometimes people remember things later that they had forgotten during the first questioning."

Jennifer sat back and crossed her legs. She gave Sally a description that pretty well matched what Alex and Lisa had given to the police.

"I do remember," she went on, "he was quite a charmer. He was smooth. You know, cool. Casual. There was something about him. I wouldn't say sexy, but…close. And he was soft spoken. I remember that. Just a nice man."

Sally wrote everything down. The more Sally learned about this man, the more intrigued she became.

Jack and Pete arrived at the McArthur residence at ten o'clock as promised. Lisa and Kendra were both ready and waiting at the door as the two agents drove up. Jack walked up the steps and greeted them both, then he sat down on the top step, inviting Kendra to sit down next to him. Lisa sat down next to her. Pete stood below.

"Kendra," Jack began, "did your mommy tell you what we are going to try to do today?"

"Uh-huh."

"Do you understand what we are trying to do?"

"You want to see the place where they took me," she said matter-of-factly.

"That's right. Now, do you think if we took this car and went back to the mountains that we might be able to find that cabin?"

Kendra shrugged. "I don't know."

Jack looked across at her mother. Lisa nodded.

"Honey," she explained, "these men think it is very important to find this place where you stayed."

"Okay."

"Would you like to ride up front with Mr. Jordon, or would you rather ride in the back with your mom?"

"My mom."

"Okay, then. Are you ready?"

"Yes."

"Pete, you drive. Kendra, do you remember which side of the car you were in when Aunt Julie and the older man brought you to the Villa?"

"I sat behind the older man. He was driving. Aunt Julie could turn and talk to me."

"Good."

Jack rose and opened the back door for Kendra. When she was safely strapped in, he went around and climbed in the front seat. Kendra was barely able to see out the window, but she managed. This worried Jack somewhat, but he pressed on.

"Let's go," he instructed Pete.

"I can save us some time," Pete volunteered. "We can catch Hampden and just go west instead of going north to the Villa. I'll just pull off at Wadsworth so she can get a reference."

"Sounds good."

Kendra proved to be quite talkative. Jack led her in the conversation, and she was able to tell them more about her stay at the cabin. She talked about the things her abductors said and did with her. She described the cabin in more detail, and she talked about the woods like they were her own backyard. In this way, the time and the miles passed quickly, and before they knew it, Pete pulled off Hampden onto northbound Wadsworth and stopped at the first light.

"There's the stores!" Kendra pointed out excitedly. "I remember. We had to stop at this light, just like now."

Pete pulled into the left lane and made a U-turn and headed back south on Wadsworth, turning west and onto the ramp to westbound Hampden. Kendra had passed her first test.

They crossed under the bridge that was part of the new C-470 highway under construction. Kendra remembered. Through the hogback, they drove and up into the hills they climbed.

"Look!" Kendra yelled. "There are the red rocks, Mommy."

To her this was becoming a game, and she was playing it quite well.

"There's the fence in the road," she pointed out as the metal crash rail came into sight. They stayed in the right-hand lane, driving at a reduced speed. The cars were lining up behind them, and each time a passing lane appeared, the cars and trucks flew by them. Some of the drivers were quite impatient. A few gestured rudely. Horns honked and headlights flashed.

"You've got some pretty rude drivers out here," Jack commented. "They're just as bad as the DC drivers."

"Well, I *am* going pretty slow," Pete confessed.

"Even so—"

Wait!" Kendra shouted.

Pete pulled over as close to the edge of the road as he could and stopped.

"What is it?" he asked.

"I think we just passed the road," Kendra said to him.

"Are you sure?"

"I think so."

Pete looked behind him. It would be impossible to back up and turn onto Parmalee Gulch Road from where he was, and he couldn't turn around.

"I'm going to have to drive up to South Turkey Creek to turn around," he told Jack. "It's no problem."

"You're doing so well," Lisa complimented her daughter. "I'm so proud of you."

She reached over and squeezed her daughter's hand.

Kendra looked up at her mother and grinned broadly.

"Yes, Kendra," Jack added, "you're doing great."

Pete turned off onto South Turkey Creek and crossed under the highway, then headed down the mountain, turning left onto Parmalee Gulch Road.

"Are you sure this is the right way?"

"Uh-huh. I remember that thing back at the corner."

"That thing" was a stone gate post. Something close to a gate on the side of the road.

"Now we need to look for a driveway on the right," Jack said, looking at his notes.

They drove on for about four miles. Jack turned and looked at Kendra.

"Do you see anything that looks familiar?"

She shook her head. "No."

"It's okay, honey," her mother reassured the little girl, "we can turn around and go back. Maybe you'll remember."

Pete checked his rearview mirror and made a U-turn then headed back toward Highway 285.

"When you see something you remember, just speak up," Pete instructed her.

"Okay."

Slowly Pete retraced the route they had just taken. Kendra sat up straighter in the back seat of the car, looking out her side window, then across through her mother's window and then back through her own window again. They retraced for over a mile.

"Anything yet?" Jack asked.

She shook her head.

Pete kept driving.

"Wait! I remember that gate!"

"You mean that gate over there?" Pete asked, pointing to an H-shaped gate with a small sign hanging from it.

"Yes. I think the other road's back there a little ways."

"All right," Jack said.

Pete turned around and slowly drove back up the road.

"There!" Jack shouted, pointing to the side of the road up ahead. "What do you think?"

Pete stopped the car at a very narrow dirt driveway. Jack got out of the car and approached the path, kneeling to inspect it closer.

"Pete! Come here!"

Pete got out of the car and walked around to where Jack was squatting and fingering a partial tire track heading into the woods. Pete knelt next to him. The two men straightened and started walking away from the road. All of a sudden, the tracks stopped. Just like that, they just disappeared.

"I think we found it, Pete, I think this is it."

They turned and walked back to the car. Lisa rolled down the window.

"I think Kendra's found it," Jack informed the two females in the back seat. "Pete? Take us in, but be careful not to mess up that track."

Pete backed the car up and turned into the almost invisible driveway and carefully drove into the woods.

"There it is!" Kendra yelled. "There's the cabin!"

The four of them sat in the sedan and stared at the building. Then Jack slowly got out of the car and approached the building. The others followed behind him.

"Come on, Mommy," Kendra said excitedly, taking her mother's hand, "let's go find some deer."

Lisa looked at Jack.

"Go ahead. Pete and I want to look things over for a while. Can you be back in fifteen minutes?"

She looked at her watch. "Sure. Be back at noon."

Jack and Pete watched as Kendra led her mother to the back of the cabin and then the two agents slowly began their walk around the cabin. The cabin was boarded up, just as Kendra had said. It looked undisturbed. In fact, it looked like no one had been near it for years, save for the slight disturbance on the ground where cars could have been parked.

They walked around to the back of the cabin. There was an old porch. Pete climbed the steps and peered through the boarded-up window in the door. There was the outhouse, just as Kendra had described it. Like the front yard, the back appeared to have been untouched for years, except that the back porch had been swept recently. Jack bent and looked under the porch. The ground looked like it, too, had been disturbed recently. Jack knelt and looked under it further. He got down on his hands and knees and crawled closer.

"What is it?" Pete asked, coming to the top step.

"Ground's been dug in recently."

Jack rose, brushed the dirt off his hands and knees and walked down to the outhouse. Opening the door, he snapped his head back. The odor told him that the place had been recently used. Not once, but several times by the look and smell of it.

"Shit," he said to Pete, who had approached behind him.

"Shit?"

"Yeah, shit. Recent. Pete, we found it"

They were walking back to the cabin when Kendra and Lisa appeared.

"I've got to go potty, Mommy," Kendra said and ran off in the direction of the outhouse.

"Kendra?"

"It's okay, Mommy. I've used it before."

Lisa looked at Jack and Pete for reassurance.

"She'll be fine. They even left a roll of paper behind."

The two men immediately looked at each other.

"Kendra!" Jack shouted. "Wait!"

He caught up with her just as she was about to enter.

"How bad do you have to go?" he asked her.

"Pretty bad," she said, scrunching up her nose.

Lisa caught up with them.

"You have any tissues in your purse?" he asked the mother.

"I think so."

She looked. "Yes. Here. Kendra, use these."

"Thanks, Mommy."

She looked at the two men standing next to her mom but did not move.

Lisa smiled and turned to Jack. "I think she wants us to leave."

"Oh," Jack said, catching on, "We'll be up there, okay?"

The little girl nodded, and when the three adults started to walk away, she entered the little building.

"Phewy!" she shouted. "It stinks!"

"She's amazing," Jack said to Lisa. "I've never met anyone quite like her before. Even my kids aren't that smart. And I think they're geniuses."

"You have kids?"

"Two boys."

He gave her a brief description of his own sons as the three of them walked back to the cabin. Jack and Pete continued on around the building while Lisa waited by the porch steps for Kendra to finish.

"I want this place gone over with a fine-toothed comb," Jack instructed his counterpart. He spread his arms to include the surrounding woods.

Have your men search out at least..." He hesitated. Make it at least a couple hundred yards in all directions. If they left paper in the john, they might have gotten careless elsewhere.

"Find me something, Pete. Find me something."

When the two agents had completely circled the cabin, Lisa and Kendra were walking up to the back porch.

"Kendra," Jack said, kneeling in front of the little girl, "you did wonderfully. And because you were so good, I'd like to buy you lunch. What would you like?"

A big grin appeared on her face, and she cried out, "A Happy Meal!"

Jack looked up at Lisa for permission and received a smile and a nod.

"A Happy Meal it is then."

He stood, took Kendra's hand and the four slowly walked back to the car.

"Pete," Jack addressed the agent when they were all settled in the car, "I want a crew up here today. And I want you in charge of the investigation. I'm going back to the office. I need to check on some things. Oh, and get a plaster of the tire print. I want to match it with the tires on the rental. It looks like there might not be too much to match the suspects to the scene. I need all the help I can get.

"You're the boss."

Sally was at the office when Jack arrived, after dropping off Kendra and Lisa and her Happy Meal.

"By the look on your face, I'd say you found the cabin," she said before he could open his mouth.

"Yep. Little Kendra took us right to it. Pete's gonna take a crew up there this afternoon."

"Congratulations, Jack."

Jack wrote down the address of the cabin and handed her the note. "Find out who owns this cabin. I can't believe anyone could stumble upon it by accident. They can't be that lucky. How 'bout you? Were you able to get anything new from the secretary?"

Sally reviewed her notes with her boss. He added a few things to the wall.

"Oh," she continued, "Washington called. *Golf World Digest* doesn't have a Jeffrey Matthews on their staff. And there are one hundred eighty-three Jeffrey Matthews in their database. They are weeding through them for a match as we speak. They'll get back to me."

"Another dead end."

"Maybe not. Jennifer gave me his business card. Maybe he left prints on it."

She smiled as she produced a little plastic bag with the card inside."

"Great! Good job, Sally. Now let's see what else we can add to the wall."

They worked through the afternoon, adding and rearranging their information. All the while, Jack's mind was at the cabin. He was hoping the crime lab boys would find something inside those four walls. His people had to be better than the kidnappers.

By three o'clock Pete was back at the cabin with a team of three crime scene investigators. There were also two FBI agents. Pete and the two agents took on the task of scouring the woods while the three investigators worked the cabins. It was hot, it was dry, and it was dirty work. Neither Pete nor the two agents were dressed for this kind of work. Traipsing through the woods was tough, and by five o'clock, their suit pants were torn and dirty. Pete agreed to sign chits for reimbursement costs for new suit pants. The three agents would be back tomorrow dressed appropriately.

They stopped back at the cabin, said goodbye to their investigators and headed back to Denver. They arrived at headquarters at six fifteen. Everyone at the office had gone home. Pete stuck his head into the conference room and saw the work that Jack and Sally had done. He was impressed. There was a noticeable amount of information added to the already spreading sheets of paper on the wall. He slowly started at the beginning and reviewed everything. It was after seven when he called his wife and told her to put the coffee on, his way of saying he was coming home.

CHAPTER 31

New Orleans, July 9

John called Monday morning and apologized to Ellen and said he would like to spend the day with them at the house. He could do his business there.

She said she'd be glad to have him.

John spent Monday night with the Cyrs and left Tuesday morning, promising he'd bring Jackie for a visit in a few months. Ellen had given him some time alone by the pool on Monday and John came up with a plan. All he needed was for Mike Morris to agree with it. He'd approach him when he and Jackie passed through Boston on their way to Ellis Bay. Nothing was said about Bertha's premonition.

Taking US 90 out of New Orleans, through Pascagoula and up into Mobile, John finally stopped for lunch. Then he grabbed Route 65 up through Evergreen and Greenville, stopping for the day in Montgomery, Alabama. He still had the temporary license paper taped to his back window. He needed to get rid of it. An out of state temporary was far too noticeable, especially one from as far away as Colorado. He needed to blend in, so, in Montgomery he made his first switch. It was simple enough. He would do this twice more before he got rid of the car. Tomorrow, with the now stolen plates attached to the Honda, he would shoot up Highway 85 into Atlanta, arriving early in the afternoon.

The drive was pleasant, a far cry from the miles and miles of nothingness that was eastern Colorado and Kansas. He passed through luxurious forests, cornfields, peanut farms, cattle grazing lands and cotton fields.

John put in several calls to Cecil from a phone booth down the street from the motel. It was eight o'clock in the evening when they finally connected. Cecil apologized, saying he took in his nephew's baseball game and just got home.

"Yeah, I been thinkin' 'bout it," Cecil answered when they finally got around to what to do with the money. "If you can find a way to get it to its proper location then go for it, man. I got no way to store it here. 'Sides, I'm not ready for it yet."

They talked for a few more minutes, and John hung up.

"Well, that solves one problem but creates another," John said, placing the phone in the cradle.

Atlanta, Wednesday, July 11, 3:30 p.m.

John pulled up in front of a modest storefront on Magnolia Street, just off Childress in East Point, and parked. The sign read TOM'S ELECTRONICS, with the address and phone number painted below it. On the front window, Tom advertised his repair service. *All work guaranteed* was written on the bottom.

He leaned over and looked out the window of his Honda through the front window of the store. He could see Tom talking to a customer. He waited and soon Tom and the customer emerged from the store. Tom was carrying a television. When he stepped out of the door, a gust of wind blew a piece of paper that had been taped to the top of the set and sent it fluttering down the sidewalk. The customer immediately chased it and caught up with it in front of the next store.

Tom spotted John through the windshield and grinned broadly. The customer returned carrying the receipt and instructed Tom to load the television into the trunk of the car parked in front of John's Honda. When this was done, and the customer had pulled out into traffic, John got out of the Honda and greeted him. The two went into the store.

After some small talk, Tom suggested that John drive around to the rear of the store to unload the delivery. Tom would meet him in back.

"It's okay. I've got my own private little delivery dock back there."

John followed Tom's directions and backed up to the dock. Tom had two empty boxes by his side by the time John arrived.

"We can load these straight from the trunk," Tom suggested.

Together they filled the two boxes with Tom's share of the ransom money. Each carried one box into the back of the store and set it on the workbench. Tom got some tape, secured the boxes, and addressed them to his store address, then set them on a shelf along with various other boxes. It all looked innocent enough.

"Well, I guess that's that," he said, approaching John. "I'm done here in about an hour. Care to come by the house? Amy makes great fried chicken."

"You're sure it'll be okay? She, um, didn't sound too happy when I called before."

"It'll be fine. Where are you staying?"

"I don't know yet, I came straight here when I got into town."

"Well then, by all means, you're staying with us. I'll call Amy and set it up."

John was grateful. A home cooked meal and a quiet bed sounded appealing.

"Okay, thanks—if you're sure it won't be any trouble."

"No trouble at all. Come on out front while I make the call."

"Hi," he heard Tom say. "I'm bringing a friend home for dinner. We still having chicken?"

There was a pause. "Um, yeah, and he's staying overnight. Could you get the guest room ready?"

Another pause. "Well, could you get it ready? We'll be home in an hour. Yes…"

Amy said something, and then, "That's a good girl. Okay, bye."

John walked over to the counter. "Everything okay?"

"Yes. Sure. Fine."

John was about to say something when Tom blurted out his confession.

"She's been having an affair."

John was taken aback.

"It just started, I guess, while we were out in Denver. One of the doctors has been sniffing around her for some time now. She used to joke about it to me. She thought he was cute in an innocent sort of way."

He continued, his voice a little quaky. "Well, one thing led to another, and he invited her out for drinks and talked her into going up to his apartment. You can figure out the rest. The night I came home, she wasn't. Didn't get in until four thirty in the morning. She lied to me when I asked her where she had been. She said she was working late. I called the hospital at 2:00 a.m. and they said she had left at ten.

"We're kind of living together under a sort of truce now. She told me all about it, and she says she's sorry. She blamed my being away for her weakness."

John felt terrible. One of the reasons he would have liked his people to be single was so that something like this wouldn't happen. When they were on a job, they had to stay focused, and when they weren't, mistakes happened. He didn't want any complications.

"Tom?"

"Yes?"

"When we get to your house, just introduce me as the major. Will you? No names, just let me do the explaining."

Tom looked him in the eyes. "Okay."

"Not that it's any of my business, but do you still love Amy?"

"Yes, I do. That's why it hurts so much."

John continued. "Tom, when we get to your place, let me do the talking. Let me explain how we came to know each other. You just listen. I think I can solve more than one problem tonight. Trust me, okay?"

"I always have, why stop now?" he said.

"Good. Let's go get us some of that fried chicken you've been braggin' about."

Tom locked the doors early with a note saying he'd be open at the regular time in the morning. John followed him home.

Amy proved to be a charming and pleasant hostess, and her fried chicken was every bit as good as Tom had said it would be. Over coffee and homemade peach pie, John got serious.

"Amy, I need to tell you something, and what I'm about to tell you must never leave this table. Do you understand what I'm saying?"

She looked at the seriousness on John's face, looked over at Tom and saw the sober expression on his face and returned her gaze to John. She nodded.

"Amy, your husband and I were stationed together at various locations around the country while we served in the Army. Did you ever hear about the Special Forces?"

She nodded. "I knew he was in that branch, but he never really talked about it."

"That's good. He's not supposed to."

John pulled his chair closer to the table. He took another bite of his peach pie.

"Yum, this is delicious. Did you make this, too?"

"Scratch," she boasted.

"Delicious. Anyway. When I 'retired' from the Army, I really didn't retire from government service. We set up a super-secret agency that even the FBI and the CIA aren't aware of." He lowered his voice. "I…" he said, looking directly into her eyes, "we…answer only to the president. We've been operational around the world now for about seven years.

"Because of your husband's unique background and training, especially in electronics, he has been invaluable to us. That's why he…can I use the word…disappears…from time to time.

"What he has done for the government of the United States cannot be measured by any medal or commendation or by any amount of money. But the government does recognize the risks and the sacrifices he has had to make.

He looked over at Tom who had the trace of a grin on his face.

"Tom was personally recruited by me, and each time that he was summoned, Tom responded unselfishly and willingly. I wish that those words could be shouted from the rooftops and printed in big bold letters in the newspapers, but they can't."

He took a deep breath before continuing, drawing closer to her as he said, "What the government has done to recognize his value and the value of others just like Tom is to set up a sort of monetary fund for him. Beginning this month, and for every month for, well, for a long, long time, cash money will be delivered to Tom's work. It may be two thousand dollars a month, it may be three or four or five the next, but every month, a nice little sum of money will be delivered to his business. This money will then be deposited in the bank by him. Of course, he'll have to pay taxes on it, just like normal people do, but that's just the American way of doing business. There will never be over five thousand dollars delivered at one time. We don't want the banks to become overly interested in his deposits. After all, Tom runs a small business, and too much additional income will send up red flags. There will be a separate set of books set up by our accountants to justify his deposits. This is the government's way of saying, 'Thank you, Tom, for a job well done.' Tom, as of now, you are officially relieved of duty.

"Now, remember, you must never say anything about this to anyone for security reasons. Is this understood?"

Again Amy nodded. This time, her eyes were like saucers.

Tom looked over at Amy. She had an almost adoring look in her eyes. John sat back and took another bite of his pie.

"Delicious," he said again.

Later that night, as John lay in the guest room bed, he could hear the passionate sounds of lovemaking coming from the couple's bedroom. He smiled inwardly. Maybe now Tom would be happy.

CHAPTER 32

Denver, Wednesday, July 11

A little after four in the afternoon the call came in. Except for a half-used roll of toilet paper, the crime unit could find no physical evidence of anyone having stayed in the cabin recently.

True, there was little dust and the ground had been disturbed under the porch, but the place yielded no prints. There was no hair. The report on the tire tracks was still pending.

The owners of the cabin were tracked down through tax records. Taxes had been paid every year since 1970 by a family in Omaha, Nebraska. The cabin had been owned by a now-deceased grandfather, and ownership had passed down to the now grown grandchildren. No, they had never seen the property, they just knew that it had increasing value and continued to pay the taxes on it. They intended to come to Colorado to see the property eventually. Now they might have to come sooner.

The next bit of bad news concerned the business card that Sally had retrieved from Jennifer. The paper was that woven kind made to look like real linen. It was almost impossible to pull up prints from it, though the FBI was able to pull up a partial. It belonged to Jennifer.

Jack was beside himself with anger and frustration. They had gathered so much more information this time and had learned so much more, and yet, what did they really know?

Nothing, he thought. How could this team outsmart the FBI? Three times now they had pulled off what was beginning to look like the perfect crimes. But there was no such thing as a perfect crime. There was always something they did or didn't do to slip up. What was it with these people? Even the car rental people had screwed up in one way or another by not checking more thoroughly. Each set of identifications had come back bogus. There was no such black person as Floyd King from Cleveland, Ohio. Of the one hundred and eighty-three known *Jeffrey Matthews* in the database, only two were even close to a match, and they both lived in different parts of the country, and each could account for his whereabouts for the past two weeks. More dead ends.

Furious, Jack tore down the sheets of paper that he had so meticulously taped to the walls. He tore them in two, crumpled them and tossed them back against the walls.

Pete, Sally, and the other agents who had stopped by just sat there silently, not daring to speak.

"What are we missing?" Jack demanded. "What are we not seeing? There's got to be something! Come on people!"

He finally quieted down, pushed up his glasses and sat down at the head of the table and looked at his hands. They held crumpled bits of paper.

"Shit! Excuse me. Damn! Did I do this?"

He looked around the table. There were nods, but only Sally and Pete were looking at him.

He laughed. "Sorry folks. Guess I got a little carried away."

Jack opened up the two pieces of crumpled paper and tried to flatten them out. He looked up at his fellow agents.

"Pete, suppose you were the leader. You now have two million dollars in cash in your possession. It fills a large blue duffel bag. It's heavy, too heavy for you to carry around by yourself, unless you are a very large, strong man. What would you do with all that money? How would you get it out of town?"

Pete looked around before answering. "Well, first of all, let's say we divide it up. Maybe five hundred thousand each. That way it would not be so hard to manage. It would be possible to stuff it into suitcases, and the four could then fly out separately."

"Or they could take a bus," Bob cut in.

"All right, Bob," Jack continued, asking the agent sitting next to Pete, "What would you do?"

"I'd probably divide and separate. Myself, I'd probably take a bus to another city, let's say Colorado Springs, and then fly home."

"Sally?"

"I don't know if I'd divide up the money just yet. If someone handed me five hundred K, I might be tempted to part with some of it. There's been no unusual cases where large amounts of money have been spent right after the last two jobs. My bet is that the money is still together. Here in Colorado? I don't know. If It were me, I'd want to get it out of the state quickly. I'd probably rent another car or maybe even buy one. But I wouldn't buy a new one. Probably something older but in good shape

"Jack? We might want to notify the Banking Commission to keep their eyes open for any large bank transfers that go out of country—"

"Already done. So you'd drive it out of state?"

Sally nodded.

"Tom? How about you?"

"I'm with Sally. I'd probably drive it out of state. Less chance of discovery that way. Only, I'd have the other three along for the ride. Honesty among thieves? I mean, is that really true?"

His attempt at a joke went nowhere.

"All right. Tom? Check the rental agencies tomorrow for anyone who wants to go out of state. Or at least as far as Colorado Springs. Or up in Cheyenne.

"We've got to assume that they didn't fly the money out. Airport security would have notified us if they had spotted anything unusual. Let's hope they didn't miss anything.

"Anything else, people?"

Jack looked around the table. There were only blank looks.

"Sorry about this," Jack said, holding up the scraps of paper in front of him. "You've all got your assignments. Let's all meet here tomorrow afternoon, say, four o'clock."

The room cleared. Sally stayed behind and began picking up the crumpled papers from the floor.

"I must have looked pretty foolish, huh?" Jack asked.

"Well, Jack," Sally said, "we all need to let off a little steam sometimes."

"A little steam! I blew the whole damn teapot!"

"Yes, you did. You really did."

Atlanta, July 12

Tom peeked in on John at seven thirty in the morning. "Amy's leaving for work pretty soon. I've got to get to the store. You're welcome to stay as long as you like. Coffee's on in the kitchen."

He turned to go and then turned back. "And, John, uh, thanks."

John gave him a thumbs-up sign.

John had made his decision during the night. He was leaving. He quickly rose, put on his pants and shirt, and hurried down the stairs. Amy was just putting her coffee cup in the drainer.

"Good morning," he said, coming through the door.

"Major! Good morning to you. I hope you slept well?"

"Like a baby. Tom says you're off to work. I just wanted to thank you for your hospitality. Dinner was great, and I haven't slept so soundly since who knows when."

"Well, we are glad to have you. Will we ever see you again?"

"Hard to say. If I'm ever in Atlanta, I promise I'll look you up. Strictly social, though, I promise."

She walked over and gave him a big hug. "Thank you," she said and walked to the door.

John was pouring himself some coffee when Tom came through the kitchen whistling softly.

"Say goodbye to Amy?"

"Yep. Nice wife you've got. I hope—"

"We'll be fine, honest. That was quite a yarn you spilled last night. Almost had me believing it. But thanks, I guess that was your way of telling me what to do with the money. But what about the books?"

"Hey. You're on your own with them. I can't think of everything."

"But you're so good at it."

"I am, aren't I?"

John held up his coffee cup in salute.

"Major, thank you," Tom said, becoming serious. "You've helped me save my marriage. And you've made our future secure. If there's ever anything I can do for you, just let me know."

"What you can do for me is to forgive that woman and be happy together. Can you do that?"

"Done," Tom promised.

"Good. Now, if you'll excuse me, I'd like to shit, shower and shave and then get out of here. I've got a lot of country to see."

"All right then."

Tom offered his hand to John. "Good luck and God bless. Remember, the door is always open. Oh, and by the way, lock it on the way out."

By nine o'clock, John was gone.

CHAPTER 33

Denver, Thursday, July 12

The first real break in the case was called into the FBI headquarters at two thirty. Pete took the call from one of his agents. He immediately reached Jack at the Marriot with the news.

"Pick me up. I'll be downstairs waiting," Jack said.

In less than ten minutes, Pete arrived.

Pete explained the discovery to Jack as they headed south on Broadway. "It seems that a John Pickett rented a car on the fifth. He returned it the following day and asked if he could keep the car and drive it to St. Louis. The guy at the rental agency said no, but he did suggest that the man talk to his brother who owns a used car lot on South Broadway. The rental agent drove the customer to his brother's lot where this Pickett evidently bought a car. Paid cash for it. Four thousand plus. Used the name John Smith. The police are down there now talking with the owner of the lot. Tom's with them."

"Good work Pete. Maybe this is the break we've been waiting for."

The two FBI men arrived at the used car lot at three. Tom led the way into the little office. Sitting behind the desk was a large man. He stopped his narration when the two agents walked in.

"Tom, Tony," Jack said, acknowledging his fellow investigators, "what have we got?"

"This is Bob Vincenza. He owns the lot," Tom said. He then brought them up to speed on the questioning.

The fat man was obviously uncomfortable. "That's about it," he said. "He said he needed to get out of town in a hurry because some very bad people were after him. He paid cash from a briefcase for God's sake!"

Tony handed Jack the paperwork on the sale of the car. "Address's a parking lot just north of the Regency Hotel off I-25 and Thirty-Eighth Avenue. And John Smith didn't provide a driver's license."

"Well, Mr. Smith, alias John Pickett, alias whatever your real name is, looks like you finally made a mistake. I want a description of this car sent out across the country ASAP. If he says he's going to St. Louis, chances are he's heading north, south, or east from there. And either he's alone or he has the woman with him. This car probably isn't big enough for all of them. That means they did split up after all. He's probably alone, but we need to be on the lookout for him or them as a couple.

"Include the temporary tag in the APB, although by now he's probably driving on stolen plates.

"Tony, instruct your department to notify you if any stolen plate notices come across the desk. I want to know about them right away."

"You got it."

Jack turned to the fat man sitting behind the desk. "You think you might be able to describe the man to a sketch artist?"

The man shrugged. "I don't know. Maybe."

Jack looked at him. "Try," he said.

Turning to Tom, he said, "I want your sketch man on this as soon as possible."

"I'm already on it."

"Now, if you'll indulge me, I want you to tell this man and me everything that happened from the time this John Smith character showed up on your lot until he drove off."

"You guys can stay if you want," Jack said to the others in the room.

"I'm going back downtown," Tony informed the FBI men. "Come on, Kevin, let's go. Good luck, Jack."

"Thanks, Tony, nice work."

Tom stood. "You need me for anything, Pete?"

"Not unless you want to hear his story again."

"Well, I guess I'll head back to the office then."

Jack and Pete took the chairs previously occupied by Tom and Tony. Jack noticed how much lower he was sitting across from Vincenza. It caused him a little discomfort.

Mr....Vincenza, how 'bout you start at the beginning and go through the whole thing again."

"But I already told those other policemen," he said, looking down at his watch.

"And now you can tell us," Jack said.

Bob Vincenza let out a big sigh and began his story again. When he was done, the only thing he had left out was the actual amount of money John Smith had paid for the car.

"You did just fine, Bob. Thank you for your help. Someone will contact you to set up a time for a sketch artist.

"Pete, I guess we've got everything we came for."

The two men rose and shook hands with the fat man.

"Oh, and in case you think of anything else," Pete interjected, "here's my card. Call me."

"I will, I will," Vincenza agreed, obviously relieved that the interrogation was over.

He walked the two men to the door and watched as they got into their car, then walked back to his desk and sat down. He looked at his hands. They were shaking. He reached into his bottom drawer and pulled out a bottle of Jack Daniels and a glass and poured himself two fingers and tossed it down, then closed the bottle and put it away.

"Fuck!" he mumbled.

Back at headquarters, Jack was moving in overdrive.

"Pete, I need a road map of the United States."

He looked around the room. They were running out of room on the walls. "I guess we can put it over there."

Jack pointed to the wall behind the open door.

"And get me some little flag pins. I have a feeling we are going to be able to track this sucker now that he's on the move. Maybe we can anticipate his movements."

Pete nodded. "I'll have Thelma bring in the map and pins."

"Good. Call your wife. It's going to be a long night. And find Sally. She called this. She should be here."

Sally arrived at eight. "Hi, Jack. Pete. What have we got?"

I think we just got our first break in the case. Seems a man fitting our description and using the names John Pickett and John Smith bought a used Honda. Said he had to get out of town fast. Said some bad people were looking for him. Paid cash for the Honda out of a briefcase. An '86 Honda coupe. Claims he's headed for St. Louis.

"We've got an APB out for the car. I realize it's been a few days now, but if he's still in the car, he's going to show up somewhere. He's driving on temporary tags. That's one way. He may steal plates. My guess is he'll do it more than once. If he does, when the plates are reported stolen, we'll be able to pick up his trail."

"Pete's bringing us a roadmap of the US in the morning."

"Are you sure this is our man?"

"It's got to be. Either he's traveling alone or he's got the woman with him. It all fits. You called this one. I wanted you to know."

Sally said, "What can I do?"

Jack glanced at Pete, then looked at his watch.

"You know what? Let's do nothing. Everything that can be done is being done. The calls are being made. The descriptions sent. I guess we're done for the night. Pete. Go home. Sally? I'm going to get a bite to eat. Care to join me?"

"I had dinner, but I'll be glad to come along. I could use the company."

At their table outside the restaurant on the Sixteenth Street Mall, Jack sat staring off into the middle distance.

"Hello, Jack!" Sally said, leaning forward so she was in his line of vision.

"Oh, sorry. I guess I was zoning. Sometimes I like to just sit and watch people go by. It's fascinating. They come in all sizes and shapes and colors. Big ones, small ones, fat, skinny, tall, short, handsome and pretty, and some are downright ugly. But each one is unique. Each one has something that sets him apart from the others. That's what we've got to remember.

"Each time we've gotten a description of these people we've been led to believe something that wasn't true. For example, the girl was a redhead. The man was older; the other man was post-hippie looking. The photographer had a tattoo on his arm. The black man was bald and had a noticeable scar on the side of his head.

"All those things we were meant to see, right? But what do we really know?"

Jack held up his index finger. "Number one, the black man, Floyd. He was big. Six three, six four. Broad shoulders, heavy through the chest and middle. Big man. Probably works out, or used to. Probably has a job that is physical, or he works out to be big for his job. Maybe he's a bouncer. Maybe he's in construction. Maybe he's a security guard. They'd all have a reason to be big.

"Number two. The girl. Julie. We know she's white, probably five three, five four. Pretty. Attractive. Age varies. Description makes her in her early twenties. My guess is she's much older. Say early to midthirties. Stands to reason each of the others is that much older. So that means she's real good at makeup. My guess is she's a beautician or something like that. She probably helped with the others' faces.

"Number three. Charlie, the photographer. Chances are he's not a photographer by trade. My guess is he's into electronics. They needed somebody to do that. That makes him our surveillance man. The bugs. He probably made them from parts that are untraceable. He's white. He's six feet tall. He's in his mid to late thirties.

"And then there's our friend, Jeffrey Matthews, slash, John Pickett, slash John Smith, slash whoever. He's been described as being in his early thirties to midforties by Alex and Lisa, and by Bob Vincenza, the used car dealer. Kendra puts him in his early sixties. Makeup. But they all agree on his physical size and general appearance."

They were interrupted by the waiter. He set Jack's sandwich down in front of him. "Will there be anything else, sir?"

Jack held up his glass of beer. He had hardly touched it. "And one of these please. Sally?"

She nodded.

"So," Jack continued when the waiter was gone, "what does this Jeffrey Matthews, a.k.a. John Smith, do when he's not kidnapping children?"

He looked at Sally.

"Oh, I'm sorry. You were asking me?"

"Um, yeah."

"Hmm," she thought. Jack had analyzed the other three so well she knew she had to come up with something good for him.

She took another sip of her beer. "I guess he'd have to have some sort of a job where he had the time to create these kidnapping plots. They have been well thought out and planned. It takes creativity. He'd probably be some sort of planner. Some sort of job that would give him time to research the families he's tracking."

"Precisely. What else?"

"Well..." She thought for a moment. "He probably knows computers. I mean, how else could he gather the information? And computers would be a great way to communicate with his accomplices. My guess is they are spread out all over the country. Unless..."

"Unless what?"

"Could it be that each one lives in a city where the kidnappings take place?"

Jack hadn't thought of that possibility. Now he had something else to think about.

"It's possible. That could explain their knowledge of the city. But that brings up the question, "what if they were recognized? No, I'm going with your theory of different parts of the country."

"That'd make him self-employed."

"Right again."

"Shouldn't we be writing this down?"

"You mean for the wall?"

"Yes, I mean for the wall."

"I already have. At least, most of it. That's why I've got you. You fill in the holes nicely."

"Why, thank you, sir."

Jack finished his sandwich. "I'm gonna have another beer. You want something?"

Sally had been eyeing a chocolate concoction at the next table. "I'm going to do something I rarely do, and something I'll probably regret tomorrow. I'm going to have one of those." She pointed to the half-eaten dessert.

"Oh, my," Jack said. "That does look good."

He signaled the waiter. "We'll each have one of those," he said, pointing to the next table. "And I'd like coffee. Sally?"

"Me too, thanks."

When the waiter left, Jack resumed his profiling of the leader.

"So. He's self-employed. He's got to be fairly well off. The obvious answer is the money from the first two jobs. But I don't think so. Somehow he's got money of his own. I think the ransom money is stashed and waiting."

"What about the others? What about their finances?"

"I think he finances them and takes his cut from the split. I don't think the others have touched their shares yet. I'm betting all the money is still in one place."

"You think it's offshore?"

"Could be, although that would take a fifth or sixth member to pull it off. They'd need an insider at a bank. They might have used one in the past, but I don't think they can today. Since Biloxi, everyone is watching. It would be impossible to pass that much money at once. And it would take too long to do it a little a time."

"So he keeps the money with him. He's probably driving around the country right now with two million in the trunk. I'd be bonkers," Sally added.

"Probably doesn't bother him too much. I think this whole thing is a game to him. And he's damn good at it."

CHAPTER 34

Charlotte, North Carolina, Thursday, July 12, 2:30 p.m.

It was Tom who had given him the idea. By the time John arrived in Washington, the money would be gone. It was a simple matter of stopping at the local FedEx offices along the way. He would get some boxes, fill them with money and ship them home. Each stop in a city would find him at the FedEx or UPS store. He kept back twenty thousand because his funds were running low.

In Charlotte, John shipped the first box to Maine. It contained three hundred thousand dollars. From Charlotte, John drove north on 65 through Greensboro where he spent the night. In the morning he used the offices of the UPS and shipped another two hundred fifty thousand. He used fictitious names as the sender and bogus addresses for the sending points. They were sent to his general delivery address in Ellis Bay.

It was in Greensboro, North Carolina, that he switched plates for the second time. This time he exchanged his stolen plates with a set of plates from Virginia. The owner of this set of plates would have a lot of explaining to do when they were finally discovered.

From Greensboro, John drove east to Raleigh. Here he sent another three hundred thousand, using FedEx. He had now shipped more than half the remaining money.

Heading east, he caught Highway 95. At a town called Lamm, he turned north. He drove as far as Petersburg, Virginia, where he sent the next shipment. Four hundred thousand left for Maine from that location. He now had a little more than three hundred thousand to send. He would drive to Richmond and send the balance. He would also spend the night there and switch plates again.

John arrived in Richmond at four in the afternoon. The first thing he did was seek a FedEx office in the phone book. He also found a bed and breakfast section and called several before he was able to find one that had available space for the weekend.

Purchasing a street map of Richmond, John located both the FedEx office and the bed and breakfast. He drove to FedEx and shipped the last of the ransom money. He now had an empty duffel bag. He deposited it in the first dumpster he found.

He drove to the bed and breakfast. It was located in an older neighborhood. Large homes lined the streets. The houses and grounds were neatly kept. Large shade trees formed a canopy and shaded the street below.

The sign hanging from a post read, "BEAUREGARD'S BED AND BREAKFAST," and below that, "ESTABLISHED 1952," and below that, "WELCOME."

The house was a white, three-story Southern colonial with black shutters bordering the front windows. A covered porch extended to the sides of the house. Screen doors gave access to the interior. He took a room and paid cash for two days.

In his room he walked to the windows. Lace curtains covered them, and they fluttered gently in the afternoon breeze. He looked down at the yard and the street below. The room faced the front. Noticing his car in the driveway, he realized it would have to be moved to the back. The less the car was visible, the better.

John decided he would ditch the car when he got to DC. It had more than served its purpose and would soon become a liability. By now, the purchase surely would have been discovered. It would only be a matter of time before it would become a problem for him.

The next morning after breakfast John found the *Richmond Times-Dispatch* next to a chair on the porch and sat down to read. He found an article on page eight regarding the kidnapping in Denver nine days ago and read it with interest. It described the abduction of Kendra McArthur, the daughter of a prominent Denver businessman, and the subsequent investigation. It mentioned that they had found the cabin where the child had been kept, but no other specific information was given about the people who had committed the act. However, several leads were being followed up. The hunt had spread out to encompass the entire country.

John put the newspaper down on his lap and stared out at the street. He was surprised that the cabin had been found so quickly. He hadn't expected little Kendra to be able to lead them to it. But then, why not? She was very bright for her age. That led him to think back to all the things the four of them had said and done. Did they leave anything that the FBI wasn't talking about? Had they said anything that she might have picked up on?

"Would you like to see Richmond?" Molly, the owner of the bed and breakfast, asked him as she came out to the porch. "You can park your car in the back and I can drive. It would save me having to give you directions all the time."

"I'd love to," John said placing the paper on the table next to his chair, but what about the house!"

"Oh, I'll just lock up. It's slow this time of year, what with the heat and all. It'll be all right.

He parked his car in the back and the two of them were off. Molly took him all over the city, showing him various points of interest: parks, buildings, statues, and other places and things that portrayed the history of the city.

That evening, after returning home from their tour and dinner, John asked her where he could find a phone. He had to make several phone calls, he said. He had decided to stay on for a few extra days and needed to tell his people of his change in plans.

Molly offered her phone to him.

"They're all long distance."

"Just add it to your bill."

"You don't mind?"

"Of course not. Besides, I feel I owe you. I had such a lovely time today."

Later, John dialed long distance.

"Hello?"

"Jackie?"

"John?"

"Who else?"

"John! Where are you? How are you?"

"Whoa. Slow down, lady. I'm in Richmond, Virginia. Everything's fine, although there's been a little glitch in our plan. I'll tell you about it when you get here. How are things going?"

He listened while Jackie went on about her moving plans. She was able to sub-lease her apartment. The furniture would stay. She was packing when he called.

She had been busy at the studio. There were some last-minute retakes that needed to be done. They were furious that she had gone out of town and couldn't be reached. The actors insisted that only she be allowed to do their makeup. Production had been tied up for five days while they tried to locate her.

She pointed out that when she left, it was understood that production was finished. She had told them she just needed some time away.

They were very apologetic when she worked her miracles and the retakes were finished. She informed the studio that she was going away for an extended period but that she would let them know where she was when she got there. She promised them that she would be available by mid-October. This coincided with the start of production on the next film.

"So it looks like I'll be arriving in DC as planned on the twentieth. That's if you still want me."

"I can't wait."

John was enjoying his stay at the inn. Molly was a delight. For an older woman, she certainly had a lot of energy. He helped her do some repairs to the inn and otherwise spent his time relaxing. He cleaned the Honda from top to bottom, inside and out. In the evenings he and Molly sat on the front porch and sipped iced tea and chatted.

He left on Wednesday morning.

CHAPTER 35

Denver, Monday, July 16

Pete pulled the message from the fax machine at two in the afternoon. One hundred nineteen reports of stolen plates were reported since the request had gone out nationwide.

Jack was operating on a hunch. If this John Smith character was their man, he would switch plates more than once. When he started was important, but where was even more so.

Pete made copies of the fax for both Jack and Sally, and the three of them sat down to analyze the information. Of the one hundred nineteen stolen plates, thirty-seven had been recovered within twenty-four hours. That left eighty-two sets still at large. By matching the dates, the plates were stolen with the locations they were stolen from, they were able to eliminate another forty-one. Smith couldn't have gotten that far in so short a time. That left forty-one sets of plates to account for. The problem was, these plates were scattered all over the country. From Seattle, Washington to Montgomery, Alabama. From San Diego, California to Boston, Massachusetts, and thirty places in between.

But it was a start. At four o'clock another fax came in. Nineteen more sets of plates had been stolen. This time there was a connection. The plates that were stolen in Montgomery showed up in Greensboro, North Carolina.

Jack went to the map and stuck in a pin in Greensboro, North Carolina.

"Pete? You got any string in this place?"

Pete checked with Thelma. In a minute a ball of string was brought into the conference room.

"All right people, we've got a connection between these two points."

He continued the string from Montgomery to Greensboro and then stepped away from the map.

"It's possible he drove from Denver to Montgomery, but why? Drop off one of the others? The woman maybe? I don't think so. Both Alex and Kendra and ah, what's her name, Darlene, the babysitter, said the black man had a slight Southern accent. If our Floyd came from Montgomery, he'd have more than a slight accent. Charlie? Maybe.

"But let's assume for the moment that he is not there to drop anyone off. He has to have a reason to be that far south.

"Sally? Any ideas? Pete? Give me some help here."

"Sally stared at the map. "Biloxi!"

Pete stared at her. "Biloxi?"

"Sure. Money laundering. Some of Biloxi's banks were caught in a big scam a few months ago," Jack informed him. "But he can't use the banks in Biloxi now. He must have known that. It was in all the papers. So where else could he go?"

The three studied the map.

Sally spoke first. "What about New Orleans or Mobile? Time frame's right. He could have driven down there."

She stood and approached the map, stared at it. "Let's try this," she finally said.

She picked up some pins. "He left Denver on the afternoon of the fifth, we'll have to assume, because that's when he bought the car. Let's say he went back to the cabin to pick up the money and the woman. If he headed east, he'd probably stop...maybe here. That's assuming he took I-70."

She stuck a pin on the map at the Colorado/Kansas border. She looked closely and said, "Burlington."

She stepped back and studied the map again. "My guess is he's doing six to seven hundred miles a day from here on out. In order to get to, say, New Orleans, he'd head to St. Louis" She stuck a pin in that location. "Then he'd drop down to…New Orleans. From there up to Montgomery, then"—she checked the map again—"then through Atlanta and up to Greensboro."

"My guess is he's headed for New York. Their route would have put him there by the tenth or eleventh. If he spent time in any of these places, I'd put him into New York by Saturday or Sunday. Question is, did he drive through the south for a reason, or just to throw us off?"

"Good theory, Sally. Problem is, there are so many places he could go."

"Washington, Baltimore. He could have turned toward Chicago. He could be anywhere." It was Pete talking.

"Theories," Jack put in. "But it does make sense. Pete, how far is it to Burlington?"

"Three, four hour's drive maybe."

"Is it a big town?"

"Not really."

"Sally? Let's say you and I drive to Burlington tomorrow and see what we can find out. Pete, make arrangements for our return to Washington on Wednesday. There's not much more we can do here. I have a feeling we'll be closer to the action back there. Oh, and pack up all this stuff for me, will you?"

The two agents left Denver and headed east at 8:00 a.m. The plains seemed to roll on forever. Past Watkins and Bennett, past Strasburg, Deer Trail, River Bend and into Limon where they stopped for coffee. Then on through Genoa, past Flagler, Stratton, finally arriving in Burlington at around noon-time.

They had lunch at a small Mexican café and then started hitting the motels. They got lucky when they stopped at the Best Western.

"Yes," the clerk said, checking his register. "A man fitting that general description and driving a silver Honda registered here on the fifth."

"I remember because the man paid cash and used the name John Smith. He sure seemed like he was in a hurry. Left early in the morning."

Sally asked, "Was he alone or was he traveling with someone?"

"Alone if I remember rightly. Don't remember seeing anyone else with him."

"Did he go anywhere while he was in town?"

"Sent him over to the Sizzler there," the clerk said, pointing to the restaurant down the street.

"You're sure he was alone?" Sally asked.

"Think so. I didn't see anyone else, and when we cleaned the room the next morning, only one face cloth and towel had been used."

Jack pulled out the composite sketch of Jeffrey Matthews.

"Did the man look like this?"

The clerk took the picture and studied it. "It could be. I don't know. I really wasn't paying much attention to his face. What'd he do anyway?"

"We just want to ask him a few questions, that's all," Jack answered. "Thanks for your help. If you think of anything else, please call this number and ask for Peter Jordan." Jack handed a card to the man.

Outside the motel, Jack said, "Let's try the restaurant."

They drove over and asked to speak to the waitresses who were on duty the night of the fifth. Two of them were working. These two did not recognize the face in the drawing. There was a third girl on that night. She was scheduled to come on at four. Jack looked at his watch. Ten after one.

"Could we call her at home?" Jack asked, producing his badge.

The manager said, "Let me call her."

He came back a few minutes later.

"She said you could come out to the house. She lives about five minutes from here."

Sally wrote down the address and directions, and they left.

Doris was waiting at the front gate when they drove up.

"Hi," she greeted them as they walked from the car.

Jack introduced Sally and showed her his badge.

"My name is Jack Donovan. Thank you for seeing us."

She invited them into the small house. When showed the sketch, she said, "Yes, that could be him. Except his nose wasn't as broad and he didn't have any facial hair. And his hair wasn't as dark."

"You remember quite a bit for seeing him only once," Jack remarked.

"I remember him because he was so soft spoken and polite. And he was kind of good-looking, you know. He had great eyes. He had a good appetite too. Besides, he didn't try to hit on me like so many single male travelers do. And he left me a big tip."

Jack wrote Pete's number on another card and gave it to her. He took down her name, address and phone number and said someone else would be in touch. Doris walked them to their car.

"What did he do?" she asked. "I mean, your card says Washington, DC. That's a long way to come to try to find someone."

Jack said, "We think he might be involved with the kidnapping of a little girl in Denver a couple of weeks ago."

"Oh no," Doris said. "Is the little girl all right?"

"She's fine, but he got away with a substantial amount of money. Thanks again for your help. Someone will be in touch."

Driving back to Denver, Jack felt elation. A few modifications to the sketch and a new face would appear. Perhaps this was the real face, one that they could send across the wires.

"Sally, I've got to hand it to you. You've called all the shots so far."

She sat back and felt good. "I've got a good teacher."

"I don't know. These things aren't taught. You've got an instinct for this sort of thing. I felt that about you the first time we met. It showed in your psych evaluation. It's going to carry you far."

Pete met them back in Denver. "I've got you both on a 10:00 a.m. flight back to DC."

"Good. Thanks," Jack said.

Jack went to the map on the wall. "He was seen here, Pete."

He tapped the map with his finger. "Here!" He stepped back from the map, rubbing his chin with his hand. He pushed up his glasses and continued. "I've got to send somebody down to Montgomery and Greensboro. If we can get a positive ID down there, then we can begin to narrow down the country. We can rule out everything west of the Mississippi."

On their last night in Denver, Jack and Sally finally had something to cheer about. Pete invited them both over for a barbeque and they accepted. Sally got to meet Pete's wife, and the two of them hit it off beautifully. Pete and Jack sat on the deck and drank beer after the food and dishes were put away.

"There's going to be a spot opening in Washington in a couple of months," Jack told his friend. "Want me to recommend you for it?"

Pete hesitated. "Sounds good. Let me talk to Annie about it. She's got some pretty deep roots here. I think she's getting tired of being uprooted all the time. And the kids like their school."

"Sounds like you like it here."

"I do. And besides. I'm coming up on twenty-eight years with the bureau. Not too many more left. I'd kind of like to ride it out here."

"Well, from what I've seen, you can't do much better. I might be inclined to want to stay here if I had all this."

He took in Pete's yard. "Nice."

They said their goodbyes at the house. Jack and Sally would go straight to the airport from the hotel. Pete would head to Burlington with the sketch artist. He would fax the results to Jack in DC by the end of tomorrow's business hours. He would also ship all the wall notes in the morning.

"Nice people," Jack said as they drove away.

"Yes," Sally agreed.

At two thirty on the eighteenth of July, the plane carrying Jack and Sally touched down in Washington, DC. They had been away for two weeks. They went directly to the office. Jack called his wife and said he'd be home by five. Sally left him at four, promising to be in the office by eight the next morning.

CHAPTER 36

Washington, DC, Wednesday, July 18, 3:00 p.m.

John drove all the way to Arlington, Virginia, on Highway 95, then cut over to US 1 by way of South Grebe Road and made his way to Washington National. He parked the car in the long-term parking lot, wiped it down, grabbed his bags and stood waiting for the shuttle. When he reached the terminal, he called for a taxi and had the driver deliver him to the Airport Sheraton.

Walking up to the counter he said, "John Parks. You've got a reservation for me?"

The girl behind the counter punched some buttons. "Yes, Mr. Parks. Suite, right? And we're glad to have you back with us."

They went through the formalities, and she rang for a bellhop. Bobby appeared promptly.

"Hello, Mr. Parks. Welcome back."

"Thank you, Bobby. Good to be back."

"How long you stayin' this time?"

"Probably through the weekend."

"You're still alone, I see," Bobby observed as he pushed the elevator button. "But you've got a suite this time. Must be expecting someone." He gave John a knowing smile.

John just winked.

Bobby accepted his tip and left John staring out the windows.

Back where it all began, John thought. He began unpacking.

John called for room service and ordered a salad and bottled water. He had to get back on a regimented diet. For more than two weeks now, he had eaten fast food, fried food, good food, and bad food. He knew he had put on weight and he knew he needed to get back to exercising. He'd spend some time at the gym tonight, tomorrow, and Friday morning.

The salad and water arrived. It didn't look especially appetizing, but he forced himself to eat it.

The phone rang at 7:00 p.m.

"Hello?"

"Hi."

"Hello? Is anybody there?" he teased.

"Hello. It's me. Hello-oo!"

"Oh, hi. What's up?"

"I can be there Friday by three."

"I can't wait."

"I'll be coming in on United Airlines." She gave him the exact time and flight number. She sounded excited.

"Ooh, I can't wait," she said. "I miss you so much."

"I miss you too."

They talked for a short time, and all the arrangements were made. When she finally said goodbye, John was as excited about her arrival as she was. He changed, went down to the exercise room, had a strenuous workout for twenty minutes, showered in cold water, returned to his room, and went to bed.

Thursday, he spent the day touring Washington by taxi and on Friday he slept late.

After exercising and having a light lunch, he was back at the airport awaiting the arrival of Jackie's flight. It was two thirty. He sat at her gate and watched the people go by until the flight's arrival was announced. He watched as her 727 pulled up to the terminal and the telescope causeway was maneuvered into position, then waited as the passengers exited.

She came through the door wearing pale blue slacks and matching, sleeveless top. Sunglasses covered her eyes. On her feet she wore a pair of Birkenstock sandals. Her brown hair was pulled back in a ponytail. She looked gorgeous.

John rose when he spotted her and hurried to meet her. She was carrying a large purse and a travel bag. Jackie spotted him as he rose and attempted to wave. With the weight of the two bags on her shoulders, it was difficult.

He caught up with her, took the traveling bag and they hugged. She felt good in his arms.

"Did you have a good flight?" he asked as they finally started moving with the crowds toward the baggage pick up area.

"Pretty good. We had some turbulence over the Rockies, but other than that, it wasn't bad."

"Well, I'm glad you're here. I've missed you."

Jackie gave him one of those seductively knowing looks and smiled. "I'm glad too."

They retrieved her luggage and took a taxi back to the hotel.

"Mr. Parks!" Bobby greeted as he opened the door of the taxi.

"Bobby," he acknowledged.

"And this must be Mrs. Parks?" Bobby added.

"You may call her that."

"How do you do, Mrs. Parks. Just call me Bobby," he said as he helped retrieve her luggage from the trunk. "Welcome to Washington, DC, and welcome to the Sheraton Hotel. If I can be of service in any way while you're here, please don't hesitate to ask for me."

"Okay, Bobby, don't overdo it," John interrupted. "You can bring her bags up to the suite."

It was obvious that Bobby was admiring the woman. Jackie had a rich bronze tan on her arms and face. The top of her outfit was open just enough to give him a hint of what was inside, and when she adjusted her purse on her shoulder, it was no longer just a hint.

Bobby caught John staring at him and gave the man a quick wink. John didn't know whether to be angry or amused by his impertinence. He chose to smile at the bellhop.

The two guests followed Bobby to the suite. When he was gone, they came together in a warm embrace. He held her to him and smelled the sweet smell of her hair and neck. He kissed her and then held her at arm's length.

"You look gorgeous, and you smell wonderful," was all he could think to say.

She smiled that sexy smile of hers and pulled away, walked to the windows, and looked out at the view from their suite. She could see the airport in the distance and watched as first one, then another of the big planes came in and landed. John walked up beside her and stared out the window with her. She reached over and took his hand in hers.

"It never ceases to amaze me how something that big can even get off the ground, let alone fly," he said.

"I know what you mean," she answered softly.

"Why don't you go and freshen up. I thought I'd call down for room service. We'll go out for dinner later."

"Sounds good to me."

She went into the bedroom, and he could hear her moving around and unpacking her bags. John called down for room service and then sat on the couch. Soon he could hear the sounds of the shower running and Jackie's humming in the background.

He felt content. He didn't realize how much he missed her until he held her in his arms. That's when he made the decision. He wanted her in his life. For now and for always.

The knock on the door brought him back to the present. He sat upright on the couch, rubbed his face with his hands and went to the door. Room service was there with a bucket of champagne, caviar, and cheese and crackers. There was also a bowl of strawberries, a bowl of whipped cream and chocolate syrup warming on a burner.

When the waiter left John opened the bottle. It popped loudly.

"What was that?" Jackie called from the bedroom.

"Just a little welcome. I'm glad you're here cheer," he called back.

"Sounds delicious. I'll be out in a minute."

He sank the bottle of champagne back into the ice bucket and went to the window. A haze was settling over the airport and the bay beyond, and shadows were beginning to stretch.

He felt, more than heard, her approach, and when she put her arms through his and squeezed him from behind, he felt the electricity that this woman generated. He turned.

Her eyes were moist. "I can't believe I'm really here. With you…"

He pulled her hands to his lips and pressed her knuckles to them. "Let's have some champagne to celebrate your being here."

He led her to the couch and poured for both of them. "To us… to your being here with me…to the future," he toasted.

They sipped the champagne, nibbled at the snacks, and talked briefly about the weekend.

"I'd like to get to Boston by Sunday. We've got a barbeque to attend with some friends of mine that I'd like you to meet. I want to show you off. You'll like them. They can't believe I've got a woman at last and want to see you in person. I hope that's all right with you."

"I'm game. It sounds like fun."

"Good. I've got reservations for dinner downstairs. I thought we could stay close to home, and maybe have a quiet evening by ourselves."

"Quiet?"

"You know what I mean."

At ten o'clock they were back in their suite.

"I'm stuffed," Jackie confessed as she went to the couch.

"Me too. Want something to drink?" he asked, going to the refrigerator at the bar.

"No, thanks. I think I've had enough."

She giggled. "You don't suppose room service will interrupt us, do you?"

"Come on, let's find out."

They fell asleep together, and in the morning, they rose and showered together. There was no awkwardness, no embarrassment or self-consciousness between them, only the newfound easiness that being in love gave them. They toweled each other off and performed their morning grooming together in front of the big vanity mirror. Then they dressed for the day.

CHAPTER 37

Brookline, Massachusetts, Sunday, July 22, 1:15 p.m.

John's Corvette pulled in front of the Morris house, it's top down, it's two occupants red from the sun. John had briefed Jackie on what to say about their relationship and what they had been doing for the past month. Everything about their past life in the military was okay to tell. If asked, she was to say that John had been in California doing research for his book and had looked her up. They had gotten together, and one thing led to another.

Jeannie met them at the door.

"John! And this must be Jackie. Welcome to our home. Come in, please, come in."

"Mike! They're here!" Jeannie yelled through the kitchen.

Jeannie hugged each of them. "Mike's out in the back firing up the grill. Please. Follow me. Oh, it's so good to see you again, John."

"John!" his friend greeted as the sliding screen doors opened. "And, Jackie? So nice to meet you. Please, have a seat. Drinks? Jackie? What would you like? Wine? Beer? Something stronger? Iced tea or coffee? Soda? You name it."

The two guests settled on iced tea and sat. Jeannie brought the tea on a tray along with sugar and wedges of lemon. Later they had steaks, grilled, and potato salad, corn on the cob and ice cream.

The afternoon passed quickly, and it was time to leave.

"Thank you so much," Jackie said to her hosts as the two visitors made their way to the front door, "it was fun."

Jeannie gave each of them a peck on the cheek. Mike kissed her cheek and shook hands with John. "I like her," he said, nodding in Jackie's direction.

"So do I, Mike, so do I."

Jackie blushed.

"Keep in touch, buddy, don't be strangers," Mike said as they walked down to the car.

"I will, Mike, I promise."

Mike and Jeannie stood on the curb as the two friends drove off, waving until John turned the corner. "She's a keeper," he said to his wife.

"Yes. I'm so happy for him."

Back at their hotel in Boston, John took Jackie's hand and led her to the couch. "Honey," he started, taking her hand in his, "these past few weeks with you have meant so much to me. I don't know when I've felt so at peace and so happy. I know now that I can't go on without you in my life. Jacqueline Chandler, will you spend your life with me? Will you be my wife? Will you grow old with me? Jackie, will you marry me?"

Tears filled her eyes and ran down her cheeks. She pulled her hand away from him and wiped her eyes. She nodded her head up and down as she did this, the words not yet forming on her lips.

"Yes! Yes, yes, yes!" she said to him, throwing her arms around his neck. "Yes, I'll marry you!"

He looked at her and a radiance coming from within her being, a glow that shown forth in her smile and in her eyes.

"Tomorrow I want to take you to a certain little jewelry shop. I want you to help me pick out a diamond and a setting."

"Okay," she said through sobs of joy, "okay."

She leaned over and kissed him and then hugged him tightly.

"When?" she said softly into his ear.

"Whenever you want, Jackie. You just pick a date."

"As soon as possible is not soon enough for me," she answered.

They talked about dates and agreed on the Friday before Labor Day.

"While you and Jeannie were in the kitchen I talked to Mike. He's letting us use his boat for that weekend. It's down on the Cape. They'll come down Saturday and we can spend the weekend together."

"They knew?"

"Well, Mike knew. If Jeannie had known, she would have blurted it out. I wanted to ask you tonight. Mike was sworn to secrecy.

Tuesday morning, they drove back to Logan Airport, picked up the rest of her luggage and drove north to Ellis Bay.

CHAPTER 38

Ellis Bay, Maine, Tuesday, July 24

"Oh, John, it's lovely." Jackie gushed as she entered the house.

John picked up the bags and followed her in, setting the bags down in the middle of the living room floor.

"Come, let me show you around. I'll have to apologize for the mess. I wasn't expecting you to come home with me when I left. Anyway, there's no one here but me. I think we're going to have to find us a cleaning person to take care of the place."

John walked her through the cottage.

"Let me show you my favorite part," he said, taking her out to the back porch. "I spend a lot of time out here, just watching the boats come and go."

He stood behind her with his arms around her as she gazed out at the harbor and the sea.

"You want to freshen up? I'll bring in the rest of the bags and then we'll go into town and have some dinner."

"That's fine. Just show me where I can put my things."

"Oh yeah. I guess you're going to need some drawer space, huh?"

"Well, I can't continue to live out of my suitcase."

"You're right. Come on."

John made room for her in his dresser, pushed his clothes together in the closet and said, "Tomorrow we'll go into town and buy you some furniture and things. I think we can move some things around to give us more room in here."

"I'll be fine."

She twirled around. "So this is the real John Burton. It's sort of like I'd pictured it to be. I love it. Now, let me freshen up a little and we can be on our way."

They went to the Anchor Café for dinner. By the time they were finished, half the town was abuzz with talk about John Burton's woman visitor.

John introduced her to Annie, and Jackie was warmly welcomed. To the other patrons, she was a newcomer who had to become accepted slowly.

"Slow are the ways and the customs in this part of the country," John explained. "It took me a while to become part of the community. Don't you worry, though, they'll grow to love you just like I did."

Jackie looked at him adoringly. He had used the "L" word. After dinner they stopped at the grocery store for milk, coffee, juice, and other essentials, then headed back to the cottage. It was after nine when they finally got everything unpacked and put away.

"Come on," he invited, "let's go out to the porch."

He grabbed a bottle of wine from the fridge, two glasses from the cupboard and led her out. Together they sat and listened to the sounds of the water breaking onto the shore and the rock jetty in the distance. The last bit of light had disappeared over the horizon.

"Mm, this is nice," she murmured, sipping her wine. "I could get used to this,"

"I hope you do, my love, I hope you do."

Jackie and John rose early and had coffee and sweet rolls on the back porch. It was a little chilly. John offered her a flannel shirt.

The sun was still low in the eastern sky and reflected off the Atlantic. Fishing boats were heading out from the harbor, their engines droning on wearily as they passed the buoy at the harbor's entrance. The clang, clang, clanging of the bell on the buoy, as the boats' wakes rocked it back and forth, cut the air, the staccato sound vibrating across the water. A foghorn sounded, and then another, as the boats signaled while maneuvering their way out of the channel and into the vastness of the North Atlantic.

"Is it like this every day?" Jackie asked.

"Pretty much," he replied.

She listened to the shrill sounds of the gulls following the wakes of the various boats as they grew smaller in the distance. It was after eight when they went inside. The coffee was long gone.

"Well, lady, are you up for a busy day of shopping, fun, and frivolity?"

She smiled and nodded. "Should we make a list?"

"Good idea."

They sat at the kitchen table and drew up plans for the day's activities: groceries, furniture and, of course, the post office. John promised to talk to the phone people *and* he'd look into getting a computer and a modem and a fax machine.

"Somebody's going to have to teach me how to use those things," he told her.

"I can help," she offered.

Washington, DC, July 24, 3:00 p.m.

"You're not going to believe this!" Sally exclaimed, bursting into Jack's office.

He looked up from his desk.

"What?" he asked, slightly annoyed.

For a week now, there had been no new developments in the McArthur case. It was as if John Smith had disappeared off the face of the earth.

"They found the Honda!"

"Where?"

"That's what you're not going to believe. The DC cops found it right here at National Airport. It's been there since last Wednesday. Our John Smith, a.k.a. Jeffrey Matthews, left it in the long-term parking lot."

"Where is it now?"

"Still there. They just found it. Locals got a call from the parking company. Seems he got careless and double-parked. After a week they called the cops. The cops called us when the plates turned up stolen in Virginia. They want to know what we want to do with it."

Jack was out of his chair and reaching for his suit coat. "Let's get it brought in."

"Figured you'd say that. I already called. It's probably being towed now." She said, looking at her watch.

"Let's go," he said and was out the door, Sally almost running to keep up.

The car was just being unloaded in the garage when Jack and Sally arrived. Lights shone on it from above.

"Who's touched this car?" Jack asked the tow truck driver.

The driver, Ed, by the nametag on his shirt, shrugged. "Me and Bob loaded it onto the truck. Cops had it taped off. Keys were on the front seat. Bob jimmied it and we drove it onto the back of the truck. We followed SOP. Nothing's been touched."

"Good."

He turned to the head of the crime investigating unit. "I want this car gone over inch by inch. Everything. Inside and out. Under the hood and in the trunk. Get me something I can use."

He stood back and looked at the car and then walked around it. He returned to where Sally was standing.

"Sally? The man parks the car at the airport in the long-term parking area. He's smart. It could have taken weeks or months for us to find it. But he double-parks. It's like he wanted us to find it. Why?"

Sally shook her head. She walked around the car and stopped at the passenger side door. Looking at Ed, she asked. Keys?"

Ed tossed her the key. She put it in the door lock and turned it, then, using her hanky, opened the door and slid into the passenger seat. Without touching anything, she looked around, inspecting the driver's side seat, floor, sun visor, console, then the floor in front of her and the visor above. Using her hanky again, she carefully lifted the cover of the middle console. It was empty. She then opened the glove box.

"Jack," she said tentatively. "Jack, you've got to see this."

He hurried around to her side and squatted down next to her, looking into the glove box as he did. Inside was the ownership pink slip, and underneath it a note, neatly folded. There was nothing else in the glove box.

"Dick? You got your tweezers with you?"

"Here," the chief investigator said, handing Jack a pair of surgical-style tweezers.

Jack reached in and pulled out the pink slip. Sure enough, it was made out to a John Smith of Denver, Colorado.

"Bingo!" Jack exclaimed. "This is it!"

Dick held out a plastic bag and Jack dropped the paper into it. Next, he reached in and pulled out the note. In neatly printed box-style letters was a short note. It read,

HI, JACK,

BY NOW YOU KNOW THAT THIS IS THE CAR I USED TO GET OUT OF DENVER. THE CAR WAS LEGALLY PURCHASED WITH MY OWN MONEY. THE CAR IS NOW YOURS TO DO WITH AS YOU WISH. I'D RECOMMEND A GOOD CHARITY. GOOD LUCK.

JS

"Son of a bitch," Jack muttered, standing up. He reread the letter out loud to Sally and the other people standing around.

"Mighty generous of him," Dick volunteered.

Jack scowled at him.

"He did want it found," Sally offered. "And I bet the car's been wiped clean as a whistle."

"All right, people," Jack said, dropping the note into another plastic bag, "you know the drill. Everything possible he could have touched. Find me some prints. Hair. Broken fingernail. Something!"

"He's cocky," Sally said, getting out of the car.

"Yes, he is. Well, Mr. Smith, a.k.a. Matthews, you're going to make a mistake. And when you do, I'll find you. Let's hope your mistake is in this car."

He stood back and looked at the car again. He walked around to the back.

"Dick, pay particular attention to the back side of these plates. He may have wiped the front side clean, but maybe he missed the back side. Oh, and get a good dusting on the gas cap. And—"

Dick interrupted. "Will you get out of here and let us do our jobs?"

"Oh yeah, sorry," Jack said sheepishly. "Come on, Sally, let's get back to the office. I want to test your theory some more."

Jack had modified the wall notes to fit on the wall beside his desk. On the opposite wall was the large map of the United States, with the pins and string attached just as they had been in Denver. It was to the map that Jack led Sally.

"Let's follow your theory and see if we can backtrack from the airport. We already know that he took the plates in Greensboro. Now we find the car here in DC. He must have come through"—he stepped back to study the map—"Roanoke or Richmond."

He pointed to both cities, leaving his index fingers to cover both of them. "My guess, Richmond," he said, tapping that location. "It's the most direct route to get here. And I'm guessing he's in enough of a hurry to get here. What's your pick?"

"I'm guessing Richmond too," Sally said. "It makes the most sense, based on his previous route. Any bets that those plates came from there?"

"I'll stake my reputation on it. It's what, about a hundred miles from here? Tomorrow you and I are going to Richmond. Who's the station man down there?"

Sally thought for a moment. "Dick Garcia, I think."

"Call him. Tell him what we know. Tell him to expect us at about ten in the morning. Get his team together. We're going to canvas that town until we find someone who saw him."

The phone rang.

"Jack," the man on the phone said, "we've got a make on your plates. They came from Richmond, Virginia."

"I know."

"You know?"

"Sally told me. Thanks."

Jack hung up and smiled at his assistant.

"We're going to Richmond. See you at seven thirty."

Dark clouds covered the skies over the DC area. Jack looked up at the sky and frowned. If it rained, it would slow progress. He hoped that Richmond would be dry when he arrived.

He climbed behind the wheel of his Buick and backed out of his driveway. By mutual agreement, he was to meet Sally at the Village Inn just off the interstate. They would have breakfast and be on the road by eight or so. That would put them into Richmond by ten. That is, if the weather didn't screw things up. And those clouds did look bad.

They were on the road by eight fifteen. It had rained the whole time they were in the restaurant, but now, only a light, intermittent drizzle persisted. The splash back from the forward vehicles causes some difficulty until they were on the highway, and then things cleared up.

Richmond was hot and muggy but at least it was not raining. Jack pulled into the parking area, then he and Sally walked into the FBI office.

Dick Garcia, Station Chief for the eastern section of Virginia, met them at the door.

"Jack, it's been a long time," he said, greeting his visitor. And you must be Sally Martin?"

She nodded.

"How many men we got, Dick?" Jack asked, getting right down to business.

"There's four of us right now. More coming later. What have you got?"

Jack pulled out the latest sketches of John Smith, a.k.a. Jeffrey Matthews. He had a dozen copies.

"We think this is a pretty good description of our man. He's wanted for kidnapping in Denver. He was here sometime last week. Maybe for a day, maybe two or three. I want to talk to anyone who may have seen him and talked to him. Check all the hotels and motels. Man had money on him. Check and see if anyone saw this man flashing money around.

"I don't know. Check stores, amusement parks, whatever. He was here, Dick. That's been confirmed. I want him, and I want him bad. Sally and I are here to help. Let's set up a game plan and get going."

Dick brought the two people from Washington into the conference room, and Jack repeated what he had told Dick to the others in the room. By ten forty-five, the team of FBI agents were dispersing to their assigned tasks. Jack, Sally, and Dick would hit the motels and hotels along the highway figuring their subject would stay close it. Each of the others had a particular type of assignment that they would cover. They planned to meet back at the office at five thirty. Jack was sure the kidnapper had been in Richmond recently, and he was anxious to get started.

By two o'clock, they had covered all the travel stops along the highway. No one had seen anyone who looked remotely like their subject. They stopped for a quick lunch at a McDonald's and continued on. By five they were exhausted. Still, they had no luck. At five thirty, they arrived back at the office, hot, sweaty, tired and a little short-tempered.

They had been so sure. It all seemed to fit. The route the man took, the stolen plates; he had to have been here. One by one, the others drifted in. Jack could tell that they too had not had any luck.

"Nothing," each of the men reported to Dick who turned to Jack and apologized. "But it's only been a day. Maybe we'll get lucky tomorrow,"

Each member of the team summarized his day's activities to Jack and Sally. As usual, she took notes. When the last agent completed his report, Jack spoke.

"Sally and I have to go back to Washington. I appreciate what each of you has done today. And Dick is right. There's always tomorrow. This job could take weeks. We know our man was here. Somebody saw him. All you need to do is locate that person."

Turning back to Dick Garcia, he continued, "I'm counting on you, Dick. We found his car. We're going to find him. Good luck. Call me tomorrow if you turn up anything. I'll be down here quicker than flies on shit."

He rose and they all rose with him. Jack shook each agent's hand before leaving, and each member made a point of saying good-bye to Sally.

On the drive back to DC, Jack asked the same question he had been asking himself from the beginning. "What are we missing, Sally? What don't we see?"

"Jack, there are a lot more hotels and motels that we didn't get to check out. As smart as he's been so far, my guess is that he might anticipate us checking motels close to the highway. What if he came closer to downtown to stay? And what if he chose one of the surrounding towns? This could take weeks, maybe even months. There's only the four of them now, unless you can free up some people from Washington."

"You're right." He slammed his hands on the steering wheel. "Sometimes I feel like Don Quixote tilting at windmills. I guess the older I get, the less patience I have."

They drove on in silence. Jack dropped Sally off next to her car at the Village Inn.

"Cheer up, Jack. We're getting close. He's going to turn up sometime. See you tomorrow."

He forced a grin. "Good night." He watched her get into her car and then headed for home.

There was a message to call Dick Halburton when Jack arrived at the office the next morning. He immediately dialed the number.

"Dick, it's Jack. What have you got for me?"

"Nothing good. Car was wiped clean inside and out. Vacuumed pretty good too. My guess is he spent a lot of time doing it, or he used one of those heavy-duty commercial vacs you find at those self-service car washes."

Jack sank down lower in his chair. "You checked—"

"Everything, Jack. Just like you said. We found squat."

"Shit. Oh, well. Thanks, Dick. I owe you one."

"That's all right. Maybe next time."

Jack hung up and put his head in his hands. Every lead was turning into a dead end.

"You fuck," he said to the image of his nemesis on the wall. "You son of a bitch. You're out there and I'm going to find you."

"Hi, Jack," Sally said cheerfully as she stuck her head in the door. "Oh...bad news again?"

"Car turned up clean. Nothing."

"I'm sorry."

Jack wiped his face with his hands; the stress of the case and the weariness of the long hours were beginning to take their toll on him. Sally didn't know what to say. And so, she said nothing. Jack watched as she crossed the hall and entered her office.

Ten minutes later she was back in his office.

"Jack? He dropped the car off at the airport, right?"

He nodded. "So?"

"So...maybe he flew out of National."

"Of course! Why didn't I think of that?"

"Why didn't I think of it sooner?" was her comeback.

He grabbed the sketch copies from his desk and stuffed them into his inside pocket. The two agents headed out to the airport.

They spent the entire day interviewing the employees of the various ticket counters and gates at the airport. No one could be certain that they had seen the man who belonged to the face in the artist's sketch. There were almost as many employees off duty as there were on. Jack finally got permission to hang copies of the sketch in all the employee lounges and in the offices of each of the different airlines.

One of the airline companies let him make more copies of the sketch, and he was able to leave one at each of the counters below the computer terminals.

Under the poster he wrote:

HAVE YOU SEEN THIS MAN? IF SO, PLEASE CALL THE FBI AT 202-555-8713 AND ASK FOR INSPECTOR JACK DONOVAN OR SPECIAL AGENT SALLY MARTIN. A REWARD WILL BE GIVEN IF YOUR INFORMATION LEADS TO THE ARREST AND CONVICTION OF THIS MAN. HE WOULD HAVE COME THROUGH THE AIRPORT ON OR ABOUT JULY 15 THROUGH JULY 18. HE WOULD HAVE BEEN TRAVELING ALONE.

This was not normal FBI procedural protocol and the reward had not been authorized, but Jack was desperate, and timing was critical. He was certain he could get approval for the reward if this all panned out. In the meantime, he was stepping gingerly along the edges of propriety.

At the end of the day, they returned to the office. Their bid to find an eyewitness had failed, but Jack was upbeat. They had missed a lot of people today but with the flyers circulated throughout the airport, and additional manpower on the case, he felt certain someone would come forward.

At least he did not have that nagging feeling in his gut, that feeling that said he was missing something. For the first time in weeks, Jack was home in time to have dinner with his family. Sally stayed at headquarters. Jack let her use his office.

She brought all her files on the McArthur case into his office and dropped them on his desk, walked around it and sat down in Jack's chair. She pulled the picture of the suspect out of her file and placed it on top of the stack of notes and reports. She stared down at it, fascinated by the image that stared back at her. The more she stared at it, the more familiar the face became.

She was impressed with the description Doris had given to the artist. It was the most detailed rendition of the suspect that had been done so far. She compared it with the sketch that the McArthur family had given them. They were quite similar, but the newest one had enough subtle differences to make it stand apart. She put the older sketch back in her file and stared at the new one again. She touched the face with her finger, tracing the line of his chin and cheek. She placed her hand over the nose and mouth, so only the eyes, forehead, and hair were visible. She stared some more. She removed her hand and then covered the eyes and forehead. The nose, mouth, and chin were the only features visible. She removed her hand and stared at the whole face again. Her mind wandered, and she swore the eyes smiled at her. She slammed her hand down on it and then pushed the picture away from her. It slipped off the desk and fluttered to the floor.

"Damn!" she muttered and bent down to retrieve it. That's when the image came to her and she remembered. She was sure of it. She had seen him in the parking lot at the Villa Italia Mall in Denver.

It was his eyes. She remembered those eyes. She closed her eyes and remembered. He was walking with a woman. Alex and Lisa had said his eyes were brown, but Doris had said they were blue. She was positive of this, but she rechecked the notes to be sure. That fact puzzled Sally until she realized that he was probably wearing colored contact lenses. That would explain the disparity. He probably had blue eyes.

She picked up the phone to call Jack, and then put it back down. No, she would wait until tomorrow to tell him. Tonight, he needed to be home with his family. This could wait.

Shuffling the pile of notes, Sally put them all back inside her folder, stood, looked at the mess of notes on Jack's walls, turned off the light and left. It was nine fifteen. She left the building and walked to her car and drove home. For the first time in a long time, Sally felt alone.

CHAPTER 39

Washington, DC, Friday, August 17

"Jack? Dick Garcia. We've got a witness."

"Say again?"

"We've got a positive identification. We've got a connection. And we've got more."

Dick explained how one of his agents had been talking to a park ranger at one of the historic parks outside Richmond who remembered a man fitting the drawing's description. The reason the ranger remembered was because he was a friend of the woman who accompanied the man to the park. He said the man had stayed at her bed and breakfast.

Jack was on the elevator on his way downstairs before he realized that Sally needed to be with him for this. He rode back up to their floor and approached her door. She was buried in paperwork when he arrived. It took a lot of patience on his part, but he managed to stand, leaning against her doorjamb, his arms folded across his chest, not saying a word until she looked up.

She saw the big grin on his face and asked, "What?"

"Want to take a ride?"

"Where to?" she asked.

"Richmond. Dick Garcia just called. We've got a witness!"

Sally let out a whoop, grabbed her purse and joined him as he led the way to the elevators. In a minute they were buckled up and heading for Richmond.

Jack explained about the park ranger and the woman who owned the boarding house. Dick Garcia was going to interview her but had decided to wait for Jack to arrive before he did.

The drive to Richmond was prolonged by an accident on US 95 that had backed up traffic just north of Thornburg, Virginia, for almost forty-five minutes. Jack called Dick on his car phone and asked him to wait for the two of them. He'd be there "whenever."

It was just two o'clock when the Buick pulled into the parking lot of FBI headquarters, Richmond. The two agents hurried up to Dick's office.

"Looks like we got lucky, Jack," Dick said, rising from his chair. "Let's go."

"Luck has nothing to do with it, Dick. It's just good investigative work. That's what it's all about. Dogged determination. Following through."

Dick drove to an older part of Richmond. He pulled up in front of a large house. The sign read: Beauregard's Bed and Breakfast.

Jack said, "How'd he find a place like this?"

"Probably in the phone book," Dick answered. "This is the fifth one like this listed in the yellow pages. These places are usually not very busy this time of year. Your man's pretty smart. Stayed away from the major hotels and motels and away from the highways. Probably figured if we'd picked up his trail we'd be checking the places closer to the highways."

Jack looked at Sally and winked. They climbed the steps to the porch. Dick twisted the little bell handle and a pleasant-looking woman appeared.

"Yes?"

"Good afternoon, ma'am," Dick began, "Special Agent Richard Garcia, FBI."

He held up his badge. "We'd like to ask you a few questions about one of your guests, if you don't mind."

"One of my guests?"

"Yes. He would have stayed here earlier this month."

"Oh? Well, all right. Come in, please."

She opened the door and held it for the three of them and then led them to the parlor and invited them to sit.

Jack spoke. "You had a guest here not too long ago." He pulled out a composite drawing from his inside pocket and handed it to her.

She looked at it and smiled. "Yes. John Parks. Such a nice man. He stayed here for…five days. Yes, he was such a nice young man. So polite. Why? Has he done something wrong?" she asked, handing the drawing back to Jack.

"We'd like to ask him some questions regarding an ongoing investigation," Jack said.

"Well, as I said, he seemed like a nice man. You said 'ongoing investigation'?"

"We think he may have been involved in a kidnapping in Denver recently," Jack said.

"Oh no, not John," Molly assured them. "He couldn't have done something like that."

Dick said, "Well, we'd like for you to tell us everything you can remember about the man."

Molly sat back in her chair and folded her hands on her lap. Sally noticed the gesture. Defensive, she thought.

The three agents took turns asking her questions about her guest. Her answers were short and simple. She said he was driving a little silver car, and that he washed and vacuumed it.

Jack described the car to her.

"Why yes, that sounds like the car."

Jack continued. "Has anyone else stayed in his room since he left?"

"Heavens, yes," she said. "I've had several different couples stay since he left."

That answer ruled out the possibility of getting a good set of prints from the room. As Jack looked around at his surroundings, he could tell that this woman was a thorough housekeeper.

Sally was next. "Did he have any visitors while he was here? Or did he make any phone calls that you remember?"

"No, no," Molly replied, "he didn't have any visitors, but yes, he did make one long-distance call that I know of," she conceded. "He paid cash for the call. I don't know where he called, I haven't gotten the bill yet."

Sally made a note to get the phone company's records.

"You said he paid cash. Did he also pay cash for his room?" This time it was Dick who asked.

"Yes. But that's not unusual…is it? Now that I think of it, he paid for everything with cash. We went to dinner and I showed him historic Richmond. He did seem to have a lot of cash in his pockets."

She smiled at her three guests. "He was such a nice man. He even helped around the house while he was here."

Sally was the next to speak. "Looking at this picture," she said, picking up the picture from the coffee table, "is there anything you would change in his appearance? Any of his features? Especially the eyes? Would you say that they are pretty accurate?"

Molly took the picture from Sally and studied it again. "Yes, those are his eyes. He had the deepest blue eyes. So kindly looking too. Yes, I would say that that's him. Maybe a little thinner in the face. I don't know."

She handed the picture back to Sally. "I hope you're wrong about him. I'm sure he couldn't have been involved in anything that illegal. He was so kind and polite."

Dick spoke up. "Could we see your register?"

Molly rose and withdrew the register from the little desk. She opened it to the page John had signed. "Here he is," she said, handing the book to the agent, He showed it to the other two.

"Do you mind if we take this with us? I promise to have it back to you in the morning," Dick said.

She hesitated and then agreed.

"Did he say where he was going when he left here?" Again, it was Dick.

She thought for a moment and answered, "I think he said he had business in Washington, DC, when he left here."

Sally wrote on her pad.

"Well, thank you, Mrs. Stuart. You've been a big help," Jack said, rising. "With your permission, I'd like to have a team of investigators go over the room he stayed in for fingerprints. I promise they will clean up when they are done. You won't even know they were here. And if you can think of anything else, please call Mr. Garcia. Dick? Your card?"

Dick was pulling a card out of his wallet as Jack spoke.

"Again, thank you. You've been a great help."

In the car, Jack asked Dick to take them to the phone company.

"I'm on my way," he responded.

It took them only five minutes to retrieve the phone number. It was registered to a Jacqueline Chandler, in Ventura, California.

Back at the office, Jack used Dick's phone to call his SAC in Los Angeles. He gave the man all the information he had and directed him to call back to Jack's Washington number after he had interviewed the girl. He also faxed a copy of John's picture to him.

Jack and Sally said thanks and goodbye to Dick Garcia and headed back to Washington.

"I wonder if this Jacqueline and Aunt Julie are the same person?" Sally asked.

"I'm wondering that myself. Jacqueline, Jackie, Julie? Could be. Aliases are most often similar to the real name. Well now, John Smith, a.k.a. Jeffrey Matthews, a.k.a. John Parks, we're getting closer. You can run, but you can't hide forever.

CHAPTER 40

Ventura, California, Saturday, August 18, 10:00 a.m.

The two FBI men rang the doorbell to apartment 203. When there was no response, they rang it again. Finally, they resorted to knocking loudly.

"She's not home," came a voice from below.

Turning, the two agents looked down at the pool. Sunning themselves next to the pool were several young women and a few men.

"She's not home," one of the young women repeated, her hands shading her eyes.

"Do you know when she will be?" one of the men asked.

"About five thirty, maybe six," a blonde answered. "Something we can do?"

The two agents walked down the stairs and entered the pool area.

"Hi," the taller of the two agents said, introducing himself. He pulled out his wallet and showed his identification card to the blonde. "My name is Paul Newman, not to be confused with the other Paul Newman. And this is Special Agent Stephen McGill."

"Any idea where we might be able to find her?" McGill asked, jerking his head in the direction of apartment 203.

A brunette spoke. "She works for an attorney downtown. I don't know which one. What's this all about?"

The man named Stephen pulled out his notebook. "We'd like to ask Miss Chandler a few questions, that's all."

"Oh, Jackie doesn't live there anymore," Gretchen responded. "She moved out a couple of weeks ago."

"She did? Do you know where she moved?" Paul asked.

The brunette cut in, giving Gretchen a quick look. "No. She upped and moved out. She did say she was going back east somewhere. She sold her lease on the apartment. Said she'd be gone until October or November."

"I see. And could I have your names please?" McGill asked.

"Why? You looking for a date?" Gretchen teased.

McGill blushed. "No, ma'am. Just need to include this in our report."

"I'm sorry," the brunette said, introducing herself as Donna Reisen. And this is Gretchen Bjork."

Newman asked, "How well did the two of you know this Jackie?"

Before Gretchen could answer, Donna said, "Not that well. We've had drinks once in a while, you know, and we've seen her at the pool. Is she in some kind of trouble?"

"We just want to ask her some questions, that's all," McGill responded. "If you hear from her, would you please give us a call?"

"Sure," Donna said, reaching for his card.

"Thank you for your help," Newman said.

"The two men went into the apartment manager's office.

"She's in some kind of trouble, isn't she?" Gretchen asked her friend while the two agents were inside the manager's office.

"I think so. If they come back, you don't know anything, got it?"

"If you say so."

In five minutes the two agents returned and stood looking down at the two women.

"Hi again."

"Hi," Donna said, giving them a big smile.

"Apartment manager said you've been collecting her mail for her. Is that true?"

"That's true. Jackie asked us to save it for her. She said she'd contact us, and we could forward it to her. We haven't heard from her yet, though."

"Mind if we go through it?" Newman asked.

Donna gave him a look of doubt.

"We could come back later with a warrant," said McGill.

"I guess it would be all right," Donna said, rising from her recliner.

Gretchen joined her, and the two agents followed them up to their apartment.

"You'll have to excuse the mess," Donna apologized as she unlocked the door to the apartment. "We usually clean on Saturday afternoon when it gets too hot to sunbathe."

"That's quite all right," Paul answered.

Donna went into one of the bedrooms and returned with a stack of mail.

"Here," she said, handing the stack of mail to Paul. "That's all there is."

Paul took the mail from her and sat down on the couch, spread the contents onto the coffee table and waded through it. It contained the usual ads, magazines, and fliers. No personal letters or anything that might give them a clue as to her whereabouts.

"No bills?"

Donna and Gretchen looked at him.

"No bills," he repeated. "There are no bills."

"Oh," Donna responded. "No. She said she paid everything off before moving out."

Paul gathered up the mail and handed it back to Donna. "Thanks. Donna, isn't it?"

"Yes."

"Well, again, thanks for your help. If you think of anything, or if you hear from her, please call us and let us know how to find her. It's extremely important."

When the agents were gone, Donna said, "Listen. Jackie's in some kind of trouble. When she calls, if I'm not here, you've got to warn her that the FBI's been here looking for her. Do you understand?"

Gretchen nodded. "But why? Jackie's the sweetest—"

"I don't know. But I think she is in trouble. We've got to be careful. Um, and when you get her mail, separate any personal mail she gets from the junk. We'll hide it until she calls for it."

Walking back to the car, agent Newman spoke. "Those two know more than they're saying. I think you could probably get something out of the blonde, what's her name? Gretchen? She kind of took to you. Donna's the smart one. She knows something. I'm sure if it."

He looked back at the entrance to the building. "We'll be back. I'm not done with them yet."

Boston, Thursday, August 16

The drive down from Ellis Bay to Boston proved to be quite pleasant. The temperature was in the midseventies when they arrived. They both took their blood tests, went over to city hall and filled out their marriage forms, picked up their rings from the jeweler, and spent the rest of the afternoon shopping.

John deposited the check from his royalties into his account at the Shawmut Bank in Boston, and then they checked into their hotel. At six thirty they met Mike and Jeannie at the Normandie on Boylston Street for dinner.

They celebrated the upcoming wedding over drinks and dinner. Mike and Jeannie agreed to stand in with the couple. "I'd be honored," Mike said, and Jeannie gushed at being invited to stand up with Jackie.

Over after-dinner drinks, John very casually mentioned a thought that had intrigued him ever since the barbeque.

"Mike? How far have you sailed the *Dram Bouie*? I mean, have you ever taken it on a long cruise?"

"A long cruise? No, we've only sailed it as far as Nantucket and Martha's Vineyard. I've been too busy for a long voyage. And besides, it's not equipped for a long journey. Why?"

"Just wondering."

John let the subject drop, and Mike did not pursue it.

The evening was a completely enjoyable affair. Finally, John and Jackie said their goodbyes and left.

Back at the hotel, Jackie said she was going to call her friends and give them the good news about the wedding. John had previously explained to her that all mail and long-distance phone calls would have to originate from Boston, and only from public phones.

"Just be cautious," he warned.

She put the call through, and Donna answered the phone.

"Hi," Jackie greeted cheerfully when her friend picked up the phone. "How are things in California?"

"Things are really strange out here," Donna answered. "The FBI has been around a couple of times looking for you."

"The FBI!" Jackie gasped and then regained her composure. "What did they want?"

"They're trying to locate your whereabouts. We haven't told them anything and they won't tell us anything. You're not in some kind of trouble are you, honey?"

"Of course not. Why would they want to talk to me?"

John was immediately beside her when he heard the acronym *FBI*. Jackie gave him a worried look as she talked to her friend. She motioned to him and he put his ear next to the receiver to listen as Donna explained about the questions and the mail search.

"No, Gretchen won't say anything. She's really much smarter than she acts," Donna assured her caller. "So what's up in your life?"

Jackie brought her up to date on her new life and her upcoming marriage to John Burton, the author, and Donna got excited. Jackie invited Donna and Gretchen to come to Boston for the wedding. She even volunteered to pay all their expenses.

"We'd love to come, honey," Donna said when Jackie was through, "but under the circumstances, what with the FBI looking for you, I don't think it would be a good idea."

"You're probably right," Jackie agreed.

There was a silence on the line. Finally, Donna spoke. "Are you all right, Jackie? I mean, is everything all right? Are you in some kind of trouble?"

"I can't tell you, Donna, but yes, I'm okay. I'm in love, I'm going to be married. Yes, everything's fine."

Again, a pause, then, "Jackie?"

"Yes, Donna?"

"Maybe it would be better if you didn't call, or even more important, if you didn't write us for a while. At least until whatever they want goes away."

"Maybe you're right."

Again, there was silence on the line.

Finally, Jackie spoke. "Donna?"

"Yes?"

"Thanks…I love you…say hello to Gretchen for me."

"I will, and congratulations."

"Bye."

"Bye."

Jackie hung up and looked at John.

"Oh God! The FBI's looking for me. How?"

"I don't know. Let me think…"

Jackie had to sit down. She was visibly shaken. John was also upset. He went over everything in his head. Had they found her fingerprints somewhere? It was all he could think of.

"No, I'm sure I wiped everything clean. Besides, you know the drill. Floyd and Allen followed me. All three of us sterilized the cabin."

"What about the car? At McArthur's place?"

"Same thing. Besides, we wore gloves. And I was careful not to touch anything. I didn't need to. I didn't even use the radio or the windshield wipers in the van. We both wore gloves. I never even touched the vase without my gloves on."

John thought some more. "Maybe it has nothing to do with us."

She smiled weakly. "Maybe you're right. But why else would they be looking for me?"

"I don't know, Honey, I don't know."

What had started out as a joyous and exciting trip to Boston had suddenly turned somber. Jackie and John watched the news and went to bed. For the first time since her arrival, they went right to sleep, and in the morning their drive up the shore was subdued.

John's mind raced as he thought of all the things he would have to do to cover their tracks. Most important, he would have to make sure that no pictures of them were ever put in the newspaper columns. It was doubly important for no mail to be sent from their address to her friends in California. Jackie assured him that her friends could be trusted, but John still had his doubts.

Washington, DC, Monday, August 20

Jack hung up the phone. Another so-called witness had just phoned wanting to know about the possible reward for information on the face on the poster. He and Sally had finally resorted to taking turns interviewing the callers. There had been dozens already. This time, though, the caller sounded legitimate.

Jack waited for Sally to get back from lunch and then the two of them headed for the airport. The witness agreed to meet with them before her shift started at 4:00 p.m. She was waiting for them when they arrived and immediately took them to the employee's lounge.

Adele Price was a tall, slender black woman in her mid to late thirties. She wore the uniform of a Delta Airlines ticket counter clerk. Her white blouse was neatly starched, and her uniform was immaculate.

As they sat down at one of the tables, she explained that she had gone on vacation the same day she had seen the man in the poster and had only been back since last Friday. She called as soon as she came into work and saw the picture.

"Only thing is," she explained, "is he wasn't alone. See, he had a woman with him."

"A woman?"

"Yes, sir. Good-lookin' woman if I remember."

"You're sure?"

"Course I'm sure. I looked it up on the computers just to be sure. Then I called you. They flew to Boston under the name Mr. And Mrs. John Parks."

Bingo, Jack thought. He asked, "And when did they fly out?"

"Sunday morning, July twenty-second. They acted like they was newly married or something."

"Could you describe the woman?"

"Not really. Didn't get a good look at her. Brunette, I think, although I'm not too sure about that. She did have a nice tan. I do remember that. She had nice skin."

"Did you get a driver's license or any other type of identification?"

"He called ahead for the tickets. Gave a credit card number if it's still in the computer. He showed me a Massachusetts driver's license when he got here, but I was so busy I didn't write it down. And they were in a hurry to catch the plane. Yes, I remember they said they were on their honeymoon. Yes, that's it. They was newlyweds."

"Sally," Jack said, "get a copy of the passenger list."

"I can help with that," Adele offered.

"Great. Adele, you've been a great help," Jack said. "If we can track these two people down and get a conviction, there will be a reward coming."

She smiled. "You be sure not to forget me now."

"Boston," Jack said when the two agents were back in their car. "You know, if all those airports had television cameras and monitors, it would make our jobs so much easier. Boston," he repeated. "You weren't too far off, Sally."

"Lucky guess," she said.

"So, lucky guesser, where do you think they're headed for now? Maybe north to Canada?"

"The thing about Boston is that there are so many towns around it. They could get lost in any one of them. Or maybe even one of the bordering states: Maine, New Hampshire, Vermont. They could have opted for some out-of-the-way town in one of those states, or even Rhode Island or Connecticut. My guess, though, is they will stay close to Boston. It makes sense. Boston is a major hub to almost anywhere."

"That's my thinking. Care to go to Boston this week?"

"Let me check my schedule," she said. "Oh, look! I've got nothing planned. I guess it would be all right."

"Oh, shut up. What say we catch the red-eye Wednesday morning? Set it up, will you? In the meantime, I'll call Bruce Sellier in Boston and tell him to expect us."

Boston, Wednesday, August 22

Jack and Sally were met by Bruce Sellier, Boston's Station Chief at six-fifty in the morning.

"Sorry to get you up so early, Bruce. Appreciate your meeting us, though. This is Sally Martin. Sally, Bruce Sellier. We worked together in Dallas a few years back. How's Susan?"

"She's fine. Taking some night courses at Northeastern. Only one more semester to go before she graduates."

"Good for her. Interior design, isn't it?"

"That's right."

They made their way up the concourse and found a coffee bar. It was busy and noisy even at this early hour and Bruce had to speak loudly to be heard.

He had an agent check out the incoming flight as Jack had requested. There was a Mr. and Mrs. John Parks on the flight manifest, just as John had said.

A check of the baggage manifest records showed nothing unusual for a couple flying into Boston; they did have two extra bags, but the weight didn't match what the agents expected; nothing unusual, just two bags for him and four for her. Jack supposed that they could have carried the cash in the bags, but he doubted it.

"I know it's a long shot, but I've got people checking the cab companies to see if anyone remembers picking them up. So far, nothing. We checked the buses. Nothing there."

"What about long-term parking?" Jack asked. "Suppose he drove to the airport and parked. We'd be looking for someone who would have parked there for three or four weeks, maybe even as much as six weeks."

"Good idea," Bruce remarked. "I'll check on it."

"So, Sally," Bruce asked, as the three agents were finishing their coffee, "how do you like working for the genius?"

Jack still got embarrassed when he was referred to as "The Genius." Sally noticed his face get red as his chin dropped onto his chest.

"I like it a lot. He's a good teacher."

They paid their bill and said goodbye to Bruce, caught their ten fifteen back to Washington, and were back in time for lunch.

Thursday afternoon Bruce called Jack. His man had interviewed all the parking and toll booth attendants. One of the toll booth attendants had remembered a late-model sports car with a couple matching the two fugitives' description on the day in question. She remembered because they had come through her gate again the next day, only this time they had luggage strapped to the rack on the trunk of the car. The car could have been either a Corvette, a Camaro, or a Firebird. She wasn't sure. She couldn't give them any more information than that except to say that the two people very attractive and seemed to be having a good time. Both times they came through her gate she had had to make change for them.

A check of the ticket stubs from that day showed that the car had been on the lot since June twenty-first. That fit with Jack's time frame. Now they had a possible car to go with the suspects: a late-model red sports car. Bruce put out an inquiry for all owners of late model red Corvettes, Camaros and Pontiac Firebirds registered in Massachusetts to the DMV. There were over forty-two hundred such vehicles registered in the greater Boston area alone. And what if the vehicle wasn't even registered in Massachusetts?"

"Keep on it, Bruce," was Jack's response.

Jack thanked his fellow investigator and hung up. He went to the wall and added the latest piece of information to it and stood back to look at the overall picture. He now had several pieces of information available to him: a description of the man that was confirmed by several people, the name of a woman who could have been Aunt

Julie, sightings of the man and woman in Boston. The net was closing around his quarry. Jack took a deep breath, feeling good about his progress, turned off the light to his office, walked over to Sally's office and relayed Bruce's phone call to her, and then went home.

CHAPTER 41

Boston, Friday, August 31

John and Jackie were married in a simple ceremony at City Hall in Boston. Mike and Jeannie stood up as best man and matron of honor. They all returned to Brookline for a quick lunch and to pick up the necessary supplies they would need for the weekend.

They would be taking the Mercedes. John parked the Bronco, his wedding gift to Jackie, in the garage. By 3:00 p.m., they were on their way. Traffic southbound on Highway 3 was atrocious. All the weekend traffic heading for the Cape had been building all day, and it took almost three hours to travel the eighty-six miles to the Bass River retreat. They had a light dinner of steamed clams and mussels, corn on the cob, coleslaw, and hushpuppies, chased with *Narragansett Beer* at the Bass River Fish Market, and were loading the boat by 8:00 p.m.

John and Jackie would spend their wedding night on the boat. Mike and Jeannie would come onboard at eight thirty Saturday morning, and the four of them would sail to Nantucket.

Mike and Jeannie stayed until after eleven, toasting the newlyweds and showing them the basics of boat life. When they finally said their goodbyes, all four were a little drunk. Mike promised to drive safely as they bid the couple a happy evening.

At last John and his new bride were alone. They sat on deck sipping their drinks, listening to the gentle lapping of the waves against the side of the boat. Overhead, a sliver of moon cut the blackness of the sky and stars twinkled. Every so often, the gentle bump of the hull against its moorings broke the quiet.

John and Jackie were content to just be together. The sounds coming over the water were relaxing. At eleven thirty, Jackie finally stood up, a little tipsy, but feeling sure of her sea legs, and began to unbutton her blouse. She looked down at her new husband with a slightly sexy smile, a twinkle in her eye.

Later, she stared deeply into his eyes through the semidarkness and said, "I love you, John Burton."

"I love you too," he answered, surprised at how easy and natural the words came.

They continued to lie on the deck, their senses absorbing the sounds and smells of the harbor and each other. Finally, Jackie spoke. "Let's get up. This floor is hard."

"Deck," John said. "This is a deck."

He knocked on the wood with his knuckles as both rose. He looked over both sides of the boat. He could see no one around. He checked the stern and the dock for as far as he could. Nothing.

"Come on," he whispered and dove over the side into the blackness of the water below him.

Jackie squealed and jumped in after him.

"Oh, God, it's cold!" she shouted, shuddering as she broke the surface.

John reached for her hand and pulled her to him, his other hand holding on to the boat's ladder.

"M-m-m," she cooed, "this feels nice."

He laughed. "I'll show you nice."

John put his hand on her head and dunked her under the water. She broke the surface squealing and laughing.

"Shh," he whispered. "Somebody might hear us."

"Let's go aboard," she said, the coldness of the water starting to seep into her. "I'm getting chilly."

He climbed the ladder and reached an arm down to help her up, pulling her wet body against him as she landed on the deck. His arms encircled her and drew her to him.

"Let's go below and dry off and put on some warm clothes," he suggested.

"I've got a better idea. Let's dry off and stay naked, you big hunk of man. I want another beer."

John went below and returned with two large towels and two more cans of beer. They dried each other off and sat on the plastic seat at the rear of the deck, towels covering their backs and shoulders.

Off in the distance they could hear the faint sounds of a band playing at one of the nightclubs that lined the street across from the harbor. The water below them was quiet now, its glassy surface reflecting the lights of the harbor in the background. Now and then the shrill sound of a seagull cut into the quiet and peace of the night.

When the chill in the air became uncomfortable, they rose and went below and went to bed, snuggled in each other's arms, the warmth of their bodies and the single sheet over them protecting them from the chill of the night air.

They were awake and had the coffee going when Mike and Jeannie arrived Saturday morning.

"Sleep well?" Jeannie asked Jackie as she stepped aboard. Jackie gave her one of those smiles and said, simply, "Wonderful."

Mike winked at John.

"Coffee smells great. How 'bout we all have a cup and then shove off. You've had breakfast already, I see."

John nodded. "We've been up since seven. You know," he continued, looking up at the clear blue sky, "I could get used to this."

Jackie came and put her arm around him. "Me too."

The plan was to sail to Nantucket, have lunch, spend the afternoon shopping and touring the island and spend the evening on the boat. Sunday morning, they would sail around Chappaquiddick Island and into Edgartown for lunch, spend the afternoon there and then cross over to Woods Hole and sail back to Hyannis, arriving there by 7:00 p.m. They would spend Labor Day night at the house in Bass River and drive back to Brookline early Tuesday morning. That way they would miss a lot of the Labor Day return traffic.

At nine thirty, the foursome set sail for Nantucket. The sun shone brightly, warming the sea below. The sound waters were relatively calm, conditions were ideal.

Jeannie proved, once again, to be an able seaman and helped with the sailing. She even taught Jackie some sailing intricacies. John was an able student so that by the time Nantucket Island came into view, both novice sailors at least understood the rudiments. The four crew members sang and laughed and thoroughly enjoyed themselves.

At eleven thirty, they dropped anchor in Nantucket Harbor. It was crowded with all kinds of boats, from the smaller catboats, sloops, cutters, and yawls to the larger ketches and schooners. Sleek, beautiful motor boats and cabin cruisers were scattered amongst them.

Furling the sails, the four sailors made their boat ready for docking. Using the auxiliary engine, Mike maneuvered the *Dram Bouie* between the other boats until it came to rest at its destination.

With instructions from Mike, John dropped the anchor, and then the two men lowered the dinghy into the water and helped the two women get into it. Mike started the small outboard motor, and they came ashore.

The weekend was a glorious affair. Each stop was better than the last, and then it was time the four friends to cast off from Woods Hole and return to Hyannis. This was when John approached Mike with an idea.

Mike was settled behind the wheel of the boat. The two women were below, packing up their things and stowing the boat's kitchen gear. As long as they headed along the same compass bearing, there was little to do.

"Mike," John began, "what would it cost to sail the *Dram Bouie* to, say, the West Indies, or maybe even the Cayman Islands?"

Mike thought for a minute. "I don't rightly know. It would require a whole lot of extra gear: sails, mast, auxiliary generators, beefed up radar and sonar equipment. GPS, ah, global positioning system, not to mention the cost of fuel and rations.

He mentally calculated. "Probably somewhere in the neighborhood of eighteen to twenty thousand dollars, I would think. Why? You planning on taking a trip?"

"Jackie and I have had so much fun this weekend. I just thought it might be fun to take a long sailing trip and maybe visit some of the islands."

"You can't sail this boat alone. It takes at least two people who know what they're doing. For a trip that long, you'd need a bigger crew."

"Well, you silly man," John said, "I wasn't talking about just Jackie and me. Suppose I was to pay for all the additional equipment and give you and Jeannie and additional twenty thousand dollars for your time. We could make a grand vacation out of it. Haven't you ever dreamed of sailing off into the sunset, sailing down to the islands? Going from island to island, just taking your time? It would be fun."

Mike just stared at him. "You're serious, aren't you?"

"Of course I'm serious. Besides. How long has it been since the two of you have had a real vacation?"

"Too long, that's for sure."

"Well?"

"Well...let me think about it. I'd like to talk to Jeannie. You're talking about practically refitting this old boat? We're talking a lot of money here, John."

"What's money? I just put a whole bunch of it in the bank, remember? And there's a lot more to be had. I don't know a lot about weather patterns and sailing, but I'm betting this month and next month could be great sailing weather."

"It should be."

"Come on, what do you say?"

Mike looked him straight in the eyes. "Let me get this straight. You're willing to outfit this boat—soup to nuts—*and* pay us twenty thousand dollars to sail this thing down to the islands?"

"That's right."

"You're crazy, you know that? Oh man. Let me talk to Jeannie. I tell you, that twenty sure would come in handy with Eric's college costs."

John knew he had him. Now, if he could convince Jeannie, then his problems would be solved.

"You said he was taking the fall semester off? Bring him along. One more deckhand could come in handy. You said so yourself. I assume he knows how to sail?"

"He knows this boat better than I do," Mike confessed. "You know, this is beginning to sound pretty good. How long a trip are we talking about here?"

"I don't know. How long would it take to sail down to Jamaica—no, let's go all out. How long would it take to sail to the Cayman Islands and back?"

"Why the Cayman Islands?"

John had to be careful here. He hadn't lied to Mike until now. At least nothing this big.

"It's for my new book. I need some background on the Cayman Islands. Plus I wanted to get a feel for the local color. Jackie and I could fly down, but since I've been on this boat, I thought this would be more fun."

"Well, if Jeannie says okay, then I guess you're on. I could close up the office, or at least, Marcie could run things by herself for a while.

The four friends discussed the sailing trip together until the entrance to Hyannis harbor came into view in the distance. Jeannie was hesitant at first, but, when Eric was brought into the equation, she consented.

Mike could rearrange his work schedule at the office to get six weeks off. It would take at least two weeks to outfit the *Dram Bouie* for her ocean voyage. They set the tentative date for departure as September twenty-second. That would give them a cushion to work with. Mike could wrap up things at the office and Eric could oversee the ship's stores and equipment. All this was discussed and reaffirmed on the drive back to Boston Tuesday morning.

John backed the Corvette out of the garage, loaded the bags into the trunk and put the top down. Jackie climbed in next to him. Mike and Jeannie waved goodbye from the driveway as the car backed out onto the street. Three o'clock. They would be back home before dark.

CHAPTER 42

Ellis Bay, Maine, Friday, September 7

Jackie picked up the phone. "Hello?"

"Jackie, is John around?"

"Hi, Mike, yes, he's out back making some notes for his book."

"John!" Mike could hear her call out over the phone. "It's Mike Morris!"

Mike waited. Finally, John took the phone from Jackie. "Mike! What's up?"

"Eric just called from the Cape. He's spent the last three days putting together a list of equipment and stores that we'll be needing to make the Cayman Islands. He just gave me the figures. You sitting down?"

"Go ahead."

"Nineteen thousand, three hundred and fifty dollars."

"Good," John responded. "Let's do it."

"You're sure?"

"You bet I am. I can't wait."

"Okay. Eric says it'll take about two weeks. We're still set for the twenty-second?"

"Sounds good to me. I'll send you a check. Jackie and I are coming down a few days early. We thought we'd meet you at the house on the Cape on Friday the twenty-first, if that's okay with you?"

"No problem here. Say, listen…Eric wanted to know if he could bring his friend, Scott, along. You know, to help with the crewing?"

"What do you think?"

"I've known Scott all his life. He's a good kid. Kid! He's twenty-two. He and Eric have been friends forever. He knows sailing like nobody's business. He'd be a big help."

"Then he's in. How much more we talking?"

"He comes with the package."

"You sly old devil. What if I'd have said no?"

"But you didn't…"

"Right. Oh, send me a list of everything Jackie and I will need to bring—clothes, toiletries, you know."

"I'll have Jeannie do that. See you soon."

Sunday, September 16

Jackie and John spent the weekend closing up the house in Ellis Bay and packing for the trip. In the back of the Ford Bronco, John had purchased for his new bride, they packed everything that they would need for the trip, except what Jeannie would have them buy in Hyannis. They also brought along two additional suitcases. Packed tightly inside the two pieces of luggage, and neatly wrapped and sealed in watertight plastic, was the money from Denver.

They would drive directly to the Cape, drop off most of their bags, and then go back to Boston where John had an appointment with the forger.

The Corvette was parked in the garage next to the house, the windows and doors secured. The post office was notified to hold the mail the phone was shut off, the newspaper canceled. All the trash was bagged up and put out for pickup. Everything that the two of them could think of was done. One last look around, and they headed off.

They reached Bass River by two in the afternoon. Eric was at the house waiting for them. John knew Eric and introduced him to Jackie.

"Eric's a junior at Harvard," John explained.

The boy was taller than his dad and strongly built. His face and arms and legs were well tanned, and his head was a mass of unruly brown hair. He was a good-looking boy, and his looks got better every time he smiled.

"I thought we'd drop off our stuff and stay here tonight. We'll be going back to Boston in the morning. There are some things I need to do before we leave.

"Sure. Ah, do you want to see the boat?"

"I'd like that, but not today. Maybe when we're done in Boston. I'd also like to meet your friend. Scott, isn't it? Your dad raved about him."

Eric nodded.

They carried the bags and suitcases into the house and up to the guest room. The bed was recently made up and the room was ready for them. Back downstairs, John and his bride bid the boy goodbye and headed off.

Boston, Monday, September 17

John and Jackie met with his man at 10:00 a.m. John needed new identification papers for the two of them: passports, driver's licenses, major credit cards, new Social Security cards. The "artist," as John referred to him, took photographs of them and promised to have the documents ready by Thursday. Because John was a regular, this time it would only cost him forty thousand dollars for complete sets.

John complained that it was highway robbery, but he paid anyway. He always wanted a backup, just in case. All his Parks and Pickett and Matthews papers and cards had gone up in smoke on the beach at Ellis Bay. It had been a good marshmallow and hot dog roast.

Mike met them for lunch, and then John and Jackie drove out to Brookline to see Jeannie. She gave them a list of essentials they would need for the voyage and assured the couple that everything they needed could be bought in Hyannis. The two travelers left and arrived back in Bass River by eight Monday evening, tired and weary, but pleased with all they had accomplished.

Tuesday morning Eric took them to see the boat. Engineers were installing the latest in navigational gear: radar, sonar, and radio equipment. Wires hung everywhere, but the workmen assured them that it would all be done by midday Wednesday. The auxiliary generators had been installed already. Spars, standing and running rigging, and the sails were stored, along with an extra rudder. Fuel and oil and all the perishable provisions would come onboard on Friday.

John was impressed. Eric was doing a fine job getting the boat ready and told him so.

"Scott and his dad have been the ones who've been the most help," Eric admitted. "Scott should be by pretty soon."

Eric took them below. "We did a complete tune-up on the engine. Runs like new. I had one of the men from the boatyard in Osterville come over. He inspected the hull, keel, rudder and all the fittings and trimming. Said everything was fine. I think when we're done here, it'll be just like new."

"That's reassuring," John said.

Another young man with a full head of uncombed curly blond hair and a dark tan was just coming aboard.

"Scott!" Eric greeted as he spied his friend.

Scott stepped aboard, and Eric introduced him to his visitors.

"Scott, these are the people I was telling you about. Mr. and Mrs. Burton, I'd like you to meet Scott Boucher. Scott, John and Jackie Burton."

Greetings were exchanged, handshakes made and then Scott spoke. "So what do you think of the old boat?"

"I'm impressed," were John's first words. "I—we, Jackie and I, want to thank you for all your help. I understand a lot of this is your doing?"

"Well, mine and my dad's," the young man admitted.

"His dad owns the marina in Bass River," Eric explained. "We got most of the equipment through him. He saved you a bundle."

"Well, that's good to know. I must meet your father and thank him personally."

"If you're still here in an hour, you can. He'll be here by then. He wants to check up on these communications guys, make sure they meet their deadline."

The four people left the boat for coffee and donuts. In an hour they were back onboard the *Dram Bouie*. Scott's dad was below, talking to the radar people when they came onboard. He came topside just as John and Scott were helping Jackie onto the deck.

"You must be John and Jackie Burton," the man said, extending his hand. "Eric's told me about you. Welcome aboard."

"Thank you." John looked at Scott.

"Oh, I'm sorry. My name is John Boucher. I'm Scott's dad."

"How do you do, Mr. Boucher—"

"Call me John, please."

"John. You've done wonders with this boat. Thank you. I understand from Scott and Eric that you had a lot to do with ordering the equipment and keeping the costs down. I really appreciate that."

"My pleasure," the man said. "I wouldn't be afraid to take this little beauty anywhere. Course, Europe's out of the question this time of year, but south to the islands? Not a problem. Well, got to be goin'. Got to get back to work. Nice meetin' you folks. And, ah, good luck."

With that the old man was over the edge and down the pier.

"Nice man," John said to Scott.

"So. What now?" John asked Eric.

"Well, Scott and I would like to teach you both some of the basic things about sailing a boat this big. Maybe tomorrow?"

"Let's plan on it. Morning be a good time?"

They agreed. Scott said, "Better plan on most of the day. There's a lot to cover. We, Eric and I, think it's a good idea to know boat safety and how to handle the old boat, just in case."

"I think it's a great idea," Jackie chimed in. "What time do you want us here?"

"We can ride together," Eric suggested, "say about eight? Hopefully they'll be done with the electronics, and they can show us how it all works by midafternoon."

"Then we'd better do our shopping today. Eric? Scott? Thank you both so much. You're doing a fine job."

The two boys helped Jackie over the side and watched as the two visitors walked up the pier.

John and Jackie spent the day walking through the shops and stores along Main Street, buying the various things Jeannie had suggested on her shopping list. By four they were ready to call it a day and headed back to Bass River.

"I can't believe all this stuff," Jackie remarked, looking at all the packages in the back of the Bronco. "We're going to have to leave some of the other things back at the house or we'll sink the boat."

"Well, you did pack a lot."

"Me! What about you? You really think you need a suit on Grand Cayman? And four, count 'em, four pairs of dress shoes?"

"Maybe you're right. We'd better both rethink our packing."

The two grabbed a quick bite at a restaurant on Union Street and went back to the house. They spent the better part of the evening sorting and repacking. When they were done, there were several items of clothing that would be left hanging in the closet.

Eric stopped by at eight and checked in, then said he and Scott were going to a party at a friend's house. He promised not to be too late.

They met Scott at the boat at 8:00 a.m. The skies overhead were gloomy and gray, clouds scudding quickly by; the forecast called for rain off and on most of the day. A chilly breeze blew in from the sea.

Scott took over immediately.

"All right," he began, "I need to know just how much you two know about a boat and how to sail it. Please excuse the questions if you think they are dumb, but this way I'll have a pretty good idea of what we need to teach you.

"Who can tell me the difference between port and starboard?"

"Oh, I know," Jackie said, raising her hand. Port is on your right and, no, wait. Port is on your left if you are looking toward the front of the boat. Starboard is on your right."

That's right," Scott agreed. "Where is the bow?"

"Up front," Jackie said quickly.

"Stern?"

"Back."

"Aft?"

Jackie looked at him in surprise. "Isn't that also the back?"

"Gotcha."

John kept quiet, amused by his wife's eagerness.

The boys covered the basics of sailing and explained the different things that were needed to sail the boat: spinnakers, shrouds, stays, sheets, booms, running lights, rigging, and so on. They then went on to explain the different terms they would hear about maneuvering and sailing the boat: sailing free, sailing downwind, sailing off the wind, or sailing before the wind, and on and on until Jackie's and John's heads were spinning.

When the boys finished, Scott asked, "Any questions?"

Jackie rolled her eyes. John saw the look and laughed.

"That's a lot to remember," he commented.

"Actually, it's all quite simple once you see how it all comes together."

Eric went below to check on the radio people. Coming topside a few minutes later, he said, "They're just about done."

"Excellent!" Scott responded enthusiastically. We can take you down and explain how all the electronics works if you want."

"Can we do that once we're on our way?" Jackie asked. "My head's spinning."

"Sure thing," Scott said. He grinned at the two novices. "I guess we can quit for today."

CHAPTER 43

Washington, DC, Tuesday, September 11

The case was growing cold. Jack knew it. Nothing new had happened since the sighting at Logan International Airport. The couple could be anywhere: Boston, New York, Canada, Mexico, Europe.

"Damn," he muttered.

He sat back and looked at the sheets of paper covering his walls. Since the couple's sighting in Boston, he had taken to calling the man John Parks. A check of all the John Parks listed with the Social Security Administration had come up blank. So they had a check of all the major credit card companies. The DMV of all six New England states and New York and New Jersey had come up with nothing. Of the hundreds and hundreds of John Parks pictures on licenses, none had come close to matching the description he had in front of him. On a hunch, he picked up the phone and called the Social Security office.

"Ted Summers."

"Ted, it's Jack Donovan. Sorry to bother you again, but I just had an idea. On this John Parks thing. What if the real John Parks is dead? What if our man somehow stumbled across the name and Social Security number? He could have created a new identity, couldn't he?"

"Well, yes, it's a possibility. Let me get on it. I'll call you back."

"Thanks, Ted. Once again, I owe you."

"No problem. Someday I *am* going to collect, though." He laughed lightly.

Jack hung up the phone, picked up the composite, and looked at it again.

"Where are you, you son of a bitch?" he asked the face staring up at him. "If only I hadn't promised the McArthur family that I'd keep this out of the newspapers, you'd be in every newspaper in the country by now. Someone has to know you. Somebody is looking at you right this very minute. Shit!

"Well, Mr. Parks, if I can't put you in the newspaper, at least I can put you in the Post Office."

He picked up the phone and had the receptionist put him through to the Post Office Department. Thirty minutes later he faxed the picture with all the pertinent information to the printing department. Within forty-eight hours the posters would be sent out to every post office in the country.

"I'm going to get you, you bastard," he said as he pushed the SEND button on the fax machine.

He waited for confirmation of receipt, and when he got it, he walked back to his office. Sally was back at her desk, deeply absorbed in her work. She too was feeling the frustration of a trail gone cold.

"Whatcha doin'?" he asked from the doorway.

She looked up. The long hours of following up leads and chasing dead ends were beginning to take its toll on her. She looked tired. Her eyes didn't quite have that sparkle, and the slightest hint of dark rings under her eyes tried to surface through her makeup.

"Just reviewing things. How 'bout you?"

"I just sent his picture to the post office. Within forty-eight hours or so it should be sent out. By next week his picture will be posted on every bulletin board in every post office in the country."

He sat down opposite her in the only chair in her office.

"Sally?" He hesitated. "Do you think I was wrong in promising the McArthurs to keep this out of the newspapers?"

She thought long and hard before answering, the top of her pen pushing against her lower lip, her eyes furrowed.

"It was their wish. You know how much of a circus it would have been had the press gotten hold of it in those first hours."

"Yes, but maybe they could have helped."

"They didn't help in Detroit, did they?"

"No."

"Houston give you any help?"

He smiled. "As a matter of fact, they really got in the way big time."

"Jack, they begged you to keep it out of the papers. You had to respect their wishes."

"I know. It's just…sometimes I think I let emotions get in the way of good judgment. This case is over two months old and what have we got? A face. A possible sighting that's already a couple of weeks old. A red late-model sports car, possibly a Corvette or Firebird or Camaro. Hell, it could even be foreign for all we know."

Sally repeated what Jack had said, holding up first one, then two, then three fingers. That's three more things than you had out of Houston or Detroit."

"You're right, you're right."

"Jack," Sally began, voicing a thought that had been running through her head when he had interrupted her. "Parks arrived in DC on July 18, right."

Jack agreed.

"He and the girl flew out on Sunday morning, the twenty-second, heading for Boston, right?"

"Right again."

"Where'd they stay while they were here?"

"You're going to tell me, right?"

"I'm going to find out. *Then* I'm going to tell you. My guess is it's along the strip near the airport."

"Yeah, go for it."

Sally looked at Jack, surprise on her face. She had not seen or heard him act this way before. Kind of humorous. It amused her.

"What?" he asked when he saw the expression on her face.

"I don't know," she said getting serious again.

"Well, let me know when you find out where they stayed."

"I will."

On her fourth stop, Sally got lucky. A John Parks had registered at that hotel. He stayed there frequently, always alone until this last time. He had been met by his wife on Friday, July twentieth. A check of the employees and Sally located Bobby, who was more than willing to help this attractive woman from the FBI.

"Mr. Parks? Sure, I remember him," Bobby began, looking at the picture in front of him. "Nice guy. Good tipper. Quiet. Pretty much kept to himself. Worked out in the gym a lot. 'Cept for the last time. He had a woman with him. She came in on a Friday, if I remember right. Good lookin'. What'd he do?"

"We just want to talk to him," Sally said.

"You know, Mr. Parks was a real gentleman. Never caused any trouble. Good tipper as I said. But there was something about him."

"Oh?" Sally asked.

"Yeah. I don't know. He was sorta…secretive. Almost mysterious, you know? I sorta sensed it right off. He had this briefcase, you know? He never let it out of his hands. Like he was protecting it, you know? Not like your average businessman. I mean, he really guarded it."

"The briefcase?"

"Yeah. You know. Samsonite. Nice. Leather. I remember I was gonna carry it for him. He practically wrestled me for it. Each time he stayed here he had that same briefcase. Dark brown. Expensive. Anyway, he wouldn't let go of it."

"You said he was a big tipper?"

Bobby looked at her. "You sure you're not with the I.R.S.?"

Sally laughed. "No, Bobby, I'm not with the I.R.S."

"I was kiddin'. Sure. He always had a wad of cash on him. Paid cash for everything, which was kind of odd, now that I think of it. I mean, he looked pretty well off, and he did have credit cards. Course, he looked pretty able to take care of himself. I think he'd give you a good fight for that wad."

"Oh?"

"Yeah. Like I said before. He worked out. Used the gym a lot when he was here. For a man his age, he was in real good shape."

"His age? How old do you think he is?"

"I'd guess early, maybe midforties."

Sally added this piece of information to the growing list of things she was learning about this man.

"What would you estimate his weight to be if you had to guess?"

Bobby rubbed his chin, picturing the man in his mind. "Maybe two hundred, two ten."

"You said his wife arrived on Friday? What can you tell me about her?"

Bobby thought for a short time, then answered. "He called her Jackie. Nice lady. Good lookin', you know? Classy. Brunette. Nice tan. Nice figure. She was younger than him."

"How old do you think she was?"

"Hard to say with a woman like that. You could tell she was a fitness nut. I'd say maybe anywhere from the late twenties to late thirties. Like I said, with her, it was hard to tell. She did a good job with makeup."

"Why do you say that?"

"Woman that attractive? She had to have had help. But you really didn't notice the makeup. It looked so natural."

"Do you think you could remember the face well enough to describe it to a police artist?"

"I think so. Face like that you don't forget very easy. Kind of like yours."

"Excuse me?"

"Well, let's face it. You're a good lookin' woman, Miss Martin. People gonna stare at you, right? They're gonna remember. People always remember good lookin' faces because they study them more. Same with ugly. You stare. Me? I study people. It's part of what I do. It's part of my job. You remember people's faces, you remember their names. You get better tips that way." He grinned when he said this.

"Good," she said to him. "I'll be sending an artist around. I certainly appreciate your help."

"Hey, no problem."

The two made arrangements for the artist and Sally left. Bobby watched her until she was out of sight.

Man, that was one good-lookin' woman, he thought. *She could ask me anything she wanted...*

He turned and signaled the front desk that he was available.

Back at the office Sally condensed her notes and prepared her report for Jack. He was in a meeting and would be tied up for the rest of the day.

He arrived back at his office just before quitting time. Quitting time for most people, anyway. Sally brought her report in and dropped it in front of him, a big grin on her face. Jack looked at the cover and then up at her. He picked up the folder.

"From the look on your face, I'd say you had some success," he said, waving the folder. "Wanna tell me about it?"

"He stayed at the Airport Sheraton. Seems he's a regular there. At least, he's been there several times. Checked the hotel's records. He was there just before he flew to Denver."

Jack looked at the file briefly and then let her continue.

"I checked the airport's records. By matching the dates when he stayed in the Sheraton, I was able to track his movements. He flew round trip to Denver as a Mr. James Pickett on May twenty-fourth, then again on June twenty-second. It's all in the report."

Jack opened the file again and read, then closed it. "Sally, this is good. This is really good detective work. This would explain how he knew Denver so well. He had, what, ten days to scope out the town? I still can't figure out how he found the cabin, though. There's no connection between him and the Cramer family that I can find. I'll have to ask him when we meet."

He dropped the file on his desk. "Good work. And this Bobby character, you think he'll remember the girl, what's her name, Jackie?"

"I tell you, Jack, that man doesn't miss a thing if you ask me."

Jack sat back in his chair, his hands clasped behind his head, and he sighed. He looked at his assistant.

"You doing anything for dinner?" he asked her.

"Nothing special, why?"

"Let me call Sue. I think you deserve a reward. How 'bout you come by the house for a little cookout. I'll throw some steaks on the grill and we'll celebrate. I think you've earned it."

Sally brightened. "I'd have to change first. What time?"

"Soon as you can get there."

He picked up the phone and called his wife.

"It's all set," he said, hanging up. "Just come on over whenever you're ready."

CHAPTER 44

Ellis Bay, Thursday, September 20

The face that stared at the Ellis Bay Postmaster from the poster was that writer fella who lived out on the point. John Burton, sure as shootin'. It was a drawing, but a darn good one. The poster said that he was wanted as a suspect in a kidnapping that took place in Denver, Colorado, in July of this year. He was considered armed and dangerous, the poster also said.

That caught Eli by surprise; that Burton was considered dangerous. Sure, he was a newcomer to the area, but at one time or another, wasn't everybody? And he seemed okay, kind of quiet. That's why It was so hard for him to call Washington, but he had to do his duty, and so he dialed the number on the poster.

"I need to talk to that Jack Donovan fella," Eli said to the receptionist, his accent thick and nasally.

"Mr. Donovan's not in right now, can someone else help you?"

Eli looked at the poster again. He debated whether to hang up or not. His eyes wandered down to the contact names in front of him. "How 'bout a Miss or Mrs. Sally Martin. She in?"

"Just a moment, sir.

He waited.

"Special Agent Sally Martin."

He identified himself.

"Yes, Mr. Snow," Sally said when he was finished, "what can I do for you?"

"Poster I'm holdin' says you're looking for this Parks, a.k.a. so-on-and-so-forth, fella. Well, I know who he is, and his name's not Parks. It's Burton. Lives up he-ah in Ellis Bay, Maine."

Sally sat up in her chair. She asked, "Are we talking about John Parks, wanted in connection with a kidnapping in Denver?"

"Ehyup. That's what the poster sez."

"And you say he lives in Ellis Bay? And that's in Maine?"

"Ehyup. That's right. That's what I said. I'm the postmaster up here. Been so for the past twenty-eight ye-ahs. I guess I know just about everybody in and around these pahts, and I'm tellin' you, this picture here is him. John Burton. Ehyup."

She asked him several questions which he answered in short sentences. She took down all the information and said she'd be in Ellis Bay in the morning and then hung up. Her heart was pumping.

"Where are you, Jack?" she called as she came flying out of her office.

The receptionist at the front desk looked up as she approached.

"Where's Jack?" she demanded, unable to control her emotions.

"He got called home on an emergency. His wife fell down the stairs and hurt herself. Her older boy found her on the floor, unconscious. He called, and Jack left right away."

Sally turned and ran back to her office and called Jack's home.

"Hello?" Jack's son answered.

"Is Jack there?"

"Just a minute."

Seconds ticked by before Jack picked up the phone. "Hello?"

"Jack, it's Sally. I just heard. What happened? Is she all right?"

"She fell down the stairs. Knocked herself out. Robbie called me, and I called an ambulance. They just arrived. She's conscious now, but as a precaution, they're taking her to the hospital."

"Oh, that's a relief. Anything I can do?"

"No. I'm going to ride along to the hospital. Robbie's going to follow along in the car."

"Jack? I think we've found Parks! He's in Maine!"

"What did you say?"

"I said, I think we've found Parks, only his real name is Burton, John Burton. He lives in Maine."

"Sally, that's great! How—"

Postmaster from his hometown called with an ID. I'd like to go up there tomorrow and check it out. Can you come?"

"Do you mind going alone, or would you like me to send another agent with you?"

"I'll go it alone. He's not in Maine right now. Witness says he'll be out of town until the end of October or the first week of November, but I thought I'd go up there anyway. Wit' says he frequently goes out of town. And, Jack? Jackie's with him. They're married now."

Sally, I've got to go now. They've got Sue in the ambulance. Good job, and good luck. Call me."

"I will. My best to Sue. I'll say some prayers."

"Thanks."

Sally hung up, her concern for Sue dulling the excitement of her news. She picked up the phone again and had the receptionist make reservations for Boston on the red-eye. She also asked for a car to be reserved. She wrestled with the idea of calling Bruce Sellier in Boston but decided against it. Burton was out of town; all she was going to do was snoop around and ask questions. She decided to go it alone.

Sally packed for the weekend and caught the flight to Boston. Her rental, a Ford Taurus, was waiting for her and she was off. She arrived in Ellis Bay by ten thirty, found a bed and breakfast, checked in, and found the post office by noon.

Eli was expecting her and suggested they have lunch at Annie's Anchor Café. They walked the few short blocks to the café and found a table by the front window.

"So tell me about this John Burton," Eli said to Sally when their orders were taken.

"I was hoping you could tell me about him," she shot back.

"Not much to tell. He's a writer. You know, wrote that Vietnam war story, *Road to Phnom Penh*. Hit the best sella's list. Moved he-ah few ye-ahs back. Pretty much keeps to himself. Comes and goes all the time. That's why he has a general delivery address I suppose. We hold his mail for weeks at a time, sometimes. Bought the old Crowell place out on the point. Lived there alone until recently. Got himself a wife now.

"Anyway, the two of 'em came in t'other day and said they was goin' away for a while. Thought they'd be gone maybe six or seven weeks. 'Goin' sailin',' he said."

"Did he say where?"

"Nope."

"Does he get much mail?"

"Not much. Bills. Government check every month. Stuff from his agent in Boston. He did get several boxes of books recently. 'Research books,' he said."

"Do you remember where they came from?"

"South. Alabama, North Carolina, Virginia, I think. Probably for his next book is my guess. I think it'll be Civil War stuff, if you ask me." He shrugged.

"And he lives out on the point you say?"

"Ehyup. On the other side of the Bay. Fixed it up real nice. Glad to take you out they-ah if you like."

"That would be nice."

"Can't believe John Burton is a kidnapper. Seems like a real nice person. But that's him on that poster. I'd bet my life on it."

"Well, we don't know if he's a kidnapper for sure. We just want to talk to him about one that happened in Denver."

Eli coughed several times, gasping for air. Finally, he stopped and sat up straight in his chair. Sally noticed the yellow stains between his fingers from long years of smoking.

Their lunches arrived, and the talk changed to life in Ellis Bay, Maine.

Eli was a talker if you gave him a chance, and Sally did.

Most of what he had to say about Burton was speculation, but it was interesting to hear.

After lunch, they returned to the post office. Eli told the clerk that he was taking Sally, the FBI agent, out to the Burton place. They rode two miles around the bay to the road that led to the cottage, turned off on the private driveway and drove down the sand and gravel drive to the gray weathered shingled cottage. From what Eli had told her at Annie's, she could see that the cottage was closed up tight. The curtains were all drawn, and the front porch was empty.

She pulled up and parked in front of the cottage. The two of them got out of her Taurus and approached the front door. Sheer curtains covered the window, but, by cupping her hands and holding them close to the glass, she was able to make out the inside living room area. It looked neat and tidy.

She walked around to the side of the house. There was a garage next to it. She continued around to the back porch and walked up the steps, peered through the glass in the kitchen door and walked down the steps. She continued around the cottage, coming once again to the front door. Eli followed her around the house but said nothing. Sally turned and hurried to the garage. It was locked, but she was able to see the Corvette through the windows in the door. It was red.

"Bingo!"

She backed away from the window and smiled at Eli Snow.

"I need to find a judge. Have you got a judge in this town?"

"Ehyup. Judge Cooper."

"Can you take me to him?"

"Don't know. It's Friday afternoon. Might be gone by now. We can try."

She turned the car around and raced back out to the road, turned right, and sped off in the direction of the courthouse. Eli reached down, put his seatbelt on and looked over at Sally.

"No need to race. Judge is either they-uh or he's not. Speeding won't make no difference."

Sally braked hard in front of the courthouse, and sped into the building, leaving Eli alone in the car. A Federal Marshall stopped her at the security checkpoint. She held up her badge and identification card for him as she said, "I need to see Judge Cooper."

"Sorry, Miss," He looked at the name on her ID, "Miss Martin, you missed him by about five minutes."

"Damn! Any other judges on duty?"

"Nope. Just Judge Cooper, and he's gone."

Sally slammed her fist down on the table in front of the Marshall. "How can I find him? It's important."

"You could try his home. It's over on—"

"Thanks," Sally said over her shoulder as she exited the building.

Eli was still sitting in the front seat of the Taurus when she raced around the front of the car and got in.

"Tell me how to get to Judge Cooper's house, please, Eli."

"Figured you'd want that. That's why I stayed. Now, you're gonna wanna head on up this street to Ceda' and turn right."

Sally shot out of her space in front of the courthouse and followed Eli's directions, finally coming to a stop in front of an old three-storied clapboard house with white columns.

"Thanks," she said, exiting the car. She hurried around the front of the car, opened the white picket gate in the fence that surrounded the house, and rushed up the steps to the front door, two at a time, ringing the bell as she came to a stop on the landing. She was slightly winded.

A silver-haired, rotund man in his sixties came to the screen door.

"Yes?" he asked.

"Judge Cooper?"

"Yes. Who's askin'?"

She held up her badge and ID. "Special Agent Sally Martin, FBI. Could I have a few minutes of your time?"

He opened the door to let her in and noticed Eli in the car.

"Afternoon Eli!" he shouted to the man in the car.

"Afternoon Judge," Eli called back.

"Come in, come in," the judge said.

Sally entered and followed him down a hall to his study. The smell of stale cigar smoke hung fetid and heavy in the air. Sally guessed that the man lived alone.

"Sit down, young lady," the judge offered, motioning to a leather chair in front of his desk. He sat down in his chair across the desk from her.

"Now, what's this all about?"

"I'm sorry to bother you so late on a Friday afternoon, Judge, but I need a search warrant."

The judge raised his bushy silver eyebrows. "And who's the lucky person that you want this search warrant for?"

"A man named John Burton. He's the author who lives out on the point."

"And why do you need this warrant? I assume you have probable cause."

"Yes, your Honor. The FBI believes he was responsible for a kidnapping that took place in Denver in early July."

"What makes you think that John Burton is your man?"

"Sally pulled out the wanted poster. "This is our man. Your Postmaster called us and said that this man lives out on the point. Secondly, there's a red Corvette parked in his garage. A man answering our man's description was seen driving a late model red sports car. Third, we believe he mailed the ransom money to his house by way of general delivery from several places in the South. Two million dollars to be precise. Eli Snow said several boxes were shipped from various cities in the South. We followed his trail from Denver through several southern cities, finally losing his trail in DC, he finally showed up again in Boston. That's where he was spotted driving the Corvette."

"Sounds like you've got probable cause to me. Tell you what. You have the necessary forms filled out and come by my office on Monday morning and you'll get your warrant."

"Monday?"

"Monday."

From the tone of his voice, Sally knew that he wouldn't budge.

"I hear tell the man has gone on some kind of honeymoon vacation. There's really no hurry now, is there?"

"No, Your Honor."

"Then you come by my office Monday morning with the proper request, and I'll be glad to give you your warrant."

The judge rose and retrieved a partially smoked cigar from a large ashtray on his desk. He reached into his coat pocket and pulled out a silver lighter, stuck the cigar in his mouth, and lit it in one swift motion.

Sally rose, offered her hand to the judge, thanked him, turned, and walked out of the room.

"Pompous ass," she mumbled.

Sally drove Eli back to the post office and dropped him off, thanking him for his help. She promised to keep him informed of her progress. She grabbed a quick bite at a fast food and returned to her room. She was asleep by 9:00 p.m.

Saturday morning, she called Jack at home. Sue was awake. She had suffered a severe concussion and had stayed overnight at the hospital for observation. They were releasing her later this morning. He was just getting ready to return to the hospital. That was good news for Sally.

She, in turn, relayed her news to him and asked him to fax a copy of a warrant request to her at the post office. She listed all the things she wanted to check on at Burton's cottage to Jack so that they would show up on the warrant.

"It's him, Jack. I've got positive identification. The Corvette's in the garage. I need the search warrant Monday morning. All we need is him. Oh, and his new wife, Jackie? She's got to be our Aunt Julie. Her description is of a younger woman. Brunette, but her physical makeup fits.

"Eli Snow, the postmaster, says Burton'll be out of town for six to eight weeks. They're off on some kind of honeymoon cruise. We can check all the cruise lines.

"Does the name John Burton ring any bells for you, Jack?"

Before he could answer, she continued. "He wrote a best seller. Jack, he's ex-Special Forces. Retired with the rank of major! Jack! It all fits! It's him! It has to be. His picture is even on the back of the book I bought, and the likeness is remarkable."

Sally spent Saturday and Sunday asking questions of the locals in town. Nobody knew him well, but everyone had good things to say about him. He was seen running on the beaches on the point every morning, come rain or come shine. He held doors open for little old ladies. He chatted openly and freely with the men at the Anchor Café. Annie herself said she'd have married him in a minute if she were a little younger. He never caused any trouble, always had a smile and a good word for everyone. The townspeople couldn't believe that he could be a kidnapper. Armed and dangerous, no way, they all agreed.

Saturday night she sat in her room and read Burton's book. It was well written, precise, and articulate. There was one interesting tidbit in the novel. There had been a kidnapping in Saigon that had gone pretty much like the one in Denver. The victim, an ARVN General had been snatched and tied up with duct tape and thrown into the trunk of a car, just like the security guard in Denver had been. Burton was meticulous in his details and in his planning. Every action was well thought out.

Sally finished the book in the early hours of Sunday morning.

On Sunday afternoon, Sally drove out to the cottage and walked around the house again. She climbed the steps to the back porch and sat in one of the chairs that she thought he must have sat in. From there she could see the channel leading to the harbor, and the jetty at the entrance to the harbor. A gentle autumn breeze came in off the water and rustled her blond hair. The sun overhead was still warm, and the breeze felt cool on her face. She tilted her head back and closed her eyes, exhaustion taking possession of her body.

When she opened her eyes, the sun was gone. Dark clouds were moving over the land. A flash of lightning lit the air with electricity and the rains began to fall, softly at first, but as she ran to her car, the rains were coming down heavier. It was a race to the car, and the rains were winning. By the time she got into the car and turned on her wipers, they could barely keep up with the downpour.

She sat there, drenched to the skin, and listened as torrents of rain pelted her car. It lasted almost ten minutes, and then it was gone. The sun broke through the clouds and a rainbow appeared off the water, the colors glorious in the clearness of the air.

Monday morning, she was waiting in the judge's outer office when Judge Cooper arrived.

"Ah, Miss Martin. A pleasure to see you so early this morning. Abby, I need—"

"Right here, Your Honor," the elderly lady said, holding up the search warrant. "All it needs is your signature."

"Good work."

He took the papers from his secretary, read them quickly and put his signature to the bottom.

"There you go, young lady. All signed and ready for execution." He chuckled at his joke.

"Thank you, Your Honor," Sally said, taking the papers from him.

She turned to leave.

"You *will* keep me informed of everything you find?"

"Yes, Your Honor, I will."

"Good day then."

Sally hurried out of the courthouse. She needed a member of the local police to be with her, so she hurried to the police station next.

By nine thirty, Sally and the officer were pulling up in front of the Burton cottage. The locksmith was already there.

"Mornin', Ephrim."

"Mornin', Bob," the locksmith replied.

"Ephrim, this here's Agent Sally Martin from Washington, DC. She's with the FBI. She's here to search the house. What we'll be needin' for you to do is open the door for her."

"No problem, what else?"

"I might be needing you to open the garage door also. I'll try to find a set of keys first."

"All right then, let's get started.

The locksmith looked at the door lock and the dead bolt and then walked back to his van. In less than a minute he was back with two keys in his hand. The first one unlocked the dead bolt; the second one opened the door handle.

"There you go," he said, grinning at the two of them. "No problem at all."

He held up the keys for the two of them to inspect. "Master keys. I changed those locks last month. Always keep a set of spares just in case. Much easier to work with, don't you think?"

Sally didn't know if he was brilliant or stupid. She only knew that she could now enter the house.

"How much do I owe you?" she asked.

"Service call. I'll just keep the keys." He thought and quickly said, "Thirty-five dollars is all."

"Do you take credit cards?"

"Proper ID I do."

"Oh, come on, Ephrim, she's FBI for Christ's sake."

"Oh yeah, well, I guess it'll be okay. You want me to unlock the garage too? I got a key."

"Please."

Sally looked at Bob. "You want to come in with me or wait outside?"

Bob was only too glad to let her search the premises herself. He went and sat in his cruiser. Sally entered the house, turning her attention to the task at hand.

The front room was masculine in its appearance, neat and tidy. There was nothing out of place. She walked through the entire house, room by room. She entered the bedroom. The bed was made up. Not a wrinkle could be found on the bedspread. "Military training," she said at the preciseness of it. On his desk was a computer. It looked new. Several computer manuals were stacked on the floor next to the desk. She knelt and examined them. They looked like they hadn't been used much. Sticking out from numerous pages were little yellow Post-its, with words written on them. On top of the desk, next to the screen and keyboard were several yellow legal pads, stacked neatly, one on top of the other. Sally lifted the cover of the top one and read a few of the notes. The notes were done in outline form: character developments, plot formation. There was no mention of the South or the Civil War on any of the notes she read.

She turned around and slowly took in the entire room. Sally walked over to the closet and slid the door open. Inside, on the left side were his clothes, and on the right side were Jackie's.

Sally fingered a few of Jackie's items and pulled them out one by one. They were designer labels, classy, but not overly expensive. She hung them back on the rack and examined a few of his shirts and jackets. The shirts were all pressed and starched and hung with a one-quarter inch separation; neat, orderly. She pulled one of his shirts out and held it, smelling the freshness of it. A faint scent of cologne touched her nostrils. Something familiar. Something from her past. She remembered. Old Spice. Her father had worn Old Spice. She hung up the shirt, careful to keep the spacing intact and turned, looking around the room one more time and then walked out.

When she entered the kitchen, she stopped. There, in the corner, neatly broken down and leaning against the wall were five medium-sized boxes. There were FedEx and UPS identifying logos on each of them. She checked the mailing labels. They were from Charlotte, Greensboro, Raleigh, Petersburg, and Richmond.

Sally sat on a chair and stared at the boxes. They were marked RESEARCH BOOKS.

This is how he got the money here, she thought. But where is it now? And how much is there? Did he have the money from the previous jobs hidden here somewhere? Perhaps buried on the beach? Or maybe inside the walls of this old house. One of the townspeople had said that he had done some remodeling. No, probably not. But if it's not hidden here, then where? The combined weight of five and a half million dollars would be too much for him to move without someone noticing. Could it be hidden in the walls? Or under the floor? The attic?"

She touched the flap on one of the boxes with her foot. This one had been sent from Charlotte. Sally pulled out her notebook and began writing.

CHAPTER 45

Hyannis, Cape Cod, Massachusetts,
Saturday, September 22, 9:20 a.m.

All the stores were onboard: fuel, masts and spars, extra equipment, food, water, and all other necessities. The suitcases were stowed below. Mike accused John and Jackie of packing far too many things but accepted all the luggage onboard.

The first leg of the voyage would take them to Baltimore. There they would replenish their supplies for the second leg of the journey. From Baltimore they would head southeast, stopping in Bermuda for two days before heading southwest into Miami. John and Mike discussed the possibility of using the inland water route south of Baltimore but decided against it. It would have taken longer for one thing, and for another, the idea of sailing to Bermuda was enticing to the Morris'. Secretly, John didn't want to be trapped in a boat with land on both sides of him should the FBI pick up his trail. They had already discovered Jackie's California address. With good weather and a fair wind, they would make Miami before the end of the month.

Eric and Scott showed up and loaded their bags onboard. Scott's father stood by, supervising and giving last-minute advice. When it was all aboard, he went below to see that it was safely stowed away. Then he came topside and pronounced the vessel ready to sail and said goodbye.

The weather reports told of fair weather and clear skies. As they prepared to cast off, the sky was an uninterrupted canopy of blue, with a bright sun shining on them.

John Boucher stepped onto the pier, waited for Mike to start the auxiliary engine, released the front and aft ropes, and tossed them onto the deck, watching as the *Dram Bouie* slowly maneuvered its way into the harbor.

Once outside the harbor, Mike set his course south by southwest; this would take them between the islands of Nantucket and Martha's Vineyard. When they were clear of the jetty and open water lay ahead, Eric and Scott put on canvas and the boat leaped forward, the air catching in its sails. The feel of the boat's picking up speed reminded John of a dog on a leash that had just been set free.

Ocean spray came over the side of the boat, wetting its occupants with a fine cooling mist. Mike adjusted the wheel slightly, and the boat settled into the water, cutting a trail through the sound waters as it picked up speed. The two boys moved about the craft like monkeys, checking the lines, getting a feel for the "lady" as they fondly referred to her.

John and the two women watched them scamper along the port and starboard sides of the boat and up and down the mast, checking everything.

"They're pretty good at this, aren't they?" John commented to the helmsman.

"They should be. Scott's been sailing almost from the time he took his first steps. Eric's not too far behind. He started sailing with Scott and his dad when he was only six. Between them they've got over thirty years' experience on the open sea.

They passed Cape Page and Chappaquiddick Island and sailed through Muskeget Channel just before one in the afternoon. Mike set a course west southwest, taking them past No Man's Island and on toward Block Island, east of Long Island. This was as far as Mike had ever sailed the *Dram Bouie*.

By late afternoon they were pulling into the inlet at Grace Point on Block Island where they dropped anchor for the night. The first day had gone well. Eric and Scott checked the boat, the engine, the sails, and all the lines, then dove overboard and checked the rudder, propellers, and keel. Surfacing, the two boys gave Mike the thumbs-up sign, then swam for the ladder and came aboard. They dried themselves off with towels supplied by Jeannie and went below. Soon, the smells of cooking filled the air.

Sitting down to a meal of steaks and salad, Mike said, "Tomorrow we set course for Baltimore. And tomorrow we start to catch our meals."

Ellis Bay, Maine, Monday, September 24, 5:00 p.m.

Slowly and methodically Sally went through the house, looking for something, anything that would tie John to any of the three kidnappings. She had called Pete Sellier in Boston, and he sent her an agent to help with the search. Ellis Bay provided an officer to assist also.

Now, with their help she went through the house in earnest. She checked all the drawers, all the cabinets, all the shelves. Nothing. She tapped the walls, listening for the sound of a hidden compartment; she moved rugs and checked floors, she checked ceilings, vents, and the attic. When she was finished with the main floor, she checked the cellar. The stairway leading down to it was old and steep, with narrow steps. She rummaged through a drawer in the kitchen and found some candles and returned to the cellar stairs, carefully descending the wooden steps, holding on to a wooden railing as she went. At the bottom of the stairs she held up the candle and scanned the basement. Overhead was a single naked light bulb with a string hanging down from it. She pulled the string, but it wouldn't light.

Sally held up the candle and surveyed her surroundings. A new cement floor had been laid down and the walls had been reinforced. It was chilly and damp, but it was clean. Boxes, cans, and jars were examined on shelves that covered the walls. A washer and dryer and a wash basin sat against the wall to the right of the stairs. Behind the staircase she found a wine rack. She checked the various bottles set in the racks. Some had dust on them; some looked like they had been placed there recently. She tried to remember the names of the bottles that had been taken from the McArthur residence and the houses in Detroit and Houston but could not. That information was in Washington. She wrote down the names on all the labels.

Carefully she examined the new cement floor, looking for signs of a false floor that might hide something underneath, but the floor was solid.

Back upstairs she checked the desk in the bedroom. In the top middle drawer, she found several deposit slips from the Shawmut Bank in Boston, and others from a local bank in town. Several of the deposits were large, but nowhere close to totaling the amounts of money she figured him for. Other deposits, all totaling the same amount of money were deposited on or about the sixth of each month in the local bank. She figured these to be his government retirement checks.

Sally made a note of all the checks that were deposited in Boston. The last one was for two hundred thousand dollars net deposit and was dated August sixteenth. She noticed that fifty thousand dollars was taken from the total amount of the check

"Fits his profile," she mused. "He likes to carry a lot of money with him, but that still is an awful lot of money to be carrying around."

She would check with the bank in Boston to see if this was normal procedure for him, but more importantly, where was this money coming from?

Sally also found an address book filled with names, addresses, and phone numbers. It was old by the looks of it. She thumbed through it quickly; there didn't appear to be any new entries that she could see. The names and addresses were scattered all over the country. Some of the entries had been scratched out, and newer addresses or phone numbers had been written in. Jackie's name was not among them. She added the book to her list of items to be confiscated.

Sally flipped the switch to his computer hoping to find something that would incriminate him. It was dead. Right, there was no power. She looked at her watch. It was after five. She had been at the cottage all day. What she had come up with so far wouldn't tease a D.A.'s curiosity.

Sally decided to call it a day. She would come back in the morning. She would have to call Ephrim and get a set of keys made so she could come back tomorrow. She wanted a go at the garage. She also wanted to check out the land around the house and garage.

She and the others locked up the cottage and drove back to town, stopping at the Anchor Café to have a bite of supper and to call Ephrim. He agreed to have a set of keys dropped at her boarding house. "No charge."

Sally hadn't eaten anything all day and her stomach was crying for food. She ordered crab cakes, tomato wedges on lettuce, hush puppies and a chocolate fudge brownie for dessert. She sat with her fellow agent, making small talk while she watched and listened as the locals came and went. When they finished, she took the other agent back to the bed and breakfast where she was able to get him a room. They said goodbye and Sally went to her room. She needed to wash her underthings. She would have liked to wash her outfits, but they required dry cleaning. She wasn't sure how much longer she would be in town. She was able to use the laundry room at the house. It was two fifteen in the morning by the time her clothes were done. She stripped to her underwear, climbed into bed, turned off the light and went to sleep. It was a troubled, restless sleep, and when she woke at 7:00 a.m., she felt more tired than when she had gone to bed.

Sally rose, showered, dressed, and came down to breakfast. Her fellow agent was already at the table.

"Good morning," he said as she entered.

"Good morning."

"We going back to the cottage?"

"Yes. I want to go through the garage. Are you staying or going back to Boston?"

"If you don't need me, I'll just go back. Do you think you can wrap things up?"

"Sure. I've got Bob again today if I need him. I'll call the sheriff's office and have him meet me out there. I want to thank you for all your help."

He nodded and smiled and then took a bite of his toast.

Sally finished her breakfast and walked the two blocks to Main Street to purchase some clothes to wear. She purchased a pair of khaki shorts which she wore with a white blouse when she headed back to the cottage, Ephrim's keys on the seat beside her. She went straight to the garage when she arrived. Throwing open the door, she was startled by the sudden appearance of a raccoon scurrying out the door. She jumped back when she saw the motion, her heart racing, as the raccoon ambled off around the corner and out of sight.

She waited outside, expecting to see more animals come out of the darkness. She turned an ear toward the inside. It was quiet. Looking around the entrance, she found a light switch and flipped it on. Nothing.

"Of course there's no light, you ninny," she said to herself, "there's no power. Duh."

Sally found a kerosene lamp on a bench in front of the car. On the bench were used cans of paint, some brushes in a coffee can, a paint tray with a roller, thinner, toolbox filled with various tools and tape, and a length of rope. Also, there were power cords, a drop light, and a portable fan.

Sally held up the lamp and surveyed the rest of the garage. Except for a few aerosol spray cans on ledges between the studs, there was nothing else in the garage. Overhead, cross beams supported the roof. There was no attic.

She walked around the car and tried the passenger side door handle. It was locked. It also set off the burglar alarm. The sound scared the hell out of her and she almost dropped the kerosene lamp. She ran out of the garage to the blaring of the horn.

She raced to the house, set the lamp down on the porch, opened the front door and closed it behind her, leaning against it to catch her breath. She could still hear the horn going on and off. And then, as suddenly as the car alarm had gone off, it suddenly went quiet. Sally continued to stand there, her hand over her heart, feeling the pounding from within.

There has to be a key to that thing, she thought. But where? I searched the entire house yesterday. The key just isn't here.

Sally walked back to the garage. It was quiet now. Entering through the open door, she stopped and stared at the red car.

"Are you going to behave?" she asked it.

Sally searched the garage, this time looking for keys. There were none. The car would have to be searched later. She walked slowly around the inside of the garage, inspecting the walls. The garage turned out to be an ordinary wooden structure. There was no money hidden here. She got down on her hands and knees and looked under the car, careful not to touch it. A cement floor with a few old dried up oil spots was all she found.

She closed up the garage and locked it, took the lamp back to the kitchen and placed it back under the counter where she had found it.

It was close to noon. She retrieved a lunch sack from her car and walked around to the porch. She set out one of the plastic chairs and ate her lunch, enjoying the breeze off the water and the smell of the salt air in her nostrils.

John Burton. I bet you spent a lot of time out here, she thought. She spent some time watching the water traffic and surveying the surrounding lands from her chair on the porch. When she was finished with her lunch, she gathered together the wrappings and trash and put it all in her brown lunch sack and dropped it into the trash can.

She removed her shoes and walked the grounds surrounding the cottage. The sand felt soft and warm under her feet. She crisscrossed the property looking for some sign of the unusual, some sign of land disturbed, but found none.

All right, John Burton, she thought, *what have you done with the money? Those five boxes did not contain books, or at least I couldn't find any books, so they had to contain the money. What have you done with it? And where are you? Surely you don't have all that money with you. What have you done with it?*

Sally looked toward the shore. Dozens and dozens of gulls were gathered along the beach, all facing in the same direction, all facing the water. Some were resting in the sand. Others were standing; others were scurrying around. Some would rise as the wind caught their wings, only to settle back onto the sand a short distance away. It was as if they were waiting for the boats to come home.

A stiff breeze blew in off the water, and with it, the air grew chilly. Sally walked back to the cottage. As she entered, the first drops of rain fell on the deck and the beach behind her. Within minutes, a drenching rain covered the land.

At four thirty, she retrieved the lamp and lit it. It was nearly dark inside. The rains had lessened, tapering down to a steady drizzle, and the wind had let up. Sally went to the window and looked out at her car. A huge puddle surrounded it. Gauging the water around the wheels of her car, she guessed that there was maybe two inches of water underneath.

"Great," she sighed. "I guess I'll have to go barefoot."

She decided she would leave and head back to town. She would have to return to the cottage one more time. Putting the lantern on the kitchen table, grabbing her note pad and purse and shoes, Sally closed the door behind her and ran to the car, splashing through the water. The water drenched her bare legs and it was cold. She opened the car door, threw her things over the other side, and climbed in. Her clothes and hair were soaked. She started the engine, turned on the radio and tuned it to a local station. The voice was talking about the storm that had suddenly come out of the northeast. The voice also talked about the fishing boats that were caught out in it and especially mentioned a trawler called the *Mary B.* that had run into trouble out on the open sea. The Coast Guard was on its way to recover the men from the sinking boat.

"More news to follow," the newsman went on.

Sally shook her head, wiped her brow, slowly backed the car up the driveway, and turned onto the road, her windshield wipers beating a steady rhythm across the glass.

CHAPTER 46

Sally spent Tuesday morning back at the cottage. She had pages of notes and an inventory of everything she wanted taken down to Boston. She walked around the cottage one more time. At eleven thirty, she locked it up and retreated to her car. Then she headed back to town.

She called Jack at noon to report in, telling him what she had in the way of inventory. She then told him she was going down to Boston to look up Burton's agent. Maybe he knew where John Burton and his new wife were. Her next call was to Bruce Sellier in Boston, bringing him up to speed and requesting a team to come to Maine to retrieve the items she had inventoried. These included, among other things, the computer, address book, the boxes—maybe the lab could pull ink traces from the money on the inside—and reams of notes that John had written. She would stop in to see him later today with the complete list that she had made. She told him she would leave the keys to the cottage and the garage with the local police department. She also told him of her plan to visit Burton's agent in the morning.

At two thirty, she was on her way back to Boston. The drive was pleasant, the air was still warm, and the trees were turning colors. Along the way Sally reflected on the case, going all the way back to the beginning. Jack's call, the trip to Denver and their return to Washington, the side trips to Richmond, Boston, her trip to Ellis Bay, all of it flashed through her mind. They were getting close; she knew it.

She was deep in thought when she noticed the red and blue flashing lights coming up behind in the rearview mirror. She glanced down at her speedometer.

"Damn," she muttered as she signaled and pulled over to the shoulder. She reached over and opened the glove box and pulled out the registration and insurance papers and then rolled down her window.

"Good afternoon, young lady," the state policeman greeted as he approached her car. "You in a hurry to be somewhere?"

Sally looked at the grinning face staring down at her from beneath his wide-brimmed blue hat. Silver tinted sunglasses reflected her image back to her. She fumbled in her purse and produced her driver's license and her FBI identification card and handed them to him. He scooped them up and looked at her picture on the cards then looked down at her.

"Well, Miss…Martin, looks here like you're FBI."

"Yes, officer."

"You know how fast you were going?"

"I didn't realize it until I saw you in my mirror and looked down at my speedometer. I guess I was daydreaming. Sorry." She gave him a weak smile of apology.

He gave a grunt, told her to wait and walked back to his car. Sally watched as he climbed in and picked up his radio.

"Damn," she said again. She had never been stopped for speeding before and she was embarrassed.

She watched him leave his car and approach in her side mirror.

"You need to pay more attention to your driving, Miss Martin. You were going pretty fast. I'm going to give you a warning this time, but please, drive more slowly, okay?"

Sally gave him her warmest smile. "Thank you, officer, I will."

Sally arrived back in Boston at four thirty that afternoon. Bruce was waiting for her at his office. She made copies of her notes for him and briefed him about what she had found and had not found at the cottage in Maine.

Together they mapped out plans for Bruce's team's search of the cottage. Sally told him that almost everything was gathered together in the living room, and what wasn't was in the notes she was giving him. She warned him about the alarm on the Corvette and admitted that she hadn't been able to find keys for it. Bruce promised to get the necessary warrants for Burton's phone records, bank statements, credit cards and so on.

He called and made arrangements for her to stay overnight in town and invited her to his house for dinner. She begged off, saying she had too much to do. She did promise to drop by the office before she headed back to Washington.

Sally left and checked into her hotel, ordered room service, and climbed into the shower. She was drying her hair when her dinner arrived. Dressed only in a hotel bathrobe, she went to the door, tipped the waiter, and pulled the cart into her room by herself. She had bought a book in the gift shop on her way up and read it while she nibbled at her dinner. She continued reading long after she was finished with dinner, and it was after ten when she finally put the book down, pushed her cart out into the hallway and got into bed.

The next morning, she found Michael Morris's address and drove over. She wanted to meet John's friend, hoping to get some personal insight into the elusive John Burton. Maybe she'd get lucky. Maybe he even knew where John Burton was.

She found a parking space less than a block away and walked the short distance to the building. Five cut stone steps led up to the door. A small brass plaque announced the name of the tenant and beneath it was a white push button buzzer. She pushed it and waited. She pushed again. And again. Still no answer.

Sally walked up the street, crossed over and entered a delicatessen on the corner. Inside she asked for and was given a phone book. She wrote down the number and asked where she could find a phone. The woman at the counter offered the use of her phone and Sally called the number.

"Michael Morris Literary Agency. This is Marcie. We're sorry, but the office is closed now. We will be out of the office for the next few weeks. I will be back on Monday, October eighth. If you will kindly leave a message, I will return your call as soon as I am able.

Mr. Morris regrets the inconvenience and will be back in the office on November 15."

There was a beep and then silence. Sally hesitated and then disconnected.

"Damn," she muttered as she calculated the days before Marcie would be back. "Twelve days. Damn! Damn! Damn! By then Burton could be anywhere."

She went back to her room to pack her bags. On an impulse, she called the MVD, identified herself and asked for information on all the Michael Morrises that lived within a sixty-mile radius of downtown Boston. She asked that they forward this information to the FBI office in Boston, to her attention. She thanked them and hung up. She decided to stay another day in Boston.

After a quick lunch at the hotel coffee shop, she headed over to the office. Bruce's people had already been in touch with the phone company and a list of phone numbers were matched up with the names and addresses. Bruce had two of his people making calls when Sally arrived. It was a slow process—many of the people were not home, some lines were busy, requiring callbacks, but at least nobody was hanging up on them.

By the end of the day, thirty-four of the thirty-nine had been accounted for. Two more were disconnected numbers and the other three were recorded messages. One was in Norwood, one in Brookline and one in Framingham. All were within thirty miles of downtown Boston.

There was nothing more to do at the office. Sally called Jack in Washington and left a message. She then went back to her hotel. It was now six thirty.

Sally awoke to the sounds of rain splattering against her windows. She opened the curtains to see rivulets of water running down the windows.

"Another day in paradise," she said to her reflection. "Oh well."

Her phone rang, startling her.

"Hello?"

"Sally?" It was Bruce. "We've located your Michael Morris. Well, at least we know where he lives. Address in Brookline. Problem is, he's not there. Seems the whole family is on vacation according to his next-door neighbor. He doesn't know where they are. Says the family will be gone for probably six to eight weeks. Thinks they might have gone sailing. No way to get in touch with them."

Sally thought, then asked, "If he went sailing, he must own a boat. Any chance the neighbor knows where Morris keeps it moored?"

We asked him. He didn't know. He's only known the Morris family for a few months. He just moved in next door in June. Says they're just sort of over-the-fence conversationalists."

He gave her the phone number. "I left him a message to call me when he gets back."

"Well, I guess that does it for now then. Damn, and we were so close. Thanks for your help, Bruce."

"No problem. Say listen, I'm going to send two men to Ellis Bay, you want to come along?"

"No. I think I'll head back to Washington. Call me when you hear from Mr. Morris, will you?"

"Sure thing. Oh, and I'll give you a heads-up when we've gone through Burton's things. Have a nice flight back."

"Thanks, Bruce."

Sally checked out of her hotel, turned in her rental at the airport, bought a one-way ticket back to DC and went to her gate. The flight wouldn't be leaving until midafternoon.

Jack was not in the office when Sally arrived back from Boston. She threw her briefcase on her desk and went down to the exercise room and worked out for thirty minutes. When she returned to her office, Jack was still out.

She waited until six and then went home. She slipped into her sweats and opened a bottle of Pinot Noir. She nibbled on cheese and crackers and drank the wine straight from the bottle.

Her alarm went off at 6:00 a.m. She rose and was in her car heading for HQ by six forty-five. She couldn't wait to get to work. There was so much to do. Thinking about the Morrises and the Burtons last night had filled her with ideas. She would call Bruce Selier first—and see if he could track down the registration for a boat in the name Michael Morris, and if so, was it currently on a cruise somewhere, and if so, where?"

She put through the call but had to leave a message. Bruce had decided to go to Maine to oversee the Burton investigation. He would be out through the weekend. She left a message telling him what she wanted and asked for a callback as soon as he found anything out.

Jack walked in at seven fifteen and stopped to say hello.

"So how's my little travelin' detective this morning? What's the latest?"

"Oh, hi, Jack," she greeted, looking up from her book. "I think Burton and his wife have hooked up with his agent Mike Morris and his wife. People in Maine and Morris's neighbor both say they went sailing on a cruise. I think they may be together."

"Good work."

"This is like trying to find a needle in a haystack. And I don't even know which haystack to start with."

"Well, you've done a remarkable job so far. I'm betting that you'll find them sooner or later."

"I hope it's sooner."

"I'll have some help for you in a little while. Good luck and keep me posted."

"Thanks, Jack. Oh! How's Sue doing?"

"She seems to be doing okay. She had some problems with headaches for a while, but she's doing better. Thanks for asking."

Miami, Saturday, September 29

The *Dram Bouie* dropped anchor in Miami at three in the afternoon. Except for a storm that had rolled over them on the evening of the twenty-fourth, the cruise had been a pleasant and uneventful one. With the exception of Jeannie, they all sported deep tans. She was suffering from a bad sunburn. Her nose had peeled off several layers of skin and was now constantly coated with a thick layer of white cream. She'd worn a wide-brimmed straw hat and a loose fitting muumuu since Baltimore.

Jackie had felt a little queasy yesterday and again this morning, finally throwing up her breakfast over the side of the boat. The men thought she was just a little seasick from a week on the water, but Jeannie thought otherwise.

At any rate, the six travelers disembarked and went ashore, glad to have solid ground under them again. They stayed in the SoBe area and went to dinner and clubbing before finally returning to the boat at around eleven thirty.

Scott and Eric went below and were soon asleep. The four adults settled in on the rear deck lounge area and sipped coffee. All around them, lights from other boats reflected off the black waters of the bay. It was peaceful. Only the sounds of an occasional boat motor, the clang of a bell, or the cry of a sea bird interrupted the quiet. They talked softly and shared their pasts.

They would leave Miami in the morning, after restocking, and sail on to the Cayman Islands, planning to arrive there in three days. Their destination would be Rum Point, off the northeast side of the big island.

John was happy. His two friends had taken to Jackie from the very beginning and she genuinely liked them. The two boys treated both of them with respect. They were patient with Jackie when she made a mistake in her sailing duties and even kidded her good-naturedly while they corrected her. By the time the *Dram Bouie* anchored in Biscayne Bay, both he and Jackie had become quite proficient and could move about the deck like able-bodied seamen. With a lot of help from the two boys, the four adults kept the boat clean and functional.

"People," Jackie began when there was a lull in the conversation, "John," she continued, looking at him and taking his hand in hers, "I have an announcement to make."

John looked into Jackie's eyes and felt like he was being drawn into them. They were so full of excitement.

"John," she said again, "I'm going to have your baby!"

Jeannie shrieked. "I knew it!"

Mike cheered, rose, came over, and patted John on the back. John stared at Jackie dumbfounded.

"A baby? A baby! We're going to have a baby! You're sure?"

John stood and pulled her up with him, his arms went around her, and he twirled her around. He was jumping up and down and shouting. "We're going to have a baby!"

Jackie was laughing and crying at once. "Yes, my darling! Yes! Yes!"

John stopped and took a step backward, his hands holding hers. "How… When… How long have you known?"

"Well, you know how, you silly, and it's been almost four weeks since my last period. You've probably noticed I've been a little under the weather these past few mornings."

Just then Eric popped his head out of the hatch, followed by Scott. "What's all the commotion about?" he asked.

Mike said "The Burtons are going to have a baby. Jackie just told us."

The boys turned to her, grins on their faces. Eric stepped up to her and gave her a big hug. "Congratulations, Mrs. Burton. That's great."

Scott followed and also hugged her.

"I think you should start calling me Jackie. Jackie and John." She nodded toward her husband.

The boys turned to John and offered their hands. "Congratulations, John."

John shook hands and accepted their congratulations, a grin as big as a Cheshire cat on his face.

And then John's protective nature took over. "Well, we've got to see a doctor. We've got to make sure everything's all right. We've—"

"Whoa. Hold on, honey. Everything's fine. We can see a doctor when we get to the Caymans. I'm fine, really. Besides, all a doctor would do would be to confirm what I already know. It's too early to do anything anyway. We'll wait until we get there, okay?"

"You're sure?" he asked. "Jeannie? What do you think?"

"She's right. All a doctor will do is run some tests on her to see if she is healthy. She'll be fine, John."

"Okay then. But we are going to see a doctor when we get there."

John put his hand on Jackie's stomach and grinned again. "We're going to have a baby."

"If it weren't so late, I'd say let's break out the champagne," Mike said, "but it is, and I don't have any champagne anyway, so I suggest we call it a night. We've got a lot to do in the morning."

They all agreed, and each went about the task of securing the boat before turning in.

Alone in their cabin, John took Jackie in his arms and held her to him. "I love you, Jackie."

They undressed and got into bed. He held her to him until they both drifted off to sleep. The last thing John murmured before he fell asleep was, "A baby. Isn't that somethin'?" Jackie smiled, and then she too drifted off to sleep.

CHAPTER 47

Off the north coast of Cuba, September 30

The *Dram Bouie* was making good time. They had left Miami and headed through the Florida Keys, sailing in a southwesterly direction. Above, only a few puffy clouds disturbed the pureness of the sky. The steady whooshing of the water as it rushed by the sides of the boat and the hissing of the saltwater as it came together again at the stern of the boat had a hypnotic effect on the travelers. The sun beat down on the sailboat, searing and relentless.

The boys put up the canopy over the rear area for shade. All sails were being used, and the boys were busy keeping everything working.

John and Mike wore swimsuits and white T-shirts, Jackie a bikini and one of John's T-shirts. Jeannie was covered with her muu-muu, and her straw hat was tied securely to her head with a bandana.

Since Jackie's announcement, John had been staying close to her and was becoming more in tune with her needs. The thought of having a baby was exciting, but it was also scary. He had never before thought about being a father. And where would they live when the baby came? There would come a time when the cottage would not be big enough any longer. Did he want the child brought up in Maine? Or did he want the child to grow up in a metropolitan setting?

The baby, he thought. *I wonder what it will be? A boy would be nice, but if it's a girl, if she's half as wonderful as Jackie, and half as beautiful, well then, that would be okay* too.

He brought her a glass of iced tea and sat next to her. She smiled up at him and sipped.

"Umm, good," she said. "Thank you."

She held the glass up to her forehead and rolled it, feeling the coolness of the glass against her skin.

"You're sure you're all right?" John asked. "You're not too hot?"

"I'm fine John, really, I am. Stop worrying. Goodness, you'd think I was getting ready to have the baby any day now. I've still got close to eight months to go. Stop worrying. And besides, I've got Jeannie here and she's had plenty of experience."

He gave her a sheepish grin and squeezed her hand.

"Land ho!" Scott shouted from the front of the boat. Land off the port bow!"

The two newlyweds stood and squinted in the direction Scott was pointing. Barely visible on the horizon rose the island of Cuba. Mike set a course to sail around it and approach Grand Cayman from the west.

Mike and John discussed where they would anchor once they reached the three islands. They could stay on the big island, Grand Cayman, or opt for one of the other two: Cayman Brac or Little Cayman. John had done his research and convinced his friend to make for Rum Point, on the northeastern side of the big island. It was quieter there, and customs and immigration were less stringent.

The *Dram Bouie*'s sails caught the breeze as Mike steered into his new heading. A spray of water rose up from the bow and caught the sun's reflection, creating a rainbow effect along the side of the boat for a brief time.

"Wow!" Jackie exclaimed.

"You don't see that too often," Mike called out from the helm. "They say that's a sign of good fortune to follow."

Jackie looked up at John and smiled. "Good fortune's already found us."

At four o'clock Eric and Scott drew in the spinnaker sail and lowered the mainsail in preparation for their afternoon meal. That's when they first heard the sound of the big engine. Coming up fast behind them was a Cuban patrol boat. Standing on the deck were three uniformed men with rifles in their hands. In front of them was an officer with a bullhorn.

"*Atencion! Atencion! Ustedes en el barco! Ocurre suceder para embarcando!* Attention! Attention! You there in the boat! Come about for boarding!"

The six members of the *Dram Bouie* all gathered in the rear of the boat and stared as the gunboat pulled up alongside.

"No hablo Espanol!" Mike called out to them. "No... comprendo!"

The officer put the bullhorn to his lips again, hesitated and then spoke again. "Drop your sail and come about. We wish to board you."

"But why? We haven't done anything wrong," Mike called back. Eric had now taken the helm and Mike stood alongside his wife and friends.

The gunboat was now only ten yards off the starboard side. The officer and his men looked menacing.

"Senor, you are inside the three-mile limit. You are trespassing in Cuban waters. We have to board your vessel and check your papers."

John turned to Mike and spoke softly. "You'd better do as he says. They don't look too happy."

"Scott! Lower the sail and secure it. Eric? Hold her steady. Prepare to be boarded."

"Gracias," the officer called out from his boat. He spoke some words to his helmsman and the Cubans prepared to board.

"Buenas dias, senors and senoras," the officer said as he boarded their boat. "I am Captain Manuel De Vargas. I am so sorry to inconvenience you, but you have sailed into Cuban waters. Please to show me your passports."

"Certainly," Mike said. "If you'll excuse me, they're below. John?"

The two men went below, returning quickly with all six passports. They handed them to the officer one at a time. He examined each one and checked the photograph against each of the faces staring back at him.

De Vargas was a small, compact man with a pencil thin moustache. His uniform was pressed and neat. He looked professional. The other men with him did not. Their uniforms were shabby, and they had stubble on their faces.

"And where are you going?" he asked as he passed the last of the passports back to Mike.

"We're sailing to the Cayman Islands on vacation," Mike answered.

The officer looked at them. "We will need to look and see that you are not smuggling illegal contraband into our country, no?"

"Oh, right," Mike answered. "Well, come along. Let me show you the way."

Jackie gave John a worried look as the captain and two of his men went below. The third guard stayed on deck with them. As the last of the Cubans descended into the boat, John gave her the slightest hint of a signal for her to relax.

Five minutes later the Cubans reappeared, followed by Mike. It appeared that the captain had been impressed with the boat and had been complimenting Mike on its beauty.

"Please to excuse our interruption, senors and senoras," the captain said as he gained the deck, "but you understand. We must be careful. Too many drugs and too much contraband comes into our little country. Sometimes we get lucky, sometimes we do not. It is lucky for you this time, no? Come," he said, turning to his men, "let us leave these people to continue their journey. Adios."

He nodded to the women and gave a casual salute to the men and boys and quickly turned and left the boat. When they were back in their own boat and heading away, Mike took the helm again and set a new course as Scott hoisted the mainsail, moving further away from the island.

"Well, that was interesting," Mike yelled out to his party. He grinned. "The captain really liked the boat."

Relief showed in John's eyes. He said, "I'm going below."

Mike began singing, "What should we do with a drunken sailor? What should we do with a drunken sailor? What should we do with a drunken sailor, early in the morning?"

Before he was done, Jeannie and the two boys joined in and together they sang the entire song.

Below deck, John went into his cabin and checked the position of the two suitcases. They had not been moved. He went back up on deck and gave an imperceptible nod to Jackie when her eyes met his. He turned to the others. "The Beachboys, you're not," he said. "But you know what? You're not that bad."

"Why, thank you, me hearty," Mike said.

Jeannie and Eric went below to finish preparations for their meal while the others watched the patrol boat sink below the horizon.

October 3

The *Dram Bouie* made the swing around the western tip of Cuba, keeping well offshore, and began its final leg of the journey, heading east-southeast toward the big island. Their anticipated time of arrival was three thirty in the afternoon.

They made excellent time, with only two fast moving squalls to contend with. Both times, Scott took charge and both times, the boat and its occupants made it through the storms easily.

Now, with the sun overhead and a gentle breeze blowing from the west, the party was relaxing in the cockpit area. Jeannie had brought brochures of the islands and was sharing them with the others, regaling them with the sights and activities offered on the islands. There was fishing and snorkeling, reef diving, a world-class golf course, pirate caves, swimming with stingrays, good food, night-life, casinos; the list went on and on. There was air travel and charters between the islands; in fact, it was only twenty-five minutes of flight from Grand Cayman to Cayman Brac if they wanted to go there to gamble.

John and Jackie didn't golf, but the others did. It was agreed that the four golfers would have to play the course while they were on the island. John and Jackie would "just have to find something to do by themselves." That was just fine with them.

"Land ho! There she is!" Scott called out from the bow of the boat.

Off to the east, barely visible, the travelers could make out the faint outline of the coast of Grand Cayman. Mike went below and returned with his pair of binoculars. He scanned the horizon and found the island in his sights.

"Not much altitude," he said. "I thought it'd be higher, you know, like the Hawaiian Islands. Maybe a mountain or two jutting up out of the sea, a volcano or something. Seems pretty flat."

He handed the glasses to John who peered into them, then adjusted them for a better look. By now, they had a clearer view of the distant island and John could count three large cruise ships docked along the bay.

"That's got to be Hog Sty Bay," John said, handing the glasses back to Mike. "That's got to be Georgetown. Jeannie? Hand me the map please."

He looked at the map and conferred with Mike. "Okay, here we are...and here's...Rum Point," he continued, moving his finger on the map. "That's our destination."

Mike turned to Eric. "Eric, set a course around the West Bay. Cayman Islands, here we come."

"Aye, aye, Captain," his son responded, turning the big wheel slightly, the cheers of the others echoing in his ears. The boat swung around, and the wind caught the sail again, filling it as the boat set its new course.

They all stood and watched as the island came closer. The two boys were amazed, even at this distance, at how large the cruise ships were, each one towering over the dock and the buildings. They would learn later that building codes allowed structures of no more than seven stories.

Large homes and condos of the wealthy, spaced well apart from each other, dominated the shoreline on the north side of the island. On the south side of the peninsula lay Little Sound, and it was here that the *Dram Bouie* anchored. It was now four ten in the afternoon.

As they anchored off the peninsula and wrapped the protective blue tarp around the furled sail, the harbormaster arrived and asked permission to come aboard. Mike gave him a hand boarding and greeted him when he had both feet on deck. He had all his papers and passports ready and handed them to the harbormaster when the man asked for them.

"Good afternoon to you all," he greeted, shaking Mike's hand.

Taking the papers, he said, "You've come a long way, I see. How was your trip?"

"The trip has been great. We were stopped by a Cuban patrol boat when we left Miami, but other than that, and two squalls, it has been an ideal journey."

The Harbormaster asked the usual questions and welcomed them to the islands. In answer to their inquiry, he recommended the Cayman Kai Yacht Club for dinner.

"Also," he added, "I'd suggest that you exchange your dollars for C.I. That would be Cayman Island dollars."

His accent was noticeably British, with a slight hint of Scots and even a trace of Jamaican. It had a musical quality to it.

"I'm afraid you'll take a bit of a bite in the exchange, but your time here on the islands will be more than worth it."

Mike posed the question that was paramount in some minds. "What is the exchange rate?"

"Oh. Well. Yes. You'll get eighty cents on the dollar. This is a good economy here. Your exchange will come in one dollar, five, ten, twenty-five, fifty, and one hundred CIs. You won't see much in the way of coinage. Too bulky, what?"

Mike was surprised at the exchange rate. John said nothing. He knew that their economy was strong, and the tourists brought millions of dollars to the islands. It was this difference that paid for all the municipal projects and salaries and all the other expenses that ran the Caymans. He knew that there was a tax on his deposits and a current rate of four and one-half percent. In the long run, his deposits would reap the benefits, but more importantly, they would be safe. The loss in the exchange rate was merely a nuisance to his way of thinking. And in truth, the taxes were a lot less than what he would have had to pay in the United States.

"Well, I'll be letting you get on with your vacation," the harbormaster continued, "have a grand time. You'll be able to get a lot of your questions answered at the yacht club: transportation, rentals, air flights to the other islands, dos, don'ts, and all that. And the Governor's Mansion in Georgetown is a wealth of information."

He tipped his hat. "Good day to you all and enjoy your stay."

The crew of the *Dram Bouie* watched as the harbormaster stepped onto his own boat and headed back to shore.

"Nice fellow," Michael commented as their visitor pulled away, "but to tell you the truth, I think if I wanted to smuggle anything onto the island, it would be pretty simple. I'd rate his inspection as cursory at best. He never touched anything."

"Well, that's because you look so honest," John joked. "Whatever would you be smuggling?"

"Oh, didn't you know about the ten tons of smack I've got stashed in the dinghy?"

"No, I guess I must have missed that."

"Well, there you go," Mike said.

By prearrangement, John and Jackie and Mike and Jeannie would be staying at the Grand Cayman Holiday Inn in Georgetown. It was famous for its beach bar. The two boys would stay on the boat and keep an eye on it. The crime rate was low on the islands, mostly drunk and disorderly and an occasional fight, but there was no sense in taking any chances.

The six travelers secured the boat, took turns in the shower, and then headed off to the Cayman Kai Yacht Club for dinner. Then it was back to the *Dram Bouie*. Their hotel reservations weren't until the next day.

October 4, 9:00 a.m.

The drive into Georgetown by taxi took forty-five minutes. They drove through Franktown and turned right through Breakers and Pease Bay and on to Bodden Town. Bodden Town was old, with fine old houses and cemeteries everywhere, even on the beaches.

Then it was on to Savannah and then South West Point, where they turned north and headed into Georgetown.

The taxi driver explained about the island's history and customs and its people. He went on to explain that he had been born here, had gone off to Jamaica for schooling and had returned here after graduation. That had been twenty-seven years ago.

He told them that the language was a mix of British, Scottish, and Jamaican with a little Texas drawl thrown in. "We get a lot of Texans down here," he went on. "They own a lot of condos along Sewen Mile Beach, and around the islands.

"By the way," he continued, "my name's Edward. Edward Bodden. You'll find that's a wery common name down here."

John noticed that Edward did not pronounce his v's; instead, his v's sounded like w's. The harbormaster had talked the same way. Even so, Edward's manner sounded refined.

"There's not much crime on the islands. After all, where can you go? Mostly it's Saturday night skirmishes and drunk and disorderly behavior. Sometimes the tourists get a little rowdy. We've had naked people on the beaches. Constabulary frowns on that sort of thing. Fact is, we're pretty conservative here on the islands. You have to wear clothes downtown—swimsuits are not allowed. And the bars and taverns? Well, they close at midnight on Saturday nights."

Edward pulled up in front of the Holiday Inn. He pulled a business card from a card case attached to the visor of his Mercedes and handed it to John.

"If you need someone to drive you around, don't hesitate to call. I'm available any time."

He got out, opened the door for Jackie, then raced around and opened the two doors on the passenger side.

"Thanks for the lift, Edward." John paid him and gave him a little something extra.

"Thank you, sir," the grateful driver said. He removed the suitcases from the spacious trunk and put them on the curb. They were immediately put on a six-wheel cart by a bellhop who waited and then followed the four travelers into the hotel, pushing the cart in front of him.

When they were checked in, they went to their separate suites, agreeing to meet at the beach bar after stowing their things in their rooms.

"We're going to have to do something with this money pretty soon. We can't leave it lying around." John said to his wife. "I'm going to go to Barclay's Bank this afternoon. I've got to make arrangements with them and the sooner I do that, the better I'm going to feel. You can make excuses for me, okay?"

"I think you're right. Having that money in here makes me nervous."

"You can imagine how I felt driving around the country with it in my trunk. I'll be glad to be rid of it."

John pulled Edward's card from his pocket and called the number. He left a message stating that he needed the cab's services at one o'clock.

He arrived at Barclay's at one fifteen and asked to see the bank president. He identified himself as Mr. Smith and gave the receptionist his account password. Within minutes, a middle-aged white-haired man in an impeccable gray three-piece suit approached.

"Ah, Mr. Smith," the man said, extending his hand. "I'm Ian Bartholomew. Welcome to Barclay's.

"Mr. Bartholomew, so good to finally meet you in person. I've heard so many good things about you."

"Yes, yes, well. Please, do come in," the man said, waving his arm in the direction of his office.

"Mrs. Bodden, see that we are not disturbed."

"Yes, sir," she nodded.

John followed the man into his office and sat in the chair that was offered to him.

"Now, Mr. Smith," the banker said, sitting opposite him and spreading his hands out on the desk as he sat, "what can I do for you?" The man spoke with a pronounced British accent.

"I'd like to make another deposit into your bank. Actually, I'd like to make three separate deposits into three separate accounts." He reached across the desk. "May I?"

He took a gold pen from the pen holder, slid a piece of notepaper from the attached pad holder and wrote down the amounts going into each account, then a series of numbers next to each deposit.

"And where are these funds coming from?" the banker asked.

"The funds will be in the form of cash currency, US, and will be delivered tomorrow morning."

"And you are aware of the taxes due?"

"I am."

"And you are aware of the exchange rate?"

"I am."

Ian Bartholomew smiled. He stood and offered his hand to his visitor. John took it and looked into the man's steel-gray eyes. "Do you have any question? I'd be glad to give you a current update on how your accounts are doing."

"As a matter of fact, a report on each account would be nice. Could you have them ready by tomorrow a.m.?"

"Most certainly. It would be my pleasure."

The banker picked up the note from his desk and walked around it to lead John to the door. Outside his office, he instructed Mrs. Bodden to furnish a report on the three account numbers he gave her.

"Actually, there's one more account, Mr. Bartholomew, if you please."

John gave the man another series of numbers, and he passed them on to his secretary. "If I could also have a report on that account, it would be greatly appreciated."

"Certainly, Mr. Smith. And will there be anything else?"

"No, I think that does it. Until tomorrow?"

"Until tomorrow."

Ian gave a slight bow toward John and John bowed back. They shook hands and John walked out of the bank and got back into Edward's car.

"Let's go back to the hotel, Edward."

"Yes, sir."

"Will you be available tomorrow morning, say about ten?"

"I most certainly can be," the man nodded. "And how long will you be needing me?"

"I don't know, but I'll be glad to pay for your services for the entire morning if that is agreeable."

"That sounds just fine to me, sir."

"Good."

John went to his room, changed into shorts and a Polo shirt, and then joined his wife and the Morrises at the beach bar. The two boys were with them. It was now two thirty.

The six travelers ordered lunch and drinks and sat under an umbrella and watched the beach activity.

After lunch, the boys excused themselves and went for a walk down on the beach. When they were alone, Mike asked, "So, John, did you get your business taken care of?"

John looked at Jackie, who rolled her eyes and shrugged, before looking at Mike and answering.

"Actually, Mike, I did."

Jeannie shaded her eyes, looking for the boys. By now they were way down the beach, almost out of sight. She spoke. "Mike and I were thinking of going into Georgetown to do some sightseeing and maybe a little shopping. You're welcome to join us," she offered.

John looked at his watch. It was just past three. "You know? I think I'd like to go to my room and take a nap before dinner. Jackie? You're more than welcome to go with them if you want. Or you can join me. It's up to you."

"You know? A nap does sound good. Jeannie? Do you mind?"

"No, no. You go right ahead. We'll call you when we get back."

Alone in their suite, lying in bed, Jackie asked, "Well, how did it go?"

"No problem. How 'bout you come with me in the morning. I really did meet with the bank president. He seems like a nice guy. Very professional. And very serious.

She snuggled closer, laying one leg over his, saying nothing. He kissed her on top of her head and smelled the freshness of it. He put his other arm under his head and stared at the slow-moving fan. The only sounds were the quiet hum of the motor and the soft, steady breathing in his ear. Jackie was asleep.

The phone ringing woke them at six thirty.

"Hey, you two, rise and shine. I got us dinner reservations for seven thirty. It'll be just you and us. The boys met up with a couple of local girls and are having dinner with them and some of their friends. Meet you in the lobby at seven."

Mike hung up before John could say anything.

John watched as Jackie walked to the bathroom. He knew he would never grow tired of looking at her. She became more beautiful to him each day, and each day he fell more deeply in love with her. A warm feeling of contentment swept over him as she turned and smiled at him before closing the bathroom door.

Life is good, he thought.

CHAPTER 48

October 5

Edward dropped them off in front of Barclay's at precisely 10:00 a.m.

"This shouldn't take more than fifteen or twenty minutes," John said.

They stepped from the vehicle as Edward released the trunk lid and retrieved the two suitcases. Taking them from the cab driver, they hurried into the bank and approached the receptionist.

John asked, "Mr. Bartholomew, please. Mr. and Mrs. John Smith. He's expecting us."

She picked up the phone and pressed a button. "Mr. Bartholomew, sir, he's here. Yes, sir, his wife. Thank you."

She hung up and looked up at John. "He'll be out in a moment."

Just as she finished speaking, Ian Bartholomew appeared. "Ah, Mr. Smith. And Mrs. Smith?"

He gave her a charming smile and took her hand in his. "A pleasure to meet you. Come in, please."

He motioned to his office with his arm and allowed them to enter first, closing the door behind them.

"Please, have a seat. I trust those are the funds we talked about?" he asked, nodding to the two suitcases.

"They are."

"Fine. Well, let's have a look then, shall we?"

John put one of the suitcases on the edge of the desk and opened it.

"May I?" Ian asked.

He slid the suitcase around to face him and started taking out the packs of wrapped bills, stacking them on his desk. He took a small knife from his desk drawer and slit open each pack, setting the stacks neatly beside each other. The wrappings went into a wastebasket next to his desk. When he was finished, he accepted the second suitcase and did the same. He then counted the entire lot and wrote down the amount on a slip of paper.

He showed the slip to John, and when John nodded, he asked, "And you want this deposited into three separate accounts, Mr. Burton?"

John's head shot up in surprise and alarm.

"I'm sorry, Mr. Burton. You see, this island is really quite small, and when word that a famous author was staying at the Holiday Inn, well, I was curious. I've read your book, and, well, your picture's on the back." He smiled at his two visitors. "Not to worry, Barclay's is a reputable bank, and we are quite discreet. Your secret is safe with us. Now, three separate accounts?"

"Yes. You have the account numbers?"

"The numbers you gave me yesterday? Yes. "He continued, closing the two suitcases and handing them back to John, "If you will just sign this form, you'll have your receipts in just a few moments.

He took the signed form back, buzzed his secretary in and gave her the necessary paperwork, instructing her to return with the finished documents.

"Now, about those reports you requested."

He reached into his drawer again and pulled out four separate reports, each one enclosed in a brown leather folder.

"I took the liberty of including the deposit amounts you gave me yesterday in the totals. I hope this is satisfactory with you."

"Quite, yes, thank you."

John accepted the folders from Ian and opened the top one. Inside were deposit figures and interest payments and a summary of the totals along with a report on how the moneys had been invested. The top report was John's. The other three were each numbered inside with the account number and had the same type of report with the totals for each of them. He found Jackie's and gave it to her without looking at it. She opened it and showed her surprise at the bottom line. She looked from John to the banker and back to John again, a bright smile on her face. Her face was flushed.

"Oh my God!" she said excitedly. "Oh, my God!"

She sat back in her chair and looked at the figures again. "Is this for real?"

John smiled and nodded.

Ian's secretary rang just then and announced that she had the documents ready.

"Well, if Barclay's can be of any further service to you, please don't hesitate to ask." He hesitated. "Um, Mr. Burton? Could I... could you..." He opened his desk drawer and pulled out a book. "Could you...?"

John reached for the book and wrote on the inside cover and handed the book back to Bartholomew.

"Thank you, Mr. Burton, thank you so much." He reached out and took John's hand and then turned and shook Jackie's hand, saying, "Mrs. Burton."

She blushed as she thanked him and held up the folder in her other hand.

John put the reports in one of the suitcases, closed it, picked them both up and thanked the banker again as he walked out of the office with them.

They stopped at Mrs. Bodden's desk and retrieved the receipts, said goodbye to Ian, and walked out of the bank. Outside, they waited as Edward drove up and stopped. John threw the two suitcases into the trunk and climbed into the back seat with Jackie.

"Back to the hotel please, Edward."

"Yes, sir."

When the two guests were gone, Bartholomew opened the book to the inside cover and read the inscription:

To Ian Bartholomew, loyal and trusted friend.
All your help has been greatly appreciated. Thanks.

John

He smiled and put the book back in his desk.

CHAPTER 49

Tuesday, October 9

Bruce Sellier and his agents had been busy since Sally's return to DC. They had thoroughly searched the cottage in Maine: fingerprinted, collected, catalogued, photographed, documented, interviewed. The collected evidence filled a Ford van. Everyone who knew John Burton was interviewed. His phone records, bank statements and records, his personal life—it was all scrutinized. Still, there was nothing that could directly link him to the kidnappings. It seemed—if he was the perpetrator—he had covered his tracks thoroughly. The only thing the FBI had was a composite drawing of a man who looked very much like John Burton.

"That's the bad news. The good news is we know where he is headed. And he is with the Morrises. They're sailing to the Cayman Islands, he and his wife, along with the Morris's son and a friend of the son's named Scott Boucher.

"We were able to track them down through the registration of the boat. From it we found that the boat's home port is Hyannis, on Cape Cod. One of my agents talked to the Coast Guard. Seems they filed a sailing plan that takes them to Baltimore, Miami and then on to the Cayman Islands. Only problem is there are three islands, and we don't know which island they're stopping at. I've just gotten off the phone with Interpol, and they are trying to track them down from their end. They are sending someone over from Jamaica to the big island. If Burton can be located, then they will interview him.

424

I'm afraid he's out of our jurisdiction down there and with so little to go on, so little evidence, I mean, there's really not much they can do for us. They will, however, keep an eye on him and keep us informed of his movements and where they all are headed when they leave the islands."

Sally listened to Bruce's commentary without comment. She now had a positive feeling in her gut. The phantom that was John Burton really did exist. She could finally put him in a physical location.

She looked at her watch. It was ten fifteen. Jack was due back in the office in fifteen minutes.

Sally paced. Her office was small, and the five steps she took pretty much covered the entire floor from wall to wall. The more she paced, the more anxious she became. Finally, not able to contain herself any longer, she left her office and approached Jack's secretary.

"Have you heard from Jack?" she asked. "Will he be back soon? I need to see him right away."

The secretary looked up at her and shrugged.

She returned to her desk, pulled a legal pad in front of her and began to write. A soft knock on the doorjamb shook her out of her concentration.

"Hi. Linda said you wanted to see me. She said you were quite agitated. What's up?"

Sally looked up and saw Jack standing there, a querulous look on his face.

"Yes! Hi!" she said. "We know where John Burton and his wife are. Well, we're pretty sure we know where they are."

"And?"

"Would you believe the Cayman Islands?"

Jack entered the room and took a seat. "The Caymans?"

"Bruce Sellier called you earlier, and when he couldn't reach you, he asked to be transferred to me. Burton and his wife, along with Mr. and Mrs. Morris and their son and a friend sailed out of Hyannis. They stopped in Baltimore and Miami—both stops con-firmed—then sailed on to the Cayman Islands. Dick got the info from the Coast Guard. They're somewhere on one of the islands now. He's notified Interpol and they're searching for them."

Jack stiffened. "I wonder if that's such a good idea? Burton might spook. We can't touch him down there. We need to wait until he's back on US soil and then we can nab him. Besides, we're not really sure Burton is our man. I don't want to strain our relationship with Interpol if it turns out he's not. Get back to Interpol and tell them to ease up. Tell them we think Burton is our man and ask them to follow and observe and report back to us, but tell them not to make contact with any of them. They can call us with his return route, and we can apprehend him when he steps foot back in America. Good work, Sally."

Sally then filled him in on the rest of Sellier's report. Jack listened without interruption.

When she was done, he said, "All the more reason to keep him at arm's length. If he is our man and we spook him, he could vanish without a trace. If he doesn't suspect us, we can approach him once he's back on American soil."

Jack sat back in his chair and pushed up his glasses. "The Cayman Islands…"

Sally could almost see the wheels turning inside his head.

"The son of a bitch is sailing the money right down to the bank. No bank wiring, no courier service, no mail. I'll be damned."

"Jack," Sally said. "What if we flew down there? We could keep an eye on them and follow them back. They're sure to leave a sailing plan. When they leave, we can fly to their destination and be there to greet them."

"Are you looking for an excuse to get out of Washington?"

"No, Jack, it's just that…well, we're getting close. I just want to be in on the capture. I want to see him up close. I want to—"

"You want to visit the islands. Tell you what. When he gets back on American soil, you can be there with the locals to bring him in for questioning. Fair enough?"

A look of disappointment crossed Sally's face for the briefest of time and then it was replaced with a wan smile.

"Okay, she said finally. "I guess that's fair enough. You want to come along when we question him?"

"Actually? I think I'll leave that up to you. You've done all the leg work and follow up. God knows you've earned this one."

She smiled brightly at that. "Thanks, Jack."

"Don't thank me," he said rising, "like I said, you did all the work. I'll call Interpol and fill them in."

He left her for his office. Sally sat back and clasped her hands together behind her head. "John Burton, your days are numbered. Someday soon you'll return, and when you do, I've gotcha."

Thursday, October 11, Cayman Islands

John exited the elevator and entered the lobby on his way to the beach bar to meet his friends. The minute he stepped away from the elevator a warning went off inside his head. Without breaking stride, he scanned the occupants in the lobby. Behind the counter were the two attendants who welcomed the guests and checked them in and out. At the counter was a young family: mom, dad, a little boy and his sister, and another couple dressed in tennis gear standing just down the counter from them. A third attendant came out of the office and handed the couple an envelope and left. Seated on one of the couches in the lobby was an elderly couple. He was laughing at something she had said. John had seen them several times over the past two days and quickly discounted all of them. All this observation took John only a few seconds.

He walked over to the newsstand and picked up a paper, paid for it, then turned around and pretended to read it as he scanned the rest of the lobby, looking for anything out of the ordinary. There, seated in a chair across the lobby was a man dressed in white shorts, topsiders, and a bright blue-and-white print shirt. He was wearing dark sunglasses, even though the lobby was dimly lit.

As John watched, the man looked in the direction of the coffee shop. Just inside the entrance was another man, dressed just as casually. That man looked at the first man, looked in John's direction and quickly looked back at the sitting man.

John remembered seeing both of them together at the coffee shop earlier. They were dressed differently at the time.

Tucking his paper under his arm, he walked out to the beach bar and joined his friends. He positioned himself so that he could see the entranceway to the lobby. Sure enough, several minutes later, the two men came out of the lobby and picked out a table across from John's party on the other side of the bar. The man John had first seen sat facing John while the other placed his back to him.

Jackie noticed the look on John's face and gave him a questioning look. He gave her the slightest gesture as if to say, "Keep quiet."

He turned to Mike and said, "So, Mike, what's on the docket for today?"

"Jeannie and the boys want to do the golf course one more time before we leave. What about you two?"

"I don't know. Jackie? You want to swim with the stingrays?"

"What?"

John chuckled. "Yes. We can go to Stingray City and swim with them. It's quite safe I hear. You just swim right up to them. We can even feed them if you want."

She gave him a funny look and wriggled her nose. "Really?"

"Cross my heart." He made the gesture on his chest and glanced in the direction of the two men. The one facing him quickly looked away.

"Whatever you want, my love."

"Okay then. Mike? Why don't we plan on meeting back here at, say, four to four thirty. We can go to dinner. Then we can all just hang out. Tomorrow we'll get the boat ready and to leave Saturday."

They agreed. Mike and Jeannie and the two boys rose and said their goodbyes. John ordered iced tea for the two of them, and when the waiter was gone, he took Jackie's hands in his.

"I love you," he said simply.

She looked deeply into his eyes and asked, "What's wrong?"

He hesitated and then speaking softly said, "I think we—I am being followed."

Jackie's back stiffened just the tiniest bit, but her expression never changed. "Are you sure?"

"I think so. There are two men sitting across the bar at a table. I saw them in the lobby earlier and I saw them twice yesterday, once while we were downtown shopping and once while we were having dinner. I don't think it's a coincidence."

"Who are they? Do you think they are the police?"

"I don't know. They could be local. The FBI doesn't have any jurisdiction down here. Could be Interpol. When we leave, we'll walk by their table. I want you to smile at them as we go by and try to memorize as much about them as you can. But don't be obvious, okay?"

She nodded, looked up and smiled as the waiter brought their iced teas. John reached over and patted her hand. He could see the tenseness mounting in her eyes.

"It'll be all right, honey. Trust me."

She smiled weakly and squeezed the lemon wedge into her drink, sucked the juice off her finger and thumb and put the glass to her lips. John did the same and took a long drink, setting the near empty glass back onto the table. They nursed the rest of their drinks for another few minutes then Jack said, "Ready?"

She nodded.

"Just be casual. There's nothing to worry about, I'm sure."

"Okay."

They rose, and Jackie walked beside him past the table. John positioned himself to her right so that he would be looking at her as he talked. She would be able to see the two men as they passed. The one facing in their direction looked up as John and Jackie passed and she gave him a slight smile and glanced at his partner.

Once inside the darkness of the lobby, they headed for the counter and stopped. John turned around and watched, waiting for the two men to enter. The second man, the one who had had his back to John at the table, came through the doors, and when he spotted the two of them, he immediately turned and entered the gift shop.

John and Jackie crossed to the elevators and went up to their suite. Once inside the safety of their rooms, Jackie fell apart.

"They're following us! What are we going to do?" she asked.

He put his finger up to his lips and motioned for her to follow him out onto the balcony. And then he turned to her, gently rubbing her bare shoulders.

"First of all, we've got to be careful of what we say—even in our rooms. I doubt it, but they could be bugged. Anyway, we're going to act like we're on vacation, and then on Saturday, we are going to sail out of here. I don't know who they are. We'll just have to wait and see."

She put her arms around him and put her head on his chest. He held her to him for a moment and then squeezed her, patted her behind and said, "Let's go swimming."

She smiled and nodded and the two of them reentered the suite. John called for Edward, and when the time came, they left the hotel.

Inside the cab John said, "Edward, I know this sounds crazy, but I think we are being followed. We want to go to Stingray City, but I want you to take the long way there. Keep an eye on your mirrors and see if anyone appears to be following us, will you?"

"You're the boss."

Edward pulled out and headed for downtown Georgetown. Sure enough, no sooner had they pulled out of the lot when a dark-colored Fiat pulled in behind them, staying no more than five car lengths behind the Mercedes.

"We got company," Edward informed them.

"Don't turn around, honey," John warned her.

To Edward he asked, "Are there two of them?" When Edward nodded, he said, "Good. Don't try to lose them but give them a chance to see the surroundings, if you know what I mean."

Edward headed into downtown Georgetown, turned onto Shedden Road, then north on Edward Street, left on Cardinal Avenue, north onto Albert Panton Street and then left onto Fort Street before heading north on North Church street.

"They're still behind us, Mr. Burton. You vant me to lose them?"

"No, let's head up to Stingray City."

"You vant me to find out who they are? I got friends who can find out for me. Maybe even talk to them if you want."

John and Jackie looked at each other.

"If you can find out who they are, there's an extra hundred dollars C.I. in it for you, but no, I don't want them roughed up, if that's what you have in mind."

"Yes, sir, you're the boss. But you jes' say the word."

"That's okay, Edward. I'm sure it's nothing. You said the crime rate's low down here. Let's just find out who they are and go from there."

Edward dropped the two of them off at Stingray City and promised to be back by three thirty. They watched as he drove off. The Fiat was parked up the street.

"Well, they're not trying to be too inconspicuous," John said, putting his arm around Jackie and ushering her inside the rental shop.

Washington, DC, Thursday, October 11

Sally brought the Telex into Jack's office.

"Jack, he's there. Interpol found him. He's staying at the Holiday Inn on Grand Cayman. He's with his wife, Mike Morris and his wife, and the two boys. They appear to be on vacation. They're doing vacation kinds of things anyway. Interpol's found the boat too. They know where it's moored. There's a team watching the boat and one following John and his wife. They're keeping back, as you requested, and will let us know when they leave and where they are going."

Jack nodded, accepting her explanation. "It won't be long now. My guess is that they'll head back to Miami. We should contact our man down there and have him get his team ready."

"We're still going to be in on it, aren't we?"

"You bet we are. I've given it a lot of thought, and I've decided I want to be in on it too. I know now I wouldn't miss it for the world. I've waited six years for this. If they show up in Miami—or wherever they've set their course for—you and I will be there."

Stingray City, 3:00 p.m.

Edward was waiting for them when they came ashore. He watched as they turned in their equipment and headed for the car.

When they were comfortably settled in the back seat, he spoke. The Fiat was nowhere to be seen.

"Those men who been following you?" he said, looking in the rearview mirror and catching John's eye. "they are a couple of agents from Interpol. According to my sources, they were sent over here from Jamaica to keep an eye on you and your wife."

Jackie reached over and took John's hand in hers, squeezing it tightly. He held it down between them and squeezed it back.

Edward pulled out of the parking lot and headed back toward the hotel. From out of nowhere, the Fiat appeared, and, keeping a safe distance behind, began to follow them.

"Fiat's back," Edward volunteered, looking in his driver's side mirror. "You vant me to lose them this time?"

"No, Edward, just head on back to the hotel."

"Listen, Mr. Burton, it's none of my business, but you've been real nice to me since you've been here. And real generous. If you're in some kind of trouble—if you need any help—well, you just let Edward know. So long's it's not illegal, I'll do what I can for you."

"Thanks for the offer, Edward, but I'm sure it's nothing. I mean, what could we possibly have done to warrant a visit from Interpol? It's probably just a mistake. Maybe they think we're somebody else."

Edward looked in the mirror again. John could see that he wasn't buying it. "I hope so, Mr. Burton, I truly do."

Edward took the direct route back to the hotel. The Fiat stayed behind them the whole way. When John exited the Mercedes, he saw the Fiat pull off to the side just up the road. On the whole ride back, Jackie had said nothing.

"You'll be available tomorrow if we need you?" John asked, handing Edward a fistful of Cayman Island dollars.

"I'm always available for you, Mr. Burton. Just call when you need me."

"Thanks, Edward."

John closed the door and walked into the hotel, his fingers on the small of Jackie's back, gently steering her into the lobby. They went to their suite and showered and changed and went down to the beach bar. Mike and Jeannie and the boys were not back yet.

"What are we going to do?" Jackie asked after their beverage orders were taken.

"We're not going to do anything. We're going to go about our business and enjoy the last days of our vacation. If they had any hard evidence against us, they would have at least brought us in for questioning. We're leaving Saturday morning and returning to Miami. I think that once we leave the islands, I'll convince Mike to sail to the Bahamas instead of Miami. Once there we can catch a flight to somewhere on the east coast and return to Maine. I think we'll be safe there for a few weeks while we decide what to do. Now, drink up, here comes Mike and Jeannie.

"Hi, you two," Mike greeted as he pulled up a chair for Jeannie. He sat down across from Jackie, took off his golf cap and wiped the sweat off his forehead. "Man oh man, it sure is hot."

He signaled to the waiter and ordered drinks for Jeannie and himself and more iced tea for John and Jackie.

"How were the rays?" Mike asked Jackie.

"Actually, they were quite beautiful and very graceful. John and I swam with them for almost an hour. One even let me hitch a ride on his back. We fed them right out of our hands. They are the most amazing creatures. And so gentle. I never would have believed it."

John turned to Mike. "How was the golfing?"

"Well, good. And thank you for asking," Mike said. "I shot four under par. Jeannie made par and the boys did quite well for themselves too."

"Where are Scott and Eric?" John asked.

"Remember the girls they met the other day? Well, they're having a cookout on the beach with some friends and asked the boys to join them. They'll take the boys back to the boat later."

John nodded. "They seem to have become pretty good friends with these girls."

"They always do," Mike said. "I mean, who can resist them?"

"Point taken."

Small talk filled the rest of the afternoon, and at seven, they went out to dinner. It was at dinner that John came up with an idea.

"Say, Mike," he started. "What if we sailed over to Cayman Brac and did a little gambling tomorrow. We could still leave Saturday for Miami. What say?"

Mike looked at Jeannie who gave a nod. He said, "Why not? I can file our route from there just as easily. And the boys have gotten everything onboard except for the fresh fruit and vegetables. We can get them on Brac. Sounds like fun."

After dinner they returned to the beach bar to watch as the sun was slowly swallowed up by the sea.

At ten thirty, just a little drunk, Mike, Jeannie, and John, along with Jackie split up and went to bed.

In the morning, slightly hung over, the four called on Edward to pick them up and they all headed back to the boat. The boys were already onboard, stowing the gear. They came topside and helped bring the luggage onboard. The two suitcases that had once contained the money now carried clothes and souvenirs that John and Jackie had bought on the island. The difference in the weights of the two suitcases went unnoticed.

The cruise from Grand Cayman to Cayman Brac took three hours and twenty-five minutes. They all went ashore for a late lunch, and then they hit the casino.

Splitting up, John and Jackie went to the blackjack tables while Mike and Jeannie hit the slots. Eric and Scott wandered around inside the casino. John slipped each of the boys one hundred dollars C.I. before they split up and told them to keep quiet about it. A quick wink to them and he and Jackie left them to their own discoveries. They all agreed to meet out front at midnight.

John found a seat at a table and asked Jackie to join him. She declined, saying she knew nothing about blackjack, but agreed to stand behind him and watch for a while.

At first, John lost. He'd make cautious bets, getting a feel for the table. He liked blackjack. It was simple, and luck played a big hand in it. But by paying attention to the cards that were dealt—there were three decks in the box—one could pretty well count each card. When the deck was replaced with new cards at the request of the player to John's right, his luck changed dramatically.

He played conservatively, not wanting to draw attention to himself, but after about two and a half hours, he was up almost ten grand. A crowd had started to gather behind him. Not wanting to be the center of attention, he collected his chips, tipped the dealer, and he and Jackie left the table and strolled over to the cashier's cage. He cashed in his winnings and then he and Jackie went in search of Mike and Jeannie.

John spotted one of his tails as he approached the steps leading down to the slots and immediately became angry. Turning to Jackie, he quietly said, "Wait here."

He walked over to the man and introduced himself. "Evening," John said as he approached. "How long have you been here?"

"Beg your pardon?" the man responded.

"Oh, come off it. You've been following us now for at least three days, both on the big island and now here."

He extended his hand. My name is John Burton, but of course you know that. I'm just curious as to why you and your partner are following us. And who the hell do you work for?"

The man's face turned red and he stuttered and stammered, trying to say something. He looked down at John's extended hand and then up at John's grinning face and took his hand.

"I'm sorry," John went on, "I didn't catch your name."

"Ah, ah, oh, quite right. My name's Geoffrey. Geoffrey Smythe-Duxton."

"Well, Geoffrey, unless you've got a good reason to be following my wife and me, I'd suggest that you stop. Otherwise, I'll have to contact the local constabulary and complain that you are harassing us. Do I make myself clear?"

John let go of the man's hand, and Geoffrey grabbed it and began massaging it. He looked John in the eye. "I don't know why we were asked to follow you, only that we were to keep an eye on you and report your whereabouts back to headquarters, and when you left, we were to notify HQ of your destination."

"That's better. And who do you work for?" John continued.

"Interpol," the man replied.

"And who requested that you follow us?"

"I don't know. We were just told to follow you. The request came down from upstairs."

"Well, Mr. Geoffrey Smythe-Duxton, you can tell your superiors that we will be leaving these beautiful islands tomorrow morning and will be sailing back to Miami. We expect to arrive there sometime Tuesday afternoon."

"Yes, sir," Geoffrey said sullenly. "Miami. Tuesday afternoon. And may I say, I personally won't miss you and yours one bit. Good evening, Mr. Burton."

Geoffrey turned on his heel and marched off toward the direction of the front entrance. John watched him make his way through the crowd. His partner met him at the front entrance, and the two of them got into a heated argument, and then they exited through the glass doors. When they were gone, John turned his attention to finding his wife. He immediately spotted her leaning against a white column staring at him. He walked over to her and saw the quizzical look on her face.

"Interpol," he said softly as he took her elbow and walked her toward the slot machines. "He said he didn't know who ordered the tail, but I don't believe him. My guess is it's the FBI. Anyway, I told him that we're heading back to Miami tomorrow and plan to arrive Tuesday afternoon."

"Was that wise?"

"Well, you see, just the boat and the others are going to Miami. We're going to Nassau."

Saturday, October 13

The day had broken cool and hazy, but the fog had cleared, and the sun was shining now.

"Eric! Scott! Man your stations! John? Jackie? Jeannie? Are you ready?"

"Aye-aye, Captain," they all chorused together.

"Cast off then," he bellowed, and the lines were released, the boat's motor fired up, and they coasted out of anchorage to begin their journey toward the Windward Passage. Their departure was noted from the shore, and when they were well away from the island, the call was made.

When, at last the island was gone from view, John approached Mike and suggested that they sail on to New Providence in the Bahamas and dock at Nassau.

"But I've already filed a course that will take us to Miami," Mike protested.

"Miami? Nassau? What's the difference? Look," John continued, pulling out a map of the Caribbean Islands, "we can stop here in Nassau and then sail on to Miami. Or we can shoot up to Baltimore from Nassau. Either way, we're going to have to sail close by the island, and we're going to have to sail through the Bahamas. Let's do Nassau, come on, what do you say? It'll be fun."

Mike studied the map, running his finger from the tip of Cuba up to Nassau and on to Miami and then from Cuba's tip into Miami.

"You're right. It's not that much out of our way, and if we shoot straight for Baltimore, it could even save us a little time. What the heck, let's do it."

John patted him on the back. "Let's keep it a secret from the girls and surprise them."

"Great idea."

CHAPTER 50

**Somewhere off the Coasts of the Southern
Bahamas, Monday, October 15**

It was after ten in the evening. The moon shone above, illuminating the few fluffy clouds that hung from the sky like silver gauze.

The water was calm, glass. Only the quiet hum of the generators and the infrequent tapping of a loose rope hitting the mast could be heard.

John and Jackie, Mike and Jeannie were asleep below. Eric and Scott were on deck drinking beer. Scott had looped a rope around the wheel, securing it so the boat would remain on a straight course, crawling along at less than two knots. Every so often he would check his bearings and make the necessary corrections to their course.

Both boys sat facing each other on the deck, their legs sprawled out in front of them, sipping their beers through their long neck bottles, talking quietly. It had been a great trip. The Cayman Island vacation had proved to be more than either of them had expected. They had swum with sharks and rays, explored coral reefs, viewed hundreds of multi-colored fish as they swam through crystal blue waters, and watched as neon-colored sponges undulated in unison in the currents that washed over them.

Up near Hell, a small town on the northwest side of Grand Cayman, the beach bristled with black dagger-like rocks, and in the shallows of Stingray City, they swam with flotillas of rays. And the girls were beautiful.

They did not hear or see the big speedboat approaching until it was less than a thousand yards away and coming fast. Eric noticed it first and casually pointed it out to Scott. Scott stood and turned as the sound of the big boat began to grow louder, bearing down on the *Dram Bouie*. By the time it was within three hundred yards, Eric was standing too. The big boat let off on its throttles as it came closer, its nose settling down in the water, its wake catching up with it and carrying it even closer. It came to the side of the sailboat, causing the sailboat to rise and fall abruptly. Eric almost lost his balance and had to grab one of the stays to keep from falling.

Suddenly a searchlight came on, illuminating the deck. The two boys shaded their eyes with their hands.

"Hola!" a voice cried out from the speedboat. "Hello!"

Scott squinted through the brightness and saw a silhouette standing on the bow of the boat. He was holding something in his arms.

"Shit!" he yelled at his friend. "Get down! He's got a gun!"

Scott ducked and crawled forward as he was yelling this. Before he could finish his warning, a burst of gunfire filled the air, cutting Eric almost in half before the boy hit the deck.

More gunfire kicked up splinters of wood along the wall of the boat above Scott's head as he made for the hatch, tumbling head first into the darkness below.

At the same time as the shooting began, the speedboat bumped into the side of the *Dram Bouie*, and three sets of feet came scrambling onto the deck.

The sound of the gunfire, the collision of the boats and the three sets of feet landing on the deck caused John and Jackie to sit up in their bunks.

"What the—" John started to ask as another burst from a gun filled the air.

The sound of a body landing hard at the bottom of the stairs to the galley cut him off.

"Pirates!" he whispered to Jackie.

"Do you have a gun?" she asked.

"No, damn it!"

The sound of heavy footsteps coming down the stairs, then another set jumping onto the floor, and then a heavily accented voice filled the air.

"Everybody, if you come out now, nobody else will be hurt, *comprende?*" Everyone! Out quickly!"

John heard the sound of a door opening and then Mike's panicked voice.

"Don't shoot! Don't shoot! We're coming out!"

John put his fingers to his lips, warning Jackie to be quiet. He could hear Mike and then Jeannie step out into the hall. He peeked through the slatted louvers in the door. Standing just up the hall from him were two men with AK-47 semiautomatic assault rifles pointed at his friends as they carefully stepped from their stateroom, their hands raised.

"Bueno!" said the one in front. "Are there any more of you?"

Mike did not hesitate before answering. "Just us and the two boys."

"Oh my God!" Jeannie screamed as she saw the body of Scott grotesquely spread out at the bottom of the stairs.

"Eric!" she screamed. "Eric! What have you done with Eric?"

She raced up the ladder, looking for her son. Mike rushed up after her, pushing the men aside as he made his way on deck. When Jeannie reached the landing, she screamed.

Lying on the deck, his eyes staring glassily ahead of him, was her son. Blood spread out and puddle under and around him, and trails of it were swimming down the deck in the grooves between each slat.

"My baby! My baby!" she wailed as she sat in a pool of blood and placed his head on her lap.

Tears flowed down her cheeks. "You bastards! Why? He was just a boy! Why?"

She held his head in her lap and rocked back and forth, moaning and crying and calling his name over and over. Mike turned to protest and was hit over the head by one of the intruders. He collapsed onto the deck unconscious. Jeannie screamed again.

Below, hidden in their cabin, John and Jackie heard it all. John's mind was racing. He had no weapon, there were at least three of them onboard already, how many more there were he did not know, the two boys appeared to be dead, and Mike and Jeannie were up on deck under the watchful eyes of their captors.

He put his lips close to Jackie's ear and whispered, "Go across to Jeannie's room and hide there. I don't expect them to look for anybody else in there, but they will come looking. I'm going to try to find a weapon. If I do, I'll bring it back to you."

She nodded.

"When I get back, we'll figure out a plan."

Again, she nodded.

John slowly opened the door to the cabin and peeked out. He could hear the yelling and the talking above. He listened vary carefully. He recognized five different voices in addition to Mike and Jeannie.

He held up all five fingers of his right hand and pointed up with his left hand and then put his fingers to his lips and motioned for Jackie to cross the hall. When she was safely inside the stateroom, he crept into the galley. He found a three-inch filleting knife. Next to it was a boning knife and he took it too. He opened another drawer and pulled out a flare gun and a box of flares. He made his way back to the cabin. He gave Jackie the flare gun, flares and boning knife and said, "I'm going forward and make my way up onto the deck. You stay here until you hear my call. I'm going to try to neutralize as many of them as I can. I count five of them onboard now. Maybe some of them will go back to their boat. We need guns. They have guns. I'm going to try to get us some. If I can overpower the men on this boat, I'll call you. I want you to come on deck and fire that flare gun into the other boat. Look for something vulnerable to shoot at. You got that?"

She nodded.

John slipped off his white T-shirt and tossed it under the bunk. He kissed her lightly on the forehead and whispered, "I love you," then slipped out of the cabin and made his way along the passageway until he reached the ladder leading up to the forward hatch. It was propped open to let in the cool night air.

He climbed the ladder's steps until his head was at the opening and then peered over the edge. The five intruders were arguing amongst themselves in Spanish. Finally, one of them climbed over the side and back onto the deck of the speedboat. Another one went below while a third one started to come forward on the deck. The shadows of the raised deck and the dinghy darkened John's spot, and he crawled onto the forward deck and slipped over the side of the boat and into the water.

He listened as the man walked the deck above him and turned and walked back on the other side of the boat. Down below, he could hear the heavy footsteps of the other man as he checked out each cabin. He heard the man call out in Spanish from the forward hatch.

"*Hay nadie aqui!* Nobody here!" He then heard the man's steps as he climbed on deck and walked back to the stern area.

More words were exchanged and then John heard a gunshot.

"Mike!" Jeannie screamed. "Oh God! You've killed him! You bastards! Mike! Oh no. Mike! Mike!"

The next thing John heard was the sound of a fist hitting flesh and Jeannie's muffled moan as she slumped to the deck.

There was laughter from the four remaining men, and John heard the sound of a body being dragged across the deck. He had worked his way toward the rear of the boat and was hidden by the curve of the hull. Overhead he could hear commotion and ducked beneath the water just as a body broke the surface and dropped out of sight below him. He surfaced and heard a splash astern. Then another one. The bodies of Mike, Eric, and Scott had been tossed into the sea.

John heard one of the men speaking. It sounded like an order was being given. He heard hustling on deck as two of the men secured lines and tossed them to the speedboat.

The bastards are going to tow it away, he thought, but what are they going to do with Jeannie?

He was getting cold in the water, and he began to shiver. The boat swung around almost drawing him under, but he managed to work his way to the stern. There were brass handles located just above the waterline, and he grabbed one of these and held on.

Two of the men returned to the speedboat; two remained behind. He could still hear Jeannie moaning and wailing above him. One of the men said something to her and then John heard scuffling and then he heard her cry out in pain.

He eased his way up until he could see what they were doing. Jeannie was lying face down on the deck while one of the men tied her arms behind her. Then they sat her back up and leaned her against the bench along the inside of the aft lounging area. One of the men said something to her in Spanish and laughed. John was less than six feet from them but didn't dare move.

His training as a Special Forces soldier came back to him, and he slid back into the water, holding onto the brass handle, and waited. The sailboat moved through the water, slowly picking up speed as it was towed along by the big speedboat. Water rushed around him and pulled at him, trying to tear him away from the stern. He gripped the handle harder, despite the pain in his muscles.

One of the men said something to the other, stood, and retreated to the galley. John looked at his watch. From the time he left Jackie, until now, had only been twelve minutes. He had to do something quickly. Slowly, quietly, he lifted himself up and looked over the transom. The man was sitting on the bench, his back to John, smoking a cigarette, staring toward the front of the boat.

John pulled the fishing knife from his belt, put it between his teeth and eased himself up and over the edge, directly behind the man. Jeannie noticed him, and her eyes became like saucers. With his right hand, he signaled for her to be quiet and then eased himself onto the boat, grabbing the knife from his teeth. He moved quickly and silently, grabbing the man's chin from behind and pulling it up. In one swift motion, he reached around and slit the man's throat, releasing a spray of blood. A gurgling airy sigh came from the man as he slumped forward, dead.

Again, John signaled for Jeannie's silence. She was close to panic and fear blasted from her eyes, but she remained quiet.

"How many of them are still onboard?" he whispered.

"One more below deck. The others are back onboard the other boat. I counted nine, including those who didn't come onboard. I think that's all. Where's Jackie?"

"She's still down below. Stay here."

John crept off, crawling silently toward the bulkhead. When he reached the top of the steps, he stopped and listened. He could hear the other man rummaging through the drawers in the galley. He crawled back to Jeannie.

"I'm afraid I'm going to have to leave you like this for a while. He needs to see you like this when he comes back on deck. Okay?"

She nodded. "John. They're all dead. Mike, Eric—"

"I know. I'm sorry. But let's try to keep the rest of us alive."

He reached around her and freed her hands.

"Stay here and don't move."

Tears filled her eyes again and were running down her cheeks. John put his hand on her shoulder.

"Hang on for just a little while, Jeannie."

With that he crawled forward again. Just as he reached the top of the stairs he heard footsteps on the ladder. He rolled to his left and got to his knees just as the other man's head appeared at the top of the stairs. The man looked at John in disbelief and ducked back into the companionway. John threw himself down the stairs, landing hard on the man who hit the floor. He tried to turn to defend himself, but John was too quick. John grabbed his head and twisted it sharply. He felt the snap and felt the man go limp under him. John felt for a pulse in the man's neck. There was none. Cold, dead brown eyes stared lifelessly down the hallway, not looking at anything anymore.

John quickly got up and headed down the hall.

"Jackie!" he whispered urgently as he slipped into the stateroom.

"Here," she called back, standing and coming around the bed. "What's happening?"

"Mike, Eric, and Scott are all dead."

She sucked in her breath. "No," she cried softly.

"There are two onboard—both dead. Jeannie's up on deck by the wheel. As long as the boat keeps moving, I think we're safe. But once it slows down and they come back onboard again, we're in deep shit. Jeannie counted seven more of them on the other boat."

"What are we going to do?" she asked, gradually regaining her composure.

"We're going to have to take them all out. We've got one AK-47. You still remember how to shoot?"

She nodded.

"Good. Now, we've got to get this one back up on deck and prop him up on the bench, and then we'll have to prop up the other one. We'll have to drag this one up. I don't want us to be seen. Come on, give me a hand."

Together they set the body up against the ladder. John crawled over him and climbed, turning to pull him up from above while Jackie helped push the body from below. When it was on deck, the two of them dragged him to a spot along the bench and then pushed and pulled him into position, all the while keeping as low as possible. John found a coil of rope under one of the benches and secured the body into position, then the two of them turned to the other man and did the same thing. Every so often one of them would check the boat towing them. So far, no alarms had been sounded.

John spoke softly to the two women. "All right, we're safe for now. I don't know where we're headed, but eventually they're going to stop and reboard us. We've got to be prepared.

"Jeannie, are there any guns onboard? Did Mike have a pistol or a rifle?"

She shook her head slowly back and forth, a dazed look in her eyes. She was going into shock. John looked her in the eyes and saw the panic there. He reached out and slapped her hard across the face and then cut off her stifled cry with his other hand.

"Jeannie," he whispered forcefully, "look at me!"

He took hold of her shoulders and shook her. "Jeannie. Listen to me. Those men mean to kill us all. We've got to protect ourselves. Does Mike have any guns onboard?"

Jeannie stuttered out a weak, "No."

"Damn! Okay. That leaves us with one semiautomatic and one flare gun."

"Against seven of them?" Jeannie asked. "I don't care about the boat, John, why don't we just surrender? Let them have the damn boat."

"Jeannie, they've already killed three people. They won't hesitate to kill us all. I'm sure that's their plan eventually. So we've got to be ready for them."

Just as John finished speaking, the roar of the powerful Chrysler inboard engine pulling the sailboat behind it began to taper off as the boat slowed. John popped his head up. They were entering a harbor of sorts. He could see a light off to his right in front of him, and another up ahead to the left. He also noted the name of the boat, *Maria Elena II, Miami, Fla.*

The drag of the *Dram Bouie* slowed both of the boats down, until, at last, there was slack on the line separating the two boats.

A voice called out from the speedboat. There was silence, and then the voice called out again. A third time the call was repeated, and then voices began shouting from the cruiser. The searchlights came on and swiveled around to sweep the deck.

"Get down!" John commanded Jackie.

The searchlight's beam came to rest on the stern of the boat. Shadows from the bulkhead blocked the pirates from having a good view, but, by maneuvering the big boat, they were finally able to flash the light into the face of Jeannie. From that angle, the man on the stern bench could be seen. Only the back of the other man was visible.

The spotlight moved slightly to provide a better view of the man at the stern. When it was shining directly on him, the blood from the gash in his neck could be seen, glistening and red as it coagulated on his neck and blue jersey.

John pulled Jeannie down onto the deck just as several shots rang out from the big boat, skimming across the deck, and then more shots were fired. A soft splash in the water as they released the tow rope and dropped it, and the cruiser swung around and passed parallel to the sailboat. The searchlight swept the deck, back and forth, back and forth.

Suddenly the air was shattered by a voice on the bull horn.

"You! Onboard! Throw down your weapons, or you will be killed!"

It was the same voice John had heard earlier. The same voice that had ordered the shooting of Mike.

"There's nowhere you can go. Surrender now and make things easier on yourself. All we want is the boat.!"

The cruiser was inching closer to the *Dram Bouie*. Suddenly Jeannie stood up.

"I surrender! I surrender! Don't shoot! I surrender!" she yelled, arms waving above her head.

"Bueno!" came the voice on the bull horn as the beam of the searchlight zeroed in on her. "Now. How many more of you are there?"

Jeannie looked down at her friends. "I'm sorry," she said, weeping.

"Two! There are only three of us left!"

"Bueno! Good. Now, tell your friends to drop their weapons and slowly stand up where we can see them!"

Jackie and John looked at each other.

"Quickly!"

Slowly Jackie placed her weapon on the deck and stood.

"Damn!" John said, and then he too stood, raising his arms over his head.

Quickly five men appeared out of the darkness and boarded the *Dram Bouie*. Each one carried a weapon of some sort. They knocked John down and kicked him, then checked on their two accomplices.

"Muerte!" one of the men called back to the man with the bull horn.

"Muerte?"

"Si!" the man called back, and then. Still speaking Spanish, he described the two dead bodies to the boss in the other boat.

The leader called back orders, and three of the men began a search of the *Dram Bouie*. Five minutes later they reassembled in the back of the boat. A slight discussion followed and then one of the men called out to the leader.

Speaking in roughly-accented English the man said that there was no one else onboard.

"Bueno!"

The leader said something to his crew, and they secured the Dram Bouie alongside the speedboat. When that was done, the leader stepped onboard. Two of the pirates pulled John to his feet and held him by the arms. The leader handed his bull horn to one of the crew and turned to face John.

John didn't see it coming, and when the man's fist caught him full in the solar plexus, he doubled over in pain. Gasping for breath, John straightened. This time, the leader struck him across the face, drawing blood from the cut opened at the corner of John's mouth. Again, John straightened, his eyes burning into those of the leader, his teeth clenched, his jaw defiant.

Jackie cried out, "No!" and stepped forward to protect him. The captain swung his hand up, catching her under the chin, knocking her backward. She almost stumbled but caught herself just before she fell.

"Jackie! No!" John yelled.

A smile appeared on the man's face. He turned to face John again, his face no more than six inches from John's.

"Senora, Jackie?" he said coldly. "Your wife, eh? Bueno."

He turned to Jackie who was now being held by two men. He said something to them and they released her, stepping back so that he could walk around her. After coming full circle, he said, "Bonita, she is beautiful, no?" He said some words in Spanish that brought laughter from his crew.

The leader then introduced himself to Jackie, bowing graciously to her.

"My name is Jorge Escovar," he said politely. "I am Captain of the *Maria Elena II*. We are, how do you say, salvagers of marooned and abandoned vessels."

The crew laughed as he spread his arms to include them. He turned and inspected Jeannie. She stood, her shoulders stooped, as he walked around her. He said something else to the crew as he came to stand in front of her. Again, nervous laughter erupted from the crew.

"So. Who is the owner of this boat?" Jorge asked.

"I am," Jeannie said in a weak voice. My...my husband and I. You killed him! You killed him, you bastard!"

Suddenly she was on him, clawing at his face, drawing blood in streaks of crimson lines down his face.

He bellowed and hit her hard in the face. Blood sprayed, splattering him and his two other prisoners.

"You bastard!" Jackie screamed.

Her two captors grabbed her before she could inflict any more damage on him.

John yelled, "Jackie! Don't!" as four arms pinioned him between them.

Escovar retrieved a kerchief from his back pocket and dabbed at his face, looking at the blood that had transferred to it. He swore in Spanish and turned to his men, anger and venom dripping from his voice. Then he turned to John.

"Senor," he began, still dabbing the cloth to his face, "your women are, how do you say, ah, yes, 'full of spirit.' This is a good thing because they will show us a good time."

He laughed loudly, and the crew joined in with him. He looked at the two men holding John and instructed them to tie him up. A third man provided the two with rope and they forced him down, tying his arms behind him and securing his legs. They fashioned a noose and looped it around his neck and drew the rope down behind him and tied all three, arms, legs, and neck together. Then they sat him down on the deck of the boat, facing aft. The more John tried to struggle, the tighter the noose got.

Jorge Escovar then spoke to his crew. A cheer erupted as their leader pulled Jackie's nightshirt from her. She was braless, and her breasts bobbed up and down. Now she wore only lace panties.

"Bonita, very nice," Jorge Escovar exclaimed.

He said something to the others who laughed, then he turned to John.

"Senor, I thank you for this most beautiful prize. From me she will learn the true meaning of love."

He threw back his head, his laugh loud and cold. Several of the others laughed with him. He said something in Spanish and some of his crew leaped upon Jeannie, tearing off her nightgown and exposing her naked body to the night air, then they threw her down on the deck. Her arms and legs were pinned, and then one after another, the crew had their way with her. She screamed at first, trying desperately to free herself. Spitting, biting, and each time, she would be slapped or punched. Finally, she gave up and just lay there, letting each of the crew have his turn.

In the meantime, Jorge Escovar had cut off Jackie's panties, and with the help of two men, forced her down onto the plastic bench along the side of the boat.

"And now, *senora,* you shall taste the power of a real man," Escovar bragged.

"Please," John begged. "She's pregnant. Don't! For God's sake, man, leave her be."

"Pregnant, is she?" he asked over his shoulder as he pulled down his pants. Then she won't mind my seed swimming around inside there."

Again, he laughed, kicked off his pants and shorts, and climbed onto her.

John screamed, "Jackie-e-e!"

She screamed back at him, turning her head to look him in the eyes. "I love you, John! I love you! Ahh!"

The leader of the pirates entered her. She managed to get one arm free, and pulling his thinning hair with all her might, yanked his head back. He punched her in the nose, breaking it. Blood sprayed everywhere. She slumped back, mercifully unconscious.

When he was done, Jorge climbed off and offered her body to the others. One by one, the men took turns violating her. Jorge returned a second time. When they were done with the two women, Jorge Escovar shot them each in the head. Jackie never regained consciousness, and for that John was thankful. The crew threw the two women overboard, naked, bleeding and bruised.

"Let the sharks finish them," Jorge said to John. "As for you, my friend, I've got other plans. Your death shall not be so sweet."

He spoke some words to his crew and they all cheered.

"I shall give my crew one hour to, how do you say, 'refresh themselves' in your galley, and then I will untie you and let them have their way with you. I hope you put up a good fight because this will be a battle to the death.

"Come, my *amigos!* Let us find food and drink!"

Escovar instructed two of his men to watch his captive, and the rest of them followed their leader down into the galley. John could hear cupboards slamming, drawers opening and closing and pots and pans clanging as the crew tore the place apart. Laughter erupted periodically. After a while, two of the crew came back on deck and relieved the first two guards. One of the new men walked over to the edge and peed over the side. He burped and found a spot across from John and sat down.

Grief and sorrow for his lost wife and for the others burned through John's entire being. The bile of overwhelming hatred ate away at his consciousness. He knew that his time on this earth was short, yet he struggled to loosen his ropes. The noose around his neck drew tighter, cutting into his flesh, drawing blood. He could feel the rope around his wrists loosening ever so slightly and strained to get it looser. He vowed to himself that before he died he would take as many of them with him as he could.

One of the two guards said something to his partner and went back down into the boat. Ever so carefully, John worked himself loose until his arms were free from his leg constraints and the noose. He worked the ropes around his legs loose. He feigned coughing and gagging and begged the guard to loosen the noose.

The guard laughed and said something John did not understand. John gagged again and forced his face to get red. The guard looked at his red face and rose to help him, calling out to his partner as he did.

As the guard reached out to loosen the noose, John's right hand, his fingers stiff, shot out and caught the man in his neck, crushing his windpipe. He went down hard. John pulled the man's knife from his belt and slit his throat viciously, just as the other man emerged from below. The man screamed, pulled his pistol out of his belt, and fired. John felt the bullet enter his side just as he slashed out and sliced through the pirate's neck, severing an artery and spraying blood all over him. He heard the sounds of other feet racing up the stairs and dove over the side of the boat just as the first man reached the top of the stairs. The man fired several shots in John's direction, one catching him in the shoulder as he entered the water. The force of the bullet hitting him caused him to twist as he splashed down and blood sprayed the hull just before he submerged. He went under as more shots rained down on him from above.

His only thought as he entered the blackness of the lagoon was, Jackie, I love you!

From the deck of the *Dram Bouie*, dozens of rounds of ammunition were expended into the dark water. The pirates shined flashlights and spotlights down onto the surface of the water, waiting for him to surface, guns aimed. They waited a long time, constantly scanning the water, but there was no sign of him. In the morning, they came ashore and searched the beach. They never did find his body.

EPILOGUE

Washington, DC, November 12, 3:35 p.m.

Jack and Sally sat in the quiet of his office, somber and subdued. Everyone else had gone home. The message had just come in from the Interpol Station Chief in Nassau.

For more than three weeks, the FBI, Interpol, and the local police departments of every jurisdiction between Kingston on Jamaica to Hyannis on Cape Cod had been looking for the *Dram Bouie* and its crew.

The Coast Guard had had ships scouring the sea and planes flying back and forth in ever increasing grids, looking for the elusive sailboat. Finally, after everyone involved had just about given up hope, a section of the rear transom with the partial name of the *Dram Bouie* and last five letters of the name Hyannis had washed up on an uninhabited beach on one of the many small islands that made up the Bahamas.

A group of scuba divers had found it and had brought it back to Clarence Town on Long Island where it was quickly sent on to Nassau. Interpol was notified, and a search party was dispatched to the island. No further parts of the boat were found.

Two days later, while swimming among coral reefs off another Bahamian island, most of an adult female human skull was found wedged between two pieces of coral. It too was turned over to the police who, in turn, sent it along to Interpol. Interpol forwarded it to the FBI in Washington, DC.

Working on a hunch, the lab people checked the dental records of Jacqueline Chandler and Jeannie Morris. The teeth were a perfect match for Jacqueline. The records were taken from her medical records on file with the US Army.

This was the information contained in the message that Jack had handed to Sally. She sat across from him and read the message for yet another time. She couldn't believe what it said.

Jackie Chandler/Burton—dead? And if she was dead, then what about the others?

All the evidence pointed to a disaster at sea. They must have been caught in a storm and the boat broke up and sank. All the evidence pointed that way, and yet, Sally could not accept it.

She would check the weather reports for the time around the sailboat's departure from Cayman Brac until the boat's tail section was found, but in her mind, she was not convinced that the boat had gone down in a storm. Something else had happened; she was sure of it.

"I just don't believe it, Jack," she said. "I know all the evidence points to a shipwreck, but I just don't buy it."

"It could have been one way for them to disappear, but what about his wife? You can't believe he killed her as part of his plan to disappear."

"No. From what those witnesses up in Maine said, they seemed to really be in love. That's the part I can't explain. And what about the others? What happened to them?"

"We may never know, Sally, we may never know."

On Monday, December 2, Jack put the file down on his desk. Sally had checked the weather reports—there had been several storms in the area during the time in question.

No further evidence had shown up.

He looked at the cover. Written on the front of it were the words, Unsolved and below that, the words Cold Case.

Now, after relaying the facts to Alex and Lisa McArthur, he felt drained. It wasn't fair. He had worked so hard—Sally had worked so hard—and to have it end this way was an injustice. And all that money. None of it was ever recovered. Five and one-half million dollars. Where the hell was it? Was it in a bank on the Caymans as he and Sally suspected? There were over 520 banks on those islands. And they were all very protective of their clients and their secrecy. Jack centered the folder on his desk, rose, took his coat off his coat tree, put it on, and walked to the door. He turned and looked at his desk one last time, turned off the lights, and went home.

Acknowledgments

To Sharon for her patience and encouragement.

To Catherine Florentz at US Bank for her input regarding banking regulations.

To Benjamin Brill for the cover art.

And lastly, to my family and friends for their support.

Without you all, this might not have been possible.

ABOUT THE AUTHOR

Richard Lippard grew up in Massachusetts. He served in the Air Force from May 1964 to June 1968. He graduated from the University of Denver in 1971 with a BA in mass communications. He and his wife have four grown children and currently reside in Lakewood, Colorado. He is retired.

CPSIA information can be obtained
at www.ICGtesting.com
Printed in the USA
FSHW021136240620
71316FS